What readers are saying about *Lily*,
book one of the Song of the River series:

"A new historical series has readers traveling by boat down the mighty Mississippi
with memorable characters who are trying to provide for themselves and their
families. These two talented authors bring to life a long-ago era of riverboat
adventures, weaving their own styles into the story line. They work very well together."
—*Romantic Times*

"*Lily* is an endearing, faith-affirming story that will leave a sigh on your lips and a
sweet 'song of the river' in your heart."
—Ramona K. Cecil, author of *A Bride's Sweet Surprise in Sauers, Indiana*
and *Freedom's Crossroad*

"Diane Ashley and Aaron McCarver have written a beautiful story of the South
right before the Civil War. You will feel immersed in the Southern culture and
setting. I felt I was right there with Lily."
—Margaret Daley, author of *From This Day Forward*

"I loved this book. Well-developed character I really cared about, authentically
detailed setting, and a story line that kept me riveted to the pages. I look forward
to the other books in the Song of the River series."
—Lena Nelson Dooley, author of *Mary's Blessing, Maggie's Journey*,
and *Love Finds You in Golden, New Mexico*—
a Will Rogers Medallion Award winner

"Brimming with romance and history, second chances and spiritual truths, *Lily*
takes you on a unique excursion that is utterly moving and delightful. Soft as a
Southern breeze, the compelling characters wrap round your heart and won't let
go. Truly a dream of a book!"
—Laura Frantz, author of *The Colonel's Lady*

"The collaboration of Diane Ashley and Aaron McCarver brings a tale as
steeped in the flavor of the South as a frosty glass of sweet tea. You'll smell the
muddy Mississippi River, her bottom churned by paddlewheel boats. You'll stand
on the dock at Natchez Under-the-Hill while the breeze off the water teases
your hair. *Lily* takes you on a pleasant journey into the colorful past. You'll be
glad you booked passage."
—Marcia Gruver, author of the *Backwoods Brides* and *Texas Fortune* series

"*Lily* swept me int⋯ ⋯ ⋯ave created a lasting tale as
poignant and deep⋯ ⋯tor of The Borrowed Book

"With the skillful use of rich and well-researched setting description, vivid scenes, and realistic dialogue authors Diane Ashley and Aaron McCarver have crafted a riveting historical romance that is sure to leave fans swooning."
—Debby Mayne, author of the Class Reunion series

"With themes of faith, family, forgiveness, and more twists and turns than a winding river, *Lily* takes readers back to the historic riverboat days in vivid detail. This charming tale of a determined, unconventional heroine and a stubborn, hurting hero is sure to capture your heart and leave you smiling at the end."
—Vickie McDonough, award-winning author of the Texas Boardinghouse Brides series

"With brilliant style, the team of Ashley and McCarver has perfectly blended Mississippi gentility and steamboat adventure. You will enter the characters' world and experience the excitement and dangers they endure in this gripping tale."
—Janelle Mowery, author of the Colorado Runaway series

"I have a special fondness for Southern literature and if the same is true for you, I think you're going to find *Lily* to be a pleasurable gem."
—Tracie Peterson, award-winning, bestselling author of over ninety-five books, including the "Striking a Match" series and *House of Secrets*

"Diane Ashley and Aaron McCarver have created a compelling tapestry of characters who live their lives, loves, and faith in a fascinating era of American history in an enchanting location—along the Mississippi. Their attention to detail helps frame the story and tempts the reader to forget the armchair in which she's sitting."
—Cynthia Ruchti, past president of American Christian Fiction Writers and author of the 2011 Carol Finalist *They Almost Always Come Home*

"Ashley and McCarver have woven a tale as gentle as a summer breeze and as treacherous as a shifting sandbar."
—Erica Vetsch, author of *A Bride's Portrait of Dodge City, Kansas*

"*Gone with the Wind* meets *The African Queen*. This book has all the action and adventure of the grand riverboat days, coupled with all the romance and grandeur of a pre-Civil-War South."
—Lenora Worth, *New York Times* bestselling author

DIANE T. ASHLEY *and*
AARON MCCARVER

Camellia

SONG OF THE RIVER

Book No. Two

BARBOUR
PUBLISHING

Published by Barbour Publishing, Inc., P.O. Box 719, Uhrichsville, OH 44683, www.barbourbooks.com

Our mission is to publish and distribute inspirational products offering exceptional value and biblical encouragement to the masses.

 Member of the
Evangelical Christian
Publishers Association

Printed in the United States of America.

Dedication

Aaron: I dedicate this book to my wonderful colleagues at Belhaven University. When Wesley College closed, I wondered if I would ever find another school where I could do more than just teach, where I could also minister to my students. God answered through you. Not only did you take me from working part-time to working full-time, you opened your hearts and took me in as one of your own. You will never understand how much this meant to me. I lost a family I had worked alongside for twenty years, but you replaced it with another that has become just as precious to me. Thank you for your love, support, encouragement, and full acceptance as a Blazer. I love you all.

Diane: For Lisa M. Davis, my sister from different parents. The hardest thing for me to do this year was tell you I was retiring from the Legislature. How could I give up the desk next to yours? How could I not talk to you every day? How could I leave you behind when we are best friends? When we count on each other to keep sane in the madness of the Capitol? Over the years, you've been there for me through hard times and good times. We've shared tears, laughter, and our deepest, darkest secrets. Even the phrase "town girl"—the one I use in my bio—came from you. And don't get me started on trips to the beach. Some things need to stay just between the two of us. The only reason I can bear to leave is the knowledge that nothing can break the bond between us. We may not talk as often, we certainly won't get to share the trivia of our daily lives. But I know when we do get together the time apart will disappear in an instant. Hang in there. I love you.

Acknowledgments

As always, we are so grateful to Becky Germany, Becky Fish, and the wonderful staff at Barbour Publishing. You truly make us feel like we belong.

Steve Laube, we couldn't do it without your invaluable assistance. . . and we wouldn't want to.

Bards of Faith, you are our anchor in the ocean of writing and publishing. Your friendships and prayers keep us grounded and fill our sails.

And most importantly, to our Lord and Savior Jesus Christ, all for You!

Chapter One

Boonville, Missouri
June 17, 1861

Jonah Thornton did not want to die.

His fingers cramped, and he loosened his grip on the trigger of his Sharps carbine. The butt of the rifle seemed grafted to his shoulder, an extra arm with deadly intent. He bent his head and sighted down the thirty-inch barrel, wondering if he could really pull the trigger. Wondering if he could take the life of another man. He raised his head and moved the rifle back to marching position, heel at waist level, barrel with bayonet over his shoulder.

A twig broke some distance away, and the tempo of Jonah's heart soared. Was it a scout looking for evidence of the force mustering in the area between the city of Boonville and the Mississippi River? Or a rabbit or deer foraging for an early morning meal?

His awareness stretched outward. Around him, the breaths of his fellow soldiers sounded loud, as did the whisper of gunpowder sliding into the throats of their muskets, followed by the snick of minie balls—a sound as deadly as a rattlesnake's tail. The moment was fast approaching when he would find out exactly what it meant to fight for his beliefs. Even to the point of risking his life in the protection of those beliefs.

Sweat sprouted on his forehead as he caught the rhythmic cadence of marching feet. The rest of the battalion was about to reach his position between two cornfields on the edge of Boonville. He had been aboard the first steamer to arrive before daybreak and had marched with the other troops toward the town where the Missouri State Guard and Governor Jackson waited.

The time to fight was upon them. His heart raced. Could he do it? Could he find the courage to leave his protected position? Could he jump to his feet and run forward when the order was given? Would the bullet from an unseen rifle tear through him? And if it didn't— if he somehow survived the assault—could he aim his own weapon at another human being and pull the trigger?

Jonah swallowed against the bitterness in his throat. *Lord, please let this end peaceably. Let them surrender without opening fire. Protect me and the other men. You know I don't want to kill. Fill them with fear and confusion so we might prevail without bloodshed. Amen.*

"Now!"

The single syllable catapulted Jonah to his feet. He ran without thought, almost propelled forward by the movement of the troops. They ran full tilt, up and over the ridge where the enemy soldiers were gathered. Cannons behind them boomed, but Jonah ignored the sound, centering his attention on one target, a man with short brown hair whose mouth had fallen open. Part of his brain noted the broad forehead, the lock of damp hair, and a pair of brown eyes wide with fear. Jonah reached for the rifle flung over his shoulder, bringing it around to his chest in one smooth movement. Tugging slightly on the trigger, he felt the movement as it began to move under the pressure.

A bullet whined past his ear, and one of the soldiers on the ridge crumpled. Still hesitating, he lifted his head slightly and realized the men on the ridge were running away from the charging soldiers. Jonah thought the battalion might prevail without further casualties until one of their officers began shouting. The fleeing soldiers halted and reached for their own weapons, apparently only now comprehending they could defend themselves.

Realizing the battle was not yet over, he sighted once more. His eyelids fluttered as he squeezed the trigger. The carbine slammed against his shoulder, and the intense fear that had been his constant companion for the past hour disappeared as the unfortunate man he had targeted jerked.

A surprised expression tautened the man's features. His rifle drooped as he looked down at his chest, at the dark stain spreading on his uniform. Then he looked up. His gaze slammed into Jonah. A scowl clouded his features. He raised his weapon a few inches before his features went slack and he crumbled to the ground.

Dead. The man was dead. He would never rise again, never laugh or speak or march again.

Horror filled Jonah as the realizations hammered him with the impact of the bullets flying between the two groups of men. He seemed frozen in the midst of the fierce fighting even though men continued to fire all around him. The sounds of battle faded, lost in the midst of the insistent ringing in his ears.

Nausea welled up, mixed with grief and remorse. He doubled over, and spasms shook him, turning his skin cold and clammy. When he thought the nausea had abated, he tried to push himself to his feet. But it was a futile effort as the horror overwhelmed him again, and his whole body convulsed once more.

It seemed to take forever before he regained control of his senses. Awareness of his surroundings crept back to him. The air was thick with smoke even though the deafening blasts of gunfire had been replaced by moans of pain.

Jonah pushed himself up and turned to survey the aftermath of the battle. Choking smoke hung low over the dirt road and clung to the few cornstalks remaining upright after the charge of the battalion. It blocked out the sun. Or had the sun set? Jonah wasn't sure of anything.

A hand clapped his shoulder, and Jonah's breath caught until he turned and recognized Cage, the dark-haired Arkansawyer who had befriended him when they met in Tennessee at the recruiting office.

"Are you all right?" His concerned gray gaze raked Jonah's face.

Hot tears pushed against his eyes, but Jonah clenched his jaw and nodded. He would not cry like a boy in short pants. He was a grown man, a soldier. He had to be all right.

Cage continued staring at him for a few moments before he nodded and cleared his throat. "You dropped this." He held out Jonah's rifle.

"Thanks." The single syllable scraped against his raw throat. When had he lost his weapon? A fine soldier he was turning out to be. Instead of reloading and killing more of their enemy, he'd run away. What if the battle had been won by their enemy? He'd likely be sprawled out on the ground, a bullet hole in his back. Jonah took his carbine from his friend's hand.

"You and I have talked about the necessity of war before." Cage nodded toward the road behind him. "We've prayed together about the Lord delivering us as He did the Israelites. 'In the world ye shall have tribulation—' "

" 'But be of good cheer; I have overcome the world.' "Jonah finished the quote for him.

Together they walked toward the riverbank to await the short voyage back to Jefferson City. Jonah knew he should be thankful for having such a strong Christian example as a friend. Over the past weeks they had spent time poring over the Word, reading from Cage's pocket Bible and discussing the significance of book, chapter, and verse.

But right now he wanted nothing more than to run from this world. To go back to New Orleans and the privileged life he'd enjoyed there. Why had he ever left home? And given the circumstances of his departure, would he ever be able to return?

ઠ૪

"I don't know how we got separated on the way back." Cage's familiar drawl brought Jonah's head up.

Jonah could have told the other man he'd purposely searched out a corner on the crowded steamboat and turned his back on the soldiers. Shrugging, he looked toward the center of their encampment where, in spite of the warm evening air, the other soldiers sat laughing around a blazing campfire. Even if Cage was a close friend, Jonah didn't want to admit the shame keeping him apart from the others.

Cage looked at him for a moment before handing Jonah a tin plate and settling himself on the nearby trunk of a fallen hickory tree.

"You shouldn't look so glum. We won the battle this morning." Cage dug into his plate of beans with gusto. "According to what the others are saying, the Missouri State Guard has been routed. We beat them with a minimum of bloodshed, at least on our side. General Lyon has succeeded in subduing the Rebels before they could infect the whole state."

"I guess so." The words had little meaning tonight. Not when the memories were so sharp in his mind. Jonah knew he wouldn't be able to force a single bite of food past the lump in his throat. He picked up his hardtack and turned it over and over in his hand.

"Do you think you're going to find any answers there?" The other man's voice held a note of sarcasm.

Jonah shook his head and let the hard biscuit drop to his plate. "I'm not hungry."

"I see." Cage swallowed another mouthful.

Feeling his friend's gaze even in the deepening gloom, Jonah shrugged. "I can't get it out of my head. He was so young, so shocked. . ."

Cage's spoon clattered as it struck the edge of his tin plate. "That will pass, kid. And it'll be a little easier the next time."

"I'm not sure that's a good thing." Now that the words were out, Jonah wished he had not voiced them. Would his friend think he was a coward? And wouldn't that be a correct estimation? Tendrils of shame curdled his stomach as he thought of his reaction during the battle. The only reason he had not died was because the Lord had protected him for some unfathomable purpose. Jonah stared at the unappealing food on his lap and waited for Cage's condemning words.

"Jonah, you're reacting to the battle. Give yourself a little more credit." He nodded toward the group of men some distance away. "Do you think they condemn you? This was your first battle, and I assume the first time you killed something other than game."

"If I could've found the strength, I would have run away." Jonah's confession brought a tiny bit of relief. He looked up at Cage and saw understanding in the other man's eyes. He tightened his jaw to dam the flood of emotions threatening to overwhelm him.

"I know. Taking another man's life is a thing no Christian should have to face. But this world belongs to Satan. Remember what we read last week. Why do you think Paul spoke of the armor of God?" He closed his eyes for a moment, his eyebrows drawing together. " 'Wherefore take unto you the whole armour of God, that ye may be able to withstand in the evil day, and having done all, to stand.' "

The verse washed over Jonah like a wave, cleansing some of the fear and shame that had hung over him this evening.

"And Paul was in prison when he wrote those words."

Jonah closed his eyes and imagined being held in chains. The fear, the discomfort, the uncertainty that must have tried to settle on Paul. Had God whispered in the disciple's ear as he looked at the Roman centurion guarding the prison? Had He suggested the comparison that Paul would send to the Ephesians? They were words to sustain Christians by reminding them of God's protection even in this world of battles and rampant sin.

"Do you remember the different parts of the armor?" Cage's voice brought him back to the present.

Jonah thought for a minute. "Is truth one of them?"

Cage's grizzled head bobbed up and down. "That's right, and the breastplate of righteousness, boots made from the gospel of peace, a shield of faith, and the most important part of all. . ."

"If I remember rightly, it's my salvation." Jonah was feeling better than he'd felt since they had come back to camp on the bank of the fast-flowing Mississippi River.

"Yes." Cage's infectious smile was as bright as a beacon. He leaned over and rapped Jonah smartly on the head. "The helmet of salvation to be exact."

A chuckle filled his throat. It felt good to let it loose. For a moment his grief and shame lifted. Jonah almost felt human once again.

One of the other soldiers, a private with blond hair and a mustache, walked over to them. He bent and glanced at Jonah's full plate. "You going t'eat that?"

Jonah shook his head and started to hand his plate to the lanky man, but Cage grabbed his wrist before he could finish the motion. "You're going to need that food. You didn't eat much this morning. If you give away your supper, you may not last another battle."

The thought of future battles made Jonah's stomach clench. He looked at Cage, recognizing the experience in his gaze. He glanced up at the private. "Give me a few minutes to decide."

The man spat at the ground next to Jonah's left boot. "I never thought you Johnnys should be allowed to join." He stomped away and rejoined the men around the campfire. A couple of them glanced back toward Cage and Jonah, suspicion showing in their faces.

"I should have just given him the food."

"We can't buy their trust, Jonah. It's only natural for them to be suspicious of us. We are Southerners after all." Cage sighed and shrugged a shoulder. "Maybe one day they'll understand why we refused to fight with the Confederacy. Until then, we have to remember why we're Federal soldiers."

He knew Cage was right, but sometimes it was hard to bear. Had he done the right thing to volunteer his service to the Yankees? Yes. Jonah could not support slavery on any level, even though he dreaded the idea of facing a friend or relative on the battlefield. Would his convictions force him into killing someone he knew? Jonah prayed not.

Cage's grunt interrupted his circling thoughts. "Private Benton will survive. There's plenty of forage if he's hungry."

Jonah picked up his hardtack and gnawed at it. Letting the tough biscuit soak up the moisture from his beans only softened it a smidgen. His thoughts seemed as hard as the food in his mouth. It was fine to talk about the armor of God, but it still didn't answer all the questions and fears that had arisen because of the battle. "What does the Bible say about using weapons to kill someone else?"

"David was a great warrior, wasn't he?"

"Yes." Jonah was somewhat surprised by the question. Everyone knew about David's many battles.

"Wasn't he also called a 'man after God's own heart'?"

Of course. The oppressive doubt and shame lifted from Jonah's heart, if only for a moment. He might not be as strong as David, but he could still spend time reading the Bible his sister had given him for Christmas last year. Once again he regretted not bringing it with him on his trip to visit his brother, Eli. But he'd never thought he would go from Memphis to the front lines of the war between the North and the South.

Eli had tried to dissuade him from joining, but Jonah had been adamant. He had known his reasons for volunteering were valid. Too bad he'd never imagined what his choice would cost him—his self-confidence, his pride, and perhaps even his life.

Jonah lifted his thoughts heavenward and prayed his sacrifices would matter. And he entreated God to someday see him in the same way He had once seen David.

The food on his plate seemed more palatable after his prayer. Jonah filled his spoon and lifted it to his mouth, savoring the smoky flavor. Even his hardtack was tastier. His appetite reawakened. He shoveled in another mouthful and chewed. Energy flowed through him like a rising tide, and Jonah realized once more how blessed he was to have such a strong Christian as his friend.

❧

Jonah ran a finger underneath the scratchy blue-black collar of his uniform jacket before entering the general's office. Good thing he'd managed to get the white pants washed and pressed by a local washerwoman. He wanted to present the best possible image to his commanding officers.

The room, a gentleman's library in the house that had been commandeered, was crowded. Soldiers and officers stood in small knots, leaned against the walls, or sat in the leather chairs scattered about. Most of them did not notice his entrance, but his captain, Drew Poindexter, stepped forward and nodded briefly.

Jonah straightened his shoulders and snapped a salute.

Captain Poindexter returned his salute before turning to a large desk covered with papers and maps. "Sir, this is the man I told you about, Jonah Thornton."

Jonah swallowed hard and saluted once again as he met the piercing, coffee-colored gaze of Brigadier General Nathaniel Lyon. He had only seen the man from a distance before this morning. Why was he here now? What possible interest could this man have in him?

"At ease, son." General Lyon nodded toward a chair occupied by another soldier. "Major Eads, clear this room. I need a moment of privacy with Mr. Thornton."

Jonah let his arm drop but stood at attention as the major carried out the general's orders. His captain turned as if to leave, but the general stopped him with a raised hand. "I didn't mean you, Drew. This is your idea after all."

The room seemed much larger without the other occupants. The general leaned back in his chair and waved a hand at the pair of chairs in front of his desk. "How long have you been a soldier, Thornton?"

Jonah's mind raced. Had his deplorable behavior on the field of battle several days earlier been noted? He looked down at his feet. "Only a few months, sir."

"I want to commend you for choosing to serve your country in spite of the leanings of many of your fellow Southerners." The general's voice was not warm, but it was not as gruff as it had been when he addressed his subordinate.

Jonah risked a glance upward. The look on the man's narrow face was one of respect. Jonah responded with a dip of his head. "Thank you, sir."

General Lyon continued studying his face for a moment. Then he turned his attention to Captain Poindexter. "Why don't you tell Mr. Thornton your idea?"

Jonah swung his glance toward the captain on his right. Poindexter's jacket was unbuttoned, but his shirt was clean and crisp. His blond hair gleamed in the yellow light of a nearby lamp. "I. . .um. . .I don't want to embarrass you, Jonah, but I saw your reaction when you shot that fellow."

Hot blood burned Jonah's cheeks. The shame had begun to subside in the intervening days, but it resurged anew. What was he doing here? He should have listened to Eli, should have stayed in Memphis. . .remained neutral. . .avoided fighting for either side. But how could he ignore his convictions? He was not the type of man to hide out until the war ended. He could not abide the institution of slavery, could not support a society that depended on slavery to succeed. So he had joined the army and come to Missouri as ordered. Only to fail his first test. "I'm sorry, sir. It won't happen again."

A hand came down on his right shoulder. "Fighting is not the only way you can serve the Union."

"Yes, sir." What other way could there be? He had no naval skills, so they couldn't be thinking of putting him aboard a ship. Maybe they were intending to assign him to the rear, an assistant to the quartermaster. Jonah braced himself. After his experience on the battlefield, perhaps it would be a relief.

General Lyon leaned forward and steepled his hands. "One of the most valuable resources in any war is information."

A memory surfaced in Jonah's mind from the first time he and his brother had traveled to visit their grandparents in Natchez. One sunny afternoon, the two of them had gone exploring in a copse to the north of town. They had looked for dangerous Indians, scared squirrels out of hiding, and chased each other around the bases of monstrous oak trees. All the sorts of things youngsters found such fun. But the fun ended suddenly when Jonah broke through dense undergrowth at the edge of a drop-off. He remembered pinwheeling his arms and trying to keep from pitching forward into the ravine. An echo of the same stomach-clenching fear he felt that day enveloped him. "Exactly what are you saying, sir?"

The general frowned at him. "This war is going to be costly for both sides. One of the ways to shorten it is to have men infiltrate the rebel ranks and bring back information on their weapons, their plans, and their manpower."

"You want me to be a spy?"

Silence answered him. The general sat back once again, his gaze boring into Jonah's face. Captain Poindexter cleared his throat and shuffled his feet, the sound loud in the quiet room.

Tugging at his collar once again, Jonah's mind returned to the past. His brother had thrown an arm around him as he teetered on the edge of a lethal plunge, pulling him back from the precipice. But who would save him today? A spy? He'd never considered such an idea. Didn't want to consider it now.

"You'll be able to return to your family." Captain Poindexter's voice brought him back to the present.

"But I would have to lie to them."

"Yes." The general's voice was firm, uncompromising. "You will have to hide the truth."

"Your efforts could shorten the war. You would save lives, perhaps even the lives of your loved ones." Captain Poindexter's voice was less stern. He seemed to be asking Jonah rather than ordering his compliance with the plan.

The general stood up and walked around in front of his desk, waiting until Jonah and the captain also stood. "My first concern will never be with those who have rebelled against their government. It is with your loyalty. After all, you could well be a spy for the Confederacy."

Jonah felt like he'd been punched in the stomach. Hadn't he volunteered for service in the army? Hadn't he accepted the slurs and suspicions of the Northern soldiers while holding fast to his belief in the rightness of the Union's position? Many of his friends and family would consider him a traitor if they discovered that he'd become a Federal soldier. Smarting from the accusation, Jonah shook his head. "I have killed for the Union. Isn't that proof enough?"

The general shook his head. "The death of one nameless man would be a small price for a Confederate soldier to pay for the information he could gather while traveling with this army. If you want to prove your loyalty, you must be ready to do whatever service you are called upon to do."

Jonah's stomach twisted. This must be what his older brother had understood when Jonah announced his decision to fight for the United States. But Jonah thought he knew better, and in the end, Eli had yielded. He'd had such high hopes, such unrealistic visions of what his future would be. Jonah thought he had considered all the privations and sacrifices he might be called upon to give. He had wondered whether he might be able to shoot someone he knew. But this? The intimate, planned betrayal of his family? Could he be that loyal to his country? Jonah didn't know the answer. "I'd like some time to pray about this, sir."

General Lyon raised an eyebrow. He exchanged a glance with the captain before nodding. "Take all the time you need. . .as long as I have your answer by this time tomorrow. And I'm sure you know you cannot mention this to anyone outside of this room."

Jonah snapped a salute, holding his bent arm stiff until a nod from the general dismissed him. He turned sharply and marched out of the room, ignoring the whispered conversation behind him. His mind raced in circles as he considered the unappealing option he'd been given. What should he do?

Chapter Two

Les Fleurs Plantation
Natchez, Mississippi

"I have to go this term." Camellia Anderson couldn't keep the pleading tone out of her voice. Her eyes stung with unshed tears. "I'll be too old to go by the fall."

"I know how badly you want to attend the finishing school in New Orleans." Her older sister stood up and moved across the front parlor at Les Fleurs. Her skirts did not have the graceful sway Camellia had practiced for hours. Lily had never taken time to practice feminine arts.

Camellia turned away from her to watch the scene from the window. The unseasonably warm November afternoon had tempted the family to spend time on the front porch. Jasmine, their youngest sister, was entertaining the rest of the family by reading to them from her dog-eared copy of *Ivanhoe* by Sir Walter Scott. Her voice rose and fell, and her free hand was splayed across her chest in a melodramatic pose.

David Foster, the young boy she and her sisters had rescued from life on the street, stood beside Jasmine. His legs were planted widely, and as Camellia watched, he reached for an imaginary sword and brandished it in the air above his head.

She could hear Aunt Dahlia's distinctive laugh as the playacting continued. It was a shame their aunt had not come with them to the parlor. She would have lent her support to Camellia. But Lily had dragged her away from the others, bringing her inside the salon so they could "chat."

Camellia unfurled her fan and fluttered it in front of her face.

Straightening her spine and concentrating on forming a pleasant smile, she turned to face Lily once more. She wanted to stomp her foot in protest, but her aunt's insistence on decorum stayed the impulse. "You promised I could go, Lily." She was pleased with the blend of pleasantness and determination in her tone of voice.

"I know I did." Lily's gaze fell. "But I didn't know then that we would be in the middle of a war."

"The war has not come here, and it probably never will, not with our courageous soldiers fighting so fiercely. They won the battles at Fort Sumter and Manassas, after all. They've whipped those Yankee aggressors at nearly every turn. Who knows, the Northerners may realize by the end of the year that they cannot win. Then the war will be over, and we'll be able to resume our regular lives. I don't see any sense in putting off my future because of fighting going on so far away."

Silence fell on them as Camellia stopped speaking. In the quiet afternoon she could hear applause coming from the porch. Why couldn't Lily understand she had to get away from here? Away from her eccentric father and melodramatic younger sister. If she was ever going to find the kind of husband she dreamed of, it was going to be through the friendships she would make at a nice finishing school—one far from Natchez.

"These are dangerous days." Lily's words brought her back to the problem at hand. "With the Union navy blockading the gulf, who knows what may happen? I want to keep my family near. Except for Blake—you, Jasmine, and Papa are the most important people in my life."

Camellia sensed a weakness she could turn to her advantage. "If I'm so important to you, why are you trying to ruin my life?"

Lily's eyes widened, and her chin lifted. "Be reasonable. I'm not trying to hurt you. I just want you to be safe."

"I'll be very safe in New Orleans. The Thorntons and the Cartiers will watch out for me. Besides, if La Belle Demoiselle could not keep their students safe, I doubt they would still have any young ladies in attendance."

A sigh from her sister made Camellia's heart ache. She didn't like hurting Lily, but she had to persevere if she was to become a proper bride for a proper husband. Her time was running out. Soon her beauty would fade, and she would find herself without any prospects, much less the kind of husband she wanted to attract.

The type of man she dreamed of marrying would not accept less than perfect manners, perfect accomplishments, and perfect breeding from his fortunate spouse. And rightly so since he would offer the same benefits to her. He would be kind and handsome and rich, so rich that she would never have to set tables, polish silverware, or count linens. She could forget about all of the menial chores Lily made her and Jasmine do aboard the paddle wheeler.

"I wish you had been able to attend Mrs. Gossett's Finishing School last year."

Camellia sniffed. "It's not my fault she decided to close her school and return to Rhode Island."

"Of course not. But I could not blame her for returning to her home state after the death of her husband. During uncertain times most people want to be near their loved ones."

There it was again. The suggestion she would only be safe on her sister's riverboat. What could she say to convince Lily to let her go to New Orleans? No new argument came to mind, so she returned to her earlier logic. "A lot of people think the war will be over soon. And if that happens, you will have ruined my future for no reason at all."

Lily folded her arms over her chest. "I don't know what to do for the best. Blake and I have prayed for an answer."

Perhaps this was the opening she'd needed. "Didn't we find a wonderful school for me to attend that is close to the Thorntons' town house?"

"Yes."

Camellia caught her sister's gaze and held it. "Then why can you not accept that God has already answered your prayer? He wants me to attend the finishing school He led us to."

Lily shook her head. "I don't think it's that simple."

"I do." Camellia reached for one of her sister's hands, prying it loose and holding it against her heart. "This is my dream, Lily, my heart's desire. When you decided to avoid Mr. Adolphus Marvin's pursuit and purchase a steamboat, you chose the life you wanted to lead."

"But I did that so you and Jasmine and I—"

"You can try to convince the rest of our family that your decision was based on noble, high-sounding ideas, but I know how much you always loved the river. You become someone different when you're out there." Camellia released her sister's hand. "Even if Jasmine and I had not been around, you would have made the same decision."

Lily's eyes filled with tears. She nodded. "You may be right about that." She stepped closer and touched one of the corkscrew curls surrounding Camellia's face. "But I was determined to spare you the same misery as Aunt Dahlia and Uncle Phillip planned for me. I want both you and Jasmine to be happy and independent. I want you to have choices."

"Then why are you taking away my choice? Why are you insisting I conform to your rules?" Camellia placed her hand over her sister's. "Can't you see you're doing the same thing to me you claim Aunt Dahlia was doing to you?"

Lily sighed and pulled her hand away. She sat down in Grandmother's overstuffed chair, her head drooping.

For a moment Camellia felt like a beast. Who was she trying to fool? Lily had always put her sisters' needs ahead of her desires. She might have packed them up willy-nilly and brought them along with her, but she had also made sure they had everything they needed and many of the things they wanted. The very clothing she wore was paid for with money Lily had earned. Guilt knotted her stomach.

She opened her mouth to apologize for her manipulative words but was forestalled when Lily looked up. "All right."

The knots tightened even further, but Camellia swallowed hard and waited. She couldn't weaken now. Not when she was about to realize her dearest wish.

"Don't you have anything to say?"

Remembering to float downward like an autumn leaf, Camellia settled on the footstool next to Grandmother's chair. "Thank you so very much. Allowing me to stay in New Orleans is the best gift you've ever given me. I promise to make you proud of me, Lily." She rested her head against her sister's knees.

Lily laid a hand on her head and stroked her hair. "I am proud of you, Camellia. You are the most polished of all of us. Everyone says so. And you're so pretty. One of these days, some man is going to snap you up. He'll take you away from us and set you up in a beautiful house."

Camellia's eyelids drifted shut as she imagined the scene her sister described. She could see a big, fancy home—even grander than Les Fleurs. The formal dining room would seat a hundred guests, and she would preside over fancy dinners dressed in expensive jewelry and the most fashionable attire money could buy. The townspeople would be envious of her and her adoring husband. . .and they would have lovable children—a dozen at least. It wouldn't matter how her father dressed or what he did for a living, or why her sister had married a former gambler.

But none of her dreams would come true until she attended the finishing school. Camellia's eyes popped open, and she raised her head. "When can we leave for New Orleans?"

A laugh slipped from Lily's mouth. "Don't be in such a hurry, dear. You're going to need new dresses. I thought we could go shopping this week."

Camellia straightened and rose from the footstool. "I know how much you dislike shopping, Lily, so I've already asked Aunt Dahlia to take me."

"Oh." A world of hurt filled her sister's voice with the single syllable.

A blush burned Camellia's cheeks. How was she supposed to know her sister would volunteer to help her? Lily had never been interested in shopping. "I'm sorry. I can tell Aunt Dahlia you want to go along."

Shaking her head, Lily stood. "Blake was telling me this morning we need to make a quick trip to Greenville and pick up some furniture and deliver it to a plantation in Tangipahoa Parish."

Relief at Lily's words eased Camellia's discomfort. "So you can go with him instead of staying here to take care of me."

Lily's smile was a little shaky, but it solidified as she nodded. "You're right. But I want you to make plans to travel with us the following week for our scheduled trip to Memphis." She walked over to Camellia and put an arm around her waist. "I want you to spend a little time with us before you go off to school."

Normally Camellia would have refused to go along with her sister's plan, but she needed to focus on the greater goal. A few boring days spent aboard the steamboat was a small price to pay, even though she'd much rather stay here and get ready for her escape. As long as she and Aunt Dahlia finished the fittings next week, her clothing should be ready in time for the beginning of the term.

"You needn't be anxious. The school won't open for almost two months."

Camellia knew it was important to keep her tone cool and logical. "I don't see how you can blame me. Not after missing out last year."

"I wish we had gone ahead and enrolled you at La Belle." Lily's brown eyes seemed to be focused on the past. "But I didn't want to take a chance at putting you somewhere until I had the opportunity to thoroughly check Mrs. Dabbs's reputation in New Orleans. Besides, you were so anxious because of the classes you had already missed."

Hanging on to her temper with difficulty, Camellia pulled away from her sister's loose embrace. She didn't remember the events in the same way her sister did. Lily was the one who had been anxious. But she wasn't going to argue the point. It was ancient history, and she didn't want to roil the waters.

"Shall we go outside and tell the others?" Not waiting for an answer, Camellia floated across the parlor. At least she hoped she appeared to be floating. What was it Aunt Dahlia said? *The road to a lady's success is trod with tiny footsteps.* Holding her head high, Camellia forced her feet to a deliberate pace. If she was going to succeed at La Belle Demoiselle, she would have to remember everything she had ever been taught about deportment and etiquette.

She preceded her sister into the hallway and out onto the porch. Blake and Uncle Phillip rose from their rockers as they arrived. Camellia met her aunt's concerned gaze with a tiny nod. Aunt Dahlia sat back, a satisfied smile on her lips.

Grandmother beckoned her to the empty chair beside her. "You have missed a fine rendition from Jasmine and David."

"Never fear, I've heard that scene several times." Camellia perched on the edge of the rocker, her spine as straight and rigid as a broomstick. "In fact, I have even been known to read the part of Ivanhoe when David is not available."

Poor David. He followed Jasmine around like a puppy. Camellia had no doubt he would lay down his life for the dark-haired girl he adored. And perhaps for that very reason, Jasmine treated him with offhanded disdain. She expected him to fall into every plan she conceived no matter his own desires or concerns. If he dared to cross her wishes, she would ban him from her presence. Eventually he would come back and ask her forgiveness, and the two of them would continue on as before. Camellia thought he would earn more respect from Jasmine if he refused to do her bidding from time to time. But that was apparently not to be.

"I have not been able to convince Camellia she would do better to wait awhile before attending the school in New Orleans." Lily's voice brought her musings to a halt.

She braced herself for her brother-in-law's frown. Blake Matthews didn't like anyone to contradict Lily. . .except himself, of course. In the first year of their marriage, Lily and her husband had spent a goodly amount of energy on arguments. But no matter what happened between the two of them, he was always eager to defend his wife against anyone who dared disagree with her.

Camellia was determined to learn from her older sister's example. Learn how *not* to act. When she married the man of her dreams, they wouldn't argue. She would be a dutiful wife. One who always put his needs ahead of her own. That was the way to conduct a marriage, not butting heads with one's spouse at every turn.

"Camellia has good reasons for being adamant." Aunt Dahlia punched her needle through the lacy handkerchief in her lap.

"I don't know, Dahlia." Uncle Phillip's long, manicured fingers worried at the cuff of his emerald-hued coat. "The Yankees seem determined to blockade the Gulf Coast and halt the flow of goods to and from Europe. They may well attack New Orleans to achieve their ends."

"I hadn't considered that possibility." Grandmother entered the discussion. Her voice carried a hint of a tremble, one that had become more noticeable in the months since Mississippi seceded from the Union.

Camellia's heart thudded, but she refused to let her consternation appear on her face. "If war does come to New Orleans, I'm sure our gallant soldiers will repulse them." Realizing her hands were clenched together in her lap, she forced them to relax into a more ladylike posture.

She'd had a lot of practice hiding her true feelings—ever since she had discovered that the man captaining her sister's steamboat was their father. Until that day she had thought he was dead, drowned in the same accident that took their mother. But he had survived. Faced with the prospect of raising three girls by himself, he had been forced to turn to his deceased wife's family for help. They had in turn wrung from him a promise to disappear from their lives, a promise Camellia wished had never been broken.

"I'm sure we could get to her before it came to a pitched battle." Her father tossed a smile in her direction. "Few men know the river as well as we do."

Guilt speared Camellia at his words. Perhaps she should not be so judgmental about Papa. He could have his uses. Her gaze drifted down the red shirt he always wore and stopped at the old-fashioned, wide-brimmed hat in his lap. If only he would not dress in such a ridiculous manner.

Jasmine pulled David onto the porch where the rest of them sat. Dropping his hand, she took a step forward, her violet eyes swirling with excitement. "I know. I could go with her."

Lily's gasp mingled with Blake's chuckle. "I don't see how that would keep Camellia safe."

Jasmine flung her ebony hair over her shoulder with a melodramatic sigh. "I was only trying to help."

Few things sounded worse to Camellia than the suggestion that her sister might accompany her to New Orleans. "Don't be silly. You're too young to attend a finishing school."

Aunt Dahlia and Uncle Phillip nodded while Grandmother and Papa exchanged a glance. Camellia sat up straighter in her rocker. Had she said something wrong? Should she not have expressed the truth in such plain language? "I'm sorry, Jasmine. I am sure you would be very welcome at La Belle Demoiselle."

"No, Camellia is right." Lily reached out to Jasmine and pulled her down onto her lap.

Camellia relaxed a tiny bit. Maybe a prayer would help. That's what the preacher had talked about last Sunday—about getting anything one asked for. Would God listen? Would He magically change the attitudes of her family? Asking for His help couldn't hurt matters. Not that she meant any disrespect.

She closed her eyes. *Lord, please forgive me for my wayward thoughts. I promise to be more circumspect if only You'll let me attend La Belle Demoiselle. It shouldn't be too much trouble for You. . . . Oh, and if You'll work this out for me, I promise to do something kind in return. I don't know exactly what, but maybe You have something in mind. Whatever it is, I'm sure we can work things out. . . .* Camellia hesitated. Should she add something else? She couldn't think of anything. *Amen.* As prayers went, it wasn't very eloquent, but maybe He would understand and give her her heart's desire.

Camellia opened her eyes and glanced around. Everyone looked the same except Jasmine, who had slumped back against Lily's shoulder and twisted her mouth into a pout.

Maybe God needed more time. She sure hoped He didn't wait too long.

❧

"What do you think of this color?" Camellia held up a length of gold silk for her aunt's approval.

Aunt Dahlia tilted her head as she considered the suggestion before nodding. "It should make a stunning ballroom ensemble with a white lace overskirt and dark gold ribbons."

Her smile widened as Camellia imagined entering a crowded ballroom on the arm of a dashing Confederate soldier. But then the dream crashed. "What if my escort is a soldier? Will the gold clash with his gray uniform?"

She held her breath as Aunt Dahlia frowned in concentration. "I don't believe so." Her aunt beckoned the owner of the dress shop to join them.

The tiny woman who ran the most fashionable shop in Natchez bustled over to them, a ticket book in her right hand and a pencil tucked into her elaborate coiffure. "You've chosen a marvelous cloth. Look at how it complements your niece's curls."

Aunt Dahlia nodded. "I know you won't have any of the suiting for men's attire, but do you have something the exact color of a soldier's uniform? My niece wants to be certain her dress will complement her escort's attire." The two women walked off, chattering about flounces, buttons, and ribbons.

Camellia was so glad her aunt was the one who had brought her to town. It wasn't that she didn't love Lily, but her sister would never understand or pay attention to all the implications of each decision they needed to make. She looked toward the counter, where the bolts of material they had already selected were piled high. By Christmas they would be transformed into day, tea, and walking dresses of white, periwinkle, jade, and jonquil. Tan broadcloth would become a riding habit for afternoon excursions. They had also ordered chemises, petticoats, and aprons from plain white cotton. She would have a short cape of black wool for fall and spring outings, as well as a long winter cloak made from a luscious length of figured navy velvet to replace the plain black wool one she currently used.

"Look at this, Camellia." Aunt Dahlia placed the bolt of gold silk on the counter and laid two swatches against it.

The pewter gray swatch was a nice contrast to the gold silk. The other swatch, a dull gold Camellia recognized as butternut, was more troublesome. She frowned but immediately forced her eyebrows back to a more pleasant position. She didn't want wrinkles. She pointed at the butternut-colored square. "I don't like that one."

"I know. Most uniforms are closer to this color." Aunt Dahlia picked up the gray swatch and held it in her hand while pointing to the square still resting on the bolt of gold material. "But what if your escort were to show up in that one?"

Camellia nodded and turned back to the table of displayed silks. She spotted another beautiful color, a bright cerulean-blue length of watered silk. "What about this one?" Her gaze met that of her aunt's, and both of them smiled at the same time.

"It's perfect. I only wish I were going to be there to see you when you enter the room on your handsome escort's arm." Aunt Dahlia walked to the table whose surface was covered with the latest dress patterns from Europe.

Following her to the table, Camellia sighed. "If only you could talk Uncle Phillip into moving to New Orleans."

"You're sweet, child. I know I shouldn't say it, but of all my nieces, you are the one who is dearest to my heart."

Camellia's lips turned up in a small smile. "I love you, too, Aunt Dahlia. I'll miss spending time with you, Uncle Phillip, and Grandmother, but we've talked about this. You know why I'm going."

Aunt Dahlia patted her hand. "You need some separation from your less. . .traditional relatives. I still find it hard to believe your sister has embraced Henrick so readily after the man all but abandoned the three of you."

Camellia glanced down at her shoes. She didn't want to point out that it was Grandfather's edict that had caused her father to disappear from their lives for so many years. She didn't want to defend the man at all.

"Don't worry." Aunt Dahlia had continued talking, unaware of her niece's inner turmoil. "I'll be busy looking for the perfect candidate to be your spouse while you're in New Orleans getting that extra bit of polish."

Thinking of the candidate her aunt and uncle had chosen for her older sister, Camellia shuddered. It was the reason Lily had purchased a steamboat and taken all three of them to live on the river. "I don't want you to try matching me to anyone like the old man you thought Lily should marry."

"Of course not." Aunt Dahlia's calculating gaze swept her from head to toe. "You are a very different girl than your sister—a beautiful gentlewoman. The man I choose for you will be of a completely different caliber. Lily, on the other hand, could have done much worse than to marry Adolphus."

Camellia remembered his atrocious sons and wondered.

Aunt Dahlia tittered and leaned closer. "As a matter of fact, she did do much worse." She glanced over her shoulder before continuing in a soft whisper. "You don't have to worry about him at all. It seems the Johnsons' oldest girl, Grace, has removed Adolphus from consideration. I have it on the best authority that they will announce their nuptials before the end of the year. I'm sure they'll host a party. Maybe we can attend it together before your departure."

"I don't think Lily will agree." Her fingers traced the outline of the topmost dress pattern lying on the counter. "She wants me to travel to Memphis with her before I start school."

"That's terrible." Aunt Dahlia shook her head and clucked her tongue. "Will she never stop interfering in your future?"

"I know, but it was the only way I could get her to agree to let me remain in New Orleans." Camellia's fingers drifted over the bolt of blue silk as she imagined the upcoming term. She would outshine every other girl at La Belle Demoiselle in a dress like this one. "At least it's only for a week, and then I'll be free to pursue my dreams."

The shop's owner returned to them then, and they began to discuss her new wardrobe. Camellia's head spun with plans and dreams as they picked and chose from the designs available. She felt like one of the princesses in Jasmine's dramas. And she would be. . .once she got to New Orleans.

Chapter Three

Lily was glad to be back on the river, even on a dreary day like this one. Winter had settled on them as they celebrated a subdued Christmas and ushered in the new year. The crisp morning air energized her as she watched the brown bank sliding past them.

A modest frame house perched on the western side of the river caught her eye. It amazed her how much the river had changed in the years since she'd first traveled its length as a young girl with her parents. Houses like the one they were passing dotted the landscape in ever-increasing numbers. She smiled and waved at a boy and girl who stood watching from the front porch. *Lord, please bless us with children of our own.*

A picture of the family's dinner table formed in her mind, the boy on one side of the table, his sister on the other. Their parents would be situated at either end. She could imagine them joining their hands as the father asked God to bless their meal. Then they would laugh and recount the day's adventures, perhaps even mentioning seeing *Water Lily* steam northward on the Mississippi River.

"You look awfully pensive on such a fine morning."

Lily jumped at the unexpected sound of her husband's voice. "Where did you come from?" She took a moment to study his masculine good looks. It never ceased to amaze her that such a wondrously handsome man had fallen in love with her, plain as she was. He could have turned the head of any female along the wide river, but he had chosen her to become his bride.

"I saw my beautiful wife standing out here all alone and came to see what might be on her mind." Blake pulled her into his arms and planted a warm kiss on her lips.

Lily melted against him as always, lost in the tender devotion he lavished on her. He was the best husband anyone could hope for—a man who sought God earnestly and worked hard to follow His leading. When they first met, he had not been as admirable in his outlook, but God had worked a miraculous change in Blake. He had taken a hardened gambler, a man who thought he didn't need anyone, and changed him into a thoughtful, kind, and generous disciple. Blake was always ready to tell anyone they met about Christ's death and resurrection and the difference His sacrifice made in the lives of all who accepted His free gift.

When he finally released her, Lily's cheeks burned in the cool air. "I love you."

"Of course you do." His eyes, bluer than the sky on a cloudless day, teased her. He wrapped her in his arms once more, this time resting his chin on her head. "I love you, too. . .more than I could ever have imagined."

A sigh of pure bliss filled Lily's lungs. She closed her eyes and thanked God for blessing her beyond anything she'd ever dreamed might be possible.

Their embrace lasted for several minutes before the long whistle of an approaching steamer separated them. Blake leaned against the rail, and she raised a hand to shade her eyes as the vessel drew nearer.

It had once been a merchant steamship much like the *Water Lily*, but unlike their boat, this one had become a warship. Steel plates covered the lower decks, featureless except for the cannons protruding from narrow openings along the side. Even the pilothouse and the great paddle wheel at the end of the boat were covered with shielding. The twin smokestacks belched black smoke, and cinders fell on the gray-suited soldiers who sat, walked, or lounged on the upper deck, their weapons close at hand.

Lily waved, even though her heart was heavy at this reminder of the terrible struggle that had been going on for nearly a full year. A few of them saluted or waved, but most of the group ignored her gesture.

She and Blake watched the boat until it disappeared around a bend in the river. "Where do you think they're going?"

Blake shrugged. "To defend one of the southern ports, I imagine."

"I'm so worried about letting Camellia attend school in New Orleans. I hate the idea of being unable to reach her."

The color of Blake's eyes seemed to change as a cloud briefly obscured the sun. "You've done everything you can to convince her, but your sister has her heart set on going to La Belle. If you don't let her have her way in this, she may strike out on her own." His lips curled in a quick smile. "She is an Anderson, after all."

Lily couldn't help the laughter that broke past her lips in response to her husband's not-so-subtle reminder of her own stubbornness. "But that was different. My aunt and uncle were trying to force me—"

"Trying to get you to do what they thought was in your best interest."

Her chin lifted. "I'm not trying to push Camellia into a loveless marriage."

"I know that, Lily. But you're the one who told me how adamant your sister is about going to that finishing school." He shrugged. "I don't see much wrong with letting her live in New Orleans. We have friends who will watch out for her safety, and if it becomes dangerous, we'll have the opportunity to rescue her and bring her safely back to Les Fleurs. Or keep her aboard with us if you want."

He was right. She knew he was right. But still she worried.

Blake dropped a reassuring kiss on her forehead. "Where is Camellia, anyway? I thought you wanted to spend all of your leisure time with her on this voyage since it will probably be the last one we manage before school begins."

"I sent her up to visit Papa." Lily glanced at the staircase behind his right shoulder. "She still seems so stilted and formal around him. I don't understand why. Camellia couldn't have felt the same way I did when I thought Papa had abandoned us. She seemed to get along well with him before she knew his real identity, and I would like to see them work out their differences before she goes away, before her heart hardens so much that—"

Blake's face, so warm and caring before her answer, hardened into a cold mask.

Remorse washed through her. "I'm sorry, Blake. . . . I didn't mean. . . . I wasn't trying to—"

He put a finger over her lips, silencing her apology. "It's okay, Lily. I suppose what I'm feeling is more guilt than anything else. Besides, we've had a similar discussion before when I was trying to get you to be more accepting of Henrick. I know I need to make peace with my own father."

Lily wanted to put her arms around Blake. She wanted to comfort him, tell him that she would always be there for him no matter what he decided to do about his relationship with his father. But she held her tongue and waited for him to finish. Her patience was rewarded after a long minute ticked by.

Blake sighed. "I just don't know if I'm ready to take that step yet. You cannot know what it was like—"

Unable to keep silent any longer, Lily interrupted him. "But I know what you're like, Blake. I've seen you grow closer to the Lord since we've been together. I love the time we spend together in devotion and prayer." She hesitated for a moment, trying to pick her words with care.

Blake smiled, but his eyes were filled with uncertainty. "But. . . ?"

Lily didn't want to cause Blake unnecessary pain, yet she owed him her honest opinion. "I can sense a hard place inside of you, a place you don't want to let Him touch. Maybe it's because I once harbored the same feelings toward my father that I recognize them in you." She put a hand on his arm, feeling the hard coil of his muscles under her fingers. "If you don't release the anger, it will consume you. I'm afraid it will make you someone different from the man I know and love. I don't want to see that happen to you. . .to us."

His head dropped toward his chest. "I know you're right, but it's not easy. I understand with my mind that I have to forgive my father, but I don't feel the truth of it in my heart. I've been praying about my father. So far, God has been silent on the subject. Maybe when things settle down some. . ."

Lily stood on her tiptoes and placed a whisper-light kiss on his cheek. "I love you, dearest, but you cannot continue to put this off. It's weighing on you too heavily."

"You're right, and I want to." His large, warm hand cupped her chin. "I have an idea."

She placed her hand over his and met his gaze, trying to encourage him. She loved him so much she felt her heart would burst, and she wanted him to see what was in her heart. "What is that?"

"Why don't you pray for God to show both of us the right time and the right way to deal with my father?"

Lily nodded. As long as both of them leaned on His strength, they would weather any storm. That knowledge also brought her a measure of peace regarding Camellia. The Lord would watch over all of them—whether they were in the same town or not.

❧

Camellia reached for another of the plates Tamar had scrubbed clean. "If I never had to spend another night on a steamboat, my life would be perfect."

"Don't you say such things." Tamar frowned at her as she continued her task. "This is your sister's chosen home."

"She can come and visit me once I get married." Camellia grimaced at the thought of her family creating a rumpus in her spotless, well-ordered plantation home. Papa's tall tales, Jasmine's dramatic posturing, and Lily's stubbornness would put an end to harmony. It would be a wonder if Camellia's husband didn't forbid their return after a single day in company with her family. "But only if she brings Aunt Dahlia and Uncle Phillip along as well."

The choked sound from the woman standing beside her made Camellia smile. Both of them knew the likelihood of Lily and Aunt Dahlia traveling together. The probability that at least one of them would expire during the journey—and not from natural causes—was extremely high.

Camellia reached for another plate to dry. "Why do you remain on the *Water Lily*?"

"Many reasons." Tamar's voice sounded serene, almost dreamy. "I suppose the main reason is that a wife's place is at the side of her husband."

The statement brought a nod from Camellia. She had finally gotten used to the romance between Blake's friend and the woman who had been a surrogate mother to her.

Tamar and Jensen first met on Lily and Blake's steamship the *Hattie Belle*. Jensen had been the cook on that ship, but Tamar was a slave, the slave who had taken care of Lily, Camellia, and Jasmine as though they were her own children. She had seemed content with her position. For as long as Camellia could remember, Tamar had been loving and kind, with a world of practical wisdom to impart to her charges.

Camellia had been surprised when her older sister went to their grandmother and asked for Tamar's freedom—and even more shocked when the newly freed woman announced she was going to marry Jensen. It gave her a whole new view of Tamar as a real person, not just the unassuming woman who made sure her clothing was mended and her hair arranged.

"But don't you want a regular home and children of your own?"

"Oh child, a home is wherever and whatever you make it. Besides, the good Lord blessed me with both of those things when He let me watch you and your sisters grow up." She sighed. "I wouldn't complain if He decided to give us a child of our own, but with things in such an uproar, I don't know if that's a good idea."

Now it was Camellia's turn to sigh. "The war affects us all, doesn't it?"

"Even though I'm free now, it may not always be that way. Who knows whether our children would be safe?" Tamar's voice was matter-of-fact.

Camellia's problems were small in comparison to Tamar's. The war had delayed her plans for the future, but whether she would be free to pursue her goals had never been in doubt.

Tamar swished her hands through the dishwater and pulled them out to reach for the towel Camellia was holding. "That's all of the dishes."

Jasmine ran into the small gallery. "We're about to dock!"

Camellia thrust her disturbing thoughts aside. Tamar was free. She had a husband and a good job. Untying her apron, she pulled it off and hung it on a peg to dry. "I'll meet you on deck, Jasmine. I just need to check my appearance."

"Looks are not the only thing that matters." Tamar's warning chased Camellia out of the room.

Ignoring the words, Camellia hurried to the room she shared with Jasmine. A glance in the mirror proved her concern was valid. Her hair was a mess, and her shirtwaist was wrinkled from leaning against the galley counter. It would take too long to heat a curling rod. Camellia ran her fingers through the blond ringlets and fastened them with combs so that they cascaded around her face.

A quick search in her trunks unearthed her short cloak. She

could use it to hide the wrinkles in her blouse. Swinging it around her shoulders, she fastened the navy frog at the neck and checked her appearance once more.

Milky complexion, wide blue eyes, generous forehead, and long neck. She would turn heads as always. Men admired her while women hid their jealousy behind stiff smiles. It was her place in the world, a place she was determined to keep in spite of everything else.

She found both of her sisters and Jasmine's shadow, David, on deck, watching as their shipment was off-loaded by burly dockworkers. "How long will we be in Memphis?"

Lily glanced in her direction. "We'll stay with Eli and Renée Thornton tonight and leave in the morning."

Swallowing her groan, Camellia pinned a fake smile on her lips. She was not going to complain, even though she had no doubt Lily knew she didn't want to stay the night in Memphis. She wanted to get to New Orleans, get settled, and begin her school term.

"Don't worry." Jasmine stepped closer and grabbed her hand. "Papa says we'll get you there in time."

Camellia pulled her hand away. She didn't want to hear what Papa had to say about anything. What did her sisters see in him, anyway? All he did was tell stories about the way the river used to be. Or preach at them about turning the other cheek and forgiving other people hundreds of times when they were unpleasant. That was fine for him, but Camellia didn't see what good his talking did for her. Why should she be the one who forgave other people?

The one time she'd tried to talk to Lily about Papa's sermonizing, her older sister had gotten all serious and talked to her about letting go of the past like she had done. Camellia didn't have any problem with Papa's past. It was his present that bothered her. She'd much rather have Uncle Phillip for a father. He was a businessman. He knew how to dress, how to act at a dinner party, how to conduct himself in public. He would never be caught dressed like someone from the Revolutionary War. She busied herself comparing Uncle Phillip to Papa as they left the *Water Lily* and climbed into a rented carriage for the trip to Eli Thornton's home a few miles east of the harbor.

Jasmine chattered as usual, pointing out every building they passed as if they'd never before stayed in Memphis. How would others see them in the carriage? She was the pretty one, of course. Jasmine was the vivacious one. And Lily? Lily was just plain old Lily. Now that she had married Blake, her life had taken on a predictable pattern—one that Camellia would abhor, but one that seemed to bring her older sister happiness.

Chapter Four

Jonah's mouth was so dry he didn't think he would be able to deliver the code phrase. "May I inquire where you got that flower? Yellow is my favorite color."

"A shop on Beale Avenue purchases them especially for me. They are quite dear, but I don't mind the cost."

It was the correct response, the one that meant he was officially a spy. Jonah's shoulders tightened. His tongue felt too big for his mouth, and his breathing was choppy—as though he'd run all the way from his brother's store. He forced himself to take a slow, deep breath. "What happens next?"

He eyed the short man whom he named Mr. Brown for the color of his frock coat. He sported long brown sideburns, a bushy mustache, and a beard. If not for the bright yellow rosebud on his lapel, Jonah never would have given him a second glance. He supposed that was a good thing for a spy.

"You're going to New Orleans, a visit to your parents."

Jonah's blood chilled. He didn't like that this stranger knew so much about him and his family. "What will I do there?"

"Ferret out information about the rebel defenses—their weapons, plans, the number of soldiers present—and pass it along to your contact."

"How will I know him?"

The shorter man hesitated. Jonah thought he smiled, but it was hard to tell through the tangle of facial hair. "Your contact is not a man."

Jonah's eyebrows climbed high. "A female spy?" What type of lady would involve herself in such a dangerous pursuit?

"Why not? She's Colonel Poindexter's cousin, a widow who runs a school for the pampered daughters of rich Southern planters. That's why the captain was involved in choosing you. He has an interest in selecting an honest man, someone who won't betray his sister and can blend in with aristocratic society. You'll elicit all the information you can and give it to Mrs. Dabbs. She's responsible for getting the information to her brother. They'll be written in code, so even if a letter is intercepted, she won't fall under suspicion."

Wondering how he would avoid suspicion when delivering the information, Jonah nodded. When he had agreed to spy for the Union in June, he'd thought the general would send him out immediately. But that was before they received orders from President Lincoln to chase down the Missouri State Guard and stop them from consolidating a base in Missouri. They marched to Springfield, anxious to end the threat. But they had lost. Lost miserably. Catastrophically. So many men died. Even General Lyon was killed in a hail of bullets as he tried to rally his remaining men.

"You'll need to make haste to New Orleans. Even now the Federal navy is considering how to capture it. They need whatever information you can glean."

"I understand." He remembered the day Poindexter summoned him. Remembered the drawn look on the man's face. A colonel's eagle had replaced the captain's stripes on his shoulders, and his kindliness had all but disappeared under the weight of his new responsibilities. He gave Jonah the two phrases to memorize and sent him to Memphis to await further development.

Jonah had felt like the prodigal son on his arrival two days earlier. Of course, the prodigal son wasn't hiding dangerous facts from his family. Renée had prepared a feast, cementing his guilt because he knew the high prices she was paying for food, especially sugar from the plantations in the Caribbean. He'd barely been able to force down a morsel of the three-layered butter pecan cake topped with caramel icing. Or join in the happy conversation between Eli, Renée, and their three sons, Brandon, Cameron, and Remington. But no one seemed to notice anything odd.

"Is that all?" He wondered why he could not have received this instruction from Colonel Poindexter, but Jonah was too anxious to end this meeting to ask.

"Mrs. Dabbs's school is on Camp Street. Arrange to meet her alone and say, 'Mr. Lincoln could end all of this fighting if he would listen to reason.' "

Jonah nodded.

"Repeat the phrase, please."

He was not a child. Jonah opened his mouth to argue with the man but then hesitated. The knowing glint in "Mr. Brown's" eyes stopped him. He was much more experienced at spying. "Mr. Lincoln could end all of this fighting if he would listen to reason."

"Good. She will say, 'Yes, but I am afraid he is too stubborn to consider the desires of the South even though I write to him of my concerns.' " The other man looked at Jonah, a hint of his impatience evident in the shuffling of his feet.

"Yes, but I am afraid he is too stubborn to consider the desires of the South even though I write to him of my concerns."

The shorter man nodded once before glancing around at the quiet square. "Godspeed. May God be with us all."

When he turned and walked away, Jonah felt his stomach plunge. Was that how he would appear to some new recruit in a few months? Would he spend the rest of this war slinking around in the shadows and meeting other spies in deserted areas? Jonah began to pray as he left the square in the opposite direction "Mr. Brown" had taken. He prayed for the wisdom to outwit his friends and acquaintances. He prayed they would not be punished if he was caught. And he prayed that the war would end before he arrived in New Orleans.

❧

Camellia was not surprised when Jonah Thornton took the seat next to hers even though he had several other choices. Most men would have chosen to sit next to the most beautiful woman in the room.

She intercepted a glance between Blake and Lily, seated at opposite ends of the table. Jasmine and David had their heads together across the table from her, and Papa sat between her and Lily. Either Jonah could choose to sit between David and Blake, or he could share her side of the table.

Satisfaction and self-confidence surged within her. She glanced at Jonah sideways, noting the well-brushed frock coat he wore over fawn-colored trousers. A white shirt, stiff collar, and silk tie completed his ensemble, showing that he was both a man of means and particular about his appearance.

"You are even lovelier than I remember, Miss Anderson." His eyes crinkled at the outside corners when he smiled. "I'm so glad you'll be in our fair city for several months."

Camellia could feel her heartbeat accelerating and wished she had brought her fan to dinner. It would have given her hands something to do and helped to hide the blush rising to her cheeks. "Thank you, Mr. Thornton. It is kind of you to say so."

Blake cleared his throat. "Let's bless this food."

Everyone bowed their heads, but Camellia peeked up at the man sitting next to her. Jonah Thornton might not have a plantation, but he was quite charming. She would enjoy bandying words with him during their trip to New Orleans. It was a pity they only had one more full day before reaching their destination. When Blake ended the blessing, she raised her head with the rest of the diners.

Lily uncovered a dish of sliced beef and passed it around the table. "How long has it been since we saw you, Mr. Thornton?"

Jonah's grass-green eyes narrowed as he considered her sister's question. "You were Miss Anderson still. And I was naught but a carefree partygoer." His smile invited all of them to join his regret over youthful indiscretions. "I wish you would call me Jonah." He glanced at Camellia for a moment before returning his gaze to the others at the table. "Mr. Thornton is my father, or perhaps Eli. I could never aspire to their heights of maturity."

Blake filled his plate with beef, creamed potatoes, and one of Tamar's fluffy biscuits. "Whether you aspire to become mature or not, you will find yourself growing old faster than you might believe possible."

"Pay no attention to my gloomy husband." Lily smiled in his direction. "He found a gray hair this morning and has felt the weight of his age ever since."

Everyone laughed at her comment, but Camellia was embarrassed for them. Why would Lily expose poor Blake to ridicule? And why did her sister think it was appropriate to speak of such intimate details in a family setting? Lily needed to attend finishing school even worse than Camellia did. Not that she would. She was too busy sailing up and down the river, stopping at every port, and dwelling in the masculine world of shipping as though her gender did not matter.

Besides, if she did agree to attend, Lily would walk out after only a week of instruction. She had never seen a need to stand on ceremony. But speaking of Blake's dressing preparations went beyond what could be considered acceptable, even in the admittedly lax world of steamship travel.

"Will you be staying in New Orleans for an extended visit?" Camellia's father asked between bites of his dinner.

Jonah shrugged. "My plans are a bit unsettled at the moment. It depends on what entertainment may be had." He glanced toward her again, his gaze threatening to burn a hole in Camellia's face.

This time her blush was so heated that even Jasmine noticed it. "I think Jonah is sweet on you."

David's pale eyebrows disappeared into the thatch of white-blond hair on his forehead. Lily sputtered, Papa laughed heartily, and Blake frowned.

Camellia wanted to climb underneath the table. She tossed a scathing look at her younger sister. "You are embarrassing all of us, Jasmine. If you cannot hold your tongue, I hope Lily will send you to your room without your supper."

That stopped Papa's laugh and Lily's sputter.

Blake's frown disappeared as he reached for his water goblet. "I hope you will forgive Jasmine, Jonah. We are fairly free with our manners when we are *en famille*."

Camellia kept her gaze locked on her plate. She couldn't bear to look up at Jonah and see the condemnation in his eyes. The sooner she separated herself from her family the better.

"I don't mind." His deep voice sent shivers across her shoulders and down the length of her arms. "I consider it a compliment to be treated as one of the family."

Gathering her courage, Camellia risked a quick glance at him. Jonah's head was turned toward Blake, so she let her gaze linger on his profile. His chiseled jaw made him appear strong and capable. He sported a dimple in his chin that she could imagine tapping with her fan. His lips were full— Her thoughts came to an abrupt halt as he turned his head and their gazes clashed. His lazy, knowing smile taunted her. Jonah Thornton was too aware of his own attractiveness. It was a quality she did not appreciate.

Camellia sniffed and turned to engage Lily in conversation. "You don't have to come to La Belle Demoiselle with me. If you'll have my trunks delivered, I'm sure I can make my own way."

Jonah's arm was close enough to her own that Camellia felt it stiffen at her words. A tiny frown creased her brow before she remembered to smooth out the muscles. What could she have said to cause such a reaction in him?

"I'm not going to drop you off at the docks like a load of cargo, Camellia." Lily glanced toward Blake for confirmation before continuing. "I was planning on spending a few days with Jonah's family before returning to the river. Besides, did you think I had forgotten your birthday? We have always celebrated together, and this year will be no different."

Papa leaned across the table. "I believe the girl is ashamed of us." His wink included everyone at the table.

Now it was Camellia's turn to sputter. She thought she'd hidden her feelings better than that. Aunt Dahlia would be disappointed to learn she had been so transparent. "I am nothing of the sort." Even to her own ears, the words fell flat. She stopped and took a deep, calming breath. "I know how hard all of you work, and I was trying to make things easier. If any of you wish to accompany me to the school, I'm sure you are most welcome." With those words, she pushed her chair away from the table. "I'll go help Tamar with the dishes."

She was determined to show them she could rise above their taunts and accusations. If she was ashamed of certain members of her family, who could blame her? Debutantes, even ones as beautiful as she, had to be very assiduous in protecting their reputations or they would find themselves old maids while other, less objectionable females snatched up the best gentlemen.

Chapter Five

*C*amellia imagined that her patience was a ball of yarn like the one Mrs. Thornton held in her lap. Blue, of course, to match her eyes. Every now and then, like the roll of wool their hostess held, it threatened to break free, land on the floor, and unravel as it rolled toward the freedom of the front door. She had to concentrate on keeping her emotions in check or she would never be able to knit a future that matched her dream. A dream that was slipping away with each year that passed. She was eighteen today, a fact that had been celebrated during lunch with a festive cake and a song. Soon she would be too old to be considered a debutante. Soon she would be an old maid.

If only everyone would stop sitting about and help her get her belongings to La Belle Demoiselle. But here they remained, stationed in the front parlor of Mr. and Mrs. Thornton's town house, drinking tea and chatting without the least degree of urgency.

Mr. Thornton was reading his newspaper, Blake sat next to Lily on the sofa, and Jasmine was standing next to the window, looking out at the street. The only one missing was Jonah. She had not seen him since they arrived at his parents' home the day before. She couldn't really blame him, though, since his father had been less than enthusiastic about his return to New Orleans.

"You shouldn't worry about your sister. The war is not likely here." Mrs. Thornton's fingers worked nimbly as she spoke, her yarn turning into a lacy doily like the one covering the back of the chair in which Camellia sat. "Things are not as dire in New Orleans as you may have heard farther up the river."

Camellia glanced at Lily to see if she would accept Mrs. Thornton's reassurance. Her mauve day dress was Lily's nicest, but it was not as new or as fashionable as Camellia's pink one. Typical. Lily couldn't care less about fashions. All she wanted was something serviceable and modest.

"I know you're right, but leaving her here seems so risky." Lily tapped her spoon against the rim of her teacup before laying it on her saucer. "We know the Federal navy is eager to take this city. They have vowed to cut off trade between Europe and the South."

Mr. Thornton, sitting in a corner of the parlor, looked up. "Two forts lie between New Orleans and the Gulf of Mexico. They will defend us."

Blake shared a glance with Lily. "My wife cannot help herself. She's like a mother hen when it comes to her younger sisters."

"Sarah's here." Jasmine turned from the window, her excitement plain to see as she announced the arrival of the Thorntons' only daughter, Sarah Cartier.

Camellia shared her younger sister's enthusiasm. Now perhaps the others would be infused with some energy.

After a moment, the door to the parlor opened, and Sarah floated into the room. Camellia approved of her ensemble, a wool skirt and jacket of muted orange plaid befitting the winter season. "I was so excited to open Mama's note this morning. I hope you have not planned too many activities for your visit. I have dozens of ideas for things we can do."

Sarah dropped a quick kiss on her mother's cheek and waved a greeting at her father before turning to Lily. "Please tell me you will be here for a few days. I am having a little dinner party." She glanced toward Camellia, her dark eyes bright. "Nothing elaborate, but we plan to have musicians in case any of the younger people wish to dance."

Lily's gaze followed Sarah's. "I don't know. We are only here to see Camellia settled at her school."

Sarah clapped her hands. "La Belle Demoiselle, *n'est-ce pas?*"

Camellia nodded. She hoped to increase her understanding of French at the school. Of course she could translate simple phrases like the ones Sarah and Mrs. Thornton were always dropping into their conversations. By employing some herself, Camellia hoped to present a more continental persona.

"It is a very good school." Sarah kissed her fingers for emphasis and perched on the arm of Camellia's chair, giving her a quick hug. "But we must make sure you have sufficient clothes for the term, *non?*"

"You should see the number of trunks we off-loaded for her clothing." Blake's voice held a hint of mischief. "If she purchases anything else, she will have to store it in a separate room."

"Men." Sarah laughed. "They don't understand the things a female needs."

Camellia returned her smile. "I'm sure you're right."

"I want to go shopping, too." Jasmine crossed the room to stand near them.

Lily groaned. "Please don't tell me you've been infected with Camellia's fever to become a fashion plate. I've always hoped you would be a bit more down-to-earth."

Although Camellia could sympathize with Jasmine's desire to shop, she was also surprised by her younger sister's uncharacteristic statement. Perhaps she was reaching maturity. Jasmine could do worse than to follow her lead. In fact, as soon as she had secured her own future, Camellia would have to turn her attention to finding a worthy candidate to marry Jasmine. "You'll have to stop spending all your spare time with your nose in a book."

Jasmine tossed her dark hair over one shoulder in a gesture fit for a prima donna. "I enjoy reading."

Camellia thought of the tears Jasmine had shed when she finished the novel she'd been reading on their way to New Orleans. "Well, at least you might limit your reading to more uplifting material."

"*Uncle Tom's Cabin* was a very uplifting story."

Mr. and Mrs. Thornton gasped in unison, and Sarah slid off the arm of Camellia's chair to look at Lily and Blake. "You let her read such things?"

What was all the fuss about? It was only a novel, after all.

Mr. Thornton folded his newspaper and laid it on the table at his elbow. "False tales designed to demonize our way of life. It's written by a woman, after all, a liberal abolitionist with a political agenda."

Jasmine looked to Lily for support, but it was Blake who answered. "I've read the book myself. It has merit."

"I've never mistreated a slave in my life." Mr. Thornton's face reddened as he spat out the words. "I clothe and feed them, make sure all of their needs are met. And I daresay most men who own slaves are like me. It makes no more sense to whip a slave than to lame a horse."

"But you are an exception to the rule." Jonah's deep voice sent Camellia's heart bounding. When had he appeared? Leaning against the door frame, he looked more intense—and much more romantic—than he had seemed while they were aboard the *Water Lily*.

At least this time she had her fan. Camellia used it to cool her cheeks as she watched him straighten and saunter into the parlor. His green gaze ignored her to scan the room, stopping for a moment when he looked toward Blake but resting only when he met his father's angry stare.

"Do you think me a fool?" Mr. Thornton jumped to his feet. "I suppose you believe your travels have made you more knowledgeable than your father."

Jonah swept a low bow before him. "Who am I to argue with your opinion?"

The older man spluttered.

Camellia hid a smile behind her fan. Jonah's travels had made him more adept in social situations.

Mr. Thornton took a step toward his son, his demeanor threatening. "I don't know how I raised such an ardent abolitionist. It's about time you saw the world as it really is."

Jonah opened his mouth, and Camellia cringed at the anger she saw in his expression. Would the two men come to blows in front of them? She had heard about hot-blooded people who lived in New Orleans, but the Thorntons had never seemed quite so volatile. Not until now.

Sarah stepped between father and son, a warning look in her dark eyes. "This is not the time to air your personal differences. Think of your guests." She swept a hand around the room. "Do not make them more uncomfortable than you already have."

The tense moment stretched out until Camellia thought it would never end. Then Jonah nodded at his sister. "You're right. I apologize, Father. My passion for those who cannot protect themselves overcame my good sense."

As apologies went, it left a lot to be desired, but it seemed to appease

Mr. Thornton. Without another word, he brushed past Jonah and left the parlor.

For a moment, Jonah's troubled gaze followed his father's exit. When Sarah threaded her arm through his, however, he smiled down at her. "One of these days, he will have to realize he cannot control me."

"No matter how old you get, Jonah, he will always be your father." She glanced around the room.

Mrs. Thornton resumed her needlework. "Weren't you planning a shopping excursion?" Her practical question gave everyone a new focus.

Sarah separated herself from her brother and shooed Camellia and her sisters out of the parlor.

For the first time she could ever remember, Camellia didn't want to go shopping. It wasn't because she already had the necessary items for beginning the school term, nor did her eagerness to get to La Belle Demoiselle play into her reluctance. She wanted to spend more time with Jonah, regain the admiring attention he had showered on her during the trip from Memphis. He was so intense, so exciting to be around. Even when his eyes seemed filled with green lightning, she found herself drawn to the man.

Of course nothing could ever develop between them beyond a light flirtation. She had her sights set on a much bigger prize than Jonah Thornton. He had neither job nor military rank, proving his lack of ambition. She adopted a pleasant smile even while scolding herself for her reluctance.

As she and her sisters donned their cloaks and gloves, Camellia made a mental list of the reasons she could not be attracted to him. Jonah had no plantation and no prospects other than running his parents' shipping business. She wanted someone of deep conviction who believed in a cause and was ready to risk everything for it. Not someone who stood on the sidelines and pointed a finger of blame at the men who were fighting for their beliefs.

Satisfied with her logic, Camellia pushed Jonah from her mind. She couldn't wait for La Belle Demoiselle to open its doors.

Chapter Six

Camellia's excitement collapsed like an unstarched petticoat when Lily suggested Papa might want to accompany them to La Belle Demoiselle. She would rather be scalded with a pot of boiling water than have to face the ridicule of her peers and the teachers at the school when they realized what a character the man was. She cast a desperate glance around the breakfast table, but no one seemed aware of her consternation. "Perhaps I should go alone."

Lily's jaw dropped open. "What?"

If she had been trying to be the center of attention, Camellia had succeeded beyond her wildest dreams. Everyone was staring at her as if she had grown an extra head. "I. . .I don't want to be any trouble."

Blake raised an eyebrow before returning his attention to the food on his plate. "I doubt your sister will send you off by yourself."

"Of course not." Mrs. Thornton smiled.

"I saw them loading your trunks into the wagon as I came through the courtyard." Jonah added the information with a hint of mischief in his voice. "Perhaps you could ride on it instead."

"Jonah!" Mrs. Thornton shook her head at her son. "You are being ridiculous. Of course Camellia will ride with the rest of us in the carriage."

When Camellia saw the moisture in Jasmine's expressive eyes, she felt even worse. Why did everything have to be so difficult? Her family seemed determined to punish her for wanting to break away, wanting to have a life of her own. She pushed back from the table. "Thank you for the delicious breakfast."

"And for your wonderful hospitality." Lily put her napkin on the table next to her plate. "You cannot imagine how much easier I feel because you are here to watch over my sister."

"Never fear." Mrs. Thornton leaned across the corner of the table and patted Lily's hand.

Camellia ignored the sardonic look in Jonah's eyes and wondered if she could slip away before anyone realized she was gone. Probably not. Unless she wanted to ride in the wagon as Jonah had suggested. Camellia's ears burned at the thought of arriving on such a pedestrian conveyance. Perhaps there were worse things than having to introduce her papa.

She went upstairs to the bedroom she had been sharing with Jasmine to gather her cloak and check to make sure she was presentable. Staring into the mirror, Camellia tried to imagine what life would be like at the school. Now that the day had finally arrived, she found herself oddly reluctant to forge ahead.

"I'm going to miss you." Jasmine had entered the room without making a sound and came to stand behind Camellia's left shoulder.

"It's not like I'll be gone for a long time. The school term will end in a few months, and I'll return to Natchez." She turned and held out her arms, enfolding Jasmine and dropping a kiss on her forehead. "But I don't want you to get any older until then."

"I won't." Jasmine could usually be counted on to giggle at her silliness, but this morning she seemed more somber. Her lower lip protruded slightly, and her violet eyes were shadowed. "Please don't forget about us."

"As if I could." Camellia leaned back and stared into her sister's eyes. "I know you don't understand why this is so important to me, but I promise to come home again."

"Lily says you'll probably be married before the end of the year." Jasmine's dark eyes filled with tears again.

What a wonderful idea. Camellia was glad her sister was prepared for that eventuality. But this was not the time to admit as much to her younger sister. "Don't worry so. It will be your turn before too much longer."

Jasmine shrugged her shoulders. "I don't ever want to get married."

Feeling the full weight of her eighteen years, Camellia drew on her own experience. "You're a warm and caring young lady who is not quite grown up yet, but wait and see. One day you'll wake up and realize that a home and children are exactly what you want most."

Jasmine didn't look convinced, but she did not argue the point, instead looking around for her cloak and bonnet.

Once she was sure they were both ready to leave, Camellia took a deep breath. She would go through with this. Nothing, not even a marauding Yankee army, was going to stand in her way.

~

Mrs. Thornton arranged her skirts with care in the crowded carriage. "I'm glad you could arrange your schedule to accompany us, Jonah."

Ignoring the beautiful Camellia, whose skirts were taking up the majority of the bench he shared with her, Jonah leaned his head back and closed his eyes. "I am happy to be of service." The thick irony in his voice was carefully contrived. None of the four females in the carriage could suspect his real motive for joining them.

"How far away is the school?" Lily was sandwiched between his mother and Jasmine. She sounded as uncomfortable as she probably was.

"Not too far," his mother answered. "The Garden District is not as close to the river as our town house, but it is a lovely area."

"Why is it called La Belle?"

Jonah lifted his head, wondering why Lily encouraged Jasmine's never-ending curiosity. One of these days it would likely put her into a perilous situation, much like those faced by an inquisitive feline. It was a pity Jasmine could not boast nine lives. She would probably need several.

"The name is La Belle Demoiselle." His mother answered the question. "It means the beautiful young girl. The man who built it, Mr. Peter Hand, was a successful architect with a very young bride. I have heard that he named his home for her. When Mrs. Dabbs, the present owner of the house, decided to open a school for young girls, she decided to use the original name."

"How romantic." Camellia leaned forward and stared out of the window as though counting the minutes until their arrival.

Wouldn't she be shocked to discover the other side of her romantic headmistress? Jonah ran through the code phrase to make sure he would not stumble when the time came to alert the woman to his identity. He hoped she was more experienced at this spying game than he. If not, the North was in serious trouble.

৵

The last one out of the carriage, Camellia put her hand in Jonah's and caught her breath. *Tranquil. . .tranquil as the surface of a pond.* The mantra helped her present a calm face even though her heart felt as though it was about to jump out of her chest. The quick squeeze he gave her gloved fingers did not help matters. What was it about this man that affected her so? Why did her cheeks burn in spite of the cold wind swirling through the quiet neighborhood?

As soon as her slippers touched the raised sidewalk, she pulled her hand from his and looked around, determined to minimize the contact. In an effort to regain control, she focused on the ornate iron fence surrounding the school property. "Is that a snowflake design?"

"Oui." Mrs. Thornton touched the gate with a gloved hand. "The story is that Mr. Hand's young wife was from New York, and she missed the beautiful winters of her youth. So he ordered the fence to ease her homesickness."

Jasmine had been quiet all the way to the school, but she brightened at Mrs. Thornton's explanation. "How romantic."

A grunt from Jonah showed his lack of appreciation for Mr. Hand's gesture. Typical.

Camellia couldn't resist adding her own interpretation. "When a marriage is based on mutual love, such wonderful gestures become commonplace."

Lily nodded her agreement, but Jonah rolled his eyes before opening the gate for the ladies.

Lacy iron formed arches between the black columns that framed the first-story porch and the second-story balcony. They reminded Camellia of picture frames. She could see herself standing on the balcony. Her soldier-fiancé would have an arm around her, and they would be facing each other as they exchanged sweet words of love and devotion.

A jerk on her arm ended the pleasant daydream. "Are you going to stand out here in the cold all morning?" Jonah's frown was like a slap.

51

"Of course not." She lifted her skirts and climbed the steps to the front porch, her head high. How dare he criticize her? This was her time. She was not going to let him destroy her anticipation.

A black woman wearing a dark dress and a fancy white apron met them at the front door. Mrs. Thornton introduced herself and explained the reason for their arrival, handing her calling card to the servant.

While they waited for Mrs. Dabbs to send for them, Camellia looked around the stylishly appointed foyer. A silver tray filled with other calling cards rested on a small table to her right. Above it was a rococo mirror. Several chairs lined the wall next to the table, a place for visitors to sit while they waited to see if the lady of the house was receiving guests.

A door opened farther down the hall, and a tall, spare woman appeared. She was probably about the same age as Aunt Dahlia, but that was the only similarity Camellia could find between them. Mrs. Dabbs moved more slowly than her aunt would, her hands folded at her waist. Her hair, parted in the center, was very dark except for a stunning stripe of snow-white tresses beginning at the V of her widow's peak. Each step she took was small and deliberate, conveying her authority and self-confidence.

"*Bienvenue, monsieur and mesdames, á mon ecôle.*" Her accent was as impressive as her entrance. Camellia wondered if she had spent time in France.

"*Merci*, Madame Dabbs. *Me permettre d'introduire. . . .*"

The words washed over Camellia. One day she would be able to carry on a conversation like the one between Mrs. Thornton and Mrs. Dabbs. It was a pity she had not studied French when she was younger, but her relatives had never seen a need for her to learn the language.

Mrs. Thornton switched to English and introduced Jonah, Lily, and Jasmine. Then she turned to her and nodded. "And this beautiful lady is of course your new pupil, Miss Camellia Anderson."

"Mademoiselle Anderson, it is a pleasure to meet you." She spoke without any trace of accent, slipping from one language to another with an ease Camellia envied.

Camellia could feel the weight of Mrs. Dabbs's assessing gaze as she curtsied.

When she straightened, the lady was smiling at her. "We are going to have such a wonderful spring, my dear. Your things arrived earlier, and they have been taken to your bedroom upstairs. Say farewell to your family, and I will take you to meet your roommate."

So soon? Her nose tingled as she turned to face the others. Parting from her sisters was going to be harder than she had realized. It wasn't like remaining behind at Les Fleurs while Lily and Jasmine took an overnight trip to Memphis or Baton Rouge. She wouldn't see her sisters for months.

The tight smile on Lily's face was an indication of her older sister's emotions. She was probably already regretting her decision. And Jasmine looked as though she might burst into tears at any moment.

"Thank you so much for letting me do this." She hugged Lily and Jasmine at the same time. "I love both of you very much."

"We love you, too." Jasmine's voice was a bare whisper.

Lily's arms tightened around her. "Are you sure you want to do this?"

Camellia nodded, her head rubbing against theirs.

"Then you'd better get upstairs before I drag you back to the carriage." Lily released her and raised her chin. "But remember that I can come get you at any time. All you have to do is get a message to the Thorntons."

"Now, now." Mrs. Dabbs stepped between them, cutting off Camellia's escape route. "Your sister will be very happy here. All of my students enjoy themselves."

Allowing herself to be pulled toward the staircase, Camellia heard a whisper from the second floor. She glanced upward and caught a glimpse of a heart-shaped face surrounded by a cloud of dark hair before it disappeared around a wall. One of the other students. She looked about Jasmine's age. Camellia glanced back over her shoulder at her younger sister, wishing for a brief instant that she would remain behind.

Then reality intruded. Jasmine would never be happy here. She barely tolerated the lessons she received aboard the *Water Lily*. La Belle Demoiselle was not the place for either of her sisters. But it was the perfect place for Camellia. She felt lighter as she moved away from the first floor, as though each step upward was freeing her, freeing her to become an irresistible combination of style and grace that would complement her physical beauty.

She looked up and met Jonah's gaze. She wished she could think of something to say that would wipe away the half smile on his face. She had no reason to blush. It wasn't like he could read her thoughts.

Jonah shook his head and turned his attention to Mrs. Dabbs. "If something happens, you will send a note around to my parents' home."

She tilted her head and stared at him. "Of course, but I believe we're safe enough here."

Camellia wondered why Mrs. Dabbs's reassurance made Jonah straighten his posture. He threw his shoulders back, looking almost like a soldier for a moment. "Mr. Lincoln could end all of this fighting if he would listen to reason."

"Yes, but I am afraid he is too stubborn to consider the desires of the South even though I write to him of my concerns."

Camellia's eyes widened. "You send letters to Abraham Lincoln?"

"Why not?" Mrs. Dabbs's smile softened her question. "If I don't ask him to stop this war, how can I expect him to grant my dearest wish?"

"How indeed?" Lily looked impressed by the lady's calm logic. "Perhaps all of us should follow your example."

Mrs. Dabbs nodded in agreement. "I encourage all of my students to do so."

"Do you really think your letters reach Mr. Lincoln's desk?" Jasmine's eyes were wide at the thought.

"I am sure of it. I grew up in Maryland, you know. It is not so far from the White House. And I got to see one of the debates between Mr. Lincoln and Mr. Douglas a few years ago. He struck me then as a man who is very approachable." Then she seemed to add as an afterthought, "As does our own president, Mr. Davis."

Lily pulled on her gloves. "Well, I hope one of them pays attention to any pleas you send. I am afraid there will be no winner in this war."

Chapter Seven

Two large beds filled the room, and a banked fire pulled dampness from the air and made the space feel warm and inviting. Camellia's trunks were nowhere to be seen, and she wondered where they might be. A large wooden desk took center stage in the room, with several books stacked on top of it and a pair of ladder-back chairs tucked on either side. A rocker filled another corner, but there was still plenty of room to move around.

Camellia looked for the girl she had caught a glimpse of as they came upstairs. Was she going to be her roommate? Pushing the question aside for the moment, she removed her gloves and hat, tossing them on the nearest bed as she moved into the room.

Mrs. Dabbs cleared her throat. "You must not get in the habit of scattering your belongings about. At least a dozen young ladies will be attending classes this spring term. You'll want to avoid the possibility of mixing up your things with someone else's."

A blush heated Camellia's cheeks. "I'm sorry."

With a wave of her hand and a quick smile, the older lady excused her actions.

Camellia snatched up her hat and gloves and looked around for a better place to put them.

"I had closets installed in all of the bedrooms last year." Mrs. Dabbs took Camellia's hat and walked to a bank of doors on the far side of the room. When she pulled on them, they parted, folding back like the spines of a fan.

Camellia's jaw dropped when she realized several of her new outfits hung from a bar inside the wooden box. "How ingenious." Her skirts looked ready to be worn. They were not crushed from lying on top of one another.

Mrs. Dabbs laid her hat and gloves on a shelf at the top of the closet before turning and dusting her hands together. "There. That's much better. One of the first lessons most of my girls learn is how to take care of their clothes. During these uncertain times, you must learn to fend for yourselves."

Camellia didn't understand the other woman's logic. She would never have to do without slaves or servants. But she was not going to start the term with an argument. She nodded and won an approving smile from Mrs. Dabbs.

"Jane Watkins, your roommate, arrived late last night. Like you, she comes from Mississippi. I'm sure you'll get along famously." Mrs. Dabbs moved to the door. "I'll ask her to come up and help you settle in before dinner. We won't start classes until tomorrow, as two of the local girls won't be here until this afternoon."

Removing her cloak, Camellia started to toss it across the foot of her bed. But then she stopped and looked toward the door. She would be a model student, learning everything Mrs. Dabbs offered whether she agreed with the lady or not.

Walking across the room, she pushed on one of the closet doors. It didn't budge. She stepped back and considered the problem. Did it act like a fan? She looked toward the floor but saw nothing except wooden planks. Raising her gaze slowly upward, she spied a pair of depressions— one on each door. She placed her fingers in one and tugged, her lips curving upward in a triumphant smile as the door glided open.

She didn't think closets would catch on. Her skirts looked odd— deflated—suspended from hooks that ran along the walls of the closet. The flounces bunched together, and the arms of her shirtwaists hung empty. Her clothing looked like it belonged on a scarecrow. With a sigh, she bunched up her cloak and tried to fit it on an empty hook. It slithered to the floor as soon as she let go of it.

"Here, let me help you."

Camellia jumped at the unexpected sound of a voice. Her ringlets bounced around her face as she turned to the front of the bedroom. Taking in the pretty girl who must be Jane, she wondered if they were going to be rivals.

Sunlight poured into the room from a large window and seemed to set Jane's thick auburn hair aflame. She stepped up to the closet and took Camellia's cloak, shook it out, and hung it on the offending hook by its collar. "There. It only takes a little practice to get the hang of this."

She giggled, her brown eyes dancing. "Get it? You'll soon get the *hang* of it."

A nervous laugh gurgled up Camellia's throat.

"Oh good. I was hoping my roommate would have a sense of humor." Jane put a hand on Camellia's arm and pulled her toward one of the beds. "You're quite beautiful, you know. I should be jealous, but that would make living with you so uncomfortable."

Camellia took in her roommate's curvaceous figure. From her long neck to her tiny waist, Jane was the very embodiment of femininity. She had thought the other girl's eyes were brown, but now that she was close to her, she realized they were more hazel. "You're pretty, too."

Jane waved away the compliment with a quick motion. "I've always wanted curls like yours, but no matter how much effort I expend, my hair has more in common with a mop than a corkscrew."

Unable to resist the urge to laugh, Camellia felt the tension and fear fading. Jane was not going to be a rival. Whatever sadness had lingered at parting from her sisters disappeared. "Your hair gleams, though, while mine is as dull as wash water."

Her new friend's mouth tightened, and the green flecks in her eyes dimmed. "I have an idea."

"What?" Assuming an equally serious expression, Camellia straightened her spine.

"I assume you're here for the same reason I am—to find the perfect husband."

Camellia wasn't sure if she was ready for this much frankness. She waited for Jane to continue.

"Think about it, Camellia. Not every man wants a vivacious, redheaded beauty on his arm."

Both of them were perched on the edge of the bed, their skirts billowing around them. Camellia thought they would present a nice picture—one dark, the other fair. Her eyes widened. She looked at Jane, who nodded. "I believe you may be the smartest girl I've ever met."

Jane squealed and fell on her neck. "Between us, we'll attract every available man in the city of New Orleans."

"Why stop there?" Camellia emerged from the embrace with a sigh. "I have my heart set on marrying a hero, someone who is willing to fight for his beliefs."

Jumping up from the bed, Jane squealed again and reached for her hand. "I cannot believe it."

"What?"

"My brother. You have to meet my brother. He's rich, handsome, and a soldier." She ran to the desk and pulled out a chair. "I'm going to write to him right away. I can't wait until we're sisters."

Camellia watched as she bent over a piece of stationery, excitement building in her. She'd known coming to La Belle Demoiselle was the right move, but she'd never dreamed she would find the perfect husband on the day of her arrival. "What's your brother's name?"

"Thaddeus. . .Thaddeus Watkins. But everyone calls him Thad."

Mrs. Thad Watkins. She extended her hand and imagined a large ring on her fourth finger. Fate had ordained her future. Maybe she'd been foolish to spend so much energy regretting the necessity of putting off her education for a year. Everything was working out perfectly.

❧

Jonah was sick of parties. He was tired of sifting through bits and pieces of information and trying to decide what was important enough to pass along to Mrs. Dabbs. At least he'd been able to report the encouraging news that the work on the two ironclads being built in the New Orleans harbor was at a standstill. Getting the supplies through Admiral Farragut's blockade had proven more difficult than expected. Furthermore, many of the men who were formerly employed as shipbuilders had volunteered in the Confederate army.

Last night he had learned that a portion of the New Orleans forces were being sent northward, further weakening the city's defenses. He needed to get that information to Mrs. Dabbs right away. If the Union showed up today, he believed they could take over the city without firing a single shot.

"Did I overhear you ordering that your horse be saddled?" His mother's question interrupted his thoughts. "I am planning to visit

Mary Lee Thompson's mother and thought you might like to join me. You seemed to be taken with her at your sister's party last week."

"No, thank you. I'm going to La Belle to check on Camellia Anderson."

"Again?" Her gaze searched his face. "You have been to see her several times in the past month. I thought the first time that it was just your sense of obligation to Lily, but I am beginning to wonder if you have other reasons to frequent the school."

Another of the problems with being a spy was the lying, especially to people he cared about. "She's pretty, but I have no interest other than that of an older brother. Besides, she has her sights set on a much bigger prize."

A frown crossed his mother's face. "I don't know why she wouldn't be flattered by your attention. Why don't you take her some flowers? Young ladies always like romantic gestures."

"Thank you for the advice, Mother."

"I know, I know. You don't need your mother telling you how to act."

At least he knew enough about the female gender to not respond to that comment.

"Why don't you invite Camellia over for a weekend visit?" His mother seemed to have taken his silence as an invitation to meddle. "I'm sure she would like to get away from the school for a few days."

"She seems pretty happy at La Belle." As soon as he made the statement, Jonah could have bitten off his tongue. Even to his own ears, he sounded too much like a jealous suitor. "I'll invite her if you wish."

"Excellent. Sarah would probably like to see her, too. And we'll all go to church together. Perhaps I can even convince your father to join us."

"I doubt that. Father cannot abide the pastor's cooperationist leanings. The last time he went with us, I thought he was going to have an apoplexy."

"He is a man of strong principles."

"It's a shame he's chosen the wrong ones."

She considered him for a moment before answering. "Youth is a glorious time. You know all the answers and could solve all of the world's problems if only you were in charge." She pursed her lips. "But things are not that simple. Your father is an ardent supporter of states' rights. He believes the federal government has grown too powerful, and he doesn't want to be ruled by the politicians in Washington."

"He would rather be ruled by the rich planters instead?"

Silence fell between them, filled with tension. Jonah wondered if other families suffered the same divisions, argued the same issues.

"Your father is a good man." His mother's voice was tender.

The tension leached out of Jonah's shoulders. He smiled at her and pushed back from the table. "I should be back in an hour or so."

Her eyes, a darker shade of green than his, were luminous with unshed tears. "I love you."

He moved to her side of the table and dropped a kiss on the cheek she raised to him. "I love you, too, Mother."

"Now go. And don't let Camellia get away from you. If you wait too long, she may fall for some other fellow's smooth talk."

It was time to make his escape before his well-meaning parent sent out invitations for a wedding. "I promise you my heart is not pining for the beauteous Miss Anderson. I'm not ready to marry anyone."

"If you change your mind, you will let me know, won't you?"

"Of course. You'll be the first." He left the house then, snagging his greatcoat on his way to the stable. A misty rain chilled the air as he threaded his way through the congested streets.

A feeling of anticipation surprised him. He wanted to get this errand behind him, didn't he? Of course he did. It must have been all the silly talk from his mother about other suitors that had him thinking of Camellia Anderson.

That was it. Jonah pulled back on his horse's reins and moved out of the flow of traffic. He had no feelings about her at all. Visiting Camellia was nothing but a ruse to protect him from exposure. He didn't even enjoy being around her. In fact, he hoped she would turn down his mother's invitation. The idea of being around her for an extended period of time filled him with nothing more than dismay, perhaps even repugnance.

Once this war was over, he would turn his attention to marriage, and when he did, it would be to someone much more serious about life. A girl who had strong faith and exhibited the qualities enumerated in the book of Proverbs. Camellia probably had no idea how to be a proper wife, and he had no desire to teach her.

Satisfied with his logic, Jonah clucked his tongue and encouraged his mount forward once more, eventually arriving in the quieter portion of the city where Mrs. Dabbs's school was located. The trick was to keep his mind on the job the military had given him. Maybe after he left the school, he would visit the Custom House to discover what the enterprising blockade runners had managed to slip past the Union navy. Feeling much more in control of himself, Jonah dismounted and tied his horse to an ornate post outside of the school. All he had to do was politely ask Camellia to visit. Then he could get on with the real reason for his visit.

Chapter Eight

I don't understand why we have to practice needlepoint." Camellia punched her needle through the piece of cotton, almost stabbing her knee through her skirt and the multiple layers of petticoats she wore. "I already know how to sew."

Mrs. Dabbs was helping Camellia with a knot in her thread. "This is not about sewing. It's about beautifying your home with handmade art."

"Every well-bred lady should be able to ply a needle with skill." Pauline, a short girl with olive skin and a long nose, added her opinion.

Fourteen-year-old Molly nodded. Camellia thought of the girl as Pauline's shadow. She had an unfortunate lisp, so she didn't speak often. Next to her sat bespectacled Catherine, who was probably doing a better job than Camellia even though she was practically as blind as a bat.

Even Jane seemed to be enjoying their lesson. She held her handwork up to the light, and Camellia could see how even each stitch was in the five-pointed star and the circle surrounding it.

She sighed and pulled her needle back through even as she realized the points of her star had an odd tilt and her circle was decidedly lopsided. She would much rather be practicing her penmanship or even adding up columns of numbers. At least those skills had some bearing on her future. If she needed artwork for her home, she would commission an artist to paint a portrait of her to be hung above the mantel in the front parlor.

A knock at the door brought Camellia back to the present. Mademoiselle Brigitte Laurent, Mrs. Dabbs's assistant, entered the room and looked straight at her. *"Excusez-moi,* Mademoiselle Anderson, *vous avez un visiteur."* The girl looked over her shoulder and blushed.

"Merci." Camellia thanked her in French without effort. Her accent was getting much better. She caught Jane's inquisitive glance and shrugged. She had no idea who might be asking for her. Standing up, she moved to place her handwork in her seat, but it was stuck on something.

A giggle from one of the other girls made her look down.

"Oh no!" The groan came when she realized she had sewn her star to her dress. Now everyone could see how poor her needlework was. She tried to jerk the pitiful cloth free, but she had no luck. She had never been so embarrassed in her life. A blush burned her throat and cheeks.

"I see you're sporting a new style."

Camellia looked toward the door and wished she had not gotten out of bed this morning. Her embarrassment increased tenfold—a hundredfold—as she saw the sardonic grin on Jonah Thornton's face. She wanted to jump out the window, sink beneath the carpets, or at least run away from the derisive laughter. Even Mrs. Dabbs had a hand over her mouth, her eyes dancing.

"Let me help you." Jane pulled out a pair of scissors and snipped the threads holding the needlework to her dress.

Bless Jane, her only friend in the world. Even though her cheeks were still flaming, Camellia lifted her chin. "I have always been an innovative thinker."

Jonah bowed, although his grin was still wide. "I look forward to seeing all the debutantes following your lead."

The smothered giggles stopped as Mrs. Dabbs stood. "How pleasant to see you again, Mr. Thornton." She nodded at Camellia. "Why don't you and Jane show Mr. Thornton the visitors' parlor? Mademoiselle Laurent will order the tea service."

Grabbing her friend by the hand, Camellia hurried to comply with the instructions. Anything to put distance between her and their stitchery lessons. She pulled Jane past Jonah before he could say anything derogatory, leading the way to a small parlor just off the central staircase.

A cheerful fire crackled in the fireplace, its flames dispelling the February chill. A small sofa provided seating for an intimate conversation, while a single straight-backed chair some distance away was for a chaperone. Camellia sank onto the sofa, her cheeks beginning to cool. She motioned for Jane to sit next to her, but her friend shook her head and moved to the chaperone's chair.

Did Jane think Jonah was a suitor? Far from it. Although she had considered him a possibility at one time, it had not taken her long to discover he was like a bothersome gnat she would like to swat. She was still staring daggers at Jane as he entered the room, having taken his sweet time to traverse the hallway.

Her heart stopped for a brief moment as their gazes met. He *was* handsome; she had to allow him that. She remembered the first time she'd seen him, his deep auburn locks stylishly disheveled, his emerald eyes swirling with mystery and challenge. But that had been years ago—almost two whole years—and she had become much more sophisticated since then.

In an effort to prove how little she cared, Camellia spread her skirts out to cover the length of the sofa. Of course he didn't understand that she wanted him to stand.

He simply raised one supercilious eyebrow and towered over her. "I'm happy to see how much you've learned about decorum since you came to La Belle."

Camellia's shocked gaze met his and read the determination stamped there. Suddenly she realized that Jonah was no longer the carefree younger son. He was a man fully grown. She huffed her irritation but gathered in her skirt. "Please sit down, Mr. Thornton."

"Thank you for the offer, Miss Anderson, but I believe I'll stand." He moved to the fireplace and leaned one shoulder against the mantel.

Infuriating man. One of these days she would get the better of him. Maybe she would even make him fall in love with her. Once she knew his heart was in her hands, she would make him beg for mercy. Then she would marry someone else, and Jonah would live out the rest of his days a broken shell of his former self.

With her plan in mind, Camellia fluttered her eyelashes at Jonah. "It's so pleasant to see you on this dreary day."

His grin widened.

Hanging on to her temper with all her might, Camellia forced herself to smile back at him. "How are your parents?"

He pushed away from the mantel, and she hoped it was because his backside was burning. After making a circle around the room, his gaze flitting from window to door, he sat next to her on the sofa. "My mother sends her regards. She and my father would like for you to come and stay with them for the first weekend next month."

Since the moment Jonah had arrived at La Belle Demoiselle today, Camellia had felt like the very ground under her feet was shifting. His statement, however, changed all that. Her world steadied. He must have told his mother he would like to court her, and sweet Mrs. Thornton had extended the invitation so he would have ample opportunity. This was a game she knew very well how to play. She would turn him down and allow herself to be persuaded by his heartfelt pleas.

She leaned against the back of the sofa and turned her head toward Jane, giving her a broad wink as a cue. "Don't we already have plans for that particular weekend?"

Jane shook her head. "I don't—"

Camellia interrupted her friend. "Oh yes, the trip to Lake Pontchartrain is scheduled for that weekend, is it not?"

Jane folded her lips together and shot her a fearful look.

Camellia turned back to Jonah only to find him not even paying any attention to her. He was looking over his shoulder at the door to the parlor. Was he interested in someone else?

A sharp pain clenched her heart, stealing her breath for a moment. Was she mistaken about Jonah's interest? "I believe my roommate is correct after all, Mr. Thornton."

"What's that?" He turned back to her, his eyes unfocused.

Had he been drinking? He was certainly acting oddly. Camellia straightened her spine. "I said I will—" She broke off as a thought occurred to her. "That is, Jane and I will be able to come for a visit on that weekend."

He nodded. "Good."

Mademoiselle Laurent entered with the tea tray, and Jane pulled her chair closer to the low, ornate table in front of the sofa. Camellia narrowed her eyes and watched to see if any secret glances passed between Mrs. Dabbs's assistant and Jonah. Neither of them seemed to notice the other, but was their nonchalance suspicious?

Camellia waited until the assistant left before pouring the tea and offering Jonah the tray of sweets. "Have you written to Mr. Lincoln?"

An odd expression crossed his face. Fear? It was gone so quickly she wondered if she had imagined it. "I have been too busy for that."

"I suppose your father must appreciate your help at his office."

"I'm not working." Jonah shook his head and glanced over his shoulder again.

Who was he expecting? Camellia looked at Jane and shrugged. "Then what is it that occupies your time?"

He looked back at her. "Escorting my sister and my mother to their numerous social engagements."

"I see." She wanted to ask him how he could waste his time in frivolity. Didn't he know they were at war? Had he no patriotic feelings? She rose from the sofa, forcing him to follow suit. "It's been nice seeing you, but Jane and I must get back to our class."

"Yes." Jonah gave her his full attention. "You certainly need all the instruction you can get."

Camellia snapped her mouth shut on the words that threatened to escape. Never before had she so clearly understood the command to not cast pearls before swine. She would make certain she followed it in her future dealings with Jonah Thornton.

❧

Jonah lingered in the parlor after Camellia stormed out. He should be ashamed of himself for baiting her, but he found the temptation irresistible. A chuckle slipped out as he considered the girl. Of course, she brought a great deal of it on herself by insisting on adhering to all the rules of society.

"It's good to hear you laugh." Mrs. Dabbs entered the room and closed the door behind her.

He shook his head. "Not while I'm on such serious business."

"Do you have new information for me?"

"Yes. Last night I learned that General Lovell's request for additional troops to defend the city has been refused for now."

Mrs. Dabbs clasped her hands in front of her chest. "That's good news for us."

"Yes, but we cannot get overconfident. The Confederacy will not give up the city unless the Union can act quickly. The troops will eventually arrive, and then it will take a pitched battle to capture New Orleans."

The older woman grew more serious. "Many lives will be lost if that happens."

"Yes."

"Can you find out exactly when the troops will be sent?"

Jonah sighed. "I don't know. I'll try."

Her sigh echoed his. "I know it's difficult, but remember that we have a worthy goal."

"You are right." He bowed and turned to depart.

Mrs. Dabbs stopped him with a hand on his arm. "I pray for your safety every night. I know God is watching over us."

"Thank you, Mrs. Dabbs. You are truly a remarkable woman." As he left, Jonah compared Camellia's personality to that of her headmistress. She would do well to emulate Mrs. Dabbs in all areas—skill, comportment, and faith. If only she could let go of her self-importance.

Chapter Nine

"I cannot believe the soldiers need any more bandages." Pauline folded her arms over her chest and sat back. "We've rolled thousands already. Enough to stretch from here to Virginia. What can they possibly need more bandages for?"

All the blood drained from Jane's face.

"Ith for doctorth to wrap around the hurth." Molly was finally beginning to talk more often in spite of her lisp, and she no longer absorbed every word spouted by the overbearing Pauline.

Camellia reached out a hand to her friend. "Don't think about it."

Jane nodded and looked at Mrs. Dabbs. "May I be excused?"

Mrs. Dabbs gave her permission, and silence fell on the room while Jane rose and slipped out of the room, closing the door with a sharp click.

Poor little Catherine's eyes grew monstrously large behind her spectacles, and a fat tear rolled down her cheek. She was a very high-strung child.

Pauline was more resilient. She rolled her eyes. "What's the matter with her?"

"How can you be so insensitive?" Camellia's hands balled into fists. She loved Jane like a sister. "Jane has never done anything to you. Don't you know her brother is a soldier? One of these bandages could be used on wounds he sustains in a battle."

"I'm sorry." Pauline's dark face blanched. "I didn't think—"

"That's right. You didn't think. You never think about anything if it doesn't affect you." Camellia could feel the blood pounding in her head.

"Enough." Mrs. Dabbs pointed to the pile of cloth strips. "If you cannot be civil to each other, then you will finish your tasks in silence."

Camellia enjoyed the practical job of rolling bandages much more than stitching stars or circles. Where would this roll go? What hands would unroll it and gently wrap it around a wounded soldier? Would this bandage save his life? She hoped so. She hoped the nameless soldier would sense the love and caring wrapped into the spiral of cotton.

Half an hour passed, and her roommate had not returned. Camellia was about to go in search of her when the door opened and Jane rejoined them. Her eyes and nose bore indications of a tearful interlude.

Reaching for a fresh strip, Camellia sent a threatening look at Pauline. She had better not say anything else untoward. Camellia wasn't afraid of her or her family.

A rustling sound brought her head up. One of the servants had opened the door, but Camellia hardly saw her for the vision standing directly behind her. He was beautiful. Tall, with shoulders so wide they looked like they would fill a doorway. His face was all angles, from his square chin to his high cheekbones. His dark eyes surveyed the room and zeroed in on one face. Camellia barely had time to register the way his smile was reflected in those delicious eyes before a feminine squeal startled her.

Jane launched herself toward the stranger and threw herself into his arms. Had she forgotten to tell her best friend about this man she obviously loved? Wistful envy filled Camellia. What a fortunate girl she was to be adored by such a fine specimen of a man. And a soldier at that. He didn't even need the gray uniform—he would have been equally handsome in civilian attire.

"Jane!" Mrs. Dabbs's shocked tones separated the two at the door.

Jane's tears were back. They trickled down her face, reddening her eyelids and nose all over again. But the wide smile on her friend's face told Camellia this time her tears were of the joyful variety.

The tall man reached into his pocket and produced a handkerchief that he offered to her.

Jane wiped her face clean and took a deep breath. "I'm sorry, Mrs. Dabbs. Please allow me to introduce a very special man." She sent him an adoring glance and reached for his hand, drawing him farther into the room. "This is my brother, Captain Thaddeus Watkins."

Camellia's heart tripled its speed. Jane's brother? The man her best friend wanted her to meet? Her whole world turned upside down. Her earlier envy turned into anticipation. He *was* the man of her dreams. Handsome, rich, and a soldier. Captain Thaddeus Watkins was almost too good to be true. She would need to be on her best behavior.

As Captain Watkins exchanged pleasantries with Mrs. Dabbs, Camellia realized that even his deep voice was perfect. When Jane dragged him across the room to stand in front of her, Camellia wondered if she was going to swoon. If she did, would he be impressed with her delicate femininity or repulsed by her weakness?

"My sister has written to me of her bosom friend." His eyes were like a cup of warm cocoa. "I have to admit she didn't exaggerate your beauty."

"I am happy to meet you, Captain. Your sister speaks so highly of you." Camellia thought she could look into his face for hours on end. For the rest of her life.

"I didn't mean to interrupt you ladies—"

"Don't give it a thought, Captain." Mrs. Dabbs beamed at him. "We were about to take our afternoon tea. I hope you'll join us."

Three parallel lines appeared in his noble brow when Jane's brother frowned. Camellia longed to smooth them away with her fingers.

"I don't want to intrude. I wanted to let Jane know that I've been stationed at Chalmette. With your permission, I will come back and visit tomorrow."

His manners were impeccable, too. Camellia knew as well as she knew her name that she was in love with Thaddeus Watkins. She hoped he didn't disagree, because she was certain they would one day become husband and wife. From the admiration in his eyes as he gazed at her over the top of his sister's head, Camellia suspected he wouldn't put up much resistance.

❧

"I have butterflies in my stomach." Camellia put her hand on the waist of her blue-gray walking dress.

"I'm just glad you want to go with me." Jane tweaked the flounce on her skirt, part of the gold ensemble that complemented her burnished auburn hair. "I promise we won't spend the whole evening talking of family members you've never heard of."

"Don't worry about that. I will be content to be next to my best friend."

They left the room together, descending the staircase with their arms around each other's waist. Camellia was aware of the picture they presented. Jane was glowing, prettier than Camellia had ever seen her. It was a good thing they were not competing for Thad's affections. Not that he could resist Camellia when she put her mind to attracting him. No one could.

He stood in the foyer, even handsomer than she remembered. His gray uniform was pressed, and he had his slouch hat tucked under his right arm. He lifted his head and watched as they floated down, his eyes glowing with appreciation.

Camellia's heart soared. She and Jane reached him at the same time, but she stepped away to allow him to hug and kiss his sister.

When he turned toward her, she sank into a deep curtsy to exhibit her gracefulness. Straightening, she extended her gloved hand for his salute.

He bent and placed a kiss on her knuckles. "I'm the luckiest man in New Orleans."

A tiny splinter of disappointment buried itself in her mind. Where was the tingle she had expected from his touch? Was it because of her glove? A more daring man might have turned her hand over and placed a kiss on the inside of her wrist. Camellia shook her head to banish the thought and allowed her lips to curve into an admiring smile. "We are the lucky ones to be escorted by a true hero."

"I'm thankful to have two of the people I love the most right here with me." Jane's pleasure was reflected in her radiant smile.

The captain helped them with their cloaks. Did his hands linger a second or two as he settled the dark velvet across her shoulders? Camellia hoped she was not imagining the tiny detail. Whether she tingled at his touch or not, she still knew Thaddeus was the man she was destined to marry.

The sun was setting as they arrived in the Vieux Carre, embarrassing the sky into a deep blush. Camellia wished she could emulate it as Captain Watkins handed her out of the carriage. She needed to get rid of her gloves. Perhaps she could leave them behind in the hotel during their meal. Frozen fingers would be a small price to pay to feel his skin on hers.

Soldiers wearing uniforms of all styles and states of repair filled the lobby. They stood in small knots, laughing and talking. But as Camellia and Jane gave their coats over to be held for them, the conversations hushed. She looked around to see that they were the center of attention. Unsettled, she looked at the captain.

His smile comforted her. "I cannot blame them for looking when I can hardly tear my own eyes from your face."

Camellia wanted to blush. That's what she was supposed to do when a man complimented her, but her heart continued its steady pace. She grabbed the fan dangling from her wrist and opened it to hide her lack of emotional upheaval.

One of the men separated himself from the others and moved toward them. His hair was so white Camellia at first thought he was an older gentlemen, but as he drew closer, she realized her mistake. He was about the same age as Jane's brother, but his freckled face was nowhere near as handsome. "Thad, you rascal, you didn't tell anyone you would be entertaining two ladies."

The captain made a face but turned to the man who had hailed him. "Jane, Miss Anderson, allow me to introduce Lieutenant Harold Baxter, a bold scoundrel who does not mind presuming on the barest of acquaintance."

Camellia didn't realize he only had one arm until he bowed and his coat sleeve dangled free. She glanced away and caught the expression of sympathy on Jane's face. It shamed her into donning a smile and turning back to the lieutenant.

"Harry, this is my sister, Jane, and her friend, Miss Camellia Anderson."

The lieutenant grinned at them. "If I weren't bold, I'd never get to meet the prettiest girls."

Other men began drifting in their direction, their gazes curious. Lieutenant Baxter held out his good arm to Jane, and he winked at Thad. "I think we'd better get these two ladies into the dining room before we are overrun by the less enterprising officers present."

Jane's brother opened his mouth to say something but was forestalled when she put her hand on the other soldier's good arm. With a good-natured shrug, Thad offered his arm to Camellia. "Don't think this means you can join us for dinner."

Lieutenant Baxter's infectious laughter drifted back over his shoulder.

Captain Watkins chuckled and leaned his head toward Camellia's. "I hope you don't mind. The poor fellow has had a rough time."

"Did he lose his arm in battle?"

"Yes, he fought with the Army of North Virginia at Manassas." The captain's face tightened. "All teasing aside, he is a good man. He and I have become fast friends since we met."

Lieutenant Baxter was helping Jane into one of the three seats as they reached the square table covered by a snowy tablecloth. A waiter dragged a fourth chair toward them, a sour look on his face.

Camellia moved toward the chair opposite Jane's, but the captain redirected her footsteps with a slight pressure on her arm and pulled out the chair on his sister's right. Then he took the seat opposite Jane, leaving the chair on his sister's left open for the lieutenant.

"Afraid to let me sit next to Miss Anderson, are you?" Lieutenant Baxter winked at her. "I can understand your fear. I'm so much more handsome than you."

His joke set the tone for the evening. Camellia could not remember ever giggling so much. Their meal was delicious, too: rack of lamb with sprigs of mint that reminded her of the meals Jensen prepared on her sister's first riverboat.

Lieutenant Baxter leaned back and sipped from his water goblet as the waiter removed his empty plate. "I still can't believe any finishing schools are still operating in the city or that your families will allow you to attend."

Camellia looked away. This conversation made her think of the time and effort she'd had to expend to convince Lily that she would be safe.

"Why not, Lieutenant Baxter?" Jane asked. "My parents believe it's important for us to continue ordinary life as much as possible."

He raised his sandy-white eyebrows. "I thought we were on a first-name basis since we've broken bread together."

"Harry." Jane looked down at the table as she spoke.

"Much better." He grew serious. "The city is filled with people who want to help the North destroy our way of life."

"Really?" Jane looked at her brother for confirmation.

Thad cleared his throat. "Let's not frighten the ladies. We don't want them to worry."

"I'm not worried." Camellia summoned a confident smile for Jane's benefit. "Not when we have such fine men defending us."

"You may rest assured that both of you will be safe no matter what happens." Thad's smile was aimed at both of them. "I promise."

Camellia finally felt a shiver rush through her at his words. How exciting to feel protected. She reached under the table for Jane's hand and gave it a reassuring squeeze. Everything was going to be just fine.

The lieutenant tried to include himself in the carriage ride to La Belle Demoiselle, but Thad sent him back inside with a wave of his hand. Camellia wouldn't have admitted it to Jane, but she was relieved. Although Harry was an entertaining dinner companion, she had no desire to listen to any more of his tall tales.

Remembering to leave her gloves in her reticule, Camellia sat next to Jane, leaving the opposite bench for Thad. She pleated the folds of her cloak and wondered if he would try to take her hand.

Darkness and silence intermingled as the carriage left the lights of town behind. She searched her memory for some interesting topic to introduce, not wanting to bore Thad with conversation about the weather or their studies.

"Spring will be here before we know it." So he couldn't think of anything either.

Then an idea came to her, sparked by his mention of spring. "Mrs. Dabbs told us this morning that we are going to host a gala as soon as the weather warms a little."

She couldn't see Thad in the dark, but she heard the rustle of his coat as he nodded. "What does Mrs. Dabbs consider a gala to be?"

"It's going to be a fancy ball," Jane answered. "We'll get to dress up in our fanciest ball gowns."

Camellia tilted her head and raised her voice a few notes in imitation of their headmistress. " 'It will give you girls the opportunity to practice the skills I've been teaching you this term.' "

Jane giggled at her imitation, and Camellia decided Jasmine's penchant for playacting must have rubbed off on her. Her friend's laughter rewarded her silliness.

Her eyes must be getting accustomed to the gloom, because she could make out Thad's features as he leaned toward them. "I'm certain you already have an escort, Camellia."

"No, she doesn't."

Camellia hoped he couldn't see her blush. Why had her friend been so quick to answer? If Thad thought someone else was interested in escorting her, it would sharpen his desire to win her affections. Or so Aunt Dahlia had always said. She stifled a sigh and tried for a nonchalant tone. "I'm not sure if any of us will have escorts since it's to be held at the school."

His hand covered hers, stilling her nervous movements. Jane might have seen the gesture, but she was looking toward the window.

Camellia's fingers fluttered under his large, warm touch. Exhilaration sent the butterflies moving about her stomach again. Now what? Should she pull her hand away or allow it to remain under his?

"My military duties will keep me occupied tomorrow, but may I call on you Saturday?" His low voice swept her away on a heady tide of success, making her almost forget her roommate was in the carriage with them.

"We can't." Jane's voice intruded in their moment like a dash of icy water.

Camellia jerked her hand away and buried it under the folds of her cloak. Her mind was still spinning. She wanted to say something, but her mouth didn't want to cooperate.

"We're going to the Thorntons' town house for the weekend, remember?"

The Thorntons' home. Of course. Jonah Thornton and his family. But how would she explain to Thad the relationship between her and the Thorntons? Camellia chewed on her lower lip as she considered how to turn the situation to her advantage. Aunt Dahlia's words came back to her as the carriage slowed and pulled up under the porte cochere.

Thad slid across the seat and reached for the door.

Taking a deep breath for courage, Camellia leaned forward and put her cold hand on his. "Wait. Perhaps you can come for dinner at the Thorntons' home Saturday evening."

He shot her an odd look. "But I don't know the Thorntons. I would not dare show up on their doorstep uninvited."

"But I know they would love to meet you. Mr. Thornton is an avid supporter of the Cause. As soon as he discovers that Jane has a brother who is a *captain*. . ." She put extra emphasis on the word and paused as though overcome. "Well, suffice it to say he would be most put out with me if I didn't invite you."

"When you put it like that. . ." His smile warmed her heart.

This was going to be perfect. He would have eyes for no one but her. By the time of the gala next month, he would be ready to propose.

She needed to get inside and start preparing. Aunt Dahlia would be so proud.

Chapter Ten

Jonah's mother studied him during the drive to La Belle. "I'm not sure why you thought it necessary to come along this morning."

"Are you saying I'm not welcome?"

"Of course not. But you cannot be that anxious to see dear Camellia again, not when she is about to spend the entire weekend with us."

He yawned to cover his inner turmoil and looked out the window. Bright sunlight heralded the impending arrival of spring. Before much more time passed, it would be summer, and the Confederate forces would arrive to bolster New Orleans' weak defenses. If the Union did not strike soon, it would be too late. The work on the ironclads in the port might be slow, but it was progressing. Now, right now, was the time to take the city. The local newspapers had carried news of the Union victories at Fort Henry and Fort Donelson in February. They even speculated that the real target was New Orleans and warned that an invading force could be expected to travel from Tennessee to attack the city. So why did the Federal forces hesitate?

Jonah fostered a smile and turned to face his mother. "Perhaps I have an ulterior motive for joining you."

Her gaze sharpened. "Oh? Is there something or someone you want to tell me about?"

For a moment, he wanted to confess his true agenda, wanted to tell his parent exactly why he had volunteered to come with her to pick up the girls. Mother was not as ardent in her support of the South as Father, and having someone he trusted to confide in would lessen the heavy burden of guilt and uncertainty.

The words burned his throat, but he choked them back. Telling her might bring him some relief, but at what cost? Involving his mother would force her to be complicit. He did not have that right. "What if I said I wanted to spend more time with the only lady who truly holds my heart in her hand?"

She sat back and laughed. "When did you become such a charmer?"

"You wound me. Are you trying to say I have not always been a pleasant fellow?"

"Of course not. But since you came back to New Orleans, you have been different. I've never known you to attend so many parties. Your father and I have begun to hope you are ready to pick a bride and settle down. And we would be delighted if your choice was a certain beautiful young student. You know how much we love all three of the Anderson girls."

His mouth tightened. "We've spoken of this before. Camellia Anderson is beautiful, but I want more in the woman I choose for a wife. Now if we were speaking of her older sister, Lily, it would be a different matter. She is a woman I admire greatly for her strong faith, her morals, and her independent spirit."

"Yes, but I can see some of those same qualities in Camellia. She only needs a strong Christian man to give her direction."

The carriage stopped then, ending their conversation, though her words echoed in his mind. As Jonah helped his mother alight, he wondered if it might be true. Was he being too hard on Camellia? Was she just young and in need of a guiding hand?

He followed his mother into La Belle Demoiselle, his eyes widening at a pile of luggage that filled the foyer. He wondered whether one of the girls had been expelled or perhaps called back home by her family. Easing his way past the stack, he nodded to the assistant, whose name he couldn't remember. Miss Lacy? Latrobe? It was on the tip of his tongue.

"Welcome, Monsieur Thornton." She smiled at him before continuing. "Madame. The young ladies are in the visitors' parlor, awaiting your arrival."

Jonah could feel his mother's speculative gaze on him, but he ignored her as he nodded. "Thank you, miss. I know the way." He strode down the hall and held the door open for his mother to precede him. Both Camellia and her friend were seated on the sofa, their heads together as they studied some magazine. He had to admit they made a pleasing picture.

Camellia stood and hurried to his mother as she entered the room, hugging her with an affection that seemed sincere. "Thank you so much for inviting us to stay with you."

"You are most welcome. I don't know why I waited so long." His mother touched Camellia's cheek. "But we will make up for my oversight by filling this weekend with a great many activities."

"We are prepared." Camellia looked back at Jane and gestured for her to join them. "Please allow me to introduce Miss Jane Watkins, my dearest friend and roommate. She is from Vicksburg."

Jonah slipped out of the room as the ladies got acquainted. He had a note to give Mrs. Dabbs—a list of the armaments planned for the *C. S. Mississippi*, the ironclad that was most likely to threaten U.S. naval ships once it was completed.

The headmistress must have gotten word of his arrival, because she was waiting for him in the hallway. "I have planned a picnic for next week. Will you have the girls back before then?"

"We'll have them back here by dark on Sunday." He pulled the note from his pocket, careful to keep it hidden in case they were being observed, and slipped it into Mrs. Dabbs's hand as he bowed over it.

"That's good, then." She wrapped her fingers around the piece of paper. "I know they'll have a nice visit with your family."

He nodded and turned away, his heart pounding as he returned to the visitors' parlor. He prayed the information would get into the right hands. Slipping back into the room a bare two minutes after his departure, Jonah was relieved to see the ladies had not missed him. He donned a bored expression and waited for a chance to interrupt.

"Are you sure you won't mind an additional guest for dinner?" Camellia's question put him on alert. What was she planning?

His mother tossed a look in his direction before responding. "Of course not, dear. Captain Watkins sounds like a fine gentleman. I'm sure my husband will be delighted to meet him."

Jonah frowned. Camellia might be a close friend of the family, but inviting a guest into his parents' home before asking their permission was ridiculous. His mother might not mind her effrontery, but he did.

"I thought this was a finishing school."

Camellia turned toward him, her face wearing a look of indignation. "What is your point, sir?"

"My point is that any *child* would know better than to invite a guest to a gathering at which she is not the hostess."

Her eyes darkened, reminding him of a stormy sky. "I don't see why it's any concern of yours. He is Jane's brother and has only recently arrived in New Orleans. Your mother does not mind if Captain Watkins comes, so I don't see why you should take exception to the idea."

"My mother is far too gracious to tell you to your face that you have gone beyond the limits of acceptable behavior."

"Jonah." Mother's voice was gentle, but it stopped him from continuing his reproach. The look she gave him was full of understanding and something else. Did she pity him? Why? Did she think he had another reason for protesting Camellia's behavior?

Jonah snapped his mouth shut. Maybe she thought he was upset because this fellow was a soldier and he was not. He wanted to tell her, tell all of them, that he *was* a soldier. But his lips were sealed by the oath he'd taken.

If she did not mind Camellia's invitation to a stranger, he could not very well continue to chastise the girl. Jonah glanced around the room. "Do you have any bags for me to load into the carriage?"

Jane and Camellia exchanged a glance. What now?

Camellia lifted her chin, her gaze still exhibiting a desire to challenge him. "Our things are in the hallway."

Jonah spluttered. "The hallway? Do you mean to tell me that mountain of luggage is what you consider necessary for a two-day visit?"

"I want to be at my best no matter what you may think." She turned up her nose at him.

"It's not all hers." Jane came to her friend's rescue. "One of them belongs to me."

"And the other dozen belong to Camellia." Jonah sighed and reached for the door handle. He'd better see to getting the bags loaded or they would be at the school until midnight.

❧

Jonah knew the first minute he saw Thad Watkins that the two of them were not going to be friends. He disliked everything about him, from his gray uniform to the way he looked at Camellia—like a wolf considering the lamb that was about to be its next meal. He practically drooled on her hand when he kissed it. And she must be an idiot to simper and preen so. Couldn't she see that he wanted to devour her?

When they'd been seated at dinner, Jonah had not been surprised to discover that the captain had been given the seat to his father's right, the space reserved for the guest of honor. His sister, Sarah, was sitting between Thad and her husband. Camellia was sitting opposite Thad and did not appear to realize anyone else had joined them for dinner. Especially not him, the man sitting next to her. She had barely spoken a word to him all evening. Perhaps she was still smarting over his amazement at the number of bags she had brought for her weekend stay.

Jonah thought she would be better served to follow her friend's example. Ironic that Jane was the hero's sister, as she had none of his brash egotism. Seated on his left side, Miss Watkins was a refined lady. She didn't flirt or try to monopolize his attention like Camellia and her "war hero." She divided her attention equally between Jonah and his mother as was proper. She had obviously paid much closer attention to their lessons on etiquette.

"What happened then?" Camellia batted her eyelashes quickly enough to raise a breeze.

Jonah's father leaned forward as though waiting for Thad's answer. He had a gleam in his eyes that seemed to disappear when he looked at his son. "What did that Yankee do when he saw you had him surrounded?"

Thad chuckled. "He dropped his weapon, fell to his knees, and begged us to let him join the Confederacy. It seems old Abe Lincoln hadn't paid him a dime in the eighteen months that he'd been a soldier."

Papa laughed out loud, leaning back and slapping his knee. "That's why the South is going to win this war. We'll never bow to Washington's tyranny. Even the Yankees know it. That's why he wanted to join up with the winning side."

Jonah could not keep silent any longer. "The newspapers don't seem to share your optimism. I read again this morning that many experts think General Grant will come knocking on our doorsteps at any moment."

Sarah, always eager to avoid family strife, frowned a warning at him.

But Jonah didn't care. They all needed to face the truth. The South was not on the winning side. It was only a matter of time. Lincoln was not going to let this country be split apart. He would keep fighting for however long it took to preserve the Union.

Instead of arguing with Jonah as expected, his father turned back to Thad. "It's true that New Orleans is very vulnerable to attack. Every time I turn around, more of our local boys are being pulled away to defend some backwoods town in Georgia or South Carolina. Abraham Lincoln has been very vocal about his plans to control the Mississippi River. Our trade with Europe is the lifeblood of the South. If we lose the river, I'm afraid we'll lose the war."

Thad's eyes narrowed. "Yes, sir, you are right. I'm not at liberty to say much, but I can assure you steps are being taken. New Orleans has not been forgotten."

"I hope you're right, young man." Jonah's father sighed. "But however this war turns out, I want you to know how proud I am of your service. I wish I could join you out on the battlefield myself, but I'm too old."

"You look like you're in your prime to me, sir."

Jonah wanted to groan aloud. Would his father fall for such blatant flattery? From the pleased look on his face, apparently he would. Right now he was probably wishing Thad was his son. But Jonah could not let that disturb him. He had prayed for wisdom before he made his decision about which side to join. He had to keep faith that God would continue to lead him.

A wisp of an idea slipped through Jonah's roiling thoughts. Thad knew things, things that could be useful to Jonah's superiors. Of all Jonah's acquaintances, none remained here who were officers in the Confederate army. He needed to use this one connection to full advantage, no matter what it cost him personally.

Jonah's mother picked up a spoon and tapped it against the rim of her plate. "That's enough talk of war and fighting. We will learn of the girls' activities at their school. Jane, why don't you tell us what you are studying."

She looked as frightened as the soldier Thad had told them about, surrounded by the enemy. "I. . .um. . .we've worked on our musical skills."

"That sounds wonderful. Do you play the piano?"

Jane shook her head, her auburn hair gleaming in the light of the candelabra that hung above the dining table.

"Don't be so modest." Camellia leaned forward, looking past Jonah. "Jane is an accomplished harpist, and she sings like an angel."

Jonah could hear the affection in her voice as she praised her friend. He found that commendable. Of course, she knew she didn't have to compete with Jane for the captain's attention. In his experience, young ladies could be quite ruthless in disparaging each other as they pursued the attentions of prospective suitors. Camellia might not be as generous with her praise if the captain and Jane were not brother and sister.

Sarah smiled at the blushing Jane. "You'll have to sing for us later this evening, Miss Watkins. I would be most happy to accompany you on my parents' piano."

Jane reached for her water and took a healthy gulp.

"Their graduation will be a formal ball." Captain Watkins's statement drew everyone's attention away from Jane.

A rising tide of irritation made Jonah want to growl. Did he have to look at Camellia with such longing?

"Miss Anderson has agreed to let me be her escort." His smug voice taunted Jonah.

Would this meal never end? Barred from reintroducing a military topic by his mother's earlier comment, all Jonah could do was think about the captain dancing with Camellia, holding her close. He shook his head to clear it of the vision. He would have to find a reason to attend their ball. . .so he could learn more from Thad, of course.

Jonah listened to the conversation flowing around him. Sarah offered to take the girls shopping for a special outfit. He expected Miss Fashion Plate to jump at the chance, but she didn't. Jane explained why when she told them about the dress Camellia had brought with her from Natchez. The ladies discussed fabrics and colors, cooing over matching ribbons and lace and all manner of folderol. How long could they continue to talk about clothes? Even his surgeon brother-in-law looked like he was about to fall asleep.

Finally his mother took pity on the men by announcing it was time for the ladies to retire. After they left the dining room, Thad and Father returned to their discussion of the war. Jonah listened carefully but discovered nothing new.

Jonah excused himself and went to his flat. Of course sleep eluded him. Until Jonah thought to get out his Bible. Opening it to the Old

Testament, he read about the trials of Joseph. At least Jonah had not been sold into slavery by his siblings. Yet Joseph had never given up his faith. And God had rewarded him and, through him, his people.

Slipping back into his bed, Jonah prayed for patience and faith like Joseph's. His anxiety lessened, and his eyes drifted shut. God would help him see the way.

Chapter Eleven

Camellia checked her appearance in the mirror. A row of tiny buttons on the front of her dress were covered in matching crimson material. She loved the tiny lines of gold that lent a striped appearance to the fabric. The sleeves, daringly simple and straight, were adorned with a single ruched band before ending halfway between her elbow and wrist. But the neckline was too plain. Draping a white scarf across the bodice, she turned to ask Jane's opinion of her embellishment, surprised by the worried frown on her friend's face. "Don't be anxious. The Thorntons' church has so many nice people. They've always welcomed me and my sisters."

Jane hid a yawn behind her hand. "I hope I don't fall asleep during the sermon."

"I promise to pinch you before you begin snoring."

"I don't snore." Jane pointed a finger at her. "You are a different matter, however. Your snoring would put a locomotive to shame."

Camellia shook her head. "That wasn't me. It was you."

They continued to banter as they headed downstairs to meet the others. Sarah and Dr. Cartier had returned home, of course, and would meet them at the church. But Camellia was surprised to see only Mrs. Thornton and Jonah awaiting them in the foyer. Mrs. Thornton was already wearing a dark cloak that hid the color and cut of her dress. Jonah wore a bottle-green coat that stretched across his broad shoulders.

An embroidered waistcoat and striped trousers completed his outfit, marking him as a gentleman of fashion.

Dragging her gaze away from his compelling features, she looked around the foyer. "Where is Mr. Thornton?"

Mrs. Thornton shook her head. "He's stopped attending services for now."

Jonah held Jane's cape for her, taking his sweet time with her friend. Determined to show she didn't need anyone's help, Camellia managed to get the heavy material of her own cloak across her shoulders without twisting her arms completely off.

"The pastor dared to express his support for abolition from the pulpit." Jonah's voice was as sour as ever. Did he always have to be so sarcastic?

Jane fastened the button at the top of her cloak and sent a grateful look in his direction. "Our pastor in the Garden District has not addressed that subject at all."

"Pastor Nolan is a good shepherd for our little flock." Mrs. Thornton pulled on her gloves. "He is a man of conscience, and his spiritual message is always applicable to our lives, even if we disagree with his political views. Coming together with other Christians is a directive from the New Testament that I will not ignore. Especially during these troubled times. I don't know how people survive when they do not have the support of a church to sustain them."

Camellia nodded. "We attend a church just around the corner from La Belle Demoiselle, even when the weather is inclement. You should see all of us following behind Mrs. Dabbs and Mademoiselle Laurent."

"Like a colorful line of ducklings?" Jonah's half smile had returned. "I'm certain you turn all the heads in your neighborhood."

She was not going to let him rile her this morning. Let him poke fun all he wanted. This was Sunday, and she was determined to be more circumspect. Didn't the Bible say something about heaping coals on someone's head? "I hadn't thought of it in exactly that way, but you're right, Jonah."

The surprise on his face at her agreement was delicious. A victory over the supercilious man at last. Squelching her glee, as it might not be considered very Christian, Camellia sailed through the door he opened and into the bright spring sunlight.

Their path to the church roughly paralleled the crescent path of the river, taking them past several shuttered homes. New Orleans had changed since Louisiana had seceded from the Union. Men had volunteered to fight, and their wives and children had fled to the safety of extended families. Those with Northern roots escaped the South rather than swear fealty to the Confederacy, leaving behind the lives they had established during the lucrative heyday of international shipping and trade. The weed-choked lawns made Camellia wonder if anything would ever be the same again. Would the residents return once the war ended? Or would those who survived remain in the new lives they had crafted? Who would one day live in these abandoned homes?

When they arrived, the pastor and his wife were standing at the front door of the whitewashed building. After brief introductions, they moved inside.

Even the church seemed subdued. The majority of those in attendance were ladies and children. Camellia wondered if that was because the men had volunteered to fight or if they, like Mr. Thornton, refused to attend.

Mrs. Thornton led the way to a vacant pew near the front, crimping her skirts to navigate the narrow space.

Camellia had meant to sit between Mrs. Thornton and Jane but somehow ended up behind her friend, meaning she would be trapped between Jane and Jonah. She wondered if she could manage to ignore him the whole time. It shouldn't be too hard. Straightening her spine, she folded her gloved hands in her lap. Presenting an attitude of humility was always appropriate in church.

" 'Thou wilt shew me the path of life: in thy presence is fulness of joy; at thy right hand there are pleasures for evermore.' " The words thundered out of the pastor's mouth, making Camellia forget all about the man sitting next to her. The reverend's gaze lifted from the Bible he held in his right hand, and he studied the congregation. "I don't know about the rest of you who are in attendance today, but I am spending hours on my knees praying for America's future."

A shifting among the pews signaled discomfort from at least some of the people. Or was that the Holy Spirit? Camellia held herself very still. If God was here with them, she didn't want Him thinking she wasn't listening.

"If we don't pay attention to God's Word, this country is doomed."

"Amen!" A male voice from somewhere behind them startled Jane.

A nervous giggle formed in Camellia's chest. She tamped it down and managed to resist the temptation of glancing at her friend, unsure if she could maintain proper decorum otherwise.

"Last night as I studied my Bible for the right message to bring to you, I was drawn to the middle of my Bible." The pastor reclaimed her attention. "I read this verse, and it got me to thinking about paths and the nature of the steps we take. Then I turned to Proverbs, the book of good advice we should all read at least once a month."

Camellia twisted her gloved fingers together, concentrating on the smooth feel of the silky material in the palm of her hand. The leather corner of a Bible appeared within her field of vision. Jonah's Bible. Curiosity turned her gaze toward the words his finger was underlining as the pastor read the verse.

" 'There is a way which seemeth right unto a man, but the end thereof are the ways of death.' "

She shuddered. Some parts of the Bible didn't appeal to her at all. Why did God have to go to all the trouble of making the way to Him so difficult? Why couldn't He make things simple? If she was running the world, things would be different. Her cheeks heated at the errant thoughts. Should she apologize to God? Was He listening that closely to her thoughts? Would He smite her where she sat?

A breathless moment of fear made her freeze again. Nothing happened, and she relaxed.

Jonah closed his Bible, his fingers stroking the worn leather cover. The book was old, worn, well used.

It sparked a new thought in her mind. Was the Bible outdated? Was it too old? They lived in a modern world, a world that would confuse the people in the Bible. She sat straighter. Maybe that was it. Maybe the Bible wasn't relevant anymore. Maybe God had instituted a new system.

The pastor had been droning on for a while now, talking about how they were all going to end in destruction. He'd probably start talking about weeping and teeth gnashing in a minute. She should have stayed at the town house with Mr. Thornton. She could understand why he refused to come.

Her head drooped lower as she studied a line of tiny stitches. It was a good thing she didn't have to make her own dresses. She caught the giggle before it escaped, but a hiccup managed to break free.

Jane elbowed her. "What are you doing?"

Jonah turned his head and looked at them, his frown stopping her answer.

Camellia pouted at him and pulled on the cuff of her glove. He didn't have to be so sanctimonious. She'd like to run his world for a little while. Send him racing down a path that no one else was on. Or was that what God had already done to him?

Her eyes narrowed, but before she could continue the thought, the pastor asked for everyone to bow their heads. After he prayed for a little while, his words running together in her mind, the pastor ended the prayer. Then it was over.

They gathered their things and began to file out of the church. Jonah offered his arm to his mother.

Jane touched Camellia's arm as they moved to follow. "Tell me what you were doing during the service."

Camellia shrugged. "Nothing much. Just trying to stay awake."

Jane shot a look at her. "I didn't have much trouble."

Ignoring her friend's censure, Camellia raised her voice so the Thorntons could hear her question. "Do you think we're on the right path?"

She could see Jonah's shoulder tighten.

It was all the encouragement she needed to continue. "I'm not sure this is the right way. It may be the path that leads to destruction."

Mrs. Thornton looked over her shoulder at them. "I'm so glad you took the sermon to heart, Camellia. I was afraid you might find the message troubling."

"No, of course not." Camellia silenced the voice inside her head. "I may not agree with his whole message, but I know he believes what he says."

Jonah stopped walking for a minute then seemed to recover himself. He continued on until they reached his family's home. But she could almost feel the storm brewing in him.

"I need to speak to you for a moment, Camellia." He practically dragged her from the foyer, his fingers making certain she didn't escape.

Camellia refused to be intimidated. Jonah held no power over her. She took a stance in the center of the room, shoulders back, head high. Aunt Dahlia would be proud of her. "What is wrong?"

"You may not. . . . No, let me start again. You obviously do not value the message you heard today."

"I don't see why the path to God has to be narrow and strewn with briars." She pulled off her gloves and held them in one hand. "And if it is, who is to say the South is not following the right path? After all, we are the smaller group. Does that make us the ones with the right answer?"

He sighed. "Is that really what you believe? That God smiles on the South and the Southern way of life?"

"If you're so sure we're wrong, why do you stay?"

His mouth closed in a straight line.

Camellia could sense she was about to win. She let her mouth relax into a smile. "Are you going to answer me?"

"You wouldn't understand if I did. Your ears have been closed. Your eyes can't see." He turned on his heel and walked out of the room.

The victory she had sensed felt hollow, empty. She slapped her gloves against her empty palm and blew out a breath of disgust. How like a man. He would never admit she might be right.

Chapter Twelve

On the Mississippi River near St. Louis

John Champion tossed another piece of wood into the boiler and slammed the door shut. "Do you want me to add more?"

The engineer pushed back his black cap and scratched his head. "No, that'll do her fer now."

Nodding, John pushed his sleeves back down and fastened them.

"Don't see why ya bother with that." The shorter man shook his head. "Ya gonna have to roll 'em up again or replace that shirt soon."

It was a habit born of his earlier years, but one John seemed unable to break. Even though it had been two years since he had last seen his home, it was hard to forgo some routines. "I'll roll them up when I have to."

The engineer's puzzled look made John laugh as he left the engine room and wound his way through hogsheads of sugar from southern Louisiana. Captain Pecanty should make a good profit this voyage. Sugar was worth its weight in gold since supply had been cut off by the Union blockade in the Gulf of Mexico. That meant John would also earn more.

Not that he had much need for money these days. Working on the *Catfish* ensured him a serviceable bunk and plenty of food. He usually stayed on the boat with the Pecantys instead of visiting the gambling dens that lined many of the towns along the river. Keeping to himself had grown easier and easier the longer he remained on the steamship.

A warm breeze pushed his hair down into his eyes. He reached up and brushed it back with an impatient gesture.

"If you didn't wear it so long, it wouldn't bother you." The feminine voice brought his head around. Almost as wide as she was tall, Naomi Pecanty had twinkling green eyes, a smile as wide as the river they rode upon, and a caring heart as steady and strong as the paddle wheel steering them northward.

She never came up on his right side, the side that bore the reminder of past sins. It was an indication of her thoughtfulness. Mrs. Naomi never asked him about the disfiguring scars that marred one side of his face. She and her husband were not the kind to ask many questions about a man's past, a fact that suited John to a T. But that hadn't stopped the kindly woman from presenting him a scarf last Christmas to serve the dual purpose of keeping his head and neck warm while covering a goodly portion of the rough, purplish-red skin left by the explosion.

"I like it long." He leaned against the wooden rail and looked out at the green hills. Of course the lock fell down into his eyes again, but this time John ignored it. He could almost feel her disapproving look. The silence lengthened until he finally gave up, sighed, and pushed back the hair once more. "Did you come up front to advise me on fashion?"

"No." The gentle tone of her voice made him feel guilty for his gruff tone. "I need to ask a favor of you."

"A favor?" He glanced sideways and met her gaze.

Something swirled in those eyes, something that made his shoulders tense. John wanted to walk away, but he couldn't. The woman next to him had practically adopted him the moment she joined the crew as the cook.

Yankees had raided her home, taking the livestock, looting the garden, and burning down the house she and Captain Pecanty had built. They decided she would be safer on the boat, so Mrs. Naomi took over the kitchen duties. John had gained at least ten pounds since she'd come on board.

"I need some supplies from Devore's in Cape Girardeau."

Their next stop would be at the small town in southern Missouri—a regular destination on their voyages. He fumbled for an excuse. "I don't know. I doubt I would come back with the right supplies."

"I made out a list for you." She pulled a folded slip of paper from her sleeve.

Tommy Bender, a short man with dirty blond hair and light blue eyes, came down the stairs and moved past them with a toothy grin. "Is dinner about ready?"

"Not yet." Mrs. Naomi returned his smile. "Biscuits will be ready at sunset."

"Don't let John eat all of 'em before the rest of us get to the dinner table."

John frowned. He should be used to the ribbing from the rest of the crew, but he wished they would simply leave him alone.

"I won't." Mrs. Naomi pushed the list toward him.

John took it and stuffed it into a pocket. It seemed the time to object had passed. He supposed he could do as his employer's wife wished. As he walked away from the rail, his shoulders twitched. Why did it feel like he had a target painted on his back?

❧

New Orleans

Camellia tucked a bit of hair under her nightcap and leaned back against her pillow. "What do you think of Jonah Thornton?"

Jane blew out their candle and shrugged. "He seems like a nice man."

Tilting her head, Camellia tried to decide if Jane was hiding her feelings. Her tone of voice was calm and matter-of-fact. But she must have been impressed with Jonah. He was quite handsome, after all. And he had been nothing but kind and courteous to Jane. He had never called her an impolite child, laughed at her faux pas, or castigated her for the number of trunks she needed for her clothing. If Jonah had been half as nice to Camellia as he had been to her roommate. . .

Camellia shook her head before the thought could complete itself. She needed to concentrate on Jane's needs. "He's well connected, you know. His family is quite popular. Sarah, his sister, hosts the grandest parties."

The bed sagged as Jane settled next to her.

A faint glow from the fireplace on the far wall was the only illumination in the room. Camellia pulled the cover up to her chin and waited for an answer.

"Yes, I'm sure you're right." Jane stopped speaking.

"But?" The word echoed in the room, but no answer came.

After several moments, Jane cleared her throat. "Nothing really.

It's just that Mr. Thornton seems so. . .so serious."

"Is that all?" Camellia let out the breath she hadn't realized she had been holding. "What he needs is a pretty young lady to help lighten that serious nature."

Her mind went back to the night when Lily and Blake had taken them to the theater. How young she had been back then. And how debonair Jonah Thornton had seemed. He'd been dashing and mysterious—grave one moment and carefree the next. He had been exactly the type of beau she wanted to snag. Camellia could feel her cheeks growing warm as she considered how he must have perceived her back then—the gauche younger sister of an unconventional family. She had made little secret of her admiration, but Jonah Thornton hadn't been interested in her. He'd never been interested in her. And he never would be. Not that she wanted him to be. . .although it would have been satisfying for him to pursue her, if only so she could ignore his advances.

She could feel Jane's gaze in the shadowy room. Camellia sniffed. "I think you should encourage him. The two of you would make a wonderful couple."

"I'd much rather spend time with someone who makes me laugh."

"Jonah is quite clever. You've only seen him at his worst." The thick down mattress made it difficult to turn over, but after a moment Camellia managed to face her friend. "It's the war, don't you see? It's made everyone too serious. As soon as our brave Confederate soldiers whip those meddlesome Yankees, everything will go back to the way it was before."

"Sometimes I don't think anything will ever be like it was before the war. Sometimes I'm afraid the South will lose and—"

"Don't say that," Camellia said, interrupting her friend's words. "Don't even think it. What would your brother think to hear you say such things?"

"I know, but that's why I don't want to spend my time with someone so. . .so intense."

The break in Jane's words made Camellia wonder if the other girl was about to start crying. She could feel her own throat tightening. If she didn't redirect their conversation right away, they would both end up bawling like a couple of hungry babies. "That's why I think Jonah would be perfect for you. I could understand your hesitation if he was a soldier like your brother. Sending them both away to fight would be difficult for anyone. But Jonah Thornton is not a soldier. He's not even interested in the war." She stopped and reached for Jane's hand under the cover. "Do you think he doesn't want to fight because he's a—a coward? I hadn't thought of that."

Jane's cold fingers gripped her warmer hand. "I don't know Jonah like you do, but from the limited amount of time I've been around him, he doesn't strike me as the sort of man who would be afraid to fight."

Camellia breathed a sigh of relief to have the idea dispelled. She nodded even though she wasn't sure if Jane could see the motion.

"I think you may be misled by appearances." Jane's voice no longer sounded as choked with emotion. "Sometimes it can take more courage to go against popular opinion than to don a uniform."

Camellia pushed up onto one elbow. "Can you see now why I think you and Jonah would make a perfect couple? You have seen something about him that I never have."

"I don't know." Jane giggled. "From the sparks that always seem to fly between the two of you, I wonder if you're not more interested in Mr. Thornton than you are my brother."

"Don't be silly." Camellia collapsed against her pillow, her low-pitched giggle harmonizing with Jane's. "Captain Watkins is wonderful. He's exactly the kind of man I hope to marry someday."

"That's good. I would much rather have you for a sister than a friend."

"I hope to be both."

A knock on the door quieted both girls. They had no desire to be chastised by either Mrs. Dabbs or her assistant.

As Camellia drifted toward sleep, she considered Jane's words. Was Jonah as brave as Captain Thaddeus Watkins? The idea seemed ludicrous. How could a man who had never fought a day in his life compare well against someone who braved danger and death in the quest for freedom for his home? The answer was simple. He couldn't.

Chapter Thirteen

*J*onah dismounted and tethered his horse before entering La Belle Demoiselle. He wondered how Camellia would respond to his visit. Just when he thought he had figured her out, she surprised him. She was as tantalizing as the first hint of spring after a long, cold winter. As refreshing as a cool breeze in the hottest part of the summer. But she wasn't the girl for him. If he ever decided to settle down and raise a family, he would not choose a young woman like Camellia. He wanted a wife who shared his faith, his ideals, and his values. Not someone as vain and shallow as she.

His heartbeat picked up with each step he took toward the house, probably because of his errand. What would Camellia think when she found out he was paying yet another visit to her school? Would she think he was pursuing her? If so, she was going to be disappointed. He had a totally different goal in mind—one that would dispel all of her pretensions.

Jonah gave his hat to the assistant who answered the door, happy to remember her name today. "Hello, Miss Laurent. I'm here to see Miss Watkins."

"Yes, sir. I'll check with Mrs. Dabbs." The girl led him to the visitors' parlor before scurrying toward the back of the school.

A pendulum clock on the mantel marked the minutes while he waited. Jonah was about to go in search of Mrs. Dabbs and her charges when the lady appeared at the door, Jane behind her. The older lady carried a basket of handwork, apparently something to occupy her while she chaperoned her charge. He gave both of them his winningest smile, a smile that barely faltered when Camellia's blond ringlets and familiar features came into view behind her friend. Why was she with Jane? His plan would not be as easy to carry out if she was going to remain in the room. He'd counted on letting her friend tell her his errand later.

"Good morning, Mr. Thornton." Mrs. Dabbs swept into the room, a question in her gaze.

She must be wondering if he had more information to pass along to her. A slight shake of his head gave her the answer.

The reason for this visit was different. He needed to secure a valid reason for attending the end-of-the-term dance. And he needed to get as close to Captain Watkins as possible. "It's a beautiful day," he said.

He bowed at all three of them as they took seats in the parlor. The younger girls sat on the sofa next to each other while he and Mrs. Dabbs sat in chairs across from them.

Camellia unfurled her fan and fluttered it with practiced ease. "Are your parents well?"

Jonah nodded at her but turned to Jane as he made his answer. "As well as can be expected since their lovely guests departed." He sent the auburn-haired beauty a smoldering look, one he remembered from his earlier days. One that had always gotten a positive response from females, whether in ballrooms or parlors.

His effort was wasted as Jane's brown gaze swept past him and settled on something behind him. "How kind of you, sir. We very much enjoyed our weekend, didn't we, Camellia?"

He wanted to look back over his shoulder to see if someone else had entered and was about to cuff him. Managing to control the impulse, his gaze clashed with the sparkling blue gaze of the minx sitting beside Jane.

Camellia's eyes danced as though she read his thoughts. "Yes, indeed. Your mother and father are *two* of my favorite people."

He swallowed a grin at the barbed comment. He got the message. He was not one of her favorite people. Jonah raised an eyebrow. "I'm sure they would want me to return the compliment." Which was not to say he would. Miss Anderson was not the only one who could use double meanings to make a point.

A slave entered with a tea tray and set it down on the table between the sofa and his chair.

"Would you care to serve?"

Jane's eyes opened wide in response to Mrs. Dabbs's question. "I think it's Camellia's turn."

"Very well." Mrs. Dabbs nodded to Camellia and reached for her embroidery, effectively divorcing herself from the conversation.

Closing her fan with a snap, Camellia rolled her eyes and reached for the teapot. "Would you care for sugar, Mr. Thornton?"

"What need have I for sugar when I'm surrounded by such sweet temperaments?"

Camellia tossed him a dirty look, one that made his smile widen.

Jane looked from one of them to the other, her brow wrinkled. She was a beauty but apparently did not understand the joy of verbal sparring with a worthy opponent.

Jonah reached out to accept the cup Camellia offered. "How are your needlework skills progressing?"

The liquid threatened to overcome the lip of the porcelain cup as she jerked. "How dare you," she hissed between clenched teeth, practically dropping the cup and saucer into his hand.

"You would be amazed at Camellia's talents." Jane came to her defense. "She understands mathematics and medicine better than anyone else here."

Jonah nodded. "A family trait she shares with her sister Lily."

"I know you didn't come today to speak of my family, Mr. Thornton." Camellia held out a tray of sweets.

Balancing his tea on one knee, Jonah picked out a cream-topped cookie. "How right you are. My reason for visiting is to ascertain whether or not Miss Watkins would allow me to be her escort for your school gala."

Jane lifted her cup and drank instead of looking at him. What was the matter with the girl? Did she find him repulsive? Did she have an escort already?

"She would love to go with you." Camellia stepped into the uncomfortable moment. "Wouldn't you, Jane?"

Mrs. Dabbs's needle stopped, and she put her embroidery down. "How kind of you, Mr. Thornton. I have to admit I have been concerned about whether or not our ball would be a success this year. So many of our Southern gentlemen are not available to act as partners."

"They are more concerned with protecting their families and homes from marauders."

Trust Camellia to take every opportunity to point out his apparent unwillingness to fight. Jonah tamped down his irritation. What was it about her disdain that made him want to defend himself?

"Camellia, you need to mind your manners." Mrs. Dabbs frowned. "Your sentiments are not shared by all."

"They are shared by those who are loyal to the South." The thump of Camellia's cup against the serving tray emphasized her words.

"God gave each of us different talents." Jane seemed to be a natural peacemaker, ready to diffuse tension. "I think those who remain at home may sometimes have the harder road."

Her championship didn't soothe him much. Jonah still wanted to blast Camellia for her ignorance. Couldn't she understand how wrongheaded she was? Or was she incapable of seeing beyond her own comfort to the needs of those enslaved to support her way of life?

Mrs. Dabbs stood. "How right you are, Jane. I'm sure you are looking forward to your entrance on Mr. Thornton's strong arm."

Jonah tried to keep his gaze centered on the girl as she nodded, but something drew his attention to Camellia. Was she pouting because her loyal friend had the effrontery to disagree with her disparaging words? Or was she the tiniest bit disappointed because he was not paying her the homage she seemed to feel was her right?

"Thank you for the honor, Mr. Thornton."

"The pleasure is all mine." He stood and bowed to her. "I'll leave you ladies to return to your studies."

Camellia's gaze burned as he took Jane's hand and dropped a kiss on it. But her glower only made him lengthen his salute.

A knock brought everyone's attention to the door. It opened and revealed the crisp gray uniform of a Confederate soldier.

Jonah recognized the beefy face of Captain Watkins before the man got all the way into the room. His teeth grated together.

Camellia rose and met the soldier in the middle of the parlor. She extended her hand, and the captain bowed over it.

Jonah didn't like being on this side of the glower. But he had not drooled over Miss Watkins's hand. And he had a responsibility to

Camellia. He might not be her relative, but as a friend of the family, he had a duty to make sure her reputation was safe. He cleared his throat.

Captain Watkins took the hint, dropping her hand and bowing to the rest of the parlor's occupants. "Hello."

To give himself the chance to regain his composure, Jonah made a show of pulling out his pocket watch. "It's been a delightful visit, but I am going to have to say good-bye. My father is expecting me at the office prior to lunch."

"We enjoyed your visit." Mrs. Dabbs rose and walked with him to the parlor door. "Please feel free to drop by at any time."

"Thank you." He bowed and left, his resolve hardening as he heard the laughter and chatter between the captain and the girls.

All the way to his father's office, Jonah lectured himself. He had a job to do here in New Orleans. A job that had nothing to do with flirtatious females. The sooner he got the needed information and returned to the battlefield, the better his life would be.

∞

Camellia brushed her hands together as if she had completed a satisfying chore. Although he had left on his own, seeing the back of the irritating Mr. Thornton was reason to feel satisfied.

She turned back to the charming captain. His chocolate-colored eyes brimmed with flattering consideration. Very different from the sarcastic green gaze and supercilious attitude of their recent guest. She felt sorry for Jane. Her friend was bound to be miserable with him as an escort to their ball. But she would make sure Jane enjoyed herself as much as possible. How could she do any less for her best friend when she was going to have the night of her life?

Captain Watkins was nothing like Jonah Thornton. Although both men were handsome and polished in their manners, the similarities ended there. Most girls would be delighted to attract the captain's attention, even without him wearing an officer's uniform. With it, he became the type of beau every young lady wished for.

Excitement coursed through her as she shared a glance with Jane. Wouldn't it be wonderful if the two of them became sisters? Of course that would only be a formality. They really were sisters. She felt as close to Jane as she ever had to Lily or even Jasmine. She and Jane were so much alike. They wanted the same things from life, and they weren't afraid to work for their goals.

"If you would care to join me?" His brown eyes caught her attention.

Captured by the admiration in his gaze, Camellia felt like she was lost in time. Thaddeus Watkins. A sigh filled her. Captain Wonderful would be a more fitting name for the man. He was so handsome. She could stare into his eyes forever. And he never poked or prodded her like the man who had just departed. No, this man could be counted on to be a gentleman rather than an irritation. Her gaze traced the outline of his insignia, and her mind recounted the other main difference between the two. It didn't matter how many excuses the others were willing to give for Jonah's actions; he was a coward. Captain Watkins believed in giving more than lip service to the things he believed in.

"Camellia seems to have lost her tongue, but I can assure you it's because she's excited at the prospect you have offered." Mrs. Dabbs's voice brought her back to earth. "Even though they have lessons, I generally set aside some time for leisure activities for the students. She has my permission as long as she and Jane wish to go."

She could see Jane's encouraging nod from the corner of her eye, and even though she had no idea exactly what she was agreeing to, Camellia took a deep breath. "Yes, Captain. We would be delighted."

"That's good, then. I'll pick you and Jane up prior to two o'clock. The troops will be performing maneuvers in Jackson Square. If you've never seen it before, I think you'll be quite impressed."

The smile that turned up her lips was genuine. She would be impressed with any destination he chose, as long as he was there to protect her. Before she could get caught up in the daydreaming his handsome physique seemed to encourage, Camellia nodded. She needed to focus or he might decide she was an empty-headed ninny, one of those giggling young women who had no ability to carry on a conversation. "I'm sure you are right. How kind of you to take time out of your busy day to escort us."

"It will be my pleasure." His smile was wide, showing his straight, white teeth.

Camellia felt like she would float across the parlor floor once teatime was over. No need to worry about the length of her stride or the sway of her skirt. Happiness would keep her feet several inches above the wooden planks.

Jane served tea to her brother with all the aplomb Mrs. Dabbs expected. He sat and conversed with them for another ten minutes before rising.

Camellia wanted to ask him to remain a little longer but knew she could not say anything of the sort. She watched him kiss Jane's cheek and bow to Mrs. Dabbs. Then he crossed to her.

She fumbled with her fan, her heart threatening to burst out of her chest. "I'm sorry to see you leave us."

"Only for a little while." He flashed that beautiful smile at her and took her hand in his. With a smooth movement, he planted a warm kiss on her skin.

Camellia's breath caught. Now that no one was looking on with disapproval, she could get lost in the moment. Her heart stopped beating altogether. This must be love. The tingling of her skin was proof. She was in love with Captain Watkins. And if the look in his dark eyes was a mirror of his desire, he felt the same way about her.

He straightened and turned to march out of the room, his stride strong and even. Everything about him was perfect.

This man had been designed specifically for her, according to her deepest desires. And she was going to do everything in her power to make certain he knew it, too. She would make him the best wife possible. How long would it be before she could claim the title of Mrs. Thaddeus Watkins?

Chapter Fourteen

The air in New Orleans had a distinct flavor all its own—a mixture of seafood from the fish market and tropical fruit from nearby plantations, with an underlying hint of the smoky odor of burning pitch used to ward off dreaded yellow fever outbreaks. Camellia raised her scented handkerchief to her nose to block out the unpleasant odors.

Captain Watkins pulled back on the reins of the restive horses leading their open barouche. "I should have procured a closed carriage."

Camellia shook her head and lowered the handkerchief, careful to take shallow breaths. A lady would never be so gauche as to agree that her escort was less than exemplary. "I'm enjoying the sunshine."

"Back home it's rarely this warm so early in the year." Jane, seated between Camellia and the captain, added her opinion. "We would have missed this wondrous weather inside a closed vehicle."

Traffic had slowed as they neared Jackson Square. Apparently most of the townspeople would be present to show their support for the Confederate forces. Ladies in large bonnets and larger skirts were escorted by men in long frock coats and followed by one or more slaves. Tradesmen and street vendors hawked everything from sweet pralines to meat pies to ready-made boots. With all the activity continuing unchecked, it was hard to believe the Union blockade had affected the flow of goods at all.

As they inched forward, Camellia realized their carriage was garnering some attention. The occupants of other carriages fluttered handkerchiefs in greeting even though they were strangers. Perhaps because of the gray uniform Captain Watkins wore.

As they neared Jackson Square, beggars crowded around them, asking for a few cents for food. Thinking of David Foster and how narrowly he had avoided becoming one of them, Camellia reached into her reticule and pulled out two folded bills.

Jane put a hand on her arm. "What are you doing?"

"We have so much. I cannot see their young, gaunt faces but that my heart is not touched."

Captain Watkins leaned forward and met her gaze. "That is laudable, Miss Anderson, but you have to be careful or one beggar will grab your purse whilst you are giving money to another."

A tiny little bubble of irritation disrupted her pleasure in the outing. Did Captain Watkins think she was an empty-headed idiot? She handed over the money to the grubby hand reaching toward the carriage seat without comment. The bubble popped after a moment. Thad was probably only being careful. She ought to be pleased with his warning instead of finding fault. Camellia summoned a smile that she turned on both of the Watkins siblings. "Thank you. I'll be more careful in the future."

The captain expertly guided their carriage to the St. Charles Hotel and handed the reins to a hostler before jumping to the ground. He came around to Camellia's side of the carriage and reached a hand up to help her.

She stepped down, coming within an inch of touching his chest.

"Steady now." His face, close enough to touch the brim of her bonnet, made Camellia's heart thump. His sideburns were neatly trimmed, not bushy like some she had seen. A shadow of stubble outlined his upper lip and the square shape of his chin.

Hot blood rushed up to her cheeks as his warm, appreciative gaze met hers. Her feet touched the ground, and he gave her hand a quick squeeze before releasing it. Needing the distraction of her fan, Camellia untied the ribbon holding her fan around her wrist and opened it. The air pushing against her face cooled it as the captain turned his attention to Jane.

She glanced around at the crowd, soaking in the festive air. A familiar voice called out her name, and Camellia turned. "Look, it's

Mrs. Thornton and her daughter, Mrs. Cartier." She smiled and waved, forgetting that she still had her fan open. An errant breeze snagged the fabric and jerked it from her hand. Without thinking, she stepped forward to catch it before it landed on the dusty street.

"Camellia, watch out!"

Jane's scream brought her head up in time to see a pair of horses galloping toward her. The men on their backs were glaring at each other instead of watching the road ahead of them. Camellia stumbled, her hands lifted above her head in an instinctive gesture, her skirts not allowing her the freedom of running to safety.

Hands circled her waist and jerked her sideways. Dizziness assailed her as she was swung in an arc. Strong arms twirled her about as though she were a child.

An unladylike *oomph* escaped her lips as she was crushed against a hard, masculine chest. Camellia's first thought was that the captain had saved her from certain death. The second was how safe she felt with his arms encircling her.

"Are you hurt?" The voice that tickled her ear was not right. It wasn't the captain's deep drawl.

Camellia bent her head back and met the bright green gaze of the wrong man. "Jonah." She struggled in his embrace. What on earth was he doing here? And how had he come to save her when it should have been Captain Watkins?

Before he could say anything more, everyone was crowding around them. Someone pulled Camellia from Jonah's arms, and he moved back a few feet. But she could still feel the weight of his gaze. And his cologne clung to her, reminding her of their closeness.

"Thank You, Lord, for protecting Camellia." Mrs. Thornton looked as though she had aged a year in the past few minutes.

Mrs. Cartier nodded her agreement. "He sent you over here, Jonah, so you could save her."

"And I thought I came to search out seats for the exhibition." His voice was full of its usual sarcasm, but Camellia had seen the concern in his eyes. Did he use sarcasm as a shield?

Before she could consider that question, Jane wrapped her in a hug. "I don't know what I would've done if you'd been hurt."

"It was my own fault." Camellia returned her hug, her mind occupied with the sight she must be. Her hat hung crookedly over her forehead, one flower dangling in front of her nose. Her flounce was dirty and possibly torn. Her fan was gone, probably smashed into tiny pieces by the very hooves that nearly got her. . .would have gotten her if not for Jonah.

Captain Watkins shook his head, a fierce frown darkening his brow. "No, I'm the one to blame. I should have been paying more attention."

Camellia heard the disgusted sound Jonah made. She might agree with Jonah, but Captain Watkins knew enough about etiquette to assume responsibility. If she disagreed with him, would she be usurping his position as the person in charge? He was obviously distraught.

"It doesn't matter who is at fault." Jane stepped between them, her voice calm. "What matters is that disaster was averted. And for that, I wish to thank you, Mr. Thornton."

"Yes." Captain Watkins turned to Jonah. "Thank you for doing what I should have done."

Jonah bowed. "I was happy to be of service, and now if you will excuse us, I need to return to my errand."

"Wait a moment, please." Jane's gaze raked Camellia's face, reminding her of her bedraggled appearance. "I don't believe I feel like observing the soldiers any longer. Perhaps you and your family can use the seats my brother arranged."

Everyone tried to argue, but Jane was adamant.

To tell the truth, Camellia felt relief. Her head ached, and she wished for nothing more than a quiet place to rest it. When Captain Watkins added his voice to Jane's, she acquiesced.

Seeing that their seats would not be used, Jonah and the two ladies agreed to take them. Mrs. Thornton promised to check on her the following day, and Mrs. Cartier invited her to visit her husband's clinic if she was not improved.

The drive back was quiet. Jane patted her hand several times but said nothing. Captain Watkins kept leaning forward to glance at her. After the fourth time, Camellia wanted to ask him if she had grown an extra head. She bit her lip instead and stared forward. He was probably upset because he'd not been the one to save her.

Camellia understood. She was disappointed, too. If he had been the one to rescue her, she might not have minded the destruction of her hat, her fan. . .and her self-esteem.

᪜

"May I help you, Mr. . . ?" The young woman came around the end of the counter, tilting her head and eyeing him with ill-concealed curiosity.

"John—" He barely stopped himself from sweeping a bow, a gesture the clerk at Devore's General Store would find odd. At least he'd managed to give her his name without stuttering. An accomplishment given the circumstances. Since landing a job on the *Catfish*, he had not spoken to many females, certainly not marriageable ones. He had stayed away from society as much as possible to hide his disfigurement. . . and to avoid temptation. "My name is John Champion." By now he should be less self-conscious, but the lie tasted sour on his tongue.

On long, dark nights when the scars on his face wouldn't let him sleep, doubts haunted John. He had been given a second chance. He wanted to do the right thing. To be worthy of the opportunity. He was determined not to make the same mistakes this time.

Mrs. Naomi was not helping, though. His boss's wife must consider herself a matchmaker. He did not doubt she had sent him to town for one purpose. . .to meet the girl standing in front of him.

"It's a pleasure to meet you, Mr. Champion." Her mouth shifted, slowly blooming into a smile that transformed her face.

Amazing how pretty she was. . . . But. . .her face seemed somehow familiar. Had they met before? Impossible. John searched his memory but came up empty.

Shifting his weight onto his right foot, he turned his body so she couldn't see the scar. It was a tactic he'd learned to spare others when they took on passengers. He wished he could grow side-whiskers on his right cheek to keep from frightening women and children, but the thick scar tissue made that an impossibility.

A curtain over an alcove in the back of the store moved, and a man wearing a white apron appeared. His brown eyes combed the store, settling on the two of them. His mustache twitched over his smile. "Anna, are you helping our customer?"

"Yes sir, Mr. Devore," Anna answered the man before turning her azure gaze back to John, her smile widening even further. "What can we do for you?"

He shouldn't return her smile. She might take his gesture as encouragement. But then again, he would probably never see her after today. They would be heading south soon, and by the time they stopped at Cape Girardeau again, she'd probably be married. So he smiled. And it felt good. As good as the first glint of sunshine on frost-covered ground.

The twinkle in her eyes made his heart turn over.

John wished he'd taken extra care with his appearance. He was clean. He bathed more often than most of the rest of the crew—a holdover from his earlier life. And he'd combed his hair. But his clothing was worn and faded, and his shoes were free of polish. He found himself hoping she would overlook his shortcomings as he fumbled for the list Mrs. Naomi had given him. "Here." He held out the folded sheet to her, noticing the creamy texture of her hand in comparison to his sun-darkened skin.

She nodded.

As she took the paper from him, his fingers grazed her palm. A tingle spread from the contact, racing up his arm and burrowing into his chest.

Her eyes widened for a brief moment, and their color went from sky-blue to the darker hues of a wave out in the open ocean. Had she felt it, too?

A bell above the door tinkled as another customer entered the store.

Anna turned to smile at the thin, sour-faced lady who had come in. The same sweet welcome she'd offered him was now expended on the new customer, and John's heartbeat returned to its normal, steady rhythm as he realized the clerk's nature had misled him. She didn't feel any more attraction to him than anyone else. She was just doing her job, greeting the customers and taking care of their needs.

The manager stepped from behind the counter and offered to help the female customer.

As John waited for Anna to fill his order, he let his gaze wander around the store. Two other customers arrived, their syrupy drawls reminding him of the Deep South. . .home. He ducked behind a display of shaving cream, not wanting to hear their gasps if they caught sight of his face.

"Mr. Champion?"

John spun around at the sound.

She stood only a foot away, her gaze caught on his face, his right cheek.

John wanted to sink through the floor. How had he missed her approach? Feeling exposed, he tried to turn away, to hide his ugliness from her.

"You poor dear." Her voice stopped him.

John looked down at her and found no revulsion, no horror. Only sympathy filled her face.

He was unmanned by the kindness of it. Most females turned away if they caught sight of his cheek—one had even fainted dead away. Children gave him a wide berth, their frightened faces turned into their mothers' skirts. Men were easier. They ignored the scars as though they did not exist.

Anna's hand reached up and softly grazed the mottled skin. "Does it hurt?"

His mouth was so dry John wasn't sure he could say anything. He shook his head, unable to admit pain that might make him seem weak to her. He looked into her eyes, lost himself in the tenderness he saw. His walls, the protection that he had slowly built over the past months, tumbled down like Jericho.

As though she realized the impropriety of touching him, Anna jerked her hand away. "I'm sorry."

"Don't be." He poured all his gratitude into the two words. How could he explain to her that he no longer felt so beastly? He might still wear the mark of Cain, but her acceptance and sympathy made his lot more bearable. He took her hand in his and lifted it to his lips, pressing a kiss on her soft skin. "Thank you."

Her breath caught, and her cheeks glowed.

John had never seen a more beautiful sight in the world. No other female could hold a candle to this tenderhearted young woman. And he knew in an instant he was in love. In love for the first time in his life. With a girl he knew only as Anna.

Chapter Fifteen

The temporary walls between the parlor and the first-floor classrooms had been removed this afternoon, and large potted plants were brought inside to decorate the large area where the ball would take place. Camellia and Jane were supposed to be napping in preparation for the festivities, but they had been unable to relax. Instead they crept downstairs to gaze at the ballroom and imagine what the evening would bring.

Jane sat in one of the chairs that lined the walls. "Are you disappointed that your family couldn't attend?"

"Not at all." Camellia took the chair next to her. She was happy with the separation between her colorful steamboat family and the social world of La Belle Demoiselle. "But I know you wish your mother was able to come."

A sigh answered her. "I'm just so worried about the situation at Willow Grove."

"Do you really think the slaves at your plantation might revolt?"

"It's happened at other places."

"That's true." Camellia reached out and took Jane's hand in hers. "But that was because of cruel owners and miserable conditions. I'm sure your parents are good to their slaves. Like at my grandmother's home. They have no reason to be unhappy."

Jane squeezed her fingers, her features relaxing as she nodded.

"Besides, we'll be going there as soon as Thad can get permission to escort us. I'm so glad you'll be with me. We're going to have so much fun."

Camellia was excited, too. It wouldn't be like Natchez where everyone knew her and her family. And of course she was looking forward to spending time with Thad. . .and Jane.

"What are you girls doing down here?" Mrs. Dabbs's voice made the two of them start.

"We were curious." Camellia stood to take the blame. It had been her idea to come downstairs, after all.

Jane stood beside her. "We'll go back to our room."

Mrs. Dabbs shook her head. "Since the two of you don't feel like sleeping, I could use some help. I have a thousand details to see to before tonight."

"What can we do?"

"Go put on your aprons and come back down." Mrs. Dabbs waved a hand toward the dining room on the other side of the hall. "The silverware needs to be polished, and then you can inspect the crystal for cracks or smudges."

Jane didn't look very happy with the instructions, but Camellia was glad for something practical to do. It would help pass the time until they dressed for the evening. The tasks were something she would be expected to oversee when she gave her own parties. She hurried her roommate upstairs, grabbed a starched apron, and returned to the first floor.

As she entered the dining room, however, Camellia began to understand Jane's reluctance. She had never seen such a pile of silver. It would take them an hour or more to finish polishing and probably as much time to inspect the crystal lined up on the sideboard. "We'd better get started." She took a seat and reached for a polishing cloth and the nearest spoon.

"Have you ever been kissed by a man?"

Jane's question startled her. "Sure I have."

"I mean someone besides your family."

Camellia's cheeks warmed. "No, of course not. Have you?"

Jane shook her head. "I wonder what it feels like."

"My sister seems to like it." Camellia could feel a deeper flush coming up now. "At least I'm sure Blake is the type of man to like kissing a lot, and she seems happy with him."

"Maybe my brother will kiss you tonight."

The skin on Camellia's arms tingled and rose like gooseflesh. Would he try? If he did, should she let him? "I'm not sure I'd like that."

Jane's mouth drooped in a pout. "I thought you wanted to be my sister. I don't think your romance will go very far if you're not willing to be kissed."

"Aunt Dahlia says a lady shouldn't let a suitor become too familiar or he'll take advantage of her innocence."

Jane's right eyebrow rose. "I don't care what your aunt says—I want to know I'm in love before I get married. It'll be too late if I discover I don't like his kisses after."

Camellia's heart, which had been fluttering, suddenly felt heavy in her chest. Jane wanted Jonah to kiss her? She wanted him to hold her close and press his lips on hers? She dropped the knife she'd been polishing, and it clattered to the floor. She leaned over to retrieve it. By the time she sat back up, she had recovered her equilibrium. "I doubt Mrs. Dabbs will let us go off alone with anyone. Can you imagine the scandal?"

Jane giggled. "I guess not, but it sure is exciting to think about."

Camellia didn't feel excited at all. In fact, she wasn't even looking forward to the ball now. She glanced toward Jane, who was concentrating on rubbing a dull spot from the handle of a serving spoon. And she wasn't sure she wanted to join her roommate at her family's plantation. Maybe she would beg off and stay here with the Thornton family until Lily could collect her. That way she wouldn't have to watch Jane flirt with anyone.

❧

The stays were so tight Camellia could hardly catch her breath.

Brigitte stepped back to reach for the hooped skirt that would form the basis for Camellia's evening gown. "*Bien. Vous sera magnifique. . . .* Beautiful."

"Merci, mademoiselle." Camellia tried to take a deep breath, but the boning around her ribs and waist would not allow it. "Can you loosen this a bit?"

Brigitte shook her head, her lips folded into a straight line as she tightened the waist of the hoop skirt.

"It will be better after a moment." Jane was already dressed, her maroon velvet gown a sharp contrast to her milky skin. One of the maids was combing her hair into elaborate swirls.

Camellia ignored the stab of jealousy. She refused to envy Jane. In fact, she would help her all she could. "I've never seen you look lovelier." Another petticoat cut off her view for a moment before it settled around her waist. Brigitte cinched it with expert fingers.

"You will surely outshine me in that dress."

"I don't know." Camellia panted while another petticoat followed the first. Then it was time for her ball gown. The silk sighed as it drifted down. It was as cool as springwater, and she knew it was a flattering color for her, but still. . . "If I look half as lovely as you, I'll be satisfied."

"Don't be silly." Jane turned her head back and forth to admire her new hairstyle. "You're at least twice as pretty as I am."

"Between us, we'll attract all of the male attention."

Brigitte clucked her tongue, looking for all the world like Mrs. Dabbs in spite of her darker hair and unlined face. But she didn't say anything.

Camellia was glad. She wasn't in the mood for a scold. Tonight was going to be difficult enough. She took Jane's place at the dressing table, concentrating on her breathing as the maid twisted her hair into a knot. Of course it sprang loose the minute the maid reached for hairpins. "My hair will never lay smooth."

Jane's smiling face appeared in the mirror in front of her. "You don't need smooth hair to be the belle of the ball. Just wait and see. You'll never get to sit down."

The maid finally managed to subdue the largest portion of her hair, but stray tendrils formed corkscrews around her face and at her neck. With that she would have to be satisfied. Jane passed her white gloves and a lacy gold fan to complete her outfit.

"Is it time to go downstairs?" Jane glanced toward Brigitte for the answer. Receiving a nod, she linked arms with Camellia. "Let's go see what my brother thinks of the woman he's going to marry."

Chapter Sixteen

Camellia and Jane were still giggling as they descended the stairs, so Camellia failed to realize some of the guests had already arrived.

"Well, if it isn't the two loveliest debutantes in New Orleans." Captain Watkins's deep voice stopped Camellia in midgiggle.

She stood still, forcing Jane to do the same or risk tumbling down six or seven steps. "Oh dear."

Jane looked from her brother to her friend, a wide smile on her face. She leaned toward Camellia. "I think it's a bit early for you to be calling him that."

Camellia's cheeks flamed. She glanced toward the small group of people in the foyer. Had anyone heard Jane's teasing remark? Captain Watkins, standing head and shoulders above the other soldiers who had come with him, did not show any evidence of having heard the words. His dark eyes were full of appreciation.

Finally, Camellia realized everyone must think she had turned into a statue. What would Aunt Dahlia say if she could see her niece frozen with fear? She would tell her to get down to her guests and present a friendly, welcoming face. The internal lecture helped her to release her strong grip on Jane's arm. Camellia took a deep breath and stepped out, her slippered feet moving as trained. She must float as though lifted a few inches above the ground. "I hope you will forgive our tardiness." She glanced past the captain toward Mrs. Dabbs, who had taken up a position at the front door.

Captain Watkins bent over her hand. "You are worth waiting for."

His voice was pitched low and, combined with the emotion in his dark eyes, caused excitement to spread upward from her stomach, bringing a rush of warm blood with it. "Th–Thank you, Captain."

Jane cleared her throat. "It's nice to see you, too, Thad."

He winked at his sister. "You look lovely as always, Sister. You're doing something different with your hair."

Camellia nodded. "Doesn't she look even more beautiful than usual?"

"Excuse me." A plaintive voice from behind Captain Watkins drew her attention to the rest of the soldiers. "I believe we should be introduced to these two ladies."

Captain Watkins's grimace made Camellia smile. She watched his features as he turned to face the man. "If you insist. This is my sister, Miss Watkins. I warn you that I will not tolerate any of you breaking her heart or treating her with the least disrespect. The same holds true for her friend and mine, Miss Anderson. Not that I plan to let you have much chance to monopolize her."

The men groaned at his words, each one bowing as Captain Watkins rattled off their names. Camellia recognized Lieutenant Baxter, the man who had dined with them last month, but the rest were a mishmash of names and faces. She might have managed one or two others, but Captain Watkins appropriated her hand as he practically spirited her away from the foyer.

With all of the candles glowing, the large room had been transformed into a magical setting akin to one from a fairy-tale world. The musicians had not started playing yet, so Camellia and the captain moved toward a section of empty chairs.

Camellia sat and arranged her skirts around her. Her waist felt pinched, but she ignored it. The admiration in her escort's gaze was worth her pain. "I'm so glad you came tonight."

Captain Watkins reached for her hand, encompassing it in both of his. "I wouldn't have missed it for the world."

Aware of the looks from some of the other students, she pulled her hand free. "Mrs. Dabbs must be delighted that you brought so many of your friends."

"Now that was a true sacrifice." He smiled at her, his teeth even and white, his eyes gleaming. "I hope I won't have to compete with them too much for your attention."

Heat warmed her cheeks once more, and Camellia glanced away. Her gaze traveled around the room as she considered how to answer him. Should she be coy? He was making his interest in her obvious. Perhaps she should let him know how much she admired him. But would that make him lose interest? For a moment she wished Aunt Dahlia had been able to come to New Orleans. She would know exactly how to advise her. But she hadn't, so Camellia had no choice but to follow her instincts. She opened her fan and let it rest against her chin in an attitude of deep thought. "I wouldn't want any of our brave soldiers to feel slighted."

The captain straightened his spine.

Camellia raised her fan to hide her smile. His reaction, the fierce frown on his face and the way he glanced about the room, told her she'd responded in the best way possible.

The musicians began playing, and the others in attendance poured into the room from the foyer. Camellia looked around and saw that Jonah had arrived. But he was not standing near Jane. Instead he was chatting with some of Captain Watkins's buddies. That was odd. What could he possibly have in common with them? She filed away the question for future consideration as the captain stood.

"Please dance with me." He held out a hand.

Camellia put away her fan, fumbling to draw out the moment. The captain knew she would accept his invitation, but why be in a hurry? By the time she put her hand in his, several couples had already taken positions on the dance floor.

She noticed that Jonah did not break away from the group he was conversing with. Jane, however, did not seem to mind. She was too busy smiling at a handsome soldier in a butternut-hued uniform who was leading her toward the other dancers.

Camellia curtsied as the captain bowed, then joined her right hand to his left and stepped forward. As the piece continued, she discovered that he was an accomplished partner. Their conversation was limited by the steps of the dance, but he never seemed to take his gaze from her face.

When the musicians struck the final chord, she expected him to take her back to the chairs, but he did not move away from the dance floor. "If you do not promise me more dances, I will simply keep you away from the rest of those dogs."

"Of course I will dance with you again." Camellia released the material of her gown, allowing it to settle around her. "You are my escort. To refuse you would be rude."

His face relaxed into his signature smile. "And I know you would never be rude."

"Never," she agreed.

He took her arm as the musicians began their next song. "Excellent."

And so the evening continued. Camellia did dance with other men, but she spent most of her time in Captain Watkins's arms. They did not stray from the strictures of propriety, however.

She could not say the same about Jonah. He had not approached her at all, but he had danced with every other girl in the room. Even some of the older ladies—the mothers, aunts, and sisters of the students. He had partnered with Mrs. Dabbs once, making that lady color and giggle like one of her pupils. Yes, Jonah had been quite the ladies' man this evening.

As Captain Watkins swirled her around the room in one of the few waltzes of the evening, she noticed Jonah had taken Jane onto the floor. He held her very close. Too close. Why wasn't Mrs. Dabbs separating them? She had done so with other men who had gotten a little too daring. Couldn't she see how inappropriately they were acting? Jonah's mouth was practically grazing Jane's ear. Camellia stumbled as she craned her head to watch them.

Captain Watkins caught her, keeping her upright when she would have fallen. "Are you tired?"

Camellia looked into his dark brown eyes, thankful he'd stopped her from making a spectacle of herself. He was kind, too. Considerate of her. "No, it's nothing. I just wondered if Mrs. Dabbs was going to stop Jonah and Ja—"

Her words were cut off as her partner swept her into a sudden turn, a turn that allowed him to see how close Jonah and his sister were dancing.

"That Cajun conniver. I should have known he would take advantage of Jane's innocence." The captain's words were laced with anger.

His anger was nothing compared to the fire that leapt to her cheeks. "Whether Jonah Thornton is a Cajun or not has nothing to say to the matter. Besides, I know your sister well enough to realize she is capable of using him to draw someone else's attention. Lieutenant Baxter, for instance."

"I can't believe you're defending him." The captain's cheeks were as red as her own, and his blazing eyes bored a hole in her. "And you call yourself Jane's friend? I cannot believe you would blame her for his poor behavior."

Camellia was so irritated with his patronizing tone that she forgot they were in the middle of a waltz. She pulled away from the captain and turned on her heel. When she saw the shocked expression of the other people in the ballroom, it was too late. For a brief instant, she considered fainting. But no. She could not bring herself to fall to the dirty floor and soil her beautiful gown. Instead she picked up her skirt and ran from the room, her eyes burning from the tears that threatened to escape.

☙

"Can you get a note out tomorrow concerning General Johnston's troops?" Jonah whispered the words to Mrs. Dabbs as they moved toward the dance floor.

"I suppose so. Are you certain the information is correct? I can hardly believe they would move a major force so far south after all these months."

Jonah nodded, his gaze centered on a rotund gentleman who was partnering with his daughter. The girl looked terrified, and he winced in sympathy as her stumbling footsteps landed on her father's feet. "I loitered near your buffet table and struck up a conversation with a soldier named Baxter. While he was talking, I overheard the captain and some of his cronies discussing it. You must send a warning. I only hope it's not too late."

The music ended then, and he moved forward to intercept Miss Watkins. It was time for him to reassume his role as the smitten escort. She was an amenable young lady, but she seemed as shallow and self-serving as Camellia. What was it about young women that made them focus on such frivolities as fashion and etiquette even while their country was tearing itself apart? Couldn't they see that their privileged world was based on a vile, destructive institution?

As they danced, he found himself unable to keep his gaze on Miss Watkins. He was too distracted by Camellia's flamboyant dress and the way her hair floated about her heart-shaped face as the captain swirled her about the dance floor. She was easily the most beautiful girl in the room. A fact borne out by the number of men eager to dance with her. She had not sat out a single dance. But it seemed to him she glowed with happiness as the captain partnered with her. Why was she so animated when the captain held her? And why did Jonah care who brought a smile to her face?

"Don't you agree, Mr. Thornton?"

Jonah dragged his attention back to Miss Watkins and wondered what she had been saying. "If you say so, Miss Watkins."

A slight frown marred her brow, so he executed several quick turns. At the same time, he tightened his hold on her waist and brought his head closer to hers, moves that should redirect her thoughts. "Will you be leaving New Orleans right away, or can I expect to see you here the next time I come to call?"

Satisfaction settled on her face, replacing the frown. Good. Better for her to count him a conquest than to wonder what really held his attention. "My brother is hoping to escort me and Camellia to Vicksburg by the end of the month. He has asked his superiors for a short leave." She giggled. "If you come before then, I will be here."

Further confirmation of the arrival of fresh troops. The smile on Jonah's face felt frozen. The Confederate leaders would not allow Captain Watkins to take leave unless they believed he would not be needed. Which would be true if General Johnston came to bolster the flagging number of defenders. Now was the time for the Federal troops to take the city. New Orleans would have no choice but surrender if Union soldiers arrived before Johnston's troops. They could cut off the South's supply lines and end the war before the year was half over. He prayed his superiors would take advantage of the information being funneled to them. Perhaps his subterfuge could end at that time, the slaves could be freed, and life could return to less battle-some days.

A commotion on the far side of the ballroom brought his head up. He was surprised to see Camellia jerk her arm away from her escort's and dash out of the room. It wasn't like her to cause a scene. She always strove hard to appear perfect. It was one of the reasons he could never resist teasing her—to witness her struggle between the desire to put him in his place and the need to maintain her flawless facade. What had happened? Had Captain Watkins offended her? Or was there another reason for her public faux pas? What could have made her break the primary rule of her very existence? The questions crowded his mind as the musicians finished playing the waltz.

Miss Watkins leaned on his arm as Jonah escorted her from the dance floor. Her brother was standing next to a large potted plant, talking to a few of his Confederate friends, so he steered Miss Watkins in that direction.

"You seem preoccupied this evening. Have I said something to upset you?" Miss Watkins pouted at him, her lips drooping.

Jonah realized she must be unaware of the disturbance between her brother and Camellia, or she would not still be trying to flirt with him. Had her back been turned to them the whole time? She would find out soon enough why the others were whispering, but for now he hoped she would remain unaware. He needed a little time to figure out what had gone wrong. "Of course not. I'm sorry. You must think me quite rude. I enjoyed our dance."

"I'm certain a polished gentleman like you must find our party boring and prosaic." Her voice was light, but he detected a slight edge to the words.

Jonah opened his mouth to answer her but was distracted by the conversation taking place a few feet away.

"Her actions show how temperamental a pretty girl can be. She'll soon learn she cannot control a man." Captain Watkins slapped one of his friends on the shoulder, and all of the group laughed.

Any answer he would have given to the girl on his arm was forgotten because of the captain's callous statement. Was he speaking of Camellia? What had he said to her? A part of Jonah wanted to confront the man right then, but he decided his first duty was to check on Camellia. Once he knew she was okay and found out exactly what the captain had said or done, he could decide the proper action to take.

"Please excuse me." He bowed to Miss Watkins, straightened, and cleared his throat to get the attention of the laughing men. "I'm certain most of these fine gentlemen are eager to partner with you."

Captain Watkins crossed his arms over his chest as the eager soldiers crowded around his sister.

Jonah's eyes narrowed as they searched the man's face. At least he could not have done her any physical harm in the middle of the ballroom. But if he'd been cruel to Camellia, Jonah would make sure he answered for it.

Turning away, he hurried to the door and into the hallway, looking left and right for any sign of Camellia. Seeing nothing, he decided to check the first-floor rooms that were not in use for the party. He crossed the hall and tried the first door. The room was dimly lit, but the yellow light of an oil lamp atop the fireplace mantel showed him floor-to-ceiling shelves lined with books. The library. "Camellia? Are you in here?"

A sniffle answered him.

Jonah's mouth tightened. She *was* crying. He entered the room and closed the door behind him. It might not be proper to shut himself in with her, but Jonah knew Camellia wouldn't want anyone to see her crying. He looked about until he spotted the bright material of her gown.

She stood beside a tall window, one hand strangling the heavy velvet drapes.

Jonah closed the distance between them and put a comforting hand on her shoulder. "It's okay, Camellia."

"Go away." She spat out the words and shrugged his hand off with an impatient motion. "Leave me alone."

He sighed. "I'll leave you alone as soon as you tell me what's going on."

She twisted to face him. "It has nothing to do with you."

"Anything that hurts you involves me." Jonah wanted to pull her into his arms and hold her close. He could see the vulnerability in her large blue eyes, could trace the pain down the wet paths on her tearstained cheeks. "Did he insult your honor?"

A brittle laugh escaped her. "Of course not. Captain Watkins did nothing wrong. All he did was defend his sister's honor."

Confusion made Jonah frown. He tilted his head as he tried to understand what she had said. Why would Captain Watkins feel the need to defend his sister? Camellia would never attack the girl. They were close friends.

Before he could puzzle out the answer, she pointed a finger at his chest. "Why did you come tonight?" Her voice was pitched low, some emotion making her tremble.

The question put him on the defensive. Did she suspect the truth? He thought he had fooled everyone. Jonah's heart was heavy in his chest. But then he realized she couldn't have any idea he was a spy. Camellia was a staunch supporter of the Confederacy. If she suspected the truth, she'd tell the soldiers to arrest him. Jonah cast about in his mind for a suitable answer, but only three words came to him. Three words that told a truth even if they didn't disclose everything. "To see you."

Her mouth formed a perfect O of shock. Her blue eyes widened. Silence filled the room as she absorbed his words. Then she shook her head. "You have some other reason. Your mother must have put the idea in your head. You only care to belittle me and my dreams. You and I both know this isn't the kind of party you generally attend."

"You don't know me at all, do you?" Jonah stepped back. "You judge me for my boyhood days. Can you not see that I am different now? I like to think I have gained a little maturity in the past few years."

Camellia shrugged, her pale shoulders catching the light of the lamp on the mantel.

"I was a child, but now I'm a man. I've put away childish things." He hesitated a moment, gathering his thoughts. "Christ is the One who guides me, not the ambitions of this world."

Her pale brows drew together.

Jonah straightened his shoulders and waited to hear the question he could almost see quivering on her full lips. He sent a quick prayer heavenward that he could properly answer whatever troubled her. That he could help turn her thoughts toward God and the real reason for existence.

She cocked her head, her curls falling across the curve of her cheek. "Is that why you're not a soldier?"

Surprise spread through him as she watched him through narrowed eyes. He almost laughed out loud. Camellia was obviously not ready to change.

The impulse to tell her the whole truth tempted him to speak. The confession would be so easy. Sharing his secret with someone he knew would be a luxury. Temptation filled him, but with an effort Jonah turned his back on the desire.

What if Camellia didn't turn him in? Then she would be a traitor to the Confederacy. Did he really want to put her life in danger for his own sake? Shame replaced his earlier surprise. "No." The single syllable was harsh even to him. Jonah swallowed and tried again. "No, that's not it at—"

"Are you afraid?"

Jonah wondered how they had gotten so far from talking about the importance of faith. "You can think what you like, Camellia. The truth is that my reasons are private."

Her gaze pierced him, leaving Jonah feeling exposed. He supposed he should credit her with looking beneath the surface for a deeper answer. But why did she have to pick tonight? Why was she searching for truth now when she'd accepted him so easily in the past? Was it some kind of test for him? A temptation placed in front of him to see if he would yield?

"I see." She turned away from him and took a step toward the door.

"Wait, Camellia." Jonah put a hand on her shoulder once more, halting her forward movement. "I'm sorry. I didn't mean to offend you."

"Don't worry about that. I'm not offended." She allowed him to turn her to face him, but she kept her gaze centered on the carpet.

He pulled her closer, intoxicated by the feel of her soft skin under his fingers and the flowery fragrance of her perfume. "I think it's time for you to realize that I can be a good friend."

"I have plenty of friends already." She glared up at him. "And I don't need the friendship of a coward anyway."

Her words bounced off of him like the first drops of a spring shower. Jonah knew he should release her, but he didn't seem to have any control over his body. He stepped closer to her, close enough to see the slight tremble in her lower lip.

Their gazes met, and her anger faded, replaced by something warmer. Something that drew his head down. His hand moved from her shoulder to cup her chin, his thumb grazing the edge of her mouth. Her eyelids drooped in response to his touch, and Jonah leaned in and let his lips cover hers.

Gently he explored her mouth with his own, teasing her, feeling her response as the kiss deepened. His heart felt as though it was about to burst from his chest. Somehow his arms had wrapped around her tiny waist, pulling her to him.

When her lips parted slightly under his, a warning bell clanged in Jonah's head. He could not allow their embrace to continue. She was too young, too innocent. Besides, hadn't he followed her in here to find out if she needed his protection?

Jonah made his hands push her away. She needed more protection from him than from the captain who had made her flee in the first place. "I'm sorry."

Her gaze fled from his, and she caught her breath with a sound between a gasp and a sob. Raising a hand to her mouth, Camellia scrubbed at her lips as though she wanted to wipe away the feel of their kiss.

He was a heel. A worm. He had taken advantage of her. Hating himself, Jonah brushed past her and exited the library. If he'd come across any other man doing what he'd just done, Jonah would have demanded satisfaction. Or at least a proposal of marriage to protect her reputation. He certainly wouldn't have allowed the fellow to slink away without repercussions.

Hesitating a moment as he considered his options, Jonah strode to the front door and jerked it open. He couldn't do anything now except put some distance between them.

Chapter Seventeen

The war didn't completely stop commerce on the river. Captain Pecanty had permission from both the Union and the Confederacy to travel on the river as long as he did not transport slaves, weapons, soldiers, or suspicious cargo. Lately, each time they made a landing, they had to allow an inspection by some authority and often lost a percentage of their cargo that was deemed to be "suspicious." It might be nails, copper wiring, sugar—anything was subject to seizure. Once they had even been commandeered as a transport ship for several wounded soldiers.

Today they had lost a hogshead of flour to the frowning Union commander. According to Mrs. Naomi, it was a small price to pay for an overnight stop in Cape Girardeau, one of her favorite landings.

Since the beginning of spring, it had become one of John's favorites, too. Miss Anna Matthews would be there, and perhaps she would be able to spend a little time with him before they had to leave. He could hardly wait to see her.

"Let's get this leather loaded." Captain Pecanty brought his attention back to the boat and the task at hand.

Two other steamboats floated next to them, a tin-clad armored boat, cannons bristling from every side, and a small, squat tugboat that had seen better days. Last year this dock would have been covered with boats, but the war had changed all that.

"They've put up another fort." Mrs. Naomi appeared from the galley in her "visiting" dress, a black bombazine with rosettes along its hem, as they finished loading the cargo. "That makes four."

The rest of the crew scattered, most of them heading to one or another of the saloons for entertainment while a few returned to the boat to stand guard.

John watched as the captain helped Mrs. Naomi climb onto the front of the wagon and then took his place beside her.

"You are coming with us, aren't you?" Mrs. Naomi sent a speaking glance his way. "I know that a certain young lady will be anxious to see you."

John ducked his head while Captain Pecanty laughed. "Leave the boy alone, Naomi. He doesn't need you to be a matchmaker, and I don't need to lose such an able-bodied crewman." He climbed up next to his wife and grabbed the reins. "But you can ride with us if you like, John."

Deciding he'd rather wash up before visiting Devore's General Store, John shook his head and waved them off. He grinned at the disgruntled look on Mrs. Naomi's face. She might have been instrumental in introducing him to Anna, but she didn't need to know how effective her strategy had been.

Devore's had several shoppers when he entered, the tinkling bell announcing his arrival. John looked about for Anna, and his heart quickened when he spotted the shining tresses of her amber-colored hair. She was helping a couple of Union soldiers find candles, so he leaned against a nearby shelf and waited. Anna was kind and patient with the men, deflecting any personal questions with ease.

As soon as she sent the men to the counter to pay for their goods, she turned toward him, her smile appearing like the first rays of the rising sun. "Hello."

"Hi. I hope you're doing well this afternoon." John took her hand and raised it to his lips, placing a soft kiss on her wrist.

Her soft intake of breath was followed by a blush, and Anna looked away from him. "I'm so glad to see you again."

John thought her embarrassment was charming. But that was not surprising. He found everything about her charming. "It's good to see you, too."

Silence enveloped them for a moment while John watched her staring at her left foot as it drew a small circle on the wood floor of the general store.

Anna looked up at him from the corner of her eye. "Do you have a list for me today?"

"Not today." He stepped toward her and took one of her hands in his. "I was hoping you could take a walk with me."

She giggled and glanced at her foot once more. "I'll have to ask Mr. Devore."

The bell over the door jingled as the soldiers left, their purchases under their arms. Her employer frowned in their direction and moved from behind his cash register. "Is that man bothering you, Anna?"

Her eyes widened, and she shook her head. "No, sir. I. . .he—" She stopped and gulped. "I mean, M–Mr. Champion has asked if he might take me for a walk."

John held out his hand to the older man. "If you can spare your assistant, Mr. Devore, I promise to bring her back as soon as you say."

Mr. Devore gripped his hand and shook it. "I don't know if her father would approve. He's the preacher in these parts, you know."

"No, sir." In fact, he knew very little about Anna's home life. But that was something he'd like to remedy. "If you think it would be better, I can apply to him for permission."

Mr. Devore studied him for a couple of minutes before shaking his head. "I think it will be all right, if she wants to go with you."

Anna nodded, the emphatic movement dislodging a lock of her hair from behind one of her ears.

John's smile felt more natural than it had for years. "Thank you, Mr. Devore. I'll take good care of her."

He opened the door for her to pass through and offered his elbow, leading her southward, toward a river bluff hosting one of the four forts built by the Union. "How have you been?"

"It's been a rather difficult summer."

Protectiveness flooded him. John wanted to protect this young woman. It was a foreign idea, but one he could not deny. He wanted to take care of Anna and make sure nothing ever disturbed her again. "Is it Mr. Devore? Is he difficult to work for?"

"Of course not. Don Devore treats me like a daughter, as does his wife, Norma Jean." Her laughter calmed his concern.

"What, then? What dragon can I slay to win your heart?"

She glanced at him and then toward someone walking toward them. A blue-uniformed soldier approached them, his rifle perched on his shoulder. As he passed them, John couldn't help but notice the bold way he stared at Anna.

As soon as they were far enough away for privacy, John halted and turned to face her. "Have the soldiers been bothering you?"

"What?" She shook her head. "No. It's nothing like that. It's just that my aunt has been ill. She has been like a mother to me since my own mother died."

John's ire began to fade. Sympathy took its place. He took her hands in his and rubbed them. "I'm so sorry. Is there anything I can do?"

She gave him a calculating look. "As a matter of fact. . .there is something."

"What? Do you need money? An extra hand back home? I'll do anything in my power."

Her smile appeared inch by inch, and her hands clung to his. "Come to church with me tomorrow morning."

She couldn't have surprised him more if she'd asked him to bring her the sun or moon. John didn't want to disappoint her, but he couldn't go to church, couldn't go anywhere with that many staring eyes. But he found it impossible to express his concern, so he fell back on an easier excuse. "I don't have a suit to wear."

Her face fell. Anna pulled her hands from his and stepped back. "I see."

John's heart clenched. But what else could he do?

≥&

John tugged on his borrowed coat one last time before stepping into the small whitewashed church. Two rows of pews marched toward the wooden pulpit, each crowded with the townspeople. Captain Pecanty and Mrs. Naomi had left the *Catfish* ahead of him, but he couldn't see their familiar faces in this sea of strangers.

What was he doing here? John would rather have faced the danger from a cauldron of boiling oil than walk down the aisle to the only empty seat he could spy. Why had he come?

As expected, he heard the gasps of the females on his right as they caught sight of the ruined side of his face, saw the way they put protective arms around their children. This was a terrible mistake. John turned on his heel, unable to continue in the face of their collective horror.

Before he could finish the move, however, the soft touch of a hand stopped him. "Please don't go." Anna's eyes echoed the plea in her words before she turned and speared one of the repulsed ladies with a glare. "You're welcome here."

John let her pull him toward the front. She sat on the first pew and looked up at him, expectation brightening her soft-green gaze. He sat and tried to ignore the whispers behind them. This was as bad as he had imagined.

Her perfume swirled around him as she leaned close. "I'm glad you came."

Suddenly the reaction of the others in the room didn't seem as important.

The Reverend Enoch Matthews entered the sanctuary, and every conversation died away as he strode down the aisle. Anna's father was a tall man with salt-and-pepper hair, whose eyes were the exact same shade as hers. He stepped up to the pulpit and laid his Bible upon it before surveying the people in the pews. "Good morning."

The people answered his greeting in a single voice, the deeper tones of the men blending with the higher notes of the women and children. "Good morning."

John started, unused to such a responsive audience.

"Let us give thanks to God for the overflowing blessings He showers on us." Pastor Matthews bowed his head and began to pray, his words flowing over John like a cleansing cascade.

He listened as Anna's father spoke to God as though they were personally acquainted. He started by praising God for His sovereignty, His loving-kindness, and His free gift of grace. The older man continued with praises for a list of things. . .everything from sleeping well to the brave soldiers who protected them from bushwhackers, the rebel guerrillas who preyed on citizens in the border states. He asked for guidance and wisdom as the church faced the challenges and opportunities of the day. He asked God to forgive them in accordance to the forgiveness they offered to others. By the time he reached the end of his prayer, the pastor's voice reverberated around the room. John was sure they had traveled all the way to heaven.

Pastor Matthews looked up once more, his face serious. "I have spoken to many of you about the future. I've listened to your fears and prayed with you for loved ones who are fighting to keep our country whole. I've shed tears with you when you found some of those same names on the lists of missing, wounded, or dead. But today, I'm here to remind you that God knew about all of this before you were even born."

He paused, his gaze moving slowly around the room. "I can see the doubt on your faces. How could God allow such pain? How could He let such terrible things happen to us if He truly loves us?"

John was riveted by the questions. He wanted to stand up and shout his agreement. What kind of God allowed such terrible things to happen to His people? He touched the skin on his right cheek. His punishment was different. He had earned it with his past deeds. But what of those who led upright, principled, honorable lives? Why were their lives full of pain?

The pastor opened his Bible and began reading from Psalm 139: " 'Whither shall I go from thy spirit? or whither shall I flee from thy presence? If I ascend up into heaven, thou art there: if I make my bed in hell, behold, thou art there. If I take the wings of the morning, and dwell in the uttermost parts of the sea; even there shall thy hand lead me, and thy right hand shall hold me. If I say, Surely the darkness shall cover me; even the night shall be light about me. Yea, the darkness hideth not from thee; but the night shineth as the day: the darkness and the light are both alike to thee. For thou hast possessed my reins: thou hast covered me in my mother's womb. I will praise thee; for I am fearfully and wonderfully made: marvelous are thy works; and that my soul knoweth right well.'

"Do you understand what this means?" the pastor asked. "The Lord God, the greatest being in existence, knew each of you before your own mothers did. And He loves you. He loves you so very much. More even than the love you feel for your children." He glanced toward the first pew, his gaze gliding past John and landing on Anna's face. "And I know how deep that love is. I know also that God's love puts my puny feelings to shame.

"This whole psalm is one I turn to often. I would read the whole chapter to you this morning, but I want to challenge each of you to go home today and read it for yourselves. Read each word. Ponder the power of our God who knows every breath each of us takes. Not just my breath. . .or Anna's. No, he also knows the breath of this stranger who has joined us this morning. He knows why this man is here and each step that led him to this place."

John's mouth dropped open. He wished more than ever that he had stayed on the *Catfish*. He wished he had found a seat in the back of the sanctuary, a place of anonymity. But somehow he knew God wanted him at this place, at this moment. The words might be issuing from the pastor's mouth, but they were coming directly from God.

Heat enveloped him. His collar was strangling him. John pulled at it with a desperate finger and wondered if he could escape. Anna must have sensed his anguish, because she touched his hand with hers. The touch did not immediately eliminate his vulnerability, but the desperation eased a bit—enough for him to remain seated on the pew.

"After you finish studying this psalm, I want you to turn to the words of the prophet Jeremiah. I want you to read my favorite verse, chapter 29, verse 11. 'For I know the thoughts that I think toward you, saith the Lord, thoughts of peace, and not of evil, to give you an expected end.' God wants you to come to Him. He made you. He is your father. Gladden His heart by turning to Him this morning. Repent and join the ranks of His fruitful children. Jesus is standing at the door and knocking. Won't you invite Him in?"

John could feel the words seeping into his soul. He was a beloved child of the Father. Even with his dark and painful past, he could still turn to God. He dropped his head and prayed to the Father to forgive his sins. He told God he wanted to be a different man. He wanted to start over and live the rest of his life according to His direction. He wanted Christ in his heart.

Tears threatened to overwhelm John, but he fought them back. Someone brushed past his left arm. John looked up and saw that two other men had come to the front of the church and were on their knees in front of the podium. Pastor Matthews was standing in front of them, his hands spread in front of him, palms up. They were praying together, a wonderful prayer of new beginnings. More than he had wanted anything in his life, John wanted to join them.

He put his hands against the pew and pushed himself up. At first he couldn't believe it was actually him moving. It seemed Something. . .Someone stronger than he was helping to lift him from the mire of his past. John stepped forward and fell to his knees, his heart full of hope—a clean, refreshing, full hope—for the first time in his life.

"Lord God," the pastor's voice washed over him, "these men come to You with repentance and hope in their hearts. They want to turn their lives over to You. They are seeking You and calling on Your promise to dwell within them forevermore. They were sinners, but now they want to be washed clean in Your holy, cleansing blood. Thank You, Lord, for speaking to their hearts and bringing them to You. We are grateful for these new brothers of the faith. Be with them as they begin these new paths to Your glory. Amen."

When John opened his eyes, the pastor was looking over their heads at the others in the church. "What a glorious morning this is. We get to welcome three more sheep into the fold."

John pushed himself up, dusted off the knees of his slacks, and turned to see Anna at his elbow.

Her face glowed with joy. "I'm so happy for you, John."

Pastor Matthews joined them. "Is this the young man you've told me about?"

"Yes, Father. This is John Champion."

"I'm pleased to meet you, John Champion." The pastor shook his hand.

John wanted to tell them the truth right then. The compulsion was very strong to come clean on this day of new beginnings. But fear grabbed him again. If he told them his real name, he would be stepping back into his past. He would be mired in his previous life. He might even once again become the monster he had been. So he nodded. "It's my pleasure, sir."

Reverend Matthews then left them to speak to others of his congregation.

Anna took one of his hands and squeezed it, her face full of joy. "Isn't it wonderful to be a Christian?"

Touched by the sincerity of her voice, John smiled. "Yes, it is. I can hardly believe how. . .how content I feel."

"I know. Walking with the Lord is a privilege." She waved one hand in an arc. "You're reborn, and from here on you can live a life of praise and thanksgiving, sure of your eternal home."

Before he could answer her, the Pecantys joined them. Mrs. Naomi hugged him, and the captain shook his hand. For a little while, John forgot the scars on his face. He forgot about his past and focused on his future. A future that was looking brighter than ever.

Chapter Eighteen

Even though almost two weeks had passed since the formal ball, Camellia's lips still tingled if she allowed herself to remember Jonah's kiss. His touch had been tender, the complete opposite of his cold voice.

"I'm sorry." The icy tone and the remorse in his eyes had thumped her back to reality.

She was sorry, too. Sorry she hadn't slapped him for taking advantage of their relationship in such a way.

Camellia had wanted to confide in her best friend, but how could she when he was supposed to have been Jane's escort? How could she admit she had been swept away by his touch? That kissing was much more delightful than they'd ever imagined?

The answer was simple. She couldn't. No one could know what had happened in this very room.

This afternoon was the first time she'd returned to the library. Mrs. Dabbs was working with some of the others on their penmanship but had sent Camellia to finish her sampler. Jane had received permission to join her.

Camellia's gaze strayed to the corner where she and Jonah had stood. With a bit of imagination, she could once again feel his warm hand on her shoulder. What had come over her? She'd been angry with Jonah Thornton right until the point at which he wrapped her in his arms. Until her mind stopped thinking and her feelings took over. Why?

What magic did Jonah have to so easily make her forget everything? Why had she felt so safe in his embrace?

"Do you think Thad will come to call this afternoon?" Jane's voice brought her out of her spinning thoughts.

Camellia shoved her needle through the square of fabric she held, careful not to stitch it to her gown as she had earlier this year. At least the time at La Belle Demoiselle had improved her sewing skills, even if she still didn't care for samplers. "I don't know."

"What about Mr. Thornton?"

A hot flush burst upward and burned her cheeks. Did Jane suspect something? "What about him?" Camellia winced at the defensive note in her voice. "I mean. . .I'm sure he has many more important things to do than frequent the school."

Jane glanced her way. "Are you feeling feverish? When Pauline's parents came to collect her last week, I overheard them tell Mrs. Dabbs that yellow jack is expected to be worse than ever this year."

Camellia rolled her eyes. "We'll be gone to Vicksburg before there's any danger."

"I suppose you're right." The two of them worked in silence for a little while, the mantel clock ticking away the minutes as the afternoon passed. "Thad has been busy lately with some secret plan, but he said he hopes to have some free time before the end of the month."

A knock at the front door made them look up.

"Who do you think that is?" Jane's brown eyes twinkled with excitement.

"Probably one of those soldiers who seemed so smitten with you at the ball."

Both of them giggled and put away their needlework. It didn't take long before footsteps echoed in the hallway. Whoever had answered the door was coming for them.

Camellia's heartbeat increased. What if it was Jonah? What would she say to him? How could she face him?

The door burst open, and Brigitte rushed inside, her cap hanging on to her curls by a single pin and a wild look in her eyes. "*C'est une catastrophe.* Come quick."

"A disaster?" Camellia translated the phrase as she and Jane rushed out of the library. Had someone been hurt? Had a doctor been called to attend one of the students? "Who's hurt?"

"Non, non." Brigitte shook her head, and her cap flew free, landing on the floor. With a cluck of her tongue, the flustered woman scooped it up before beckoning them to follow. "Soldiers are here. *Vite.* Hurry."

As they rushed behind her, their hands clasped, Camellia heard thumps and bumps coming from upstairs. It sounded as though the second floor had been invaded. What was going on?

Brigitte passed the door to the visitors' parlor and the private parlor, heading toward the dining room behind the stairwell. As she opened the oak door, the sound of feminine sobbing was punctuated by the deeper sound of male voices. "I have brought the last two."

Jane stopped in her tracks, her grasp holding Camellia back. "I'm scared."

"Camellia? Jane?" Camellia recognized Mrs. Dabbs's voice, although it sounded strained to her ears.

"Don't be scared." Wishing she could follow her own advice, Camellia swallowed against the lump in her throat and pulled on Jane's hand. "It's going to be all right." She took the last steps to the open doorway and glanced inside, shock making her let go of Jane. What she saw did not calm her.

The remaining students were congregated in the far corner of the room. Three soldiers surrounded Mrs. Dabbs, their rifles pointed toward the ceiling. But the serious cast to their features was more than a little intimidating. Brigitte's eyes were large in her face as she positioned herself between the soldiers and the students as though intent on protecting them.

But what protection did any of them need? These were not invading Yankees. These soldiers wore the gray uniforms of the Confederacy.

Mrs. Dabbs stood as Camellia and Jane entered the room.

One of the soldiers, his face hidden by a thick brown beard, swung the point of his rifle down. The bayonet flashed in the light coming from the windows.

Red splotches stained Mrs. Dabbs's cheeks. "Put that weapon away before you hurt someone."

He looked toward the taller one, who shrugged. After a moment, he shifted the weapon so it rested on his shoulder. "Is this all of them?"

Mrs. Dabbs sent him a disdainful glance. "I have seven students remaining. Count for yourself."

"What's going on?" Camellia took a step toward Mrs. Dabbs.

The tall soldier, who had blue eyes and a freckled face, frowned at her.

Camellia ignored him, moving forward and taking the older woman's hands in her own. They were as cold as icicles. "Are you all right?"

"Yes, dear." Mrs. Dabbs sighed. "But I'm afraid these gentlemen are going to insist on my accompanying them. As the oldest student, you'll need to help Mademoiselle Laurent notify everyone that the school is closing immediately. Thank goodness many of them have already departed. You should have no trouble getting the rest of them to their relatives."

"But why?"

A noise at the door took Mrs. Dabbs's attention away from her face. An exclamation from behind her brought Camellia's head around. Jane had run to the door and flung herself on the man standing there.

Relief spread through Camellia, and she squeezed Mrs. Dabbs's hands. "Captain Watkins, thank goodness. Now everything will be fine."

He hugged his sister briefly, keeping one arm around her as he entered the room. He ignored everyone else as he nodded to the soldiers in the room. "I'll take over in here. Riley, Hamilton, stand guard at the front door. Don't let anyone in or out until I've cleared them. Adkins, go help the search out back."

The three men hurried to do his bidding.

Camellia let go of Mrs. Dabbs's hands and summoned a bright smile for his benefit. He was forgiven for his boorish behavior the last time she'd seen him. "I'm so glad you're here."

"And I wish you and Jane were not." His handsome mouth did not relax into a smile. He didn't look angry. But he glanced toward Mrs. Dabbs, and his face hardened. "I wish I could spare all of you girls, but your families will no doubt read of it in the newspaper. Traitors cannot be tolerated. Not when so much is at stake."

Camellia put a hand to her mouth. It couldn't be true. But then she saw the defiant gleam in Mrs. Dabbs's eyes. The lady looked as though she was proud of her actions. Camellia took a step away from her.

Jane sidled to her and put an arm around Camellia's waist as she directed a question toward their teacher. "What have you done?"

Mrs. Dabbs rolled her eyes. "Why don't you ask the brave captain?" She directed a frown at him. "I assume you have thoroughly searched the rooms upstairs?"

Captain Watkins nodded. Then he looked at Camellia and his sister. "We intercepted a letter she tried to send to Captain Poindexter, a man who happens to be her cousin."

That didn't sound too bad. Camellia supposed she had relatives who were Yankees. Would she be arrested if she wrote to one of them? She sent a questioning gaze toward the captain.

"It contained information we planted during her party."

Now he had everyone's attention. Even the younger girls stopped sniffling to listen to his story.

"We've had reports of a traitor—maybe one person, maybe more—who is passing information to the Yankees about our troop movements. Of course the letters are in code. They appear to be innocent, but in reality they are detailed descriptions of our plans, weapons, and troop strength. We got a lead on Poindexter and decided to set a trap, something that would flush out the guilty party. We planted false information about the impending arrival in New Orleans of General Joseph Johnston and his troops. Then we waited for someone to take the bait."

He drew a folded sheet of stationery from his coat pocket and opened it with a snap. "This is all the proof we need to arrest Mrs. Dabbs. It's taken more than a week, but we finally broke her code. This letter warns her cousin of Johnston's arrival and begs him to come and conquer the city while our defenses are weak."

Camellia's stomach clenched so hard she felt nauseated. "What will happen to her?"

"We'll take her to prison." The captain's eyes blazed with scorn. "I hope they hang her."

Jane gasped, and several of the students began crying again.

Camellia tightened her jaw against the nausea, reminding herself that she had to be strong for the other girls. She could feel their gazes on her, awaiting her response. "We'll pray for her."

Captain Watkins's expression softened a smidgen. "Your sympathy is admirable if misplaced. I'll check on you and Jane as soon as I can." He took Mrs. Dabbs's arm and urged her to the door.

As he led their schoolteacher away, Camellia turned toward the distraught students, wondering what had driven Mrs. Dabbs to take such drastic steps. Why had she turned on the system that supported her students? Her school?

And what did this turn of events say about Camellia's ability to judge others? She had respected Mrs. Dabbs more than most, as much as Aunt Dahlia. She could no longer trust anyone, even if her own powers of discernment said differently.

≈҂

"I hope Thad doesn't arrive before we get back from delivering Molly to her parents." Camellia glanced toward the little girl who huddled in one corner of the carriage.

"I'm sure he'll wait." Jane coughed and waved a scented handkerchief in front of her face. "The smoke seems worse than this morning."

Camellia nodded her agreement. "I wish they would stop ringing the alarm bells. Surely no one in New Orleans is unaware of the danger." She thought about the report Brigitte had brought them while they were getting ready to leave.

Mrs. Dabbs's assistant had gone to Jackson Square to discover why the alarm was being sounded. Apparently everyone expected the Yankees to arrive at any moment. The shipyards across the river at Algiers were in flames. Bales of cotton had been dragged out of warehouses and put to the torch. Even boats on the river had been set afire and loosed from their moorings to drift down the river.

"I hope my parents are all right." Tears puddled in Molly's eyes.

"I know you're frightened." Camellia hid her fear behind a brief smile. "Don't worry. I doubt the Yankees are really coming. Don't you remember all of the handsome soldiers who came to dance with us?"

Molly looked a little happier as she nodded.

"Those silly Yankees wouldn't dare to attack them, now, would they?"

Molly shook her head and sat up straight as the carriage made a turn. "Are we there?"

Camellia leaned forward, careful to keep her spine straight as she'd been taught. No matter what the future held, she was determined to present a polished and serene image. A curve in the drive showed her a double row of moss-draped oaks, a fitting entrance to a grand plantation home. " I believe we are."

She and Jane helped gather Molly's belongings, but before they could alight, a short lady with dark curls and worried brown eyes was at the door to the carriage. When Camellia saw the woman's rounded stomach, she realized why Molly's mother had not been able to come

138

collect her daughter. She was going to have a baby, a little brother or sister for Molly.

"Merci. My husband is in the army, but we have much room if you would like to stay here with us."

For a moment Camellia was tempted to take up Molly's mother on her offer. Farther from town, the air seemed clearer, the danger not so immediate. They could hide out here and hope the war would pass them by.

But then a picture of Thad's earnest face appeared in her mind. His dark eyes boring a hole into her, his arms coming around her, his lips—Camellia slammed the door on the memory—not of Thad but of Jonah. Why was he the one she thought of?

No matter, they had to go back to the school or *Thad* would be worried. She shook her head. "We have family in town."

The older woman nodded her understanding. Putting an arm around her daughter's waist, she led Molly between a pair of white columns and onto a shady porch. They both turned and waved as the coachman backed the carriage and began the drive to town.

When a bend in the drive hid the graceful, two-story home from sight, Camellia turned to Jane. "What do you think will happen to them?"

"We should pray for their safety." Jane sighed.

As the carriage trundled through the countryside, each retreated into her own thoughts. Camellia wondered why everything had changed. Why was her life so out of control? No matter what she did, nothing ever worked out as planned.

First she was kissed by the wrong man. Then Thad, the man she hoped to marry, appeared to arrest Mrs. Dabbs. He had single-handedly closed down the school, although she supposed she couldn't blame Thad for his actions. But couldn't they have just intercepted the letters and waited to arrest Mrs. Dabbs once the term was completely over? And now the Yankees were practically knocking at their front door. How much worse could things get?

The thoughts continued to roll in her mind until the carriage came to a halt. "What now?"

Jane's eyes widened. "Do you think it's. . .Yankees?"

A shudder passed through Camellia. "I hope not."

The coachman climbed down and opened the door between them.

His dark face was drawn in a frown. "There's some kind of speechifying going on up on the Levee Road. I can't get through right now. Did you ladies want to get out and walk about while we wait?"

Without waiting for Jane's agreement, Camellia moved toward the door. She needed to get out of the stuffy carriage. As soon as her feet touched the ground, she looked about. A crowd had gathered around a man of average height whose mustache blended with his side-whiskers. Curiosity drove her forward.

"Wait for me." Jane's voice came from behind her.

The heat pounded on her shoulders, and the smoke was worse once more. Camellia choked back the urge to cough. When Jane drew even with her, they linked their arms and picked their way around the ruts in the road to stand on the outskirts of the crowd.

The man tugged on his uniform and cleared his throat. "That's why I feel it would be best to withdraw from the city."

A collective groan greeted his statement. One of the ladies fainted. Her escort caught her and lowered her to the ground before returning his attention to the man speaking.

"We will be within easy reach should you need our military support, but I don't want the Yankee navy bombing the city. If no one remains within New Orleans but workingmen, women, and children, I believe they will not take action against you."

Camellia was horrified at his suggestion. Without a military presence, the city would undoubtedly fall into Yankee control. Since her sister was directly involved in the world of commerce, she understood what it would mean to the South to lose the city. The free flow of arms and goods would be halted. It would be a devastating blow, one that might mean the end of the war, the end of everything that mattered to her.

Chapter Nineteen

"You cannot remain here all alone." Jonah held on to his patience with an effort. The woman standing in front of him had to understand the dangers she and her friend might face. "Now that Admiral Farragut has landed, New Orleans must surrender to the inevitable."

Camellia opened her mouth and closed it with a snap. "If you believe that, you're an idiot. Our soldiers will defend us."

"Is that what you think? Do you expect Captain Watkins to ride in on a white horse and save the day?"

Her eyes darkened, distracting him.

All he wanted to do was take her in his arms once more and feel her soft curves yielding to him. Jonah shook his head to clear it. This was definitely not the time to be thinking about romance. He needed to convince Camellia and Jane to leave the school and take up residence with his family where he could keep an eye on them. Just to make sure they were safe, of course.

"I'm sorry. I shouldn't have said that." He pivoted and walked to the far side of the visitors' parlor, his footsteps echoing in the empty house. Maybe some distance would help him keep his focus.

She sniffed. Had he made her cry? Jonah glanced over his shoulder, relieved to see that her lips were folded in a straight line. She might be angry, but at least she wasn't falling apart.

A thought occurred to him. Was she angry with him because of this afternoon? Or was she upset about the way he'd acted the last time they were together? "Camellia, I'm sorry for what happened that night, and I know what you must think of—"

A disdainful roll of her eyes stopped his words and made his jaw tighten.

Jonah took a deep breath and began again. "I promise I won't come near you if you'll only consent to moving to the town house. Father will fuss about the Federals, and Mother will fuss over you and Miss Watkins—"

"Jane. Her name is Jane."

He was glad to get past the apology, so Jonah ignored the needling tone in her voice. "You and *Jane* cannot remain here without Mrs. Dabbs."

"We couldn't very well abandon the younger girls to suit your sense of propriety." Camellia raised her chin in a defiant gesture. "Jane and I have spent the past two days getting messages out to the families of the other girls and delivering the ones who could not be picked up."

Jonah sighed. "It's not my sense of propriety, Camellia. I'm impressed that you took it upon yourself to reunite the remaining students with their families or send them home, but that responsibility is completed. I saw no sign of any servants, so I assume they've run away. It's time for you to leave, too. Thieves are taking advantage of the confusion and panic to break into homes and steal whatever they can find. And they don't care if they hurt someone in the process."

"Wait a minute." Camellia's chin lowered a notch, and her gaze studied him. "How did you know Mrs. Dabbs wasn't here? We haven't told anyone, and it hasn't been in the newspapers."

She was too quick for her own good. Jonah could hardly tell her he'd received a report from another sympathizer who was stationed at the prison. Nor could he kiss her again to distract her. He looked away, his mind grasping for a plausible answer. "That captain sent me a note about it and asked me to make sure the two of you were safe."

The suspicion on her face didn't abate. "Why would he do that? When did the two of you become such fast friends?"

He forced a laugh. "I wouldn't call our relationship friendly, but you're the one who introduced him to my family. He was worried about you and couldn't check on you himself. It's no wonder he contacted my father."

"I thought you said he sent a note to you."

"I—I meant that I read Father's note." Jonah summoned up all the innocence he could muster and met her gaze openly. It was time to put her on the defensive. "Why are you so concerned about how he addressed the message? What really matters is that you and Miss. . .Jane pack a bag or two. I could not bring the wagon through the streets, so don't pack too much." He held his breath as he watched the emotions play across her features.

She finally shrugged and moved to the door. "I don't suppose we have much choice. But I'm going to take Thad to task when I see him next for sending a note to you—or your parents—when he couldn't be bothered with letting us know what was going on. Jane and I have been worried sick about him since he failed to show up yesterday afternoon as expected."

"I'm sure he wanted to." Jonah kept his tone light. "Go on and get your things. We need to leave as soon as possible."

The moment the door closed behind Camellia, Jonah collapsed onto the striped damask sofa. That had been a close one. He would have to send a missive to the captain reassuring the man about the girls' whereabouts. And he would have to hope his subterfuge was not discovered.

As long as Camellia was around, Jonah would also have to watch every word he uttered. If she realized his true mission, she would run straight to Captain Watkins with the information. Then his usefulness as a spy would be over. He wouldn't be able to rescue Mrs. Dabbs, and he'd probably have to run for his life to escape imprisonment or hanging.

❧

"Mayor Monroe sent a note back that if Farragut didn't like the flags flying over our government buildings, he would have to remove them himself." Mr. Thornton's laughter rocked the carriage.

Camellia hoped the noise their host was making wouldn't bring unwanted attention to them. Fog and smoke swirled outside the window, barely visible in the predawn hours. She stretched her senses to their utmost, trying to hear above the *clip-clop* of their horse's hooves on the pavement. Did a shadow detach itself from the alley they passed, or was it only her imagination?

"Are you sure the boat will leave this morning?" Jane's question brought her attention back to the interior of the carriage.

Accustomed to the dark, she saw Jonah's nod. "Don't worry. Everything's arranged."

Why did his voice sound so kind when he addressed Jane? When Jonah spoke to her, which had been an infrequent occurrence over the past three days, it had been in distant monosyllables. When she had asked if he'd seen the Yankee boat, he'd answered yes. When she questioned him about further messages from Captain Watkins, he'd simply said no. No explanation, no comment. As though they were strangers. It was very perplexing.

As she returned her gaze to the dark landscape, Camellia's thoughts turned to home. Wouldn't Lily be amused that she was so anxious to board a steamboat? A pang speared her. She couldn't wait to see precious Jasmine. Had her baby sister memorized any more dramas? Or had she grown out of that fascination? She had no doubt that Lily and Blake were still happy in their odd, argumentative way. And what about Aunt Dahlia and Uncle Phillip? Had they found her a better suitor than Thaddeus Watkins, Esquire? She couldn't wait to show all of them how much she'd matured. Even Grandmother would be impressed by her improved skills.

If only she'd been able to convince Mrs. Thornton to come with them. But the lady had refused, stating that she would not abandon her husband and children. Camellia shuddered to think of any of them caught between the opposing forces. The men in the family would try to protect Mrs. Thornton and her daughter, but would it be enough?

She would have to pray that the Yankee admiral would give up and slink away. Wasn't it enough that his ships were blockading Confederate waters? Did he have to threaten the cities, too?

Camellia glanced toward Jonah and wondered what he would say if she voiced her opinion. Would he stick to monosyllables then? She was tempted by the idea of engaging him in a discussion, even if it was an argument.

She knew she should be thankful he was keeping his distance from her. They could not afford a repeat of that moment in the library at La Belle Demoiselle. Her cheeks heated, and a chill that had nothing to do with the damp morning air raced through her. A part of her wanted to repeat the experience, if only to prove that the emotions of that night had been a result of the excitement of the dance rather than a response to his kiss.

A shout interrupted her thoughts and brought Camellia's attention back to her surroundings. The carriage came to a halt as they reached the port. How different it looked without all the steamships lined up along the docks. Before the war, she would not have been able to see the oak trees on the west bank, but as the sun began to rise above the horizon, she could easily make out the widespread limbs and gnarled trunks lining the opposite shore.

The pungent odor of burned cotton seemed to hang over them as Jonah opened the door and jumped out, turning to offer a hand to assist them.

Camellia waited for Jane to alight then took Jonah's hand. She realized her mistake as soon as her bare hand touched his. No admonition to be as tranquil as a lake's surface could stop her reaction. Grabbing hold of a lightning bolt could not have caused a greater sensation. A flash in Jonah's dark eyes told her he had felt the same thrill. Time stretched out as she leaned against his strength, as she relied on him to keep her from tumbling to the damp pavement. Then her foot touched the ground, and the moment ended. Her heart was fluttering in her chest like a frightened bird. What had happened? What power was it that Jonah had over her? Why could the mere touch of his hand cause such a furor?

Jerking away from him, Camellia caught her breath and looked around them. The fog dampened all sounds, giving the area an eerie, deserted feel. Gooseflesh arose on her arms. She wanted to reach for Jonah's solid form again but moved closer to Jane instead. "Where is the boat?"

Behind her, the horse whinnied and the coach creaked as Mr. Thornton disembarked. "It ought to be right over there."

"I don't see anything." Concern filled Jonah's deep voice. "I thought he was going to wait here for us."

Jane put an arm around Camellia's waist. "Perhaps he had to move to a berth farther down the river?"

Mr. Thornton walked to the water's edge and raised a hand to his brow, searching in both directions for any sign of the boat. "Nothing. I don't see anything but water."

Camellia's heart sank. Would they not be able to escape after all?

A bright light shone from the opposite bank, piercing the fog that seemed to grow denser with every passing moment.

She pointed toward it. "Is that the boat?"

"That doesn't make sense." Jonah took up a position on the other side of Jane. She could almost feel the tension rolling off him. "Why would it be on the west bank?"

Camellia squinted, trying to discover the source of the light. It seemed to expand, becoming several points of brightness. Was that the effect of the fog? Or something more ominous?

"I think it's a fire." Jane whispered the words as though afraid to say them out loud.

The lights jumped higher and spread out wider at the same time, casting a yellow reflection on the dark water of the river. For a moment she thought someone might have set fire to one of the old oaks, but then Camellia recognized the outline being made—a steamship.

A blast rent the air, and the sky filled with burning debris.

"Watch out!" Jonah turned and caught both of them in his arms, bending his torso to form a barrier between them and the dangerous missiles.

She could hear the thunks and splashes as the pieces rained down all around them, but Camellia was more aware of the scent of Jonah's cologne, the strength of his arms, and his protective stance than the danger they were in.

As soon as the noises abated, he dropped his arms from them. "Father? Father, are you all right?"

"I'm fine." Mr. Thornton was no longer standing where he had been.

Camellia looked around, relieved when she saw Jonah's father and the coachman emerging from the space under the carriage. "There they are."

"Look." Jane's voice brought their attention back to the river.

The decks of the steamer were completely enwrapped in a blanket of flames. The paddle wheel still churned, however, its great blades pushing through the muddy water and sending the boat downriver.

Camellia looked for the name on its side, her heart sliding downward as she made out the last three letters: H–O–E. "It's the *Ivanhoe*." Her voice cracked on the last word.

"Don't worry." Jonah stepped toward her. "We'll get you out of New Orleans."

"How?"

"We'll find another boat."

Camellia wanted to believe him, but his eyes told her a different story. "There aren't any more boats."

He put a hand under her arm and guided her back toward the carriage. "I'll do whatever is necessary, Camellia. If I have to carry you out of here on my back, I'll see that you reach your family safely. You can count on me."

And somehow she knew she could.

Chapter Twenty

$\mathcal{J}$onah wondered how the mayor could continue refusing to bow to Admiral Farragut now that everyone knew both forts guarding the river below the city had surrendered. It was only a matter of time before troops arrived and put the city under marshal law. He ought to be proud that his work had helped make a bloodless victory possible.

Even his father had accepted the inevitable and freed their slaves. A couple of the older ones stayed, but most of them were happy to seek out brighter futures than they had once dreamed possible. Jonah had given them all the cash he could collect, a gesture he hoped would help them during these difficult times.

A knock on the front door went unanswered for a moment until he rose with a grin. Along with his parents, he was going to have to remember to wait on himself. He crossed the marble floor of the foyer and pulled the door open, a frown drawing his eyebrows together when he recognized their visitor. "Captain Watkins."

"Are my sister and Miss Anderson staying with you?"

Jonah bowed and stepped back begrudgingly. "They're safe." He wanted to voice the unspoken words *thanks to my efforts* but decided that would be an unchristian remark.

"Captain Watkins!" Camellia didn't run to the door, but she moved faster than her usual sedate pace.

Jane followed, her smile mirroring the wide one Camellia wore.

The two girls pulled Thad into the parlor.

Jonah decided to ask if anyone in the kitchen could prepare a tea tray. As he waited for Selma to finish steeping the tea, he wondered what conversation was going on in the parlor.

"We got a few more pralines, Master Jonah, but no cookies to go on the tray."

Maybe that would keep the captain from returning. But Jonah knew better. They could forgo tea altogether for that matter. He was here to regale Camellia and Jane with his derring-do. He would gloss over the conditions under which the Confederates held poor Mrs. Dabbs with the excuse that he didn't want to upset the girls.

Jonah gulped as a new thought hit him. If Camellia thought to upbraid him for his supposed message to the Thornton household, she would find out Jonah had made up that story. Grabbing the tray from Selma, he hurried back to the parlor, the rattle of the china announcing his arrival.

". . .and how much longer the city can hold out." Captain Watkins sat on the sofa between Camellia and Jane.

Jonah's father and mother sat across the tea table from them in the pair of overstuffed chairs. Jonah was relieved to see his parents in the parlor, as it meant the conversation would be centered on the war.

"As long as it takes." Father banged his hand on the arm of his chair. "We're not a bunch of sniveling cowards like the men at those forts. I still find it hard to believe they surrendered without a fight."

A fact for which Jonah was profoundly thankful. He attributed the event to God's intervention. As He had done to the enemies of the Israelites, God had filled the Confederate soldiers with a spirit of fear. According to the reports Jonah had heard, they had spiked or dismounted the cannons, insisting on surrender no matter what their superiors promised. The route to the city was open, and he expected to see troop ships sailing into the port city any day.

"Unfortunately, our batteries at Chalmette are intended to revoke an attack by land. There's nothing we can do to protect the city at this point."

Jonah put the tray on the tea table and straightened. "So what will you do?"

What the captain might have answered was lost as the sound of marching feet outside grabbed their attention.

Jonah was the first to the door. He wrenched it open and strode to the sidewalk, followed by his parents and their guests.

Soldiers marched through the street, their faces stern, the brass buttons on their blue uniforms gleaming under the noonday sun. The familiar red and white stripes of the U.S. flag waved bravely above their heads.

"This is a disgrace." His father's voice was gritty with disgust. "A day of shame for the South."

"It's the end of the war." Relief flooded Jonah. Southerners would have to realize they could not win now. They could return to their homes, free their slaves, and vow fealty to their country.

Captain Watkins rested a hand on his sidearm. "Not quite."

What was the idiot going to do? Fight the Union all by himself? Jonah failed to see how Camellia could admire the captain.

"Come, girls. Let's get out of the street." Mother's voice was quiet, emotionless. "The rest of you should come inside, too. No need to risk being shot."

Jonah ignored her suggestion, watching until the soldiers disappeared from sight. He supposed they were headed to city hall to replace the Louisiana state flag.

It was over. Without access to the Gulf of Mexico, the blockades would succeed in stopping the movement of troops and goods. He had no doubt May 1, 1862, would go down in the history books as the day the War Between the States was won.

∽

Camellia turned over and punched her pillow. Settling back with a sigh, she studied the ceiling and wondered why sleep was so elusive. Was it because of the soldiers they'd seen marching through the streets? What would happen tomorrow? And when would they ever get out of the city? No Confederate steamships would come; that was for certain. Not unless they intended to fight the Union navy.

According to both Jonah and Thad, all was lost for this city and probably for the war. While a part of her mourned the defeat, another part of her was glad it was ending. Maybe now her life could get back on an even keel. Thad would be able to woo her without the distraction of his military duties. Yes, the more she thought of it, the better things were looking.

She rose from her bed and looked out the window, noting the rain that had begun falling. A figure on the street caught her attention. Her hand went to her throat. The stories of looters had begun to abate, but the danger was still there. Another figure joined the first, slipping from shadow to shadow as they traveled down the street and onto the Thorntons' front lawn.

A scream rose to her throat but then halted when she saw the smaller figure raise a hand to knock on the door. Burglars wouldn't knock, would they? She ran to her bed and pulled on her dressing gown. She used the tinderbox on the mantel to light a candle then slipped out of her room, one hand guarding the flame while the other grasped the balustrade.

Light flowed up the spiral staircase, indicating the late-night visitors had roused someone in the household. Voices from below were hushed, but she heard her name clearly. The voice was familiar. Her feet moved faster, and Camellia was suddenly glad she'd been unable to sleep.

"Lily?" She reached the foyer and threw herself at her sister, excitement stripping away her decorum and the training she'd received at La Belle Demoiselle. But for the moment she didn't care. Camellia wrapped her arms around Lily and squeezed her like a fresh lemon. "What are you doing here?"

Lily returned her hug. "We came to get you, of course." Her voice choked. "Did you think we wouldn't?"

"I'm so glad you're here." She leaned back a little, her smile encompassing her brother-in-law as well.

"Why don't you come into the parlor and tell us all about it." Camellia had not realized Mrs. Thornton was in the foyer until she spoke.

Lily shook her head. "We don't have much time. You'll need to pack one set of clothing, Camellia. Your other things can come to Natchez by wagon."

"I understand."

"What? No argument?" Blake's blue gaze held a twinkle. "I'm beginning to think that school was a good idea after all."

"What's going on down here?" Jane looked down on them from the first-floor landing.

Camellia beckoned to her friend. "Come down and meet my family." She performed the introductions, leaving out the fact that Jane's brother was the man she was going to marry.

Lily and Blake exchanged a glance, some wordless communication passing between them. "We'll gladly take you with us, Miss Watkins, if you wish."

"I hate to leave, but I do think it would be best. Thank you."

"Then both of you had better get upstairs." Blake gestured toward the stairwell with his chin. "And remember you cannot bring more than one valise each."

Camellia rushed to do his bidding, wadding up underclothing, a nightgown, and a shirtwaist and stuffing them into the bag she had stored under her bed a week earlier. She dragged on her smallest hoops and tied them loosely around her waist. Her black skirt looked a little lopsided, but perhaps no one would notice.

By the time she returned to the parlor, it seemed everyone in the household was awake. Even Jonah had come over from his *garçonnier*, his auburn hair gleaming in the candlelight. He was standing in a corner of the room, talking to her brother-in-law. Was he going to come with them? The thought made her heart race.

Mr. Thornton was asking Lily about commerce north of the city, a subject that seemed unimportant to Camellia. As steeped as she had been in the standoff between the mayor and the Yankee admiral, she had forgotten the rest of the world might continue business as usual. When he saw her, however, he stopped. "I'd better call for the carriage."

Jonah raised a hand to stop his father. "I'll drive them."

"It's not too far for us to walk." Blake took Camellia's valise from her. "As soon as your friend is ready, we'll leave."

Jane entered the room as though on cue, a bit of lace trailing from her valise. "I'm here."

"I insist on taking you. It'll be much safer." Jonah straightened and moved to the door. "I'll meet everyone outside in a few minutes." Since no one argued, he disappeared through the door.

At least he would be with them a few more minutes. Now that it was time to go, sadness swept through Camellia. She hugged both of the Thorntons and thanked them for their hospitality.

Lily hugged them, too. "Are you sure you won't come with us?"

"Not now." Mr. Thornton shook his head. "Maybe in a week or two when we can be certain our daughter and our home are safe."

Blake handed the ladies into the carriage before joining Jonah up front. Since they had no lantern, Camellia knew it would take both of them to avoid obstacles.

She peppered Lily with questions on the way to the river, learning that Jensen and Tamar had stayed on board to protect the *Water Lily*. Seeing their former nanny and her husband would be more pleasant than dealing with her father once more. Odd how when she'd been wishing to sail away from New Orleans, Camellia had not once considered the most colorful member of her family. A familiar vise settled around her chest. It was a reminder of the reason she'd fled to New Orleans in the first place. How had she ever forgotten that?

Yet when she looked out the carriage window to see the white decks and tall stern-wheeler of her sister's steamship, Camellia wanted to applaud. Safety was finally within reach.

The carriage halted, and Jonah pulled open the door. Mindful of her experience the last time he'd helped her out of a vehicle, Camellia pulled back. Jonah handed Jane out. Then Blake appeared and caught Lily around the waist, pulling her out amid giggles and whispered demands that he be more serious.

Camellia rolled her eyes, but inside a part of her rejoiced to be near them once more. She moved to the door quickly and stepped down without any assistance. It might not have been her most graceful exit, but at least Jonah's touch didn't electrify her.

Her father, Jensen, and Tamar stood at the rail of the boat, waving toward the dock.

Camellia returned the gesture, moving closer to Jane. "It won't be long now before we'll be back in Confederate-controlled territory."

A grunt made Camellia look behind her. A nearby lamp played against the planes of Jonah's face, highlighting his disgust. Why? Because of her words? Even if he wouldn't fight, he still supported the Confederacy. . .didn't he? He had chosen to return here. What other reason could he have for remaining?

The answer to her question smashed into her with the force of a runaway train. He didn't like the Confederacy, was opposed to all of its goals. He didn't want independence, and he was here to make sure the Cause failed. The reason he'd come to La Belle Demoiselle so often had nothing to do with her or Jane. He had come to pass along information to Mrs. Dabbs. All the little incidents, all the glances, words, and gestures played through her mind, ending with the kiss. Was that nothing more than another of his lies?

Jane crossed the gangplank with dainty footsteps while Camellia, thoroughly shaken by the monumental realization, stared at Jonah, not wanting to believe he could have betrayed his country, his friends, his family.

"What's the matter with you?" His whisper came out sharp, like the buzz of a wasp.

Camellia shook her head. "You're a spy." She watched him carefully, hoping he would deny the accusation.

His shoulders drooped. "You don't understand anything."

No denial. No attempt to hide the truth now that it was too late for her to do anything about it. "I ought to send a note to Thad."

"Camellia, my work here is done. The city is in the hands of the United States."

"If not for people like you and Mrs. Dabbs, New Orleans might still be safe."

"Or thousands could be dead, including my family." He sighed. "Why do you think Farragut has not bombarded us with his cannons?"

He stepped closer to her, wrapping his hands around her upper arms and squeezing them with gentle strength. "Because of people like me who assured him there's no need. You haven't seen the horrors of war. . .the destruction and death. What I've done has spared New Orleans. Can't you see that?"

Madness. Even now, even when she knew how he had lied to her, Camellia wanted to lean into him. She wanted to rest her head against his broad chest and let his argument convince her. But she couldn't. "I see nothing but your betrayal of the people who care for you." She stepped back, wondering if he would try to stop her.

But he released his hold on her arms. "I wish you weren't going. Not now. Not like this."

The words were soft, tempting. Like the look on his face. But what could she believe from a man who lied to everyone around him?

Camellia grabbed her skirts and ran across the gangplank, eager to put physical distance between them. Tamar was there, and Camellia fell into the older woman's arms, thankful for the familiar welcome from the woman who had raised her and her sisters. But the ache in her chest did not ease. Overwhelmed by a loss she didn't completely understand, Camellia sobbed into Tamar's collar.

"There, there." Tamar patted her back. "You're safe now, dearest."

The words were empty to Camellia. In the last few days, everything had changed. Two people very close to her—her teacher and her. . .what was Jonah to her exactly?—had proven to be the opposite of what she had thought. She didn't think she would ever feel safe again.

Chapter Twenty-one

"You're here!" A feminine squeal split the morning air, and weight landed on Camellia's bed.

Disoriented for a moment by the familiar walls of the bedroom she had grown up in, Camellia squinted at the dark-haired girl perched on her bed. Almond-shaped eyes the color of violets stared back at her. "Jasmine."

It was the only encouragement her younger sister needed to launch herself at Camellia and envelop her in a tight embrace.

The nightmare of the dark journey home began to fade. She was home. Home where everything was still normal. The scourge of war and soldiers and traitorous spies had not touched Natchez, and she hoped it never would.

Emerging from Jasmine's hug, Camellia leaned back and stretched her arms over her head. "What time is it?"

"Noon."

The single word caught her in midyawn. "It can't be that late."

"Grandmother said we should let everyone sleep this morning." Jasmine hopped off the bed and went to the pair of long windows on the far side of the bed. She pulled back the claret-hued curtains, and golden sunlight flooded the bedroom. "But everyone else is up, even your friend Miss Watkins. So Aunt Dahlia said I could come wake you."

Camellia pushed back the quilt and swung her legs over the edge of the bed. "Find something for me to wear, please. I had to leave nearly everything in New Orleans."

"There should be an old outfit around here somewhere." Jasmine moved to the bureau, opening and closing drawers in her search.

Surveying the familiar room, Camellia was comforted by the floral wallpaper, marble mantel, cane-backed chair, and dressing table. It was good to be home. She sat in front of the mirror and unbraided her hair.

"You don't look much different." Jasmine held up a white shirtwaist and a gray wool skirt with a patched hem. "What did you learn at that fancy school?"

"Too much to tell you about right now." Camellia dragged a brush through her hair to remove snarls. "Where are the servants?"

"Uncle Phillip said they were a danger, what with all the rumors of an uprising, so he shipped them to some island in the Caribbean."

The brush halted. Obviously not all things had remained the same during her absence. "Who does the chores?"

"Cook is still here, and we hire out some of the work, like the laundry." Jasmine took the brush from her hand and started pulling back the curly locks. "I help Grandmother with her buttons, and all of us have chores in the house. When Lily and Blake are here, things are much easier."

"What about the fields? Surely we are not reduced to picking cotton or cutting sugar cane."

"No, silly." Jasmine giggled. "Uncle Phillip hires workers, some black, some white. Everyone who has not gone to fight in the war needs work. Everything has gotten very dear because of the blockade."

"Why didn't anyone tell me what was going on?" Camellia thought of the letters she had received. Not a hint of any troubles had been apparent. Feeling chastised and a little miffed, she dressed in silence.

Jasmine continued chattering, however, apparently unaware of her sister's emotions.

As they trod downstairs, Camellia trailed her hand along the rail of the stairwell, noticing it lacked its usual glossy sheen. Would she be reduced to dusting the woodwork and polishing the silver?

A vision formed in her imagination. She wore an apron and carried a dustpan in one hand and a broom in the other as she welcomed guests to Les Fleurs. What kind of suitor could she hope to attract in such a situation? Maybe Aunt Dahlia could give her some advice.

Feeling a tiny bit better, Camellia took a deep breath, threw back her shoulders, and followed her sister into the front parlor. Whatever the future held, she would face it with the aplomb and gentility she had learned at La Belle Demoiselle.

❧

Camellia set the pitcher of lemonade on the tray and picked it up with both hands.

"You sure you can handle that by yourself?" Tamar watched her with a doubtful expression on her face.

"Don't worry. I made the lemonade, didn't I?" Proud of her accomplishment, Camellia walked out of the kitchen and around the side of the house to take the refreshment to Aunt Dahlia and Jane on the front porch. She kept one eye on the grass and the other on the slices of lemon threatening to slosh over the top of the pitcher. Arriving without mishap, she set the laden tray onto the table between the rockers.

Aunt Dahlia was crocheting a doily while Jane was working on the sampler she'd managed to bring with her from New Orleans two days earlier.

"There you are." Aunt Dahlia pulled on the spindle of white thread and continued looping it. "I was about to come in search of you."

Camellia shook her head, and several ringlets came loose. She swept them away from her face with an impatient hand. "I hope I didn't keep you waiting too long."

"Not at all." Jane put her sampler in her lap and smiled. "Your timing is impeccable as always."

The sound of an approaching horse stopped Camellia's answer as she turned to see who was coming up the drive. Gray fronds of Spanish moss obscured the rider as he rode between the oak trees that lined both sides of the path, but she could tell he was a soldier from the gray uniform he wore. She raised a hand to shade her eyes.

Jane gasped. "It's Thad." Her needlework hit the floor as she jumped from the rocker and raced down the steps just as Thad reached the house.

He dismounted and held out his arms, folding them around his sister and dropping a kiss on her head.

"Well." Disapproval filled the single syllable from Aunt Dahlia.

"Captain Watkins is Jane's brother," Camellia explained as she smiled on the two of them.

"Oh. I should have noticed the resemblance right away."

Camellia nodded and descended the steps with less exuberance than her friend had showed. But she didn't try to hide her pleasure.

The captain kept one arm around his sister but bowed to her. "I'm happy to see you and my sister are safe."

"I could say the same about you. When we left New Orleans, we didn't know if you would be taken prisoner by the Yankees."

"Were you worried about me, Miss Anderson?"

Jane rolled her eyes. "Of course she was. We all were. I hated leaving you, but when Camellia's family asked me to accompany them, I thought it best to go."

He squeezed his sister once more before letting go of her. "Thank you for making sure she is safe."

Camellia's cheeks warmed under his approving gaze. "L–Let me introduce you to my aunt."

Captain Watkins tucked his cap under one arm and followed the two of them to the front porch.

Camellia performed the introductions and served lemonade as Jane peppered him with questions.

Aunt Dahlia's fingers once again twisted her thread as her rocker moved back and forth. "I still cannot believe the Yankees have taken New Orleans."

"It should not have happened." The captain shook his head, a mixture of sadness and anger pulling at his features. "But now we must concentrate on taking it back into the Confederacy and regaining our base of operations there."

Hope blossomed in Camellia. "I knew all was not lost."

"No, indeed." He sipped from his glass. "Our first step will be to retake Forts Jackson and St. Phillips to the south. Once we cut off the support of the ships that have their guns trained on the city, they will realize their mistake and withdraw."

"Is that the mission that brings you to us, Captain?" Aunt Dahlia stopped her handwork for a moment while she waited for his answer.

Thad looked down at his glass of lemonade. "I really can't talk about my mission. I hope you understand."

"Of course we do." Jane reached for his hand.

Aunt Dahlia frowned. "Do you think we cannot hold our tongues?"

It was time to turn the conversation in a different direction. Camellia leaned forward. "Thank you so much for sending Jonah Thornton to collect us after Mrs. Dabbs was arrested."

One of Thad's eyebrows rose. "What?"

Camellia should have known. Jonah had lied even about that. He had not one truthful bone in his whole traitorous body. Her mouth tightened. "I thought Jonah said you had sent him a note. I must have misunderstood."

His gaze remained on her a few moments.

During that time, the temptation to blurt out the truth was strong. But she could not do it. What would happen to Mr. and Mrs. Thornton once New Orleans was retaken by the Confederates? Would they pay the price for their son's stupidity? She couldn't afford the luxury of confessing what she knew to Thad. He would be honor bound to pass the information along to his superiors. No, this was one secret she had to keep.

"You will not believe how harrowing our trip to Natchez was." Jane's statement ended the uncomfortable moment. She began to describe the way she and Camellia had boarded the *Water Lily* and the trip through the darkness.

The captain listened intently, making exclamations at the right points and sitting back when she finished. "I can only conclude that God was on your side."

"My papa is a very religious man," Camellia offered. "Perhaps his prayers were heard."

"He is a very sweet man, too." Jane smiled in her direction. "But Camellia's whole family is wonderful. They've taken me in without complaint."

"I'm glad for that, Sister, but I can get you a berth on the boat that will take me north. I know you're enjoying your visit to this beautiful home, but our parents must be worried about your welfare."

Camellia sent a desperate look toward her friend. Without Jane around, what would she do with her time?

Before she could express her concern, the other women in her family came outside, and Captain Watkins stood. She cringed at Lily's brown skin, but at least Grandmother and Jasmine looked presentable. Performing the introductions, Camellia watched the captain's reactions, pleased when he seemed so accepting, even of Lily's life on a steamboat.

If this was a test, he had passed it with flying colors. Aunt Dahlia smiled at her, her meaning clear. Captain Watkins was an excellent candidate for a husband.

Looking back at Thad, she wondered. Only a few short weeks ago she would have agreed. He was handsome, polite, wealthy—all the things a girl should want in a husband. Of course he was the perfect mate. A Confederate soldier for goodness' sake. He was exactly the man she'd always dreamed of marrying. Wasn't he?

Chapter Twenty-two

This riverboat was more spacious than the *Water Lily*. Camellia's fingers straightened the sterling knife on the right side of her plate. It caught the light of the chandelier above their table, almost seeming to throw off sparks as it moved. The linen cloth covering the table was spotless, the crystal sparkled, and the china was decorated with a delicate floral design. Aboard the *Kosciusko* she could almost forget the war that had wrought such change in her life.

A white-gloved hand filled her goblet with water and then withdrew. Another hand, this one female, removed her napkin from the table, shook it, and placed it on Camellia's lap. She could grow used to such deference. It was much better than having to clean dirty dishes as she'd once done aboard her sister's boat.

"I'm honored your family entrusted me with your care." Thad's voice brought her out of the past.

Camellia smiled at him. "I'm honored to be escorted by a true hero of the Confederacy."

"I don't know about all that." He looked troubled, as though uncertain of himself. Or was he concerned for the future?

The desire to ease his concerns filled her. Was this what it would feel like to be married? Being a helpmeet to such an honorable man would be a wonderful way to spend her life.

His hand rested on the table next to the assortment of forks on the left side of his plate.

Camellia reached to pick up her goblet and let her hand brush against his. The contact brought a sense of daring. . .but no romantic thrill. Thad's eyebrows climbed up toward his hairline, and a blush heated her cheeks. She had been too forward.

"I haven't written to our parents." Jane's voice came from Thad's far side. "They're going to be surprised when we show up on their doorstep."

Thad turned away from her to answer his sister's comment.

Camellia took a deep breath and brought her goblet to her lips. As she sipped the cool water, she wondered if her misstep would cause him to reconsider his pursuit. The platters of food on the laden table lost their appeal. What if Thad considered her too forward?

A young man on her left cleared his throat and asked her to pass the saltcellar. Camellia complied. He looked about her age, his cheeks still showing the roundness of youth. His auburn hair gleamed richly in the glow from the chandelier. He looked like a younger, more innocent version of Jonah Thornton, bringing a smile to her face. He blushed and shook a copious amount of salt on his serving of roast duck. The incident reminded her of the usual effect her attention had on members of the opposite sex. If she set her mind to it, she could certainly win her way back into Thad's affections.

"Where are you going?" The young man's voice cracked in the middle of his query.

"I'm visiting friends in Vicksburg."

He looked taken aback by her answer. "This is a perilous time to be making social visits."

Camellia dabbed her mouth with her napkin as she considered him, watching as his cheeks turned a deeper shade of red. "Our escort will see that we arrive safely at our destination."

"Of course." The young man took a bite of his dinner. An expression of shock widened his eyes.

Camellia watched as his Adam's apple worked up and down and the corners of his mouth turned down. She hid her smile and took pity on him. Looking behind her at the line of white-coated servers, she signaled to one and asked for a fresh plate.

He threw her a thankful glance and started his dinner afresh, paying much closer attention to the amount of salt he applied to his food.

When dinner was over, Jane and Camellia joined the other ladies in their lounge.

"How much longer will our trip be?" Jane settled in one of the upholstered chairs.

Camellia shrugged as she sat next to her. "It depends on how many stops the captain makes, but we should arrive before dark."

"I hope so." A short, older lady sniffed. "All of our lives are in danger from those marauding Yankees, especially after dark."

"My brother, an officer, is aboard." Jane crossed her legs at the ankles. "He'll make sure no one gets aboard without proper papers."

"I'm scared, Ma." A young girl with brown hair the color of Mississippi mud buried her face in her mother's lap. "I don't want them Yankees to get me."

A black woman in a dark dress and starched apron entered the room with a laden tea tray balanced in her hands.

Camellia waited for her to put the tray on the low table in the middle of the room and then depart before answering. "You don't have to worry about Yankees. Did you see all the men in their handsome uniforms at dinner? They'll protect us."

"That's right." Her mother stroked her daughter's hair. "And you remember what your pa said about them old Yankees. It'll take a dozen of them to fight just one of our soldiers. If they see how many we have on board with us, they'll run away and hide."

Camellia thought of Jonah. He was the only Yankee she knew. But was a Yankee sympathizer the same thing as a Yankee soldier? She thought of his strength of character and his physical prowess. If Jonah was typical of the caliber of man fighting for the North, they were in for a desperate fight.

Even if he wasn't, the rebel forces had run when the Yankees showed up with one little boat at the dock in New Orleans. The soldiers at Fort Jackson and Fort St. Philip had also surrendered without a fight. They had not even tried to stop the Yankee navy from steaming up the river to take the city.

Maybe what this mother was saying to her child was wrong. Camellia was beginning to wonder if it took a dozen Confederates to overcome one Yankee. And if that was the way of it, they would all be Yankees before long.

"Natchez has fallen." Thad crumpled the newspaper between his hands and threw it into the fireplace. "I cannot believe they didn't fight. Why have the cannons on the bluff if they are not going to use them?"

Camellia's stomach knotted. She felt as though they were running across a bridge that was disintegrating immediately behind them. If Natchez had fallen, would Vicksburg be next? She looked at Jane and her mother and saw the same fear mirrored on their faces.

"I must go on to Memphis immediately." Thad's announcement made all three of the women gasp. "The Confederacy needs every able-bodied man now."

"But what will happen to us?" His mother rose and moved across the room to stare out the window of her home.

Camellia knew she was not really looking at the rolling hills outside or the well-tended grounds surrounding her plantation. The faint movement of the older woman's shoulders indicated that she was choking back tears.

Jane got up and went to her, putting an arm around her mother's tiny waist. "It's going to be all right, Mama. I'm here now. You won't be alone."

"No." Mrs. Watkins broke away from her daughter and turned from the window. She faced her son with a determined look. "You must take Jane and Camellia with you."

Thad frowned. "Impossible. I won't be able to protect them once I have rejoined my regiment."

"The danger from the encroaching navy is greater. If they continue to advance this quickly, it won't be long before they are knocking on my door."

Camellia considered their options. There must be some place they could go. Would Lily and Blake come to Vicksburg to rescue them as they had in New Orleans? It might be better to wait here and see. Thinking of her sister put her in mind of stops they had made in the past. "I have it."

All three of the Watkinses turned to her.

"Mr. and Mrs. Thornton have a son in Memphis. Eli and his wife, Renée, will take us in. Surely we'll be safe with them." She turned to Mrs. Watkins. "You can go with us, too."

Mrs. Watkins's lips turned up, but sadness filled her eyes. "I cannot leave my home."

"Mama, you can't stay here alo—" A catch in Jane's voice stopped her for a moment. She gulped and raised her chin before continuing. "It won't be safe for you if the Yankees really do come."

"Don't worry about me. Your father will have returned from Barbados before long. I am determined that he will have a home to return to." Mrs. Watkins took a deep breath and nodded. "I'll keep everything running here."

"Then I won't leave you behind." Jane was a younger version of her mother's determination.

Camellia could feel pride and admiration filling her. The women of the Confederacy were as strong in their way as their husbands and sons.

"Don't be silly." Mrs. Watkins summoned a frown for her daughter. "I can manage here until your father returns, and I will sleep much better knowing you and Camellia are safe."

"I think Mama is right." Thad nodded. "You and Camellia can come with me to Memphis. I'll make sure you are safe with Camellia's friends. Once the South has retaken Natchez, Baton Rouge, and New Orleans, you can return. I'm certain it will only be a matter of days or weeks before things return to normal. As soon as our troops arrive from Virginia, we'll push those Yankees out of our waterways and restore order."

Camellia smiled in his direction. As long as men like Thad were in charge, she could rest easy. The South would overcome even these dark days. "I'll write a message to my family in Natchez. I don't know if packets will be allowed back into the city, but in case they are, I would like them to know where they can find me."

Mrs. Watkins smiled in her direction. "They will appreciate any news. I know how much I awaited letters from Jane and Thad when we were apart."

Jane sighed. "I can't believe we need to pack our belongings so soon."

"Limit yourselves to one trunk each." Thad raised his eyebrows toward his sister.

Camellia's mind flew back in time. Her cheeks burned at the memory of Jonah's incredulous voice as he surveyed the mountain of luggage she'd packed for the weekend with his parents. What innocent days those seemed in retrospect, when all she had to worry about was fashion and etiquette.

Well, she knew better now. A lady might desire all the comforts of home when traveling, but as long as she had a few basic necessities, she could get by. Camellia wondered what new lessons she would learn as the war dragged on. And what her life would look like once the fighting finally ended. Would she find herself married to Thad or someone like him? Or would she remain single, becoming a burden to her family as her beauty faded?

Everything seemed to be careening out of control. As she prepared to flee once more, Camellia found herself wishing for stability and some measure of normalcy. She wished to return to the past. She even wished for the days she'd spent with her sisters aboard Lily's boat.

Given her disdain for life on the river, she could imagine the shock her sisters would exhibit if they had any inkling of her thoughts. But that did not protect her from the yearning inside her, a yearning for something she would probably never again enjoy.

Chapter Twenty-three

$\mathcal{J}$onah's heart thudded in his chest as he made out the shape of four, no, five Union ironclads. Their armored plates and bristling gun ports became more distinct as the sky lightened. He prayed the Confederate officers would realize the overwhelming odds against them and surrender. If they did not, the South would lose many brave men in the ensuing battle. And he might be one of them since his officers had once again sent him into enemy territory as a spy. That was how he found himself on this Confederate ship, locked in a fierce battle near Memphis.

The eastern horizon glowed pink as the sun began to rise, but before it could make its appearance, the boom of a cannon drew his attention. A deadly whistle accompanied it as the missile passed over their heads and crashed into the bank behind their cotton-clad ram.

Jonah prayed for God's protection. It was the only thing that would keep them alive on their outgunned, out-armored boat.

"Man your stations." The command from above sent him and the other sailors running.

Another explosion rent the air. Another missile whistled past them. But when it splashed into the water, Jonah could tell it was closer than the first shot. The Yankees were closing in. They would sink this ship in a matter of minutes.

"Cannoners post!" At least he wasn't part of the seven-man team who would have to man the cannons on either end of the ship. "Solid shot load!"

The deck shuddered under Jonah's feet as twin explosions announced their intention to fight. The sky above was filled with smoke so dense and gray he could no longer tell the time of day.

Jonah wondered if he should jump overboard and take his chances in the strong currents of the river. Or should he remain aboard and try to convince the commander to surrender? The side of the Union ironclad expanded, growing larger and larger until he could see nothing but its dark hull in front and above them. Too late. He was too late to do any good at all.

"Brace for impact," the Confederate officer warned the crew.

Jonah slung his rifle over one shoulder and wrapped his arms around the tall mast at the stern. He closed his eyes and prayed, the words lost in the sounds of battle raging around him. Then it happened. As their prow rammed into the side of the ironclad, a cannon found them. It slammed through the tall stacks of cotton and pierced the deck with devastating results.

Water gushed upward in a dirty fountain as it mixed with coal, splintered wood, and blood. Jonah tried to hold on to the mast, but he was thrown away from it like a droplet of water shaken from a dog's back. He scrambled for another purchase as he slid headfirst toward the edge of the steamship. In the last possible instant, his questing fingers latched onto something. What they found was not important. What mattered was that he had not plunged into the muddy water between the two ships. That way was certain death.

Another barrage of cannon fire warned him the danger was not past. Screams of fear and pain were punctuated by the endless booms of the cannons. He managed to drag himself to his knees and look around. The deck was on fire, and he saw several men lowering buckets to the river. The attempt to stop the deadly flames was doomed. The ship was sinking faster than he would have thought possible. He had failed, completely and utterly. He would not be able to save a single life.

Explosions rocked the water around them, but at least the ironclad had drawn back some. It gave the sailors a better chance to escape in the river without being caught up in the churning water of the paddle wheels or rammed by the heavy hulls. As he crossed to the starboard side of the boat, a groan stopped him.

Jonah glanced around, his eyes streaming from the thick smoke enveloping the ship. At first he saw nothing, but then the groan came again, and he saw a slight movement to his right. A young man, a boy really, lay on the deck, his legs pinned beneath the heavy mast that must have broken during the battle. Jonah fell to his knees to assess the situation.

"I think my leg's broke." The boy coughed. "I don't wanta die."

"You're not going to die." Jonah made the promise even though he had no idea how to keep it. He glanced around them, looking for something to use as a lever. Several men staggered past them, but no one stopped. Each was fighting to save his life, climbing to the far side of the boat as it listed at an ever-steeper angle.

Remembering the rifle on his back, Jonah pulled it forward and wedged it under the mast. Pushing with all of his strength, he managed to move it an inch. "Can you move?"

The boy stopped moaning and pushed up onto his elbows. He managed to move a few inches. The battle faded around them as hope shone on his face. After a few minutes of sweating and grunting, he pulled free.

Jonah released his hold on the mast with relief. Placing an arm around the boy, he helped him stand. "Is it broken?"

The boy shook his head.

"Praise God."

They limped together to the edge. The black water of the river was full—bobbing heads, debris, oil. Jonah took a deep breath, pushed the boy, and jumped. Water closed around his head, and the whine of bullets whizzed past him. Fear pushed him forward. Something slammed against his legs, catching him and trying to drag him under. Then another obstacle hit his shoulders, his chest, his head. Jonah couldn't tell any longer which direction he should be swimming. His lungs ached to breathe. It was done. Fear was replaced by sadness that he had failed to do so many things.

"Today shalt thou be with me in paradise." The promise brought peace and acceptance to Jonah as he lost consciousness.

❧

Camellia thought Thad was as handsome in regular clothes as when he donned his uniform. But on this voyage, he was in disguise. If the packet they were traveling on was stopped by Union forces, he would appear to be nothing more than an escort for his sister and her. Of course anyone searching his bags would know better, but that was a remote possibility since this portion of the river was still controlled by the Confederacy.

She watched the way he sipped coffee from a china cup. His exceptional manners were apparent even in this prosaic setting. Their breakfast came without frills—black coffee, dry biscuits, and a piece of jerked pork that Camellia had no intention of touching. She crumbled the edge of her cold biscuit with a thumb and finger. "When should we arrive in Memphis?"

"Later than I had hoped." He set down his cup and smiled in her direction. "The captain delayed our departure because of a rumor that the Union navy is headed this way."

Jane pushed her plate to one side, apparently as unimpressed as Camellia with the plain fare. "I hope we have not made a mistake to leave Mama alone in Vicksburg."

"I worry about her, too." Thad's brows lowered. "But she was quite insistent."

Silence enveloped them. Camellia wondered about her own family. The reports from Natchez were encouraging. . .as encouraging as possible considering they were in the hands of the enemy. Since the town had surrendered without a fight, most homes were safe. No casualties, no injuries. While a part of her wished the city council had not given up so easily, she was relieved at the lack of bloodshed.

Shouts from outside drew her attention to the window. Crewmen ran back and forth, pointing at something in the river.

She pushed her chair back and stood, aware that both Thad and Jane had done the same. "What's happened?"

"I have no idea." Thad strode to the door and opened it.

Camellia and Jane stood immediately behind him, both trying to hear what was being said.

Someone was in the river.

"We have to help the poor soul." She tried to push past Thad.

"Wait, Camellia." Thad put a hand on her arm. "This could be a ruse to draw passengers out where they can be picked off by sharpshooters in the woods."

Her heart faltered, but then she frowned. "If that's the case, it seems they would have picked off a few of the crewmen already." Pulling her arm free of his grip, Camellia stepped to the edge of the boat. What she saw made her stomach heave. A gray uniform was draped across a large tree trunk floating in the water. The poor soldier's head hung down, hiding his face, but she would recognize those distinctive auburn curls anywhere. She ran to one of the crewmen who had a boat hook in his hand. "Please help him. I know that man."

"What?" Thad had followed her outside.

"Yes." She pointed at the form as it drew even with the boat. "That's Jonah Thornton."

The captain shouted an order to halt the boat while the crewman snagged Jonah's sleeve.

Camellia winced as they dragged his limp body aboard. Was he dead? Her heart stopped beating at the thought. He couldn't be dead. Half-forgotten prayers surfaced as the men laid him on his back. Jonah's face was as white as fish scales, and his eyelids remained closed. Was he breathing?

Ignoring her hoops, Camellia dropped to the deck next to him and took Jonah's cold hand in her own. "Bring me some blankets." She put her head against his chest and listened, not daring to draw a breath for fear of missing some evidence of life.

Dimly, slowly, his heartbeat sounded. He was alive.

"Thank You, God," she whispered as someone spread a blanket over him.

"What's wrong with him?" Jane stood next to her. "Is he dead?"

Camellia shook her head. She didn't see any evidence of a gunshot wound. "His heart's beating."

Thad pulled her up and took her place on the deck, sliding his arms under Jonah's shoulders. "Someone take his legs. Let's get this man to a bed."

Camellia and Jane followed him, their hands linked.

"What on earth is Jonah doing here?" Jane's question echoed her own. "And why is he in uniform? I thought he wasn't the fighting type."

If he had decided to join the army, he certainly wouldn't have joined the Confederacy. Not when his convictions had led him to spy on his friends and neighbors. He was a traitor. His uniform was more likely a disguise to allow him to infiltrate new areas and send vital information to the Union. She should be glad he was wounded. In fact, she ought to be hoping for his demise. But though Camellia considered herself a patriot, she could not go that far.

Thad carried Jonah into a room reserved for passengers. "You girls stay out here."

Camellia opened her mouth to argue, but seeing the look on Thad's face, she remained silent.

"Trust me. I'll take care of your friend and let you know how he's doing." He kicked the door closed.

Jane pulled on Camellia's hand. "Let's go back upstairs. Maybe we can learn more about what's going on while Thad sees to Jonah."

They climbed the stairs to the main deck. Only a handful of passengers had joined them on this trip. They stood in a cluster at the bow of the boat, whispering and pointing at something in the water. Did someone else need to be rescued?

Camellia stepped to the rail, relieved when she saw that a small fishing boat had pulled up alongside the packet. "What's going on?"

"There's been a huge battle at Memphis." A man with a large mustache pulled off his spectacles and wiped them with a handkerchief before continuing. "The Confederate navy was scuttled in little more than an hour."

Jane gasped, and Camellia felt like crying. Their hope for a safe harbor had been snatched from them once again. What would they do now?

Chapter Twenty-four

No doctor traveled with them, so nursing their half-drowned passenger fell to Jane and Camellia. As the men discussed the next move to be taken, the two friends cleaned the scrapes and scratches on Jonah's face and limbs. After an hour or so, Camellia sent Jane to find out what was going on while she stayed behind to watch over Jonah.

He was so still she could hardly believe he was still alive. Yet she could see the faint rise and fall of his chest under the bedcovers. If he would simply open his eyes and smile at her. Her anger and frustration faded away as she sat next to his bed and watched him breathe. She wanted him to wake up, if only so she could turn him over to Thad.

That would serve Jonah right. While she might be able to admire him for standing up for his principles and joining the wrong side of the war, she could not understand how he could reconcile those same principles to the lies he'd told his family and friends while he spied on them. She could only conclude he had no principles at all. So why did she want him to awaken so desperately?

The door opened, and Jane entered. "They've decided to remain here for the rest of the day and await further news."

Camellia wondered what they hoped to hear. Did they think the original report of complete defeat was wrong? The fishermen had seemed to her to have very detailed information about the battle just north of Memphis, including the number and names of the Union ironclads.

"How's our patient?"

"Much the same." Camellia dipped her cloth in a bowl beside the bed and wrung it out before placing it on Jonah's forehead again. "He still won't awaken."

"Don't worry." Jane hugged her before slipping into the chair on the opposite side of Jonah's bed. "He's strong. I'm sure he'll pull through."

"I hope you're right."

Silence invaded the room. As the day wore on, Camellia prayed. She tried to bargain with God, but she could not think of anything to offer Him equal to Jonah's life.

Jane cleared her throat. "You should get something to eat."

"I'm fine." The growl of her stomach belied her words, but Camellia ignored the sound. "Why don't you take a break?"

The door opened, and Thad's shoulders filled the space. "Is he any better?"

"He's no worse," Jane answered for both of them.

"Perhaps in his mind he's still in the belly of the whale."

Camellia looked up at Thad's words. "Like Jonah in the Bible?"

Thad nodded. "Jonah of Nineveh spent three days and three nights there. Maybe your friend is frightened of waking up and finding himself swallowed alive. Maybe he'll wake up in a few days all rested and ready to return to the fighting."

Her heart took wing, and Camellia sent a grateful smile toward Thad. "I hope you're right."

He held out a hand to her. "I'm sure that's all it is. We found no sign of a serious injury. Jonah Thornton is just showing us how stubborn he is."

Camellia allowed him to pull her up.

"I think it's time you took a break."

"I'm fine."

"I know that very well, Miss Camellia Anderson." He smiled down at her. "Few women would expend so much energy over an unresponsive soldier. You're a shining example of patience and hope. But even though you are very fine indeed, I believe you should come with me now for a walk around the deck. Jane will let us know if Jonah's situation changes."

Allowing herself to be pulled out of the room was a little like departing from her family when she left to attend finishing school. But she knew Thad was right. She had been stooped over Jonah's bed for hours. With one last glance at his pale face, she turned and left on Thad's arm. As she walked, the knots and kinks in her back, arms, and chest began to loosen. "Have you any more news?"

"Yes, and it's not good."

Camellia felt her worries descend once more. "What will we do? Where can we go that is safe?"

"The captain has an idea about that." He patted the hand resting on his arm. "Are you familiar with Jacksonport in Arkansas?"

She shook her head. "Where is it?"

"It's on the White River. We'll overnight here and return south tomorrow to the place where the White River empties into the Mississippi. As soon as we leave the main course of the river, I think we'll be safer. Although we'll have to take our time and make sure the Yankees haven't gotten ahead of us once more, it should be an uneventful voyage. And the advantage is that the passengers can disembark there. I can join the forces in Jacksonport and return to my duties knowing you and Jane are safe."

Camellia nodded. Perhaps Jacksonport boasted a doctor who would know how to treat Jonah's injuries.

As though he could read her mind, Thad sent a keen glance in her direction. "I know you and Jane are not experienced nurses, but I appreciate your efforts with Mr. Thornton. Who knows? One day I may be the unconscious soldier in need of care." He raised her hand to his lips and pressed a warm kiss on it. "I would like to think it might come from someone as lovely and caring as you."

Blushing, Camellia looked away. If only Thad realized what kind of man Jonah really was, he'd probably throw him back into the river. But she couldn't tell him what she knew about Jonah. The information she was hiding from Thad was like a wall between them. A wall she wasn't sure she wanted to breach.

❧

The little packet crept around the curves in the river, sliding down its length like a snake, taking to the bayous whenever other boats were spotted.

Camellia kept watch over Jonah, but he remained unchanged. This morning Jane had brought her sewing basket with her and was even now busily plying her needle. Wishing for something to divert her own attention, Camellia decided to go look for writing paper and a pen. She could send word to her family of her whereabouts so they wouldn't worry.

"I'll be back in a few moments." She spoke in a normal voice. Perhaps they were being too quiet in the room since they wanted Jonah to awaken.

Jane nodded.

Camellia walked down the passageway of the small boat and decided to take a turn on the lower deck to breathe some fresh air. The river here was so wide it looked like a long lake. Oak, walnut, sweet gum, and magnolia trees shaded the banks, their wide trunks making a convenient cover for their boat. Of course, they also provided excellent hiding places for ambushes. Even though the day was warm, her thoughts made the skin on her arms prickle.

"We're about to reach the mouth of the White River." Thad's deep voice made her jump. "I'm sorry, I didn't mean to startle you."

A giggle threatened to escape, but Camellia managed to choke it down. "It wasn't your fault. It's just so quiet. I was thinking about soldiers hiding in the woods with their rifles trained on us." She leaned against the rail and tried to see past the wall of hardwoods.

Thad moved closer, his arm brushing hers.

A tingle that had nothing to do with warfare spread from her fingers upward, and Camellia caught her breath. Was she actually beginning to feel something truly romantic for Thad?

If he noticed, he said nothing.

They stood that way for several minutes, neither speaking, as the river widened even further. The riverboat turned westward and poured steam into its engines to break free of the Mississippi's powerful current. After several moments, the water narrowed, the trees closing in on either side of them.

A crewman appeared with a sounding weight and began taking readings, calling out the depths in a distinct voice so the captain could avoid shallows and sandbars. From having watched her own father on Lily's steamship, Camellia knew this captain would also be keeping an eye out for snags formed by fallen trees and floating debris.

The thrash of the paddle wheel faded into the background as the sounds of the swamp surrounded them. The plop of alligators and snakes falling into the water as they fled for safer bayous. The caw of birds warning their brethren of approaching danger. The scream of a large cat, either a panther or a bobcat. The swamp was a place of darkness, danger, and mystery.

Camellia moved a tiny bit closer to Thad for security, her heart thundering. She didn't like swamps.

Thad slid an arm around her and pulled her close. His presence was warm and reassuring. His closeness calmed her heart and allowed her to breathe more easily.

She let her head fall onto his shoulder, so tired from her vigil at Jonah's bedside that she didn't give a thought to the impropriety of her action. Or what signal she was sending to Thad.

His hand under her chin should have been a warning. When Camellia looked up to see what he needed, she realized what was happening. Thad's gaze scalded her, setting off a warning in her head. But it was too late for her to fight now. Besides, wasn't this what she wanted? Thad was an honorable man. Kissing her would be tantamount to a betrothal. She would become Mrs. Thad Watkins, perhaps before they even returned to the waters of the Mississippi.

So why did her body stiffen in protest? Why did she pull free of his embrace? Why did she lower her head and turn away? Camellia couldn't understand the instinct, but she also couldn't resist it. "I—I'm sorry."

"Camellia, forgive me." He reached for her. "I didn't mean any disrespect."

"I know you didn't." She twisted her hands together and wished she had never left Jonah's side. "Let's just forget about this. We can go on as before, can't we?"

Confusion filled his handsome face. He opened his mouth, but before he could put his thoughts into words, a shout interrupted them.

"Torpedo!"

The single word made him turn his attention to the water. What had almost happened was forgotten as they both searched for a glimpse of the threat.

"There it is."

Camellia squinted. All she could see was an empty barrel floating on the surface of the water some distance away. It didn't look particularly dangerous to her.

"Get back inside." Thad shouted the command at her as he rushed up to the hurricane deck. "All stop. All stop!"

Curiosity kept her at the rail. The paddle wheel fell silent, but they continued drifting toward the barrel, their forward motion stronger than the river's current.

Thad ran back downstairs with a bundle of dyed cloth in his arms. He didn't slow down to tell her again to leave the deck, instead running to the flagpole. With efficient movements, he lowered the white flag they had been flying and tied on the corners of the material from his bundle below it. She watched as his strong arms worked the ropes and a new flag spread out over his head.

It took her a moment to realize what Thad had done. A bright red background was crossed by a blue X with white stars on it, the flag of the Confederacy. Thad was flying their true colors, hoping the torpedo was being manned by a Confederate soldier.

She held her breath as they drew even with the barrel. It scraped the hull of the packet, the sound distinctive in the thick air, but it didn't explode. Then they were past it.

Camellia closed her eyes for a moment. She was thankful Thad was so smart. If not for his quick action, they might now be sinking into a watery grave.

Two near disasters in such a short time weakened her knees. She needed time to calm her emotions. To think about what had almost happened.

She ought to linger on the deck and see if Thad returned to take up the conversation about their future. But she took the cowardly route, returning to her room.

How could she explain her muddled feelings to him when she didn't understand them herself? Thad was everything she'd dreamed of, but was he the right man for her?

Chapter Twenty-five

*J*onah floated in inky blackness, the screams of dying men all around him. It was too much to bear. The pain was physical and emotional as well. He didn't want to live any longer. He wanted to join those who had gone before him. Jonah wanted to sing in a celestial choir and walk on streets of gold. He wanted to enter the mansion Jesus had prepared for him.

The first emotion to hit him as he opened his eyes was disappointment. Heaven should not be dark. He turned his head and was surprised to see Camellia sitting beside him. What was she doing here? She was far too young, so full of life and beauty. "Are you dead, too?" His voice was cracked and dry, a mere shadow of what it had once been.

But the sound seemed to please Camellia. Her mouth widened in a smile, a genuine smile of gratitude and happiness. Her warmth eased some of his physical pain. "Of course not, and neither are you." She reached for his hand, her fingers encircling his wrist, causing his pulse to skyrocket.

"I don't understand."

"I'm not surprised." Camellia let go of his hand and shook a finger at him. "You had us terrified that you wouldn't wake up at all. You didn't seem to be seriously hurt, but you wouldn't wake up even for meals."

"How long have I been asleep?" He tried to prop himself up on his elbows, but his arms refused to support the weight of his upper body.

She reached for a pitcher and glass from a small table next to his bed. The splash of the liquid made him realize how dry his throat felt. She held the glass to his lips, her free hand supporting his head and shoulders so he could swallow the water without choking.

Jonah still sputtered a little, unaccustomed to having someone else control the glass.

"It's good to see you drinking on your own." Camellia moved the water away from his mouth and gave him a moment to breathe. "For three days and three nights we've had to coax broth into you, feeding you one spoonful at a time."

"What?" The urge to rise from the bed swept him again. "I have to get up."

Camellia put a hand on his shoulder, holding him down with little trouble. He was as weak as a newborn babe.

"Not so fast. Didn't you hear what I said? Your body needs to recover its strength. Don't worry. You don't have any battles to fight today."

"Where am I?" Jonah fought against her grasp.

Her frown deepened. "Aboard a packet bound for Jacksonport, Arkansas. We fished you out of the water after the battle in Memphis. A battle we lost because of the efforts of men like you."

The sting of her words was like a physical slap. He fell back against the pillows, his breath coming in gasps. "You don't understand anything."

"I think you've forgotten how much I do understand, Mr. Thornton." She set the glass on the table with a punctuating *thump*. "I may not understand everything that's transpired since we parted in New Orleans some months ago, but I know exactly why we found you masquerading in a Confederate uniform when we pulled you from the water."

Dread of prison or a hanging filled him. "Have you already told them who I am?"

Her face hardened. "Of course. I could hardly do less. Did you think I would try to hide your identity?"

"I see." His mouth grew dry all over again, as though it were filled with cotton bolls. "I suppose I should be thankful I'm not already in leg irons."

"Yes, indeed." She turned from him, her chin held high, her golden curls bouncing with the strength of her convictions. "I'll make certain that the situation is remedied before you regain your strength. We can't afford to allow a traitor to escape."

181

He had no answer for her, so Jonah remained silent.

Camellia busied herself with folding a towel and placing it on the table that held the water pitcher. Then she filled a spoon with some kind of concoction from a small brown bottle and tipped it against his mouth.

Jonah drank reflexively, making a face as the bitter draught slid across his tongue. He coughed, wishing for another swallow of water but determined to conceal his weakness.

"Why did you do it?" She put down the spoon and reached for his glass of water, holding it to his lips.

Another cough rattled him, but Jonah managed to drink. His chest relaxed as the cool moisture spread through his body. When she took away the glass, he had regained the strength he needed to answer her. "Become a spy, you mean?"

Camellia nodded, her harsh expression at odds with the gentle touch of her hand on his brow.

"It's not like I awoke one morning and decided I should lie to my family and friends in the service of my country."

She blew out a sharp breath. "You live in the South."

"Yes, the southern part of the United States of America. Not some cobbled-together rebellion that has but one purpose—the continuation of slavery."

"You twist everything about until it makes no sense. Why can't you be like everyone else and simply accept that we are trying to preserve our freedom, our way of life?"

Jonah wanted to answer her, but the room was growing fuzzy, distant. He couldn't keep his eyes open any longer. Yet even as he sank into oblivion, Camellia's face hovered over him, but it looked as though a long tunnel had formed between them. She was saying something to him, and her hand reached through the tunnel to touch his cheek. Turning his face into her hand, he relaxed and let the void take him to a more peaceful place.

❧

"Jonah seems better." Camellia looked toward Thad. "We've managed to get more food down him, but I wish we were in Jacksonport. Jane and I aren't doctors."

Thad pushed his empty plate away and tossed his napkin on it.

"We're taking things much slower than normal. We have to spend most of our time in bayous and shallow waterways to avoid falling into enemy hands. The boilers need fresh wood every day, and the snags are worse because the snag-boats have been pressed into service for one side of the war or the other."

"Have you seen any more torpedoes?" Jane's eyes were shadowed by lack of sleep and worry.

Camellia knew the same could be said for her. Both she and Jane had worn themselves out taking care of Jonah. They divided their time between sitting at his bedside, preparing and feeding him nourishing broths, and administering medicinal concoctions the cook made for them.

Those who had remained on the packet worked hard each day, even old Mr. Carlton, the silver-haired man who walked with a cane. Several of the passengers and one of the original crewmen had decided to take their chances on land after the near disaster with the first torpedo. Only five men had remained on board the packet—the captain, the engineer, the cook, Thad, and Mr. Carlton.

"Not since the one on Wednesday," Thad answered his sister.

Camellia pushed a curl back with her right hand. Her coiffure had suffered from the lack of proper facilities and the help of a lady's maid. She had learned to thread a ribbon around her head to keep her hair out of her face. Aunt Dahlia would be appalled, but then, Aunt Dahlia had never had to survive aboard a boat without any of the basic necessities. Deciding to dwell on more positive matters, she summoned a smile. "What fine stories we'll have to share with your parents and my family about this excursion."

Mr. Carlton nodded and pushed his chair from the small table at which they sat. "If that handsome fella there didn't have an eye on you, little missy, I'd try to woo you myself."

A blush heated Camellia's cheeks. She found it impossible to look toward Thad. Since the day he'd almost kissed her, she had kept some distance between them. That wasn't hard to do, of course, since she had to see to Jonah. She began to gather the dishes from the table, having fallen back into the habit she'd learned when living aboard Lily and Blake's steamship. "Come along, Jane. We need to check on the rabbit stew for Jonah."

A male chuckle followed them out of the dining room, but Camellia didn't look back to see if it came from Mr. Carlton or Thad. In the past she might have remained with the men and flirted with both of them. But now she had more important matters to see to.

≈

The next time Jonah awoke, Jane Watkins was sitting beside his bed. He coughed, and she held a glass of water to his lips as Camellia had done. He told himself he was not disappointed that Jane's hand was the one supporting his shoulders. Had he only dreamed Camellia had caressed his cheek as he fell asleep?

"Good afternoon, Mr. Thornton. I hope you're truly on the mend now."

After he'd drunk enough to moisten the inside of his mouth, Jonah indicated he was done with a shake of his head. She removed the glass and let his head fall back against the pillow.

He sent a smile in her direction. "Thank you."

"You're very welcome."

Jonah studied the young woman, a beauty in her own way. Did she feel any kindness toward him? Would she help him escape? Would the time she had spent around him and his family influence her decision? She was certainly being considerate of him now. But that might change as he got stronger. If she was filled with the same misplaced zeal for rebellion that had infected Camellia, she would never countenance his escape.

The door to his room opened, and Jonah squinted toward the newcomer. His heart climbed up toward his throat when he recognized Jane's brother in full dress uniform. Whether or not he could convince Jane or Camellia to help him became immaterial. As long as Captain Watkins was aboard, Jonah's chances of escaping dwindled to nothing but a vain hope.

"How is the patient today?"

"He's awake." Jane smiled at Thad. "Why don't you ask him yourself?"

Thad nodded and entered the room. "How do you feel?"

"Tolerably well, I suppose. Camellia said y'all fished me from the river."

"Yes." Thad sat on the end of his bed. "You were a pretty sad sight. I was all for leaving you behind, but the girls would not hear of it."

"Thad!" Jane's scandalized response made Thad smile and raise an eyebrow.

Realizing the man was trying to introduce a note of levity, Jonah managed to force his parched lips into a weak grin. "I don't blame you. I probably would have done the same thing if you had been the one in the water."

Thad laughed out loud and slapped the bed. "At least you're strong enough to give as good as you get. The girls have been nursing you nonstop this past week. If you recover your health, you have them to thank for it."

Jonah hid his surprise that so many more days had passed. "I'm thankful to both of them."

Thad turned his attention to his sister. "Why don't you go and get Camellia? I have a couple of things to say to your patient."

Both of them watched her leave the room. Jonah tried to brace himself for the worst. Though his chest felt heavy with congestion, at least he was a little stronger than the last time he'd awakened. But was he strong enough to face what was coming? If he'd been unconscious for another three days, their boat would have had plenty of time to arrive in Jacksonport. Would Thad arrest him now and have him dragged away to a prison? He tried to choke down his cough, but it would not be denied. When the paroxysm ended, he lay back against his pillow and waited to hear the bad news.

"That's a bad cough, Thornton. I hope it won't delay your return to action." Thad stood and moved to the chair his sister had vacated. "I have to admit I had my doubts about you when we met in New Orleans. But in light of the fact that you've decided to volunteer, I am willing to put our differences aside. The Confederacy can use every able-bodied man whose heart is in the right place."

Shock held him still. Camellia had not spilled his secret after all. If he could keep his wits about him, he might yet escape hanging or prison. Jonah's grin turned rueful. While he didn't want to mislead Thad, it was necessary. "You're right about that. I'm glad you're willing to overlook my past, and I want you to know I'm determined to do my part to finish this war."

"Good. I'm glad that's settled." Thad put a hand on the doorknob. "The girls seem to think your body is mending well. You've had plenty of time to catch up on your sleep, so I'll hope to see you on deck in a day or two. I could use the careful eye of another soldier."

Jonah's head fell back on the pillow once more as Thad left him alone. He closed his eyes and began a prayer of thanksgiving. It was only through God's grace that he'd not been found out. His grace and the unfathomable intentions of a Southern belle who had little reason to protect him.

Chapter Twenty-six

John watched each bend in the river as they once again approached Cape Girardeau. It had been too long since he last saw Anna, but he'd thought of her every moment of those weeks. The sound of rain on the surface of the river became the tinkling noise of her laughter. He imagined building a home for the two of them. A home filled with faith, love, and laughter. It was a dream that he hoped would one day become a reality.

The walls of the southernmost fort came into view, the formidable black eyes of its cannons unblinking.

"Are you going to ask that girl to marry you?" Mrs. Naomi's voice startled him.

He couldn't keep the grin from his face. "Who told you such a thing?"

"I'm a woman." Her eyes twinkled. "No one had to tell me."

John sobered. "Do you think she'll have me?"

"You and I've been working together for more than a year now. I know people well enough to tell the difference between a scoundrel and an honest, Christian man. If that young lady doesn't snap you up, she's not half as smart as she looks." Mrs. Naomi laughed and patted his hand. "Don't you worry. She'll fall in your arms as soon as you open them for her."

The captain signaled that it was time for the crew to begin making preparations for their landing, so John moved away from Mrs. Naomi. He picked up a coil of rope and twisted it into a loop, throwing it over his shoulder and measuring the distance to the pier. The large paddle wheel slowed and changed the direction of its rotation. Churning the water in reverse, it slowed the *Catfish* and brought her closer to land. John tossed his rope expertly, catching the upright piling on the first try. He heard two other crewmen toss separate ropes, and soon they had the boat securely tied.

He waited with barely leashed patience as their ship was inspected by the harbormaster and a couple of Union soldiers. As soon as they were cleared, he went onshore and strode up the hill to the central part of town. The sun was sinking toward the western horizon, but he calculated it was only about three in the afternoon. Anna should still be at work.

The moment John pushed open the door, he knew something was wrong. Devore's looked like an unkempt child. Items were crowded every which way on the normally orderly shelves, and a film of dust dulled the shiny counter behind which she and Mr. Devore usually stood. The latter was helping a female customer, but John could not see Anna anywhere. Another lady stood in her place behind the counter. His heart thudded to a stop. Where was Anna? Had there been an accident? Was she sick?

Lord, please let her be safe and healthy. The plea filled John's head. He walked to the counter, his mind dwelling on the macabre possibilities. They lived in a dangerous time. Anything could have happened to her—a snakebite, the attack of a wild animal, yellow jack fever. His mind spun.

"Are you all right?" The lady in Anna's place looked at John with concern. From Anna's descriptions, he knew the attractive woman must be Norma Devore, Don's wife.

More concern washed over him as he realized she must be assisting her husband due to Anna's not being able to work. "I'm fine. I was hoping to see Anna. I'm John Champion."

"Anna's at home," Mrs. Devore said. "Her father had an accident, and she's been nursing him."

At least she was not hurt—or worse, dead. John thanked the woman and hurried out of the store without asking any more details. He had to get to Anna. Make sure she had what she needed. His gaze remained fixed on the road in front of his feet, the prayer in his mind becoming wordless as he cast his cares before his Lord.

A knock on the door of the Matthewses' place brought a middle-aged woman to the door, Anna's aunt Tessie.

"Is Anna home?"

Before she could answer, John heard a sound in the hall behind her. Aunt Tessie stepped back, and there she was in front of him. His Anna. His gaze took in her appearance in an instant, cataloging the dark circles under her eyes, the droop of her shoulders, and the desperation in her gaze.

"John?" Her expression eased a little. "I can't believe you're really here."

Aunt Tessie finally took care of the social amenities as he and Anna could only stare at each other. "Come in, young man." He then noticed the same mixture of weariness and fear in her face, too. "Why don't you take him to the parlor, and I'll see if I can fix a tray for the two of you."

John followed Anna down the hall, noticing the general air of disorder here, too. "How is your father?"

Anna shook her head and opened the door to the parlor. She sat down in a rocker that dwarfed her and leaned back. "He's failing." A catch in her voice made John want to gather her in his arms and comfort her. "I don't know what to do. Aunt Tessie is doing everything she can, but she's still recovering from her illness."

"What happened?"

"Pa was cutting down a tree out back because it had begun to lean and he was worried it might fall and take down part of the house." Anna parroted the words as though she'd told the story many times before. "I don't know exactly how, but the tree fell the wrong way, and Pa was caught underneath it. Aunt Tessie was resting in her bedroom and couldn't hear him calling for help. By the time I got home several hours later, he was b–barely hanging on."

John closed his eyes for a moment, seeking words of comfort for her. Something that would let her know how much he regretted everything that had happened to her and her family. "I'm here now, and I'll do anything I can to help you."

She looked up at him, her eyes watery with unshed tears. "Thank you, John. Just seeing you is a blessing to me."

"What can I do?"

"Pray. Pray that God won't take my pa until he and my brother have made their peace with each other."

John frowned. "You have a brother? You've never mentioned a brother before."

"I haven't seen him in nearly a decade. The last letter I had from him is more than five years old."

"Where is he?"

She shrugged. "The last time Blake wrote to us, he was living in a town in Mississippi. . . .Natchez or Vicksburg, I can't remember exactly."

"Blake Matthews is your brother?" John's knees weakened, and he collapsed on the nearby sofa. In all of his dreams of what this day would bring, he'd never imagined such a calamity. He'd never thought a nightmare of gargantuan proportions would swallow his future whole. He'd never thought that the woman he'd fallen in love with would bring his doom on him.

প্ত

Camellia watched as Jonah's health returned slowly over the next days. His deep cough still worried her, but he shrugged it off with a quip. He even spent a few hours each day sitting in one of the two chairs in his room, his legs modestly covered with a blanket whenever she or Jane was with him.

Today, however, he had spent the morning sitting up, so now he rested in his bed as he finished the light lunch she had brought.

When Jane left them alone while he ate, Camellia decided to tackle the subject they had both avoided since he'd first awakened. "I don't understand how you can betray everyone you care for."

His sigh was long and led to another cough. As soon as it passed, he picked up his tray and handed it to her. "You do understand that a soldier must follow orders, right?"

"Yes."

"Thad is following his orders, isn't he? He might choose to get you and his sister to safety before completing his mission, but he cannot. His duty must come before family obligations or others will suffer."

"Yes, but—" A sudden jerk of the boat threw Camellia forward. The tray hit the far wall, and she sprawled across his lap with an unladylike grunt.

"I know you find me attractive, Miss Anderson, but you really must control yourself." Jonah's laughter brought his cough back.

Camellia bounced off of him as though she had springs under her. "I'm sorry."

As soon as he stopped coughing, he raised his head and stared at her. "I can't say that I am."

Her face flamed. Trust the man to make a joke at her expense. Shouts and the sound of feet running down the passageway provided her with a needed distraction. She moved to the door and peeked out. "I wonder what's happened."

"It's time for me to get out of this bed and find out."

A rustle behind her brought Camellia's head back around. Jonah had thrown his sheet back and was putting his feet to the floor. She gasped at the sight of his bare legs sticking out from the tail of his nightshirt. "Jonah!"

"You may want to leave if you don't want to be offended." His voice was grim and determined. "I refuse to lie here and wait to find out what disaster has overtaken us now."

Camellia picked up her skirts and fled. As she ran to the room she shared with Jane, she realized the paddle wheel was not churning. Had they hit another snag? A sandbar? She threw open the door and found her friend trying to lace up the back of her dress. "Let me help."

"Do you know what's going on?" Jane looked over her shoulder, a concerned look on her face. "Have we finally made it to Jacksonport?"

"I don't know." Camellia finished with the lacing. "Let's go see."

The main deck was empty. Camellia glanced at Jane, who reached for her hand. Had the men deserted them? That made no sense. Thad would not leave them voluntarily. Her heart thumped.

"We must get free. We may lose another day." Thad's voice came from the far side of the boat.

Jane and Camellia followed the sound to discover the men, even Jonah, standing in ankle-deep water just off the bow. That's when she realized that the packet was sitting at an angle. They had run up onto a sandbar. She looked at the gangplank that had been swung to the bank to allow the men to see the extent of the damage done.

"I didn't realize we were on a schedule." Jonah's voice was still weak, but he had managed to negotiate the gangplank, a definite improvement.

Jane squeezed her hand and pulled her forward. "What's wrong?"

The captain scratched his head, dislodging the slouch hat he wore.

"I was trying to avoid a snag and ran us into more trouble."

Another of the men sighed. "We'd better get busy."

"Can we help?" Camellia hoped the answer would be no.

Jonah laughed and exchanged a glance with Thad. "Not unless you can handle a shovel."

"Look at that." Jane's voice sounded sad to Camellia.

She looked toward the bank and saw what had drawn her friend's attention. A stunning plantation had once commanded a view of this bend in the river. All that remained of it, however, was a burned-out shell. The spreading limbs of live oak trees formed a path from the bank of the river to the front steps. Five tall columns were spread out as silent sentinels across what had once been an inviting veranda edged with a profusion of azaleas, bougainvillea, and roses.

Visions of slave uprisings and Yankee marauders made Camellia's head spin. "I wonder what happened there."

Mr. Carlton stomped out to join them, his gaze surveying the ruined estate. "Most likely lightning." He pointed with his cane at a tree Camellia had not noticed earlier, its trunk blackened, its bare limbs reaching toward the sky. "See the hole in that wall? Once the fire breached the house, it was too late to do anything. It would have burned in less than an hour."

Camellia turned to Jane. "Are you feeling adventurous?"

"Not me." Jane shook her head and shrank back.

"Come on. We can spend the afternoon exploring while the men do their work." Camellia drew her forward. "It'll be fun."

Jane squealed as the gangplank bounced under their feet, the river water rushing a few inches beneath their feet. "I don't think this is a good idea."

Thad shook his head and waded back to the bank, meeting them before they got halfway across the narrow wooden planks. Walking three abreast was impossible, so he took his sister's arm and guided her to the bank. Then he turned back to where Camellia stood with one hand clutching the packet's rail. Instead of offering her his hand, he bent and scooped her into his arms.

Caught off guard by his unexpected action, she had no choice but to rest her head against his chest.

Mr. Carlton chuckled and she heard the *tap-tap* of his cane as he moved away. The captain was giving instructions to his crewmen, ignoring the women and Thad.

Jonah was a different matter, however. He stood at the end of the gangplank, his face a mask of fury.

Thad put her feet on the ground, his hand settling around her waist. "Is there a problem?"

Jonah's hands clenched and unclenched. "As a friend of Camellia's family, I can be considered a chaperone. I don't know how you've been comporting yourself while I've been indisposed, but I'll thank you to act like a gentleman now."

Stepping away from her, Thad straightened his shoulders. "My actions are in keeping with the man who will one day be Camellia's husband."

Camellia's mouth dropped open, but before she could say anything, she saw Jonah sway.

His complexion had grayed to almost the same hue as his uniform. His gaze went to her face. "You're engaged to be married?"

"I am not." She shot a look of warning toward Thad. "And this is not the time or place to discuss such matters."

To his credit, Thad moved to Jonah and steadied him. "I'm sorry if I spoke out of turn, Camellia, but it cannot be a secret that I care about you greatly. And now that we've spent all this time practically alone on the river, everyone will expect us to—"

"Enough." She stomped her foot on the ground, coughing at the dust it raised. "You might make the same argument about myself and Jonah, or even Jonah and your sister. We've been adequately chaperoned the whole time, so I will hear no more on the matter."

Both Jonah and Thad looked at her, their faces slack. Then Thad glared at Jonah. "You ought to get inside before you fall over and I have to carry you, too."

Jonah snorted but never took his gaze off her face. Even as she walked toward the ruined house, she could feel a prickle on the back of her neck. Why did the man have such fire in his eyes? And why did she feel so bruised? She ought to be glad two men were vying for her attention, but all she felt was persecution. She hadn't done anything to deserve their attention or their scorn. She would not feel guilty.

❧

Mist had settled on the water overnight. Now it rose in wraithlike tendrils, first hiding then revealing the surface of the river.

Jonah settled into a chair provided by the engineer and watched as the plantation home receded in the distance. It had taken the men all night to move enough sand for their boat to float free. How much longer would it take them to reach Jacksonport? And what would happen to him when they did?

"How do you feel this morning?" Camellia's voice pulled him away from his thoughts.

Jonah looked at her, standing so demurely in front of him. He had thought her beautiful when she wore glittering finery, but she was even more so out here on the river without her fancy coiffures and fancier dresses. Her eyes were bluer than the sky, her lips as soft as the petals of a rose. Even though she looked as delicate as porcelain, he knew better. Many women would have spent their time weeping and bemoaning the danger and privations of this trip. Camellia had not complained even once. He could not afford to give in to the tenderness flooding him. "Not as tired as your fiancé."

"Don't call him that. Thad spoke out of turn."

Her denial made his heart pound. "Are you saying you don't love him?"

She looked past his shoulder, a frown on her lovely face. "I. . . Oh, I don't know how I feel. I always thought I would marry someone like Thad, but now I don't know."

"He's a good man—honorable and caring. You could do worse for a husband." What impulse made him defend the Confederate soldier? She could see for herself what kind of man Thad was. Jonah didn't need to push her in that direction. But somehow her happiness was important to him, more important than his own.

Her head shot up at that. "Are you saying you want me to be engaged to him?"

"Only if it will make you happy." Jonah sighed. "I've known you for years, Camellia. I've seen you during good times and hard times. I've seen you act the part of a supremely egotistical debutante. Your physical beauty is undeniable, but at times I've thought I glimpsed something else in you. . .something admirable, something warm and caring and honest."

A tear slipped free and trickled down the curve of Camellia's cheek.

Jonah's breath caught. "I'm sorry. I didn't mean to make you cry. I only want you to be sure you love Thad before you agree to marry him."

She rubbed a finger across her cheek. "Sometimes I don't know what I'm doing. I think about that sermon. Do you remember? The one at your church where the pastor talked about the narrow path that leads to salvation. I thought he was being silly. Everyone I knew felt the same way. We all believed in the South, the Cause. But I'm not so sure anymore. War is a harsh, scary thing. How many men will give their lives for an ideal that has nothing to do with God? How many lives will be ruined when husbands, brothers, or sons never come home again?"

Jonah took a deep breath. He didn't want to say the wrong thing now. Their conversation had taken a much more serious turn, a turn that could lead her either to a closer relationship with Christ or to a life of discontent that ended in eternal destruction.

He closed his eyes and prayed for the right message to give her. She was the missing lamb, the one the Shepherd left His flock to find. For the first time, Jonah understood why the Shepherd would risk everything to bring one lost lamb back into the fold. "Hundreds, even thousands will be affected before the war is over. It's the nature of war."

Her gaze came back to him. "That's the real reason, isn't it?"

"I believe the South is wrong. I believe the soul of every person is precious to God, no matter the color of a person's skin. I believe slavery is an abomination that must end if our country is to survive." Jonah paused. Should he tell her everything? Let her see how far he would go. . .had gone? "Even before the war began, my brother, Eli, and I helped slaves escape to safe havens. He didn't want me to volunteer to fight because he understood what you are just now seeing, the death and destruction. But I couldn't stand on the sidelines. Following God's urging is more important than my comforts, my life, or even my family."

Emotions chased each other across her face—fear, knowledge, understanding, and finally determination. "What can I do to help?"

Her question made him want to shout with joy. And in that moment, he knew why Thad's announcement had caused him so much pain. He was deeply, completely, irrevocably in love with Camellia Anderson. If she married someone else, it would be a disaster of monumental proportions. He wanted to extract a promise from her to wait for him. He wanted her to vow not to marry Thad. But he could not. He would not. So he shrugged. "Keep your eyes and ears open. God will give you the answer in His time."

Chapter Twenty-seven

The landing at Jacksonport should have been crowded with townspeople and soldiers in the morning, but Camellia could see no sign of activity.

White tents littered a clearing nearby; lazy tendrils of smoke rose from cooling campfires. Gray-coated soldiers with bayonets attached to their rifles patrolled the edges of the camp, their faces hard as they watched the packet approach the empty landing.

As soon as the gangplank was lowered, Thad marched across it and headed toward a tent over which a Confederate flag waved.

Jane came to stand next to Camellia and placed an arm around her waist. "You've seemed different these past few days. Is that scene with my brother troubling you?"

Camellia would have liked to blame her problems on such an easy target, but she could not be untruthful to her best friend. "No."

The other girl was silent, as though waiting for an explanation. But Camellia had none to give her. She couldn't reveal her changed feelings about the war and slavery without exposing Jonah, and she couldn't very well ask her friend to betray her brother by hiding Jonah's secret.

"I suppose we're all tired."

Camellia sighed. "It has been a long trip."

"At least Jonah seems back to normal. Even his cough is easing."

Thanking God in her heart, Camellia smiled. "That's true. Perhaps we have bright futures as nurses."

Jane shivered. "I don't think I have the stomach for it."

"You don't find it rewarding to see Jonah's recovery?"

"Of course I do, but it's not like he had any gaping wounds or sores. His problems were more internal."

Thad's reappearance stopped their conversation. He was escorted by an older man, a civilian.

"Here they come. I wonder what your brother has learned."

They soon found out. Jacksonport had been in the hands of the Union until only a few days earlier. Camellia wondered what might have happened if they had arrived then. Would they have been taken prisoner, or would Jonah have come forward and worked to ensure their freedom?

The Confederate commander who had retaken the town had a number of wounded on his hands, and he needed to arrange transport back to Vicksburg where they could receive proper care. Even though their packet was small, he thought it would meet his requirements.

Thad described the proposition as a choice, but Camellia viewed it as a command. They would transport the wounded soldiers to Vicksburg whether they wanted to or not.

She and Jane spent the afternoon scrubbing out the unused guest quarters. Soldiers drove nails into the walls and hung hammocks inside the cleaned quarters. By the time the sun was setting, the boat was almost ready.

The commander's assistant, a pale man with a long beard and pale eyes, joined them for dinner. It was a fancier dinner than they had enjoyed for the weeks they'd been on the White River. Colonel Thomas Scoggins regaled them with stories of battles and skirmishes they had managed to avoid in their time on the river.

As a result, Camellia found herself unable to eat any of the fried squirrel or rice. From the colonel's descriptions, they would surely encounter Union gunboats if they tried to return to the Mississippi. Would she and Jane spend the rest of the war in this small town in Arkansas?

"I'm surprised Mr. Thornton is not present for dinner this evening." Mr. Carlton's innocent comment set Camellia's heart thumping. "I would have thought he would be anxious to make a report of the activities at Memphis."

Colonel Scoggins raised an eyebrow. "Who is this?"

Thad explained how they had fished Jonah from the river after the battle above Memphis and watched him sleep for three days and nights. Colonel Scoggins expressed a desire to interview Jonah, and the conversation at the table became more general.

But Camellia knew it didn't bode well for Jonah. She had to warn him and see that he avoided talking with the sharp-eyed soldier. She had no intention of seeing him hanged for his actions—not now that she understood the truth.

∼

Two days later the packet had taken on a whole new identity. Fresh paint blazoned the word HOSPITAL on the housing that protected the paddle wheel, declaring to all that she should be allowed to pass without being fired upon. Camellia hoped both armies would respect the packet's purpose.

She had never been more tired in her life. Her legs hurt, her arms felt too heavy to lift, and her neck was as stiff as a board. And still the wounded and sick were brought onto the boat in a never-ending flood. Women from the town came aboard, too, with offerings of fresh bandages, soap, and herbal remedies.

The doctor had Jane and Camellia organize their supplies and start a list of their patients' names. Along with Mr. Carlton and some of the other crewmen, they talked to the men, holding their hands, cleaning their faces, and making them as comfortable as possible. The stench was nearly unbearable, but somehow Camellia managed to get around the crowded room.

Jonah caught her in the passageway at noon on the second day. "I want you to come to the dining hall with me."

"I don't have time to eat." She tried to push past him but was halted when he spread his legs and crossed his arms over his chest. "Get out of my way."

He uncrossed his arms and touched her cheek with a gentle finger. "You cannot keep spending all your time with the wounded."

"That's what Thad told me when I was tending you."

Jonah's head snapped back as though she had slapped him.

Remorse flooded Camellia. "I'm sorry."

"Don't be. I don't mean to irritate you, Camellia. But I'm worried about your health. You're exhausted." He took her by the shoulders and turned her to face one of the passageway windows. "Look at yourself. If you keep up this pace, you'll expire before those men in there."

Tears burned her eyes. Couldn't he see she was doing this because of him? Because he had helped her see the truth? "What do you want from me?"

"Come with me." He dropped his hands from her shoulders and pulled her toward the exit. "I have something I need to tell you, and spending an afternoon in the sunshine will make you feel better."

The fresh air did smell good. And the warmth of the sun on her skin was a welcome relief. Strangers, the soldiers who came and went from the Confederate headquarters in a never-ending flow, watched them disembark. But no one challenged Jonah. Had he convinced them that he was one of them? Was he even now gathering information that would be used to defeat them? "Where are you taking me?"

Jonah didn't answer her, just kept a guiding hand under her elbow. They walked down the dusty street, passing a mercantile and half-a-dozen houses. And still he walked. Over a slight rise, through a valley of tall grasses.

Camellia was beginning to think her legs would fall off. "I have to stop."

"It's not much farther now." Jonah's promise encouraged her to continue.

Finally he turned into the woods, following a path only he could see. Trees surrounded them, hiding them from civilization. She could hear something new ahead of them, a sound like thunder. Where was he taking her?

And then she saw it. The thunder was water rushing across huge boulders. "A waterfall?"

Their gazes met. He looked like a mischievous kid. "One of the local men told me about this place. I thought I would offer to stand guard while you refresh yourself." He held out his hand, his palm open to show her a sliver of soap.

Suddenly the layers of grit and grime on her skin were intolerable. She took the soap from him, imagining the feeling of the cleansing water surrounding her. "Really?"

He nodded and turned his back to the waterfall. "Be careful. I'd hate to have to offend your modesty."

Camellia felt her blush, though she knew he couldn't see it under the dirt. She moved to a pool at the base of the waterfall and stripped off her clothing one layer at a time. Dressed only in her chemise, she stuck a toe in the water. It was cool, as refreshing as she'd hoped. She glanced back over her shoulder to make certain Jonah was not watching. His back was barely discernible among the tree limbs. Satisfied, she walked forward. The water climbed to her waist then to her neck. Camellia held her breath and plunged her head into the water. She lathered the soap and used it to melt the dirt and grime. She rinsed the suds away and started over again, scrubbing her scalp, her skin, every part of her body she could reach.

"Are you still in the water?" Jonah's voice reminded her of his presence.

"Yes. It's wonderful, Jonah." She rinsed the soap off a second time and stepped out of the pool. Getting dressed was not easy, but with a bit of squirming and straining she managed the laces and buttons.

Squeezing the water out of her curls, Camellia walked back up the path to the place where she had parted from Jonah. "Where are you?"

He appeared from behind a large oak. "Right here." His crooked smile made her breath catch.

"Thank you."

"Did you enjoy yourself?" He offered his arm.

Camellia nodded. "It was worth the walk. I feel I could take on the whole world again."

They wandered down the path again, at peace with each other. The sun was beginning to approach the western horizon.

Jonah sighed and stopped walking just short of the town's edge. "I have to leave."

Although she'd been expecting this moment from the start, Camellia's heart fell. "When?"

"Now. A couple of days ago Colonel Scoggins sent a messenger to my battalion to report my survival. As soon as he realizes my commanding officer doesn't have any record of me, he'll realize I'm a spy." Jonah heaved a sigh. "I wish I could stay, but it's impossible."

"I could go with you." The words slipped out before Camellia could stop them.

He shook his head. "Thad will take care of you."

Camellia promised herself she would not cry. She would not let him see how his refusal hurt her or how much she would miss him. She choked back her emotions. "Godspeed, then."

"Camellia, I want you t—" He bit off the word and shook his head. "Thad is a good man. You could do worse than marry him."

She shook her head. "Please don't say such things." They had been through so much together. The memory of his kiss came back to her with startling clarity. She wanted to do nothing more than repeat the experience. Before she could talk herself out of it, Camellia lifted herself on tiptoe and pressed her lips against Jonah's.

After a brief hesitation, his arms embraced her, holding her close. His lips moved on hers, and a shock like lightning shot through her. Time stood still as the bond between them strengthened. For a moment she seemed to melt into him, become a part of him in some way that she didn't understand. Then it was over.

Jonah put his hands on her shoulders and slowly pushed her away. "I have to go." His voice was rough, but she could see the remorse in his gaze. Then he turned on his heel and walked away, disappearing into the woods without a backward glance.

Pain tore through her, and Camellia sank to her knees and wept. She wept for past mistakes and present dreams; she wept for lost causes and separate pathways. But mostly she wept for the brave man who would not shirk his duty no matter the cost.

Chapter Twenty-eight

The note was delivered by a young boy who put Lily in mind of David, the child they had rescued from the streets of Natchez Under-the-Hill. Dirty and barefoot, he was another of the "throwaway" children who should be staying at the foundling home. She must remember to mention him to the orphanage's matron.

"I have a note here for y'all. The scary man said you'd pay me for it." He held up the folded sheet.

Lily frowned. "The scary man?"

The child nodded, his brown eyes solemn.

Wondering who had given the child a note, Lily shrugged. She reached for the reticule at her waist and drew out a gold coin. "Is this enough for your long walk?"

The child's eyes widened at the generous offering. "Yes, ma'am."

She held out the coin, smiling as he snatched it from her hand.

He handed her the note and skipped off the veranda. Lily imagined the tales he would share tonight in whatever hovel sheltered him. Perhaps the money would buy him a good meal and a real bed or stretch to a new pair of shoes. She hoped so.

Returning to the front parlor, she sat next to Blake. "I had hoped this would be a note from Camellia, but it's addressed to you."

Blake took the note from her hand. "One of my admirers, no doubt."

She punched his arm.

"Lily, control yourself, please." Aunt Dahlia sniffed.

Blake adopted an angelic expression and nodded. "Thank you. I have told Lily again and again that she should adopt your manners."

The older woman preened, and Lily felt like punching his arm again. If she had followed Aunt Dahlia's advice, they never would have met. She never would have purchased half interest in a steamboat, and he probably would have been shot by some unhappy gambler by now. Deciding to take the higher road, she forced her lips into a congenial smile. "Are you going to open your note?"

His unrepentant grin teased her.

Lily folded her hands in her lap and gazed at the fireplace. She refused to be drawn into further tomfoolery.

Blake sighed and pulled a small knife from the pocket of his trousers.

Aunt Dahlia gasped and fanned herself, apparently overcome to find a lethal weapon in their parlor.

Lily regaled her aunt and grandmother with a description of the boy and his "scary man" while her husband perused the note. She didn't realize anything was wrong until the sheet of paper drifted to the floor. She turned to look at her husband, surprised to see the anguish in his navy-blue eyes. "What is it?"

Blake shook his head and leaned back against the sofa, his hand covering his eyes. Was he crying?

Lily scooped up the note and read it:

Dear Mr. Matthews,

I am sorry to inform you that your father has suffered a serious accident and is not expected to recover. By the time you receive this note, it may already be too late, but your sister has expressed a desire for your help, as she has no other male relative to support her during these trying and dangerous times. As a friend of the family, I have taken it upon myself to contact you and request that you repair immediately to your family's home in Cape Girardeau.

The note was signed with a flourishing *J*.

Grandmother put down her teacup. "What has happened?"

"It's Blake's father. He's been in some sort of accident."

"Your father?" Aunt Dahlia looked at the man beside her. "I thought you were an orphan."

Blake lowered his hand, and Lily noticed that the skin under his eyes seemed moist. The urge to protect her husband took hold of her. "Blake had a difficult childhood and had to break free from his family."

Aunt Dahlia's jaw fell. After a moment, she snapped it shut. "I suppose I shouldn't be surprised."

What she left unsaid was a phrase Lily had heard often enough. . . *from a gambler*. She frowned at her relative. "Not everyone is as comfortable or blessed as we have been. Blake deserves your admiration for succeeding in spite of the setbacks he's faced."

Blake patted her hand. "It's all right, Lily. You don't have to defend me. I have never corrected your relatives' mistaken assumptions about my past."

"But—"

A look from him stopped her words. "I believe the time has come for me to take your advice." He stood and reached for the note.

Lily bent her wrist away from his hand. "Don't think I'm going to let you take this trip alone."

Grandmother cleared her throat and sent a look in Aunt Dahlia's direction. "I believe we need to inspect the linens upstairs." It was her tactful way of offering them privacy.

Aunt Dahlia's mouth curved downward, but she nodded and rose from her rocker.

Lily waited until both of them exited the parlor before returning her attention to her husband. "We can pick up Camellia on the way. I think it's time she rejoined her family. I really miss her."

"It's too dangerous for you to come. Every day we receive more reports of battles and skirmishes along the river." He reached for the note once more.

Shaking her head, Lily stood and held her hand behind her back. "You are no more impervious to bullets than I."

"Lily, be reasonable. I must go." He cupped her chin with one hand.

She refused to be swayed by his tenderness. "I suppose you mean to take *my* boat and *my* father."

"I can catch a ride on a different boat. Captains will be eager to travel north for goods they can sell to us at inflated prices." He slid his hand down the length of her arm, raising gooseflesh.

Lily shivered and failed to hold on to the note.

Blake snatched it from her hand and stepped back, a teasing smile on his lips.

"I can't stop you if that's what you want to do." Lily returned his smile with deceptive humility. "But whether you're aboard or not, the *Water Lily* will be making a trip to Cape Girardeau."

๏

Camellia wept for the first soldier whose shroud-covered body slid into the dark waters of the river. She cried over the next one, too. But then her heart seemed to scab over, hardened by experience. Fever swept the packet ship, and more of them died. Helplessly, she swabbed their foreheads and listened as they spoke of home.

"I'm afraid Michael won't last another day." One of the soldiers traveling with them whispered the information as she took his place beside Michael's hammock.

Camellia nodded and removed the warm cloth from the patient's forehead, dropping it into a pan with other dirty cloths. Later she would boil the contents of this pan in a large pot with lye soap. "I think they might do better if we could carry them to the deck." Replacing the soiled cloth with a fresh one, she thought of the way she'd felt that bittersweet day when Jonah had taken her to the waterfall.

How impossibly far away that moment of hope seemed to her now. Jonah was gone, and all that was left was sickness, pain, and death. Helplessness and hopelessness were her constant companions. Sometimes she felt she would lose her mind.

Moving to the next hammock, Camellia peeled the dirty cloth from the soldier's head, wrung out a fresh one, and laid it gently across his face. As she turned away, however, this man put a hot, dry hand around her wrist. "Are you an angel?"

Camellia shook her head.

"I've never seen anyone as pretty as you."

"Of course you haven't." Michael coughed, and she turned back to look at him again, noticing the gray cast to his face. "That's 'cause she *is* an angel, only she can't tell anyone."

Her heart broke again as she put a hand on his shoulder. No one could say these men weren't brave. Even now, as their broken bodies failed, they could find something to make each other smile. "Of course I'm not an angel. I'm just a girl from Natchez."

"Didn't I tell you?" Michael nodded before sinking back against the hammock. "She can't tell anyone what she really is."

Shaking her head, Camellia looked up and saw Thad entering the sickroom. He looked troubled, and her heart pounded in response. How much more would they have to bear before this nightmare ended? She picked up her bowl of rags and moved toward him.

"We need to talk." His voice was as grim as his face. His back was as straight as a ramrod as he escorted her out of the sickroom.

"What has happened?"

They walked through the passageway to the deck. Camellia glanced about for evidence of a new threat, but she could see nothing more than the trees and banks they were sliding past.

"We've received news about Jonah Thornton. It appears he's been masquerading. . ."

Camellia's mind spun as Thad talked. Had Jonah been apprehended by the Confederates? A vision of his lifeless body dangling from a hangman's noose sprang to life in her mind. She couldn't seem to catch her breath. Couldn't make sense of the words flowing from Thad. What would she do without Jonah? Without seeing that half smile of his, the fire in his green eyes? What about his parents? His sister? The brother in Memphis?

"If I see his conniving face again, I'll put a bullet in him myself."

The truth burst upon her like the blast of a torpedo. He was not dead. Was not even languishing in a Confederate prison. Her heartbeat quickened. Jonah was alive. And free. Something of her joy must have shown on Camellia's face, because Thad stopped talking and frowned at her. "You don't seem surprised at my news." His brown gaze pierced her.

Camellia realized she had best step warily if she didn't want to be branded a spy herself. "Jonah told me there was a problem with his enlistment."

A harsh laugh from the man beside her stopped her careful words. "The problem with his enlistment is that it's a sham. Wait a minute. . . ."

She looked up at him.

Thad was gazing into the distance, his mind busy with implications. "He's the missing piece!"

"What do you mean?" Camellia forced the words through her tight throat.

"He's the one who was passing classified information to Mrs. Dabbs. And he's the one who most likely orchestrated her escape before we left New Orleans." Thad no longer looked suspicious of her. His gaze settled on her hair, and he reached up to tuck a stray strand into her bun. "It all makes sense now."

Before Camellia could say anything, he bowed to her. "I have to report this to my commanding officer. He needs to know exactly how nefarious Jonah Thornton really is."

She watched Thad march away and wondered where it would all end. Would Thad someday kill Jonah?

Guilt assailed her, and she felt her heart being torn in two parts. Thad was a good man. He had all the qualifications to make her happy. But her heart wanted to be near Jonah. If only he wanted the same thing, too.

Chapter Twenty-nine

Thunder rumbled in the distance as the packet-turned-hospital reached the Mississippi River. Camellia wondered if it came from the dark clouds in the sky or yet another confrontation between the United States and the Confederacy. She leaned against the rail and turned her face to the wind.

"It won't be long before we reach Vicksburg." Jane came up behind her and removed her apron.

"I wonder if the Union navy has taken it as well."

"Thad says no. Vicksburg may be the only city the Confederacy can hold, but it will never fall into the hands of the Yankees."

Camellia wondered if Thad could be wrong. But she had seen the high bluffs. She had heard the men talking about Vicksburg's refusal to surrender even after New Orleans, Natchez, and Baton Rouge had fallen. And she could see for herself the ardent desperation of Confederate soldiers to win the war against all odds.

Ahead of them the river seemed to come to an end, so deep was its curve. The hairpin curve just above Vicksburg.

Jane's dark hair whipped around her head in the brisk wind. "Isn't it ironic that we tried to stay away from the fighting but only managed to get ourselves mired in it?"

"I read something about that in my Bible this morning."

"I'm not surprised. You've spent more time with your nose stuck in your Bible during this trip than you did the whole time we were at La Belle." Her fingers tried to tuck the errant strands back into her coiffure. "Exactly what do you hope to find?"

"Answers." Camellia sniffed. "Isn't the Bible supposed to have all the answers?"

"I suppose so. . .if you're a preacher."

"The book of Proverbs has good advice for everyone."

Jane wrinkled her nose. "I suppose you're right, but you have to weed through all the ones that don't apply to get to the good ones."

Camellia could remember thinking the same way, so she knew nothing she said would change Jane's mind. All she could do was pray for her friend to have an awakening that would open Jane's heart and mind to the importance of each verse in the Bible.

Thad walked up to them, and Jane moved over to make a space between her and Camellia. He stepped into it. "What are my two favorite ladies discussing?"

The question made Camellia's brows rise. This was the Thad she remembered from New Orleans—the kind, debonair escort with a ready quip and winning smile. She liked him much better than the angry, bitter man who spoke of vengeance and reprisals.

"We were talking about the Bible," Jane answered.

He looked up at the sky and pursed his lips. " 'Blessed are the peacemakers: for they shall be called the children of God.' "

Camellia wondered why that verse had sprung to his mind. Did he wish to be a peacemaker? This was indeed a change, one that could only be wrought by God. She looked at him with new eyes. "Can you imagine listening to Jesus on that hillside?"

Thad looked at her, his gaze seeming to penetrate to her very soul. "His words are no less valid today or they wouldn't be included in the Bible."

Jane's voice broke the deepening spell between them. "I'm beginning to think we're at church."

Camellia turned back to the vista. "Look, there's the city."

A boat bristling with cannons approached them, and Thad sighed. "I'd best leave you two to pack your belongings while I go reassure those gentlemen that we are no threat."

Jane left to do as her brother suggested, but Camellia didn't care if she never saw any of the clothing she'd brought on this trip. Most of it was too filthy to even be given away. As soon as she got back to civilization, she would order a whole new wardrobe.

Men in worn gray uniforms walked past her with serious looks on their faces. Camellia watched as they checked every nook and cranny of the boat. Thad talked with one of the other officers. Eventually the soldiers left, and the boat continued to the port. As they drew nearer, her gaze swept the boats tied together at the dock. Tugs and schooners towered over canoes and pirogues. The distinctive smokestacks of other steamships filled the air with black steam and cinders. At least this area seemed untouched by the war.

Her breath caught when she noticed the lettering on one of the steamships. It couldn't be. And yet there it was. The *Water Lily*. Her family was in Vicksburg. Camellia's heart leapt in her chest. She wanted to shout at the captain to hurry.

Jane came back to the deck. "I'm ready."

"Look." Camellia pointed to her sister's boat. "My family is here."

"I'm happy for you." Jane gave her a brief hug. "I hope this doesn't mean you're planning to leave me after we land."

The unalloyed joy she'd felt was pierced by sadness. She put an arm around her friend. "Maybe we can all go back to Natchez together."

A shake of her friend's head negated that idea. And Camellia understood why. It was the war. Jane would want to remain on Confederate soil so she could stay in touch with her brother, the soldier, and her father, the blockade runner.

"Maybe your family has fled to Vicksburg, and all of us can stay here."

Given her sister and brother-in-law's views, Camellia doubted that possibility, but she kept her own counsel. And prayed for God to work out the things she could not see. A feeling of peace settled on her shoulders as the verse she'd read that morning came back to her. *"A man's heart deviseth his way: but the Lord directeth his steps."*

❧

"Camellia! Look, there she is!"

She waved her arm in a wide arc. "Lily! Blake!" Her feet flew across the gangplank. As soon as they hit the dock, she was caught up in a three-way hug.

"Are you hurt? Where have you been?" Lily's question melded with Blake's.

Laughing, Camellia added one of her own. "How long have you been here?"

Before they could answer, another person joined them. "I know this wretched creature is not my dainty Camellia."

Freezing at the sound of her father's voice, Camellia turned. And smiled. "I'm afraid it's me."

He opened his arms, and she walked into them. For the first time since she'd learned this man's real identity, she felt a connection with him.

Lily and Blake crowded around them. Questions and answers flew through the air like the gulls that followed behind fishing boats. By the time all of the stories had been sorted out, the packet was empty. Camellia looked around for Jane and Thad.

"Your friends have gone to their home ahead of us." Blake answered the question in her gaze. "We rented rooms in a hotel downtown, but we'll ask them to join us for dinner if you'd like."

"Of course she would like." Lily smiled at her. "She's in love with that handsome soldier, remember? That's the reason we let her go to Vicksburg."

Camellia opened her mouth to disagree but decided this was not the time to try to explain her divided loyalties. "But I have nothing to wear."

"Never fear." Her father's eyes twinkled. "Your sister brought one or two of the things that arrived from New Orleans after you left."

Lily nodded. "One or two trunks, he means. You should have heard Jensen complaining about their weight."

"Jensen is with you?"

"And Tamar, too. They are watching Jasmine." Blake put two fingers in his mouth and whistled. A carriage rolled away from the curb toward them, and all four of them climbed in.

A short ride later brought them into the central part of Vicksburg. Camellia was conscious of the stares her tattered garments and gnarled hair garnered in the lobby, but her family closed ranks around her and whisked her to a room. It looked huge to her, with a four-poster bed, two bureaus, a dressing table, and a sofa.

She turned to look at Lily who had followed her into the room. "Who's staying with me?"

"No one." Lily hugged her once more. "This whole place is for you."

Camellia perched on the edge of the sofa. "I feel like a princess."

"And you're going to look like one, too. But first, why don't you relax and take a nap. You've lost so much weight."

"I know. I've become a hag."

"No, no." Lily sat next to her and put a hand on her shoulder. "You're beautiful. All you need is a little rest, some fresh food, and your clothes. You'll feel better in no time."

It felt good to wash her face and hands, to strip off her clothes and choose something from the bureau Lily had filled with the clothing from her trunks. It felt even better to climb into the soft bed and pull the cover up to her chin.

The only things that remained troublesome were the grass-green eyes that chased her into oblivion.

❧

"I wish you weren't leaving in the morning." Thad's soulful brown gaze pricked her conscience. "We need you. . .*I* need you. . .here."

Camellia stepped back as required by the dance and curtsied. Her smile was not as firm as it should have been. She took two steps forward and curtsied again. "I have to go with my sister. She's upset that I left Vicksburg with you last time."

"I know. But that was my fault. I should have realized the danger."

"Don't be silly." Her smile relaxed into a more natural curve as she sought to allay his guilt. "No one could have known what would happen in Memphis. Lily should be glad you were there to protect us on our trip to Jacksonport."

The music ended. Thad offered her an elbow and escorted her from the dance floor. Camellia was immediately besieged by other handsome soldiers. She was the most popular girl at the party. She should be giddy with excitement, but a strange emptiness filled her with each new partner. Some stepped on her toes while others regaled her with stories of their exploits on the field of battle. She had never been so ready to leave a party.

Jane and Thad talked nonstop on the way back to the hotel, neither noticing that Camellia hardly spoke. When the carriage came to a halt, she gathered her wrap and reached for the door handle.

"I'll be right back, Jane." Thad's hand covered hers on the handle.

Camellia jerked her hand away as though his touch burned it.

Jane settled in the far corner of the carriage. "Don't hurry on my account. I may even take a nap." She lowered one eyelid at Camellia before turning her head away.

Thad stepped down, unaware of the byplay between Jane and Camellia. He reached a hand toward her, and Camellia allowed him to help her from the carriage.

"Thank you for a lovely evening." She turned to go inside.

His hand encircled her elbow. "Wait a moment."

She sighed. "I know what you're going to say, Thad. I'm sorry I can't stay in Vicksburg, but it's out of the question. My family needs—" Her mouth dropped open when she turned to look up at him, ending the speech she'd prepared.

Thad had dropped to one knee. His head was lower than her shoulder.

"Please get up, Thad."

"No." He reached for her hand, raising it to his lips and placing a warm kiss on it. "I have something to ask you, Camellia."

She wanted to pull her hand away, but his grip was too strong. "Thad, please. You're embarrassing me."

"Camellia, you are the most beautiful woman I've ever met. But that's not the best thing about you. Looks fade, but not the things in here." He thumped his chest with his free hand. "You care about others. I've watched you under the most extreme of circumstances. You didn't break. You never complained or whined."

"Neither did Jane."

His smile lifted only a corner of his mouth. "I'm not in love with my sister, Camellia. Now will you hush and let me finish?"

She gave him a slow nod.

Another carriage pulled up at the front of the hotel, and a couple got out. They stared at Camellia and Thad. The woman giggled.

"Camellia, I love you." His words came faster. "Please say you'll marry me and make me the happiest man alive."

"I. . .uh. . .I don't know what to say, Thad."

He stood and brushed dirt from the knees of his trousers. He didn't pull her into his arms but stood with his arms hanging loose at his side. "The obvious answer is yes."

She shook her head. "I can't. . ."

"Don't answer right now." He put a finger on her lips. "Not unless you're going to give me an emphatic yes."

Camellia couldn't bear to see the hurt in his eyes, so she looked past his shoulder and remained silent.

"I thought so." He turned to walk toward the hotel entrance and held the door open for her. "Just promise me you'll think about your answer while you're gone."

Tears sprang to her eyes. What woman would be silly enough to turn him down? Yet she couldn't accept his offer. Not until she sorted out her muddled feelings. "We've been living in each other's pockets for more than a month now. I think spending some time apart is a good idea."

Silently, he bowed and watched her with his sad brown eyes.

Camellia entered the hotel and went to her room. As the maid helped her undress, her mind kept going over Thad's proposal. She knew she'd done the right thing by not accepting him. So why did she feel like she'd kicked an innocent puppy?

Chapter Thirty

"You need to get out of that sunshine before you turn yo' skin as dark as mine." Tamar stood at the entrance to the parlor.

Camellia blinked away her drowsiness. "I'll go get a hat."

"T'ain't no hat to protect you from the glare off the water. You need to get inside here and help with the mending."

Making a face, Camellia pushed herself out of the chair she had been resting in. "I can't sew at all."

"Humph. A fine job they did at that fancy school, then. Now you go help your sister. I'm going to check on Jasmine and make sure she's doing the schoolwork Lily assigned." Tamar disappeared into the shady interior.

Camellia wondered if Tamar ever worried about losing her freedom. She had lived most of her life as the property of Camellia's grandparents, and she had never seemed unhappy with her situation. She had lavished affection on all three of her charges. But that had been before Lily bought a steamship and before Tamar fell in love with Jensen. Camellia had been thrilled when the woman who raised her gained her freedom and married Jensen, Blake's friend and employee.

Their situation gave the issue of slavery a human face. If Tamar had remained a slave, she would have had to petition Grandmother for the right to marry. How many other Tamars and Jensens were denied the chance for happiness because of slavery? The question made her heart ache and brought Jonah's arguments back to her. Yet without slavery, so many plantations would fail. Was there not some middle ground that would work for everyone?

Putting away the question for later, Camellia moved into the parlor, pulled out a chair, and sat next to her sister.

"Oh good. I can use an extra hand." Lily nodded her head at the pile of starched linen and clean socks that hid the surface of the table in front of her. "I don't know how I can get so far behind."

Camellia made a face. "I'd rather be scrubbing the deck outside."

"I know you've never enjoyed handwork, but surely you learned enough at La Belle to be able to sew a straight line." Lily handed her a needle and some thread. "Why don't you show me what they taught you?"

"I doubt you'll be impressed." Catching her tongue between her teeth, Camellia concentrated on threading the needle. Nostalgia brought a sad smile to her face as she recalled the day she'd sown her sampler to her skirt. Life had seemed so much simpler then. . .before she'd seen the ugly face of war. Camellia glanced toward her sister. "Do you ever wish you could go back into the past?"

Lily shook her head. "I'm happy to be where I am. If you spend time always looking back over your shoulder at what was, you'll miss out on a lot."

"I just wish things were not so complicated."

"It's true that adults have more responsibilities than children." Lily inspected the napkin she was working on. "But many of our problems are as simple as theirs."

Camellia huffed her disbelief.

"No, it's true. We tend to think everything is complicated. Think about how the Pharisees tried to trip up Jesus. They asked him to list the commandments in order of importance."

"How complicated could that be? There are only ten commandments, after all."

Lily raised her eyebrows. "Whole volumes of laws have been written to support those ten rules, but that's not even the point. Jesus pointed out a simple answer. He said that we must first love God with all our hearts, souls, minds, and strength. Secondly, we are to love our neighbors as ourselves. He told the Pharisees to forget about everything else and concentrate on those two things alone."

"It can't be that easy."

"I didn't say it was easy, Camellia. I said it was simple. Even the most ardent Christians may struggle at times with loving God with everything in them. And it's extremely difficult to love someone who is trying to harm you."

"But if everyone did the same thing. . ." Camellia let her voice trail off, trying to imagine a world without strife.

"Someday we will. When Christ comes again, everyone will bow to Him."

Another thought occurred to her. "If everyone will bow to Him then, why do we worry about following His Word now? I mean, if everyone will be saved when He comes back, what difference does it make how we live?"

"I didn't say everyone would be saved. Christ promised that some will claim to be His children, but He will not know them. Those pitiful souls will be separated from God for all eternity." She shivered and reached for another cloth to mend. "I know you believe in God and that He sent His Son, Jesus Christ, to die for your sins, Camellia. Listen to God, always keeping your heart in repentance toward Him. Love Him and love the people around you. God will take care of the rest."

It sounded too easy to Camellia. And how was she supposed to apply her sister's advice to the problem she was facing? What answer was she going to give Thad the next time she saw him?

"Camellia, I've prayed a lot about your future." Lily hesitated before continuing. "I worried that you might not have the right priorities in mind. But I've seen the difference in you since the beginning of the year, and I have confidence you are seeking the path God intends you to follow. It will not be the same path as mine or Jasmine's, but that's as it should be."

Her sister's words washed over Camellia like a cleansing flood. If Lily believed in her, she must be doing something right. The little voice trying to insist that she still didn't know what to do was firmly squashed.

She didn't need to make the decision today, after all. Once they arrived at Blake's family home, they would probably stay at least a month. Perhaps she would figure out what to do before the voyage home.

❧

"Heave to." The order was punctuated by a blast from a cannon.

Blake bounded up the steps from the engine room, his gaze landing on Lily before swinging to the gunboat stationed near their bow. "Are you all right?"

Papa stared down at them from the hurricane deck. "You may want to shut off the boiler and weigh anchor before those fellows get nervous."

Jensen appeared from the galley and moved toward the anchor, releasing the pin with a minimum of effort.

Blake disappeared down the steps into the engine room once again, and Lily heard the hiss of steam being vented. The paddle wheel stopped, and they were still in the water, ready to be boarded.

The tin-clad steamer, not much larger than the *Water Lily*, was fully outfitted for battle. Three large cannons poked muzzles through the tin that offered protection to the sailors manning them. She could still see smoke rising from the one that had fired a warning shot past them.

Both wooden decks and the pilothouse were encased in sheets of tin that would stop a hail of bullets. As she watched, sailors in dark blue poured from the interior of the ship, bayonetted rifles in their arms. Above them the familiar flag of the United States waved its colors.

Blake came up next to her and slipped a comforting arm around her waist. "You should probably go inside with Tamar and your sister while your father and I talk to the officers."

"I'm not afraid of them."

"That's not the issue here, Lily." Blake kept his tone light, but his fingers squeezed a warning. "I don't want the captain or his men to be distracted. Let me show them our papers, and we'll be on our way in no time. Both of us want to reach Cape Girardeau before the sun sets."

She cupped his chin with her hand. "Just make sure you don't get shot or impressed. I wouldn't relish being left on the bank while the Union navy sails away with my boat."

Camellia, Jasmine, and Tamar met her at the door to the parlor.

"What will happen now?" Camellia's face was as white as a bleached napkin.

Tamar didn't look as concerned as she had the night they crept into New Orleans to rescue Camellia and Jane. She stood next to the doorway, her legs spread and her arms crossed over her chest.

Lily encouraged them to sit down, enclosing Jasmine in her arms. The men would talk to the sailors, show them the papers that cleared the *Water Lily* for travel along the Mississippi and Ohio Rivers. Before leaving Natchez, she and Blake had signed sworn statements of fealty to the United States to receive their clearance. At the time she had thought it an unnecessary precaution to take. They had never been stopped by either side before. But now she was glad Blake had insisted.

The minutes passed slowly, but Lily took comfort in the fact that no one was shouting or shooting. She closed her eyes and prayed for the safety of their crew and the men on the gunboat. Peace blanketed her as she took her petition to God, and Lily opened her eyes.

Camellia had moved to the window and was watching the action through a slit in the curtains.

"What's going on?"

"Not much. One of the Yankees—"

"Federals," Lily corrected her sister.

Camellia sighed and started over. "One of the *Federals* is talking to Blake. . . . Now he's going back to his boat. . . . Blake's waving at our father. . . . I don't see Jensen."

The sound of the anchor chain as it was being wound back up told them what Jensen was doing.

"I'll be back." Lily released Jasmine, rose, and put her hand on the door, surprised when it moved under her hand. Had a deserter sneaked on board while the two boats were lying side by side? She took a step back, breathing a sigh of relief when Blake's dark hair and blue eyes appeared.

"Are all of you going to lollygag in here the rest of the afternoon?" His smile teased her. "If this is the effect your debutante sister is going to have on you, we'll have to leave her in Cape Girardeau."

Lily rolled her eyes. "And to think I was praying for your safety."

"And a good thing, too." He caught her in a hug and dropped a quick kiss on her forehead. "That was the USS *Rattler*. Her captain is spoiling for a battle and seemed a bit put out that we weren't blockade runners or spies."

She looked at him more closely to see if he was still teasing. What she saw made her heart stutter. Whatever had transpired outside had been a close-run thing. Visions of Blake, Jensen, and Papa being carried off in chains while strangers in blue uniforms commandeered the *Water Lily* took form in her head. Lily closed her eyes and thanked God for His protection before following her husband to the engine room.

The sun had not quite sunk below the horizon as they passed under the guns of a fort south of Cape Girardeau and began looking for an overnight berth. The dock was crowded with warships—steamers, screw steamers, and schooners. All flew the Stars and Stripes, and most bore evidence of contact with Confederates.

They tied up at the end of a pier, and Blake met with the harbormaster before returning to report to the others. "He says we can stay here tonight, but tomorrow we'll need to come back and move to make way for ships that are currently out on patrol."

Lily nodded. "Does he know where your family is?"

"He's heard of a sick preacher who lives a couple of miles downstream."

"Do you think that's him?"

Blake shrugged. "It's as good a place to start as any. After we get the boat settled tomorrow morning, I'll walk down there and see whether or not it's my father's home."

Touching his arm, Lily gave him an encouraging smile. "I'm glad we're finally here. As soon as we find your father, we'll get him on the road to recovery."

"I hope you're right." Blake put an arm around her waist. "But no matter what we find, I know God will help us face it."

She rested her head on his shoulder. "I love you."

"I love you, too."

The kiss he dropped on her cheek was sweeter than honey. How blessed she was to have such a godly man as her husband.

Chapter Thirty-one

Blake pointed toward the river. "If we're about to reach my father's house, we could move the *Water Lily* over there and tie her up."

Lily nodded. "It would be nice to have Papa, Jensen, and Tamar close at hand."

Feeling a trickle of sweat down her back, Camellia wished they would reach the house. She had told Lily she could stay on the *Water Lily* as Jasmine was, but her older sister had insisted she wanted Camellia with her.

It seemed they had been walking an hour. At first Camellia had enjoyed the view of the colorful hills. The reds, golds, greens, and browns of the leaves made them look as though God had rained paint down on them. But all these months on board one riverboat or another had meant little walking. Her legs ached, she was huffing like a racehorse, and one of her hat pins was drilling a hole into her head.

"Is that it?"

Lily's question brought her head up. A small house squatted at the end of a twisty lane. Camellia frowned. It looked like a face to her. The door was a nose flanked by two window "eyes." The steps up to the porch looked like a mouth, and the roof continued the image with its brown shingles rising steeply above the porch in imitation of a head of hair. It was smaller than Lily and Blake's boat.

Blake bounded up the steps and knocked on the front door, but Lily and Camellia waited on the lane behind him.

After a moment, the door opened a crack. Camellia thought it might be a woman who answered, but she wasn't certain.

Blake said something, and the door flew open.

A girl about Camellia's age flung herself into Blake's arms and hugged him tightly. "It's a miracle."

Blake put his arms around her and bent his head. "How have you been, Anna?"

After a moment, he turned and waved to Lily and Camellia. "I have some special ladies I'd like you to meet."

Camellia planted a smile on her lips as he performed the introductions. After hugging Lily and welcoming her to the family, Blake's sister turned to her. "You're ever so beautiful, Camellia. I hope we're going to be good friends as well as sisters-in-law."

She noticed Anna's threadbare cuffs and the old-fashioned cut to the dress that was partially hidden by her apron. She looked tired, too, and her figure was certainly not as rounded as Camellia's. But she did have a pleasant face and natural gracefulness. With a little time and effort, she could be made into a very presentable young lady. "I'm sure we will."

Anna waved them into the house. "Aunt Tessie, come to the parlor. I have the most wonderful surprise for you."

The older woman who came to greet them had silver-touched brown hair and light blue eyes. Her smile was warm and welcoming as she surveyed them. Then her expression froze as she recognized who stood in the doorway to the parlor. "Ezekiel." Joy rose in her face like the first rays of the morning sun. "You've come home to us."

Ezekiel? Camellia saw the frown on Blake's face even though it was quickly absorbed into a smile of recognition. "Aunt Tessie, you've not aged a day since I was fourteen."

She waved a hand at him. "Go on with you, Ezekiel. You still haven't lost that slick tongue of yours."

"Aunt Tessie." Anna's voice brimmed with concern. "You know Blake prefers to be called by his middle name."

"I know, I know. But old habits die hard. You'll always be Ezekiel to me, dear, but I'll try to remember." Blake's aunt hugged him before turning to Lily and Camellia. "And who are these lovely ladies?"

"This is my wife, Lily, and Camellia, her—"

Aunt Tessie's shriek interrupted him. "You've gone and gotten married!"

Camellia watched, bemused, as Blake's aunt pulled Lily out of her curtsy and wrapped her in an enthusiastic embrace. Then it was her turn to be bear-hugged. At least she could set aside the concern that her family might embarrass Blake. If this lady was any indication, his family had at least as many eccentric characters as hers.

"God bless the two of you for bringing Ezek—" She halted and shook her head. "Blake back to us."

The parlor was small. A sofa, whose worn covering was imperfectly disguised by several doilies, looked like a castoff. The rest of the furniture looked old, too, including several wooden chairs that boasted neither cushion nor upholstery. At least the tables in the room gleamed with furniture polish, somewhat softening the air of spartan frontier existence.

Camellia and Lily sat next to each other on the sofa, leaving sufficient room for Blake to join them. Anna and Aunt Tessie took two of the straight-backed chairs.

"You're an answer to prayer." Anna twisted her hands in her apron.

"Pa?" Blake's voice trembled with the single syllable.

Anna looked out the window for a minute as though gathering her thoughts. "He's growing weaker every day. After the accident, his leg wouldn't heal, and the doctor had to. . .had to remove it. Since then, it seems he's lost the will to live." She put a hand up and swiped at a tear.

"I've tried every remedy I know to help him recover, but your father's an obstinate man." The aunt continued the explanation while Anna recovered her composure. "I'm at my wits' end, as is your sister. But perhaps all that is about to change now. Maybe seeing you will give him a reason to get out of his bed and resume his life."

Blake's face looked as though it had turned to stone. Wasn't that why they were here? Lily had told her that Blake and his father had had an argument years ago. This trip was supposed to give him a chance to make amends. So why did he look so frozen? "I won't feed his ego just to keep him alive."

The words fell into the silent room, and Camellia wished she could be somewhere else. Was there something she could say to diffuse the tension? The weather? The trip to Cape Girardeau? Nothing seemed appropriate, so she kept her gaze trained on her lap and waited.

"No one's asking you to lie to Pa." Anna stood and paced across the room, her stride too wide to be considered proper for a young lady. Mrs. Dabbs would have corrected her, but no one said a word in this parlor. "But I hope you can find it in your heart to forgive him for whatever wrong he's done to you."

Blake stood and walked to his sister. Camellia looked up and caught the determined look on her brother-in-law's face. "I'll do my best." His words, like his face, were filled with determination. "That's all I can promise."

Anna reached up and touched his cheek. "That's all anyone can ask of you."

"How long will you and your family be staying with us?" The aunt turned her attention to Lily.

Lily glanced at her husband for an answer, but he was still talking to his sister. "I'm not really certain. We weren't sure what the situation would be. The note Blake received was rather cryptic."

"You received a note?"

"Yes." Lily took a deep breath. "The note said Reverend Matthews was very sick and that y'all needed Blake's support."

A frown appeared on the aunt's face. "I wonder who sent the note? It had to be someone who knows us and who knew Blake and where he was."

Lily shrugged. "I'm just glad whoever it was took the time to let us know. Blake would have been distraught if he'd learned about this when it was too late to help."

"We'll be happy to have you as long as you'll stay." Anna left her brother and walked to the door. "I'm going to let Pa know you're here before I leave for my job at Devore's. I'll be back before dark."

"Oh no." Her aunt also stood. "Your lunch is not ready yet. I forgot all about it in the excitement."

The two of them exited the room.

Lily stood and moved toward Blake. "Are you okay, dear?"

"I suppose so." His tone was bleak. "So much has changed since I left."

Camellia stood and cleared her throat. "I think I'll go see if I can help someone do something."

Neither of them said anything, so she exited and looked around the foyer. What was she supposed to do with herself now?

Blake felt his shoulders tense as he passed through the doorway into his father's bedroom. The curtains were drawn, seeming to shut out light, hope. . .and life. In the dimly lit interior, he could make out the posters at each corner of his father's bed, but he could not make out the man's form behind the thick bed curtains hanging between them. "Pa?"

"Who's there?" The voice was querulous and shaky.

Blake's memory of his father's voice was much stronger, deeper, frightening. He glanced at Aunt Tessie, who was sitting a few feet away from the bed, a book in her lap. "It's your son come to visit you."

"Ezekiel?"

Blake grimaced at the name. He'd hated it as a child. Even after his parents had told him about the prophet he'd been named for. Ma had taken pity on him and began calling him by his middle name—her maiden name—Blake. But Pa had never called him anything else. "Yes, it's me, sir."

Silence filled the room. Blake wondered if the man had fainted from shock. Or was he struck dumb with horror?

Long, pale fingers pulled back one of the bed curtains a few inches. Blake could feel the chill of his father's gaze. It reminded him of the past—of being pierced by his parent's wrathful looks and fiery accusations. The hand fell back. "Why did you come?"

"Enoch," Aunt Tessie said as she rose from her chair and placed her book on it, "that's no way to treat your only son."

" 'The son shall not bear the iniquity of the father, neither shall the father bear the iniquity of the son: the righteousness of the righteous shall be upon him, and the wickedness of the wicked shall be upon him.' "

Blake's ears burned as he realized his father was quoting from the book of Ezekiel. He knew because he'd turned to that same verse many times as a young man. It had been comforting to him then to believe that his father's sins wouldn't be passed on to him. He had enough sins of his own to be concerned about. "If you're trying to say that I should not blame my mistakes on you, then you don't need to worry. I'm man enough to take responsibility for my mistakes. But I am not sure God will judge either of us righteous."

A whispery sound came from behind the curtains as his father apparently shifted his position in the bed. This time when the fingers appeared, they jerked back the cloth between Blake and his father.

Schooling his features to show none of his surprise, Blake looked at the man who had always stirred such fear in him. Propped into a sitting position with pillows behind him, his pa seemed much less frightening now. Wispy tendrils of graying hair fell over his forehead. His cheeks were gaunt from privation, and his faded blue eyes seemed filled with sorrow and regret. His mouth worked, but no words issued from it.

The years of bitterness seemed to melt away as Blake looked at his father's bent shoulders and lined face. Should he bow? Offer his hand? Try to hug the feeble man? Uncertainty kept him rooted to the floor a few feet away from the edge of his father's bed.

"I've prayed for this day." His father reached out his arms. "Please say you'll forgive me."

In all the times Blake had imagined facing his father, he'd never once thought the man would ask him for forgiveness. He'd expected a thundering scold, a litany of his shortcomings, or perhaps a demand that he leave immediately. He shook his head. "It wasn't all your fault, Pa. I shouldn't have run away."

"I've missed you, Son."

Blake moved toward the bed and hugged his father, his own eyes filled with tears. "I'm sorry it took me so long to come home."

"The important thing is that you're here now." Aunt Tessie's practical voice reminded Blake she was still in the room. "God has a way of working things out once we give Him our obedience." Her words resounded with faith and truth.

Blake closed his eyes and thanked God for giving him and his father this moment, this chance to heal the wounds of the past. "I know you've had a hard time over the past few months, Pa."

"They took my leg, Ezekiel. I'll never walk again." His father's voice was choked with unshed tears. "I'll never stand at the podium and look out over my church."

"I know, Pa." Blake straightened and took his father's hands in his own. "But we'll make some crutches for you. With prayer and hard work, we'll have you moving around this house like you always did. By spring you'll be back in your church telling them about doing all things through Christ."

Pa looked down at the sheet covering him and said nothing.

"That's right. God's got a lot of things for you to do. If He didn't, you'd be gone from here." Aunt Tessie pulled back a curtain to let the afternoon light into the room. "It's about time you remembered you're here for His purposes, and I'm pretty sure He didn't intend for you to lie about in here any longer."

Watching his father's head and shoulders rise at his aunt's words, Blake felt hope flooding him with the thought that it wasn't too late. His father's indomitable spirit might return. And he intended to stay here long enough to see that it did. No matter what difficulties they had ahead of them, they would face them together.

Facing difficulties together reminded him that his father had a few other surprises in store for him. "Pa, I've changed a lot since the last time we saw each other, and I owe a lot of that to a young lady I want you to meet. Her name is Lily. . .Lily Matthews."

"You're married." It was more a statement than a question.

Blake nodded.

"Well, go get her." His father leaned back against the pillows and closed his eyes.

Concerned that he had overtaxed his father's strength, Blake patted his hand. "It can wait, Pa. You rest a bit. She'll still be here when you wake up. We're not going to leave anytime soon."

"Good."

Blake leaned closer to hear his father's whisper.

"I want to thank her for bringing my son back to me."

Chapter Thirty-two

Camellia looked up from the letter she'd been trying to compose as Lily and Aunt Tessie, as she'd insisted Camellia call her, entered the warm parlor. "How is Mr. Matthews feeling this morning?"

Lily looked more than a little unsettled, her face paler than normal.

"He's feverish." The older woman's face wore a worried frown. "I'm going to the kitchen to prepare some tea that should reduce his fever and make him more comfortable."

Camellia put down her letter, her mind going back to the voyage from Jacksonport to Vicksburg and her helplessness as the sick and wounded soldiers grew weaker. She wanted to learn how to treat illness, how to mend young men instead of grieving over their deaths.

The letter to Jane could wait another day. "May I come with you? I'd like to learn more about making medicinal concoctions."

"Of course you can." Aunt Tessie gave her an approving nod before glancing toward Lily. "Would you like to come with us?"

Lily shook her head. "I'm not very good in the kitchen. Unless you think you'll need my help, I'd like to walk over to the boat and check on Papa, Jasmine, Jensen, and Tamar. I want to make sure they haven't had any problems since Blake and I saw them last week."

"Of course, dear." She beckoned Camellia toward the hall, where they headed to the back entrance and outside.

The air was cold, quickening their footsteps as they crossed the distance between the house and the separate, one-room kitchen. Warmth replaced the chill as they entered the functional room, and Camellia breathed in the mixture of pleasant smells. Coals smoldered in the fireplace that took up one wall, their heat warming her cold cheeks.

She glanced up at the copper pots and black, cast-iron cookware suspended from the ceiling beams overhead. A pair of shelves on the wall to her left was crowded with jugs, tall bottles, ladles, clay crocks, and tin plates. Sitting in a corner beneath the shelves, a wooden butter churn waited for fresh cream. To her right, she noted a tall safe holding bowls, baskets, and an impressive supply of canned vegetables. The fourth wall was used for drying. Herbs with their stems pointing toward the ceiling were fastened in neat bundles, hanging between and over two long tables next to the safe. The plank surface of one of the tables held labeled jars filled with leaves, seeds, creams, ointments, and wood shavings.

Aunt Tessie handed her an apron before she walked to the table with the labeled jars. She picked one up and shook it before removing the lid. "I'll need you to draw some water and put it on the fire to boil."

Camellia tied her apron strings and picked up a black kettle from the hearth. She worked the pump as Aunt Tessie got out some cheesecloth and filled it with curls of bark. "How did you learn about taking care of people?" Camellia asked.

"Experience mostly." The older woman waved a hand toward the safe. "My mother taught me which herbs, flowers, and roots to grow or gather. Sweet myrtle for congestion, aloe for burns, willow bark for fever, and many others. Most of the plants out there in the woods can be used as remedies, but you also need to know which ones to avoid."

"Will you teach me?" Camellia suspended the kettle on the cooking arm and waited for Aunt Tessie to drop in her packet of willow bark before swinging it over the coals.

"I'd be delighted to. Anna has never had time or the inclination to learn."

While they waited for the kettle to boil, Aunt Tessie began the lesson. It didn't take long for Camellia to realize she would need to take notes, so she ran back to the parlor to retrieve her stationery and writing implements. By the time she recorded the information from Aunt Tessie, the tea was ready.

Aunt Tessie arranged the teapot, cup, and saucer on a serving tray.

"If you will get some of the ginger cookies from that jar, we'll be ready to take this to my brother."

Camellia followed the older lady up the stairs, opening the bedroom door for her. "Do you want me to wait out here?"

"No. Come on in and help me check our patient's dressing." Aunt Tessie put down the tray and turned to Mr. Matthews's bed.

Embarrassment attacked her as Miss Tessie examined Mr. Matthews's leg, but that disappeared as she concentrated on the wound and learned how to check for infection. Black sutures held the skin together where the leg had been removed below the man's knee. She could not imagine what pain he must have gone through.

Their patient was querulous and restive until they pulled the bedcovers back over him. "I don't want any of that nasty swill of yours, Tessie."

"Come now, Mr. Matthews." Camellia smiled at him. "I am anxious to see how effective our remedy will be."

He frowned but didn't resist as she plumped up his pillows and helped him sit in a more upright position. "We've got some ginger cookies for you, too. What if we dip one of them in the tea to sweeten it some?"

"I suppose."

She flattered his efforts and coaxed him to continue trying until he downed a full cup of the willow bark tea.

"You have a natural talent," Aunt Tessie complimented her as they left the bedroom. "And you're so pretty that men seem to naturally want to please you."

Camellia almost stumbled on the next step. She grabbed hold of the balustrade to keep from tumbling to the floor. Was her physical beauty an attribute God had given her for some reason other than snagging a rich husband? Like a stone plopping into a quiet pond, the thought rippled through her past assumptions, changing them forever. Had Aunt Dahlia been wrong in advising her to pursue wealth and ease as her primary goal in life? Jonah's face flashed in front of her, and she heard again his condemnation of her shallow dreams and plans. He'd been right all along.

Aunt Tessie stopped and looked over her shoulder. "Are you dizzy?"

"No. I j–just realized something." How could she explain what had happened? Her life had changed. She felt like a veil had been ripped away and now she could see the banality of her existence. Nothing would ever be the same again.

Raising an eyebrow at the enigmatic answer, the older woman continued her descent.

After a moment, Camellia loosened her grip and followed her to the first floor. She didn't have time right now to ponder her epiphany. She had a lot of things to learn if she was going to fulfill her purpose.

&

"His name is John. . .John Champion." Anna's pale green eyes seemed to have caught a spark from the nearby fireplace. Her smile was at once tentative and hopeful. "He is a very handsome man, even with his scar. . . ." She blushed. "At least he is to me."

Imagining someone who looked like Tamar's husband, Jensen, Camellia tried not to cringe. She was determined to avoid making assumptions based on appearance as she once would have done. "What kind of work does he do?"

She followed Anna's glance around the room, but everyone else was engrossed in their own conversations. Aunt Tessie and Blake were talking about his father, making plans for a special wheeled chair to help him move about. Blake's father considered his next play on a chessboard while Lily and Jasmine sat opposite him, joining forces in an attempt to defeat him.

"He works on the *Catfish*."

An image of a saddle being placed over the back fin of a splashing fish took form in her mind before Camellia realized Anna must be referring to a steamboat. "He works on the river."

"Yes, and he should be coming to town within the next week or so." Anna gazed into the distance and sighed. "His captain generally comes through here before the Missouri River freezes and puts a stop to northbound travel."

"Maybe you can invite him to dinner so all of us can meet him," Aunt Tessie piped in.

The opportunity of getting to know this man intrigued Camellia, too. She would like to see if he cared for Anna or if the romance was one-sided. He didn't sound like much of a Lothario, but Anna was such an innocent when it came to matters of the heart. How could she be otherwise, living on the edge of the frontier?

A vague sense of discontent had begun to awaken in Camellia as the end of the year approached. Neither Blake nor Lily seemed anxious to return south. Papa, along with Jasmine, had left Jensen and Tamar to guard the *Water Lily* and moved into the Matthewses' home, which was beginning to feel quite crowded. He led the worship service at the church in town and spent the rest of his time helping out with the chores that had been left undone after Mr. Matthews's accident.

Jasmine and Lily cleaned house, Anna worked at the store, and Aunt Tessie spent most of her time in the kitchen, preparing meals for the large household. She had told Camellia she felt free to do so as her pupil was taking such good care of her brother. Reverend Matthews's recuperation had occupied Camellia's time. . .until now. Since he was doing better, she found herself with too much time on her hands. She had written to Jane and to Thad, and she helped out with the chores, but she wanted to do more. She wanted to do something meaningful.

"He won't come." Anna's sad voice dragged her back to their discussion. "But he does attend church if his boat is still here on a Sunday."

Making a face, Camellia considered the young woman sitting next to her. "That's good, but it would show more serious intentions if he were to come calling at your home."

"I've invited him before, but he always refuses."

Camellia put a finger on her chin as an idea popped into her head. "We'll have to see what we can do to fix that problem."

"What do you mean?" Anna's concern was apparent in the frown on her face.

"I'm not very adept with hairstyles, but we can go to the *Water Lily* and ask Tamar to do one of her special arrangements." She looked at Anna's shapeless gray wool dress, her excitement growing as she considered the possibilities. "We'll need to see if any of my clothes will fit you."

"I—I don't know if that's a good idea."

"Trust me." Camellia imagined the finished product. She would take Anna's pleasant looks and turn her into a real belle. If he was not toying with her affections, this man for whom Anna pined would have to declare his intentions or risk losing her to some other suitor. "It's a wonderful idea."

She stood and glanced toward Lily. "Anna and I will be upstairs."

"That's nice." Lily waved at them before returning to her game.

Camellia grabbed Anna's hand and dragged her up the staircase and into the bedroom she shared with Jasmine. "I think you should wear my blue-and-beige walking dress. The cut is very modern, and the colors will complement your skin."

"I don't think I would dare wear one of your dresses to Devore's. What if I spilled something on it?" Anna's eyes rounded as Camellia held up the silk gown. "I could never replace such a beautiful dress."

"You don't have to replace it, silly. All you have to do is wear it to work." She held the dress up to Anna's neck. "This will make your beau realize what a lucky man he is."

Anna blushed. "I. . .I don't—"

"Do you want him to notice you?"

Anna nodded.

"Do you want him to hold your hand and give you compliments?"

Another nod.

"Then you're going to have to trust me. I have a great deal more experience in these things than you. If you'll do what I suggest, you'll soon have Mr. Champion bowing to your every whim."

"But I'll never be as pretty as you."

"To a man who loves you, you will be prettier than any other woman born." Camellia smiled in her direction. "We just have to make sure he realizes that he does love you. Then you'll see. Your Mr. Champion won't have eyes for anyone else."

Over the next several days, Camellia coached Anna in the ways to walk, talk, and flirt with a fan. She called on all of the lessons she'd received at La Belle Demoiselle. She walked with Anna to the store each morning and watched her interact with the customers, dispensing advice and tips after each visitor departed. By the time Blake and Lily came to collect her around noon, the store would be filled with eager customers.

It took until the middle of December, but Anna was now much more polished and self-confident. She could exchange banter with the customers while taking care of their shopping needs. Mr. Devore was happy with the increase in sales and encouraged Anna to listen to her sister-in-law's advice.

Soldiers came by more often and spent more time, and more money, each visit. Anna blamed this phenomenon on Camellia's presence more than any changes in her. But Camellia gave all the credit to her sister-in-law as winter settled in around them.

Anna had blossomed, even though the weather was not warm at all. As long as she followed Camellia's advice, she would surely be a bride by the time spring returned to Missouri.

Chapter Thirty-three

$\mathscr{J}$ohn strode into the store, hope riding high in his heart. He'd begun to think they would never reach Cape Girardeau before the Mississippi became impassable. Every bend in the river seemed to harbor yet another Union ironclad that wished to check their cargo and crew. They had spent more time docked each day than actually moving along the river. But they were finally here.

At least the delay meant he didn't have to worry about running into Blake. That would be a disaster of untold proportions. He felt certain the man would have come and gone in the months since he'd received word about his father's accident. He only hoped Blake was able to lift some of the burden from Anna's shoulders.

Worry nibbled at the edge of his mind as John wondered if Anna was still in Cape Girardeau. What if her father had died? What if she and her aunt had gone to Natchez with Blake? It was a possibility that had occurred to him some weeks ago. He didn't know what he would do if Anna was forever removed from his life. But a return to Natchez was out of the question. Everyone would be far better off if he never went ashore in that town again.

The little bell tinkled as he pushed open the door. John's heart clenched in his chest when he saw a pretty blond standing behind the counter. He could not see her face as her back was turned to him, but she was not his Anna.

A rustle of skirts from the end of the main aisle was accompanied by a quick intake of breath. "John, is it really you?"

His heart began beating once more as he turned and saw her. "Anna." He reached for her hand as he searched her face.

"I was beginning to worry something had happened to the *Catfish*." Her slow smile spread across her face, and her beautiful eyes filled with joy and welcome.

John felt like he'd come home. "It was a slow trip. The war, you know."

"You weren't caught in any battles, were you?"

He shook his head. "But every inch of the boat has been searched over and over again by suspicious officers. Not even a Confederate grasshopper could have traveled with us to Missouri."

Her giggle was like music. Was it his imagination, or had Anna undergone a change since his last visit? He couldn't quite put his finger on it, but something was different.

"I have someone I want you to meet." She put a hand on his arm and pulled him to the counter. "A new member of my family."

The blond who had been standing next to Mr. Devore looked up as they approached, a smile of welcome on her face.

Dismay and fear mingled in John's chest. He tried to separate himself from Anna, but she would not release him. He couldn't break free without drawing even more attention to himself.

"Don't be shy, John. You're going to love her."

He should have seen this coming. He should have made inquiries before walking into the store. But he'd been so focused on seeing Anna. And he'd been certain enough time had passed. Trapped by his impetuousness, John still realized all was not lost. The girl at the counter might not even recognize him. For the first time, he found himself glad for the scars that obscured his features. He managed a shaky smile as Anna introduced him, but not much more.

He needed to escape, get out of the store, get out of town. His pleasure at seeing Anna was overcome by the necessity of keeping his identity hidden. "I'm sorry, but I have to leave now."

Lily's younger sister frowned at his abrupt announcement.

Disappointment stole Anna's smile. "Is something wrong?"

John shook his head. "I'll come back later." He pulled his arm free and began to back away.

As he reached the front door, the bell tinkled, and a couple entered the store. Out of habit, he turned the burned side of his face away to keep from frightening the female.

She was chattering at her escort but stopped in midsentence with a gasp as she caught sight of him. "Jean Luc?"

With those two words, his whole world crashed around him.

৯৪

"Stay out here, Camellia." Lily ignored the huff of irritation from her sister and strode to the stockroom door.

Anna was already in the room, turning up a lamp to bring light into the windowless room. Blake was right behind her, and Jean Luc lagged farther behind.

Lily was impressed by the cleanliness of the spacious area and the order in which Mr. Devore kept his extra stock. Floor-to-ceiling shelves held everything from baking soda to jewelry, all neatly labeled. It must make reordering simple.

Blake snapped the door shut as soon as Jean Luc entered. His brows were pulled down by a ferocious frown, and he stood with his feet spread and his arms crossed over his chest.

Anna moved away from the lamp and faced her brother. "I don't understand what's going on. How do you know John?"

"First of all, his name is not John." Blake spat out the words. "He's Jean Luc Champney, a wastrel, a thief, and a scoundrel. He has tried to cheat me out of everything I ever cared for."

Lily was as surprised as Anna by Blake's denunciation. "He saved your life and mine that night after the *Hattie Belle* was set on fire."

"It's more likely he was trying to cover up his own culpability and failed to get off the boat in time."

Anna looked from one of them to the other before turning to Jean Luc. "Please, would someone start at the beginning?"

"I will." Jean Luc stepped forward, his shoulders drooping. "I deserve all of your brother's scorn and enmity. I've done things. . .terrible things. I thought at one time that I could start over, leave behind all the mess I caused, and begin my life with a clean slate."

Lily's heart fell as she heard the man's confession. She prayed for guidance to navigate the murky currents of their shared past. Peace settled over her like a warm fur coat. Glancing toward Blake, she could see the condemnation on his face. She stepped closer to him, letting her shoulder rub his arm.

"It all started the night I lost my boat in a card game."

"Half a boat," Blake said, correcting Jean Luc's statement.

Jean Luc nodded. "My father was very angry, even threatening to keep me away from his business. Then Lily bought the other half of the boat, a controlling half, and I decided I could regain the *Hattie Belle* through her."

Lily put a hand to her chest. Jean Luc had never been romantically interested in her. The realization stung, but looking back over the events of the past, she realized she was more than happy with the way God had worked things out. And very thankful she hadn't lost her heart to him.

"When all my efforts failed, I hired a couple of men to tear up a couple of the staterooms." Jean Luc turned to her, confusion apparent in the twist of his eyebrows. "Even that didn't stop you. So I hired them again and told them to do more damage, enough to keep your boat docked for a few days until I could figure out another way to succeed."

The disappointment of learning Jean Luc had not been enamored of her faded as she listened to his tale in growing horror. "You set the *Hattie Belle* on fire?"

"That was never my intention."

"You see now why Jean Luc isn't an acceptable suitor for my sister." Blake's voice was smug. "He's dangerous. He needs to be locked up for trying to destroy our livelihood and for attempted murder."

"I cannot argue with you." Jean Luc held up his hands, crossed at the wrist, and bowed his head. "I'll go with you to the constable. I'll confess to my misdeeds."

"Wait a moment." Lily stepped between the two men. "That story is all fine and dandy, but it has a few holes in it."

"I don't know what you're talking about." Blake kept his voice low.

"I'm talking about the fact that I never heard this from you." She pointed a finger at her husband. "I'm talking about your letting me believe Captain Steenberg and his henchmen were the culprits. You never mentioned that Jean Luc had any part in the mess they left."

"Why should I?" Blake shrugged. "He was dead. Why upset his grieving parents further? You and the rest of the town were saying he was a hero for sacrificing his life to save our lives and the other boats in the harbor. I didn't see any reason to reveal the truth."

Lily tried to set aside her feelings of betrayal to consider Blake's explanation from a logical standpoint. Would she have done the same thing? She didn't know. "I still wish you had told me. Now I have to wonder what other things you have failed to tell me about because you see no need to 'reveal the truth.'"

Blake's arms fell to his side. He looked startled by her words. "I'm sorry. I thought I was protecting you."

"I would have thought you would know I'm not some delicate flower that needs to be protected from the bumps and bruises of life."

An arresting look entered his blue eyes. "You may be able to stand on your own, but you must allow me to protect you. It's my right and my pleasure as your husband."

"Rest assured we'll talk about this later when we're alone, but what we need to focus on right now is Jean Luc and Anna."

"You needn't worry about that." Anna stepped directly in front of Jean Luc. "Did you set my brother's boat on fire?"

He straightened his shoulders, his facial features showing resignation. "Not directly, but it was still my fault."

"Did you try to murder Blake?"

"No." The word shot out of him like the blast from a cannon. He glanced at Lily. "I was trying to free him, remember? I knew someone had to get the boat out into the river, so as soon as I knew you and Blake were safe, I went to the pilothouse."

Lily nodded. "I remember."

"It's true he was not the one who tied me up."

"I almost died that night." Jean Luc touched the scarred side of his face. "When I woke up in a strange town, I thought God had given me a second chance. I returned to Natchez several months later, but everyone thought I was dead. It was wrong of me to try to escape the consequences of my terrible decisions. I know that now. I see that it was cowardice on my part, a desire to escape punishment. But at that time, I convinced myself it would be kinder for my parents. They had gone through so much already. I was content to make a living on the river. I knew I didn't deserve anything more because of what I'd done. But then I met you, Anna, and everything changed. I fell in love with you. . .with your honesty and purity."

A new thought occurred to Lily. "You're the one who sent us the note about Blake's father."

Blake's head jerked as if from a slap.

Jean Luc nodded. "Anna was struggling to survive. She needed your help."

"Didn't you think I would recognize you when I saw you here?"

"I thought you might have left again when I didn't see your boat in the harbor." Jean Luc shrugged his shoulders. "Besides, I couldn't stay away from her any longer."

Blake put his hands on his sister's shoulders and moved her to the side before pointing an accusing finger at Jean Luc. "You'd better learn how to stay away from her, because I'm telling you now that you won't be seeing her again."

Anna gasped. "Blake, please. I'm a grown woman. I can make my own decisions."

"No, he's right." Jean Luc lifted his chin. "You're much too good for me."

"Yes, she is."

Lily could feel the heat of her husband's anger from where she stood a foot away. Jean Luc looked so dejected. While she could not agree with his decision to run from his problems, she could understand how high a price he'd paid for his actions. At this moment, he reminded her of her father. He'd run away when he should have stayed and persevered.

Blake reached for his sister's elbow, but Lily stopped him with a shake of her head. "While I appreciate your concern for your sister, you should give Anna the chance to decide her own future now that she knows the truth about Jean Luc."

He turned his frown on her, but Lily would not back down. She knew she was right about this. Reaching for his hand, she pulled him toward the door. "Let's leave them here to thrash out their problems."

"That's a good idea." Blake's frown did not abate at all. "And I can use the time to hunt down the sheriff and lodge a complaint against him."

Lily seemed to be the only one who heard his threat. She shook her head, dragged the door open, and pushed him through it. "You have five minutes. I doubt I can hold my husband off for any longer than that."

❧

"I'll never understand women." Blake took aim at the piece of wood on the chopping block and split it with his ax.

"I don't think we're meant to." Henrick Anderson picked up the two halves and placed them on the growing pile of firewood. "It's our job to love them and protect them. But as for understanding them. . ."

"Lily is barely speaking to me. She seems to think I had some nefarious reason to keep her in the dark about Jean Luc's treachery."

"Did you?"

Blake grunted. "Of course not. The *Hattie Belle* was gone. By the time I woke up, everyone was saying what a noble thing he'd done to sacrifice his own life for the sake of the other boat owners. Like everyone else, I thought the man was dead. I thought he was beyond taking responsibility for his actions, and I didn't see why his parents should suffer for his misdeeds."

"That sounds logical to me."

"Then why is Lily so miffed?" Blake put another piece of wood on the block. "Why can't she see the truth?"

"She probably can." Henrick chuckled. "But if I know my eldest daughter, she is wondering if there are other things you've been less than truthful about. For your own good reasons, of course."

"That's ridiculous." Blake concentrated on his chore for several minutes—splitting the wood released some of his irritation.

Sweat trickled into his eyes, and he stopped to wipe his brow. "I don't understand Anna, either. She ought to be glad she found out who 'John Champion' really was before she committed herself to him."

"The girl's heart is bruised if not broken." Henrick spoke gently. "Since Jean Luc has disappeared—"

"A fact she seems to blame on me."

"Yes, well. . .I'm sure you didn't arrange for his boat to leave Cape Girardeau, but you probably weren't unhappy to learn of the man's departure."

Of course he wasn't unhappy. Blake didn't want to have to go to the authorities and swear out a complaint against the man. And he wouldn't. . .as long as Jean Luc stayed away from Anna. He put down the ax, crossed his arms over his chest, and waited for Henrick to continue.

"So now that Jean Luc is gone, you're a convenient target for her disappointment."

"That makes no sense at all."

Henrick shrugged. "As I said, it's our job to love the women in our lives, not understand them."

The man sounded just like Camellia—shallow, foolish Camellia— the girl who had told him earlier this morning that he should bide his time. She'd actually suggested he might give the other two women a little time to recover from their disappointments instead of trying to defend his actions. When had she become so mature? When had she grown more levelheaded than Lily?

First she had become Aunt Tessie's assistant, nursing his father and learning how to make remedies. Then she had taken Anna under her wing and showed her how to be more self-confident. Now she was dispensing advice to him. It made absolutely no sense.

"This world would be a sorry place without the ladies." Henrick chuckled again. "Logical or not, we're much better off with them than without them."

"That's easy for you to say." Blake glanced toward the house. "You're not married to a single one of them, nor do you have a sister to watch over."

"No, only three daughters. And I thank God every day for putting them back in my life."

The older man's words struck a chord in his heart. Shame hit Blake. He should be focusing on his blessings—having a wife and a sister who loved him in spite of his shortcomings. They might be put out with him now, but one day they would forgive him. At least he hoped they would.

Chapter Thirty-four

Mrs. Naomi plopped down beside Jean Luc as he whittled a piece of driftwood. "What are you making?"

Hunching a shoulder, he looked at the pattern of grains. "A bird, I guess."

"A seagull!" She clapped her hands together. "You have a fine talent at whittling."

Jean Luc shrugged. What did it matter? His life had come to another dead end. He never should have fallen in love with Anna Matthews. He should have kept to himself, kept his heart free of entanglements. Hadn't he learned yet that he had nothing to offer others? Blake had been right when he'd condemned Jean Luc. He couldn't blame the man for his anger or for the way Anna had run from him that day.

"You've been moping around here for more than a week." Mrs. Naomi's soft voice pulled him from his roiling thoughts.

Jean Luc looked at the river, its muddy surface sliding past them. "I don't know what to do."

"We'll be back in Cape Girardeau by Christmas Eve. Why don't you plan on going to the church service? Your sweet Anna should be there."

"I can't."

Mrs. Naomi squinted at him. "I don't understand what happened between you and that young lady, but I know how much you care for her. And it seemed to me she was taken with you, too."

"That was before her brother told her about my past. He knew me when I was a different man. I tried to hurt him and his wife. And I almost succeeded in getting all three of us killed."

"I see." Mrs. Naomi put a hand on his arm. "I have to admit that sounds pretty awful."

Jean Luc grunted as the knife in his hand slipped and pinked his thumb. A dot of red appeared in the fleshy center of the appendage. He concentrated on it to keep his emotions at bay. When he was sure he could speak without betraying himself, he looked at her kindly face. The captain's wife had been a good friend to him, almost a second mother. But how could she understand? "It was—and is—inexcusable."

"You have given your life to Jesus, haven't you?"

He shrugged. "I guess so."

"No." She shook her head. "There's no guessing when it comes to this. Either you are a child of God or you are not. Jesus died on the cross because He is committed to saving you from eternal damnation. If you've asked Him into your heart, He's washed away your past sins. Even God does not see them anymore."

"But the earthly consequences are still there."

"Yes, and you have to face up to those. But always remember that Jesus loves you. He knows not only what you did but also every thought inside that thick head of yours. And He still has His arms wide open to you."

A faint hope entered Jean Luc's chest. In the turmoil of having to admit his past, he'd neglected Christ's love and acceptance.

Mrs. Naomi winked at him. "As soon as we dock, I want you to go to that girl and lay your heart in front of her. If she rejects you, it will hurt, but you can survive her rejection with God's love to sustain you."

Jean Luc flattened his palm and studied the spread wings of the bird he'd whittled. He could feel his own heart soaring with the freedom Mrs. Naomi's words were bringing to him. "You're a very wise woman."

"I couldn't sit still and let the devil convince you with his lies. He'd like nothing better than to separate you from God, but don't you let him get away with it. No matter what happens in Cape Girardeau, you can always lean on Him."

He offered the seagull to her, but Mrs. Naomi shook her head. "You're going to need a gift to give your girl for Christmas."

Jean Luc smiled. For the first time since seeing Blake and Lily, he began to believe everything might turn out all right.

&

"When are we going back to Mississippi?" Camellia looked down at her feet as they walked the path to the church on Christmas Eve.

Lily thought for a moment her younger sister had returned to the immature girl she'd once been, the girl who thought of nothing beyond the next social occasion and the newest fashion plates. Then the likely reason for Camellia's question occurred to her. "Are you missing that handsome Captain Watkins?"

"No, that's not it." Camellia lifted her skirts to avoid a puddle. "I would like to see Jane of course."

"Of course." Blake joined the conversation as they walked three abreast.

Lily frowned at him before returning her attention to Camellia. "I've been so impressed with you, Camellia. You've always had a tender heart when it comes to taking care of others, but now you've turned that talent into a calling. You've learned so much about healing and effective treatments. You should be proud of yourself."

"That's just it." Camellia sighed. "Blake's father is getting better now. He really doesn't need me anymore. I want to be useful. I want to make a difference. If you're right and God has given me a calling, I need to find a way to use it. I thought I was helping Anna, but now look at her. She's practically walking on air since Jean Luc showed up this afternoon."

"I know." Lily glanced toward the couple walking a few yards ahead of them, their heads inclined toward each other. "Isn't it romantic?"

"I don't see why everyone else is so pleased to see Jean Luc and my sister together," Blake complained. "Have all of you forgotten what he did?"

Lily planted her feet in the path and tugged on his arm to make him face her. "Your sister is happier right now than she's been since the day she discovered who Jean Luc really was."

"I always thought you had a soft place in your heart for that man, but you're letting your emotions rule your head."

"That's like the pot calling the kettle black." Lily heard Camellia mutter something and move away. She waited a moment until she was sure no one would overhear her words. "If you're wondering whether or not I ever loved Jean Luc Champney, you can rest easy. Yes, I did have a bit of a soft spot for him. His parents tried to force him into their idea of a proper future the same way my aunt Dahlia and uncle Phillip tried to do to me. But that's all it ever was." She pointed a finger at him. "You're the only man I've ever loved."

"I didn't mean—"

"While we're on the subject of Jean Luc, I want to point out a few things for you to consider. First is that he has lost a lot more than you or I have. Sure, we lost the *Hattie Belle*, but I thought you were happy on the *Water Lily*. I know I have been. And God has blessed us abundantly. We have family and friends and a life that has not been spent hiding from our past."

She could see that her words were beginning to get through to her husband. He was finally starting to understand why she'd been so put out with him lately. She had waited for him to discover these truths for himself, but maybe she should have been more direct back when they first found out whom Anna had fallen in love with.

"So you think he should be forgiven? Allowed to escape the consequences of his actions?"

"What I think is that we are not supposed to judge him. Anna has told us he's a Christian. He is our brother as surely as Anna, Camellia, and Jasmine are our sisters. By taking on the role of judge, you are inviting bitterness to creep back into your soul." She took hold of one of his hands and held it to her cheek. "You have only recently rooted out the bitterness you had against your father. Can't you see that you are inviting more pain into your life—our lives—by holding on to this anger against Jean Luc?"

He raised his other hand and cupped her face. "You're a very smart woman, Lily Matthews."

"That's right." Happiness brought a wide smile to her lips. "And don't you ever forget it."

Blake laughed with her, dropped a light kiss on her lips, and grasped her hand in his larger one. "I have the feeling that if I dare to forget, you'll remind me."

❧

Henrick read the story of Christ's birth from the Gospel of Luke to the church that evening. As he spoke of the wonder of that night, the promises of the host of angels, and the birth of the world's hope, Blake closed his eyes and prayed.

He laid at Christ's feet the anger he'd been carrying toward Jean Luc and the worry that his sister had fallen in love with the wrong man. He asked for forgiveness and felt Christ's answer deep inside. Peace and reverence filled him.

By the time the service was over, he knew what he had to do. As they left the church, he asked Henrick to take all of the girls home while he talked with Jean Luc. He could see Lily's worried frown and Jean Luc's fear, but he smiled at both of them, shooing his wife away as he waited for the church to empty.

"I'm sorry about what I did to you and Lily." Jean Luc shuffled his feet and looked at the door with longing.

Blake sat down in one of the empty pews. "I'm sorry, too. I'm sorry you felt cheated and that you had to pay such a high price for your immaturity."

As the words rolled off his tongue, he praised God inwardly. It was only through His power that Blake could utter such phrases and mean them.

"Thank you for understanding."

"You are the one who sent me that note about my father, aren't you?"

Jean Luc nodded. "I didn't know she was your sister. Not until the day she told me that she wished her brother was here in Cape Girardeau. When she told me your name, I couldn't believe it."

Blake tried to imagine what the man must have felt. He wondered if he would have done the same thing if he'd been in Jean Luc's shoes. "It must have been a hard thing for you, knowing you would have to face your past."

With a sigh, Jean Luc sat in the pew opposite Blake. "I knew I had to do it. I still hoped to evade you, you know. I stayed away from Devore's for several months, even when the *Catfish* docked here. I wasn't sure Anna would still be here."

"Why did you come back?"

"I love your sister."

The four words were spoken with an intensity Blake could not ignore. He remembered too well the feeling that he had to get back to Lily no matter the cost. He held his hand out to Jean Luc, who took it after a brief hesitation. "You're invited to come back to our home tomorrow and have dinner with us."

Jean Luc's hope shone as bright as the sunrise. Even the scars on the right side of his face couldn't detract from his joy. "Thank you, Blake. I promise to make your sister happy."

"I still have hope she'll turn you down." Blake clapped him on the shoulder and rose, smiling at the other man to show that his words were not to be taken seriously. He had the feeling his sister was going to accept Jean Luc's offer, and he was beginning to find peace with the idea of welcoming him into the family.

❧

The food on the Matthews family's table was as sumptuous as any of the meals Jean Luc had eaten with his parents, but the atmosphere was very different.

Anna presented him with a platter filled with succulent slices of meat. "Did you try any of the roast duck? It's one of Aunt Tessie's specialties."

Jean Luc patted his stomach. "I couldn't eat another bite if I had to."

She nodded and returned the platter to an empty space on the far side of her plate. "I'm glad you came."

"I'm happier to be here than you can imagine." He touched his napkin to his mouth. "It's the best Christmas I've ever enjoyed."

"Excuse me." Blake stood and tapped his water goblet with a spoon to get their attention. "Now that we've all enjoyed a wonderful meal, my wife and I have an announcement to share with you."

Camellia, sitting on his left, squeaked and put both hands over her mouth. Did she already know what Blake was about to say?

Jean Luc turned his attention to the foot of the table as Lily stood next to her husband, her gaze locked on his face. Blake took her hand and brought it to his lips, kissing her knuckles in an open display of affection that surprised Jean Luc. He loved Anna. He knew that for certain. He could not imagine a future without her in it. But he wasn't sure he would ever feel comfortable letting others see his feelings so clearly.

Lily blushed and tugged her hand away, apparently sharing some of Jean Luc's discomfort. But the affection in her eyes never dimmed.

Blake turned his attention back to the other diners. "Lily just told me this morning that we're going to have a baby."

The room filled with noise. The women squealed and pushed back their chairs, even Anna. They surrounded Lily and practically carried her out of the room, their eager questions and exclamations trailing behind them.

"Congratulations." Lily's father raised his glass to Blake. "Having a child is one of the most rewarding, challenging experiences you'll ever have."

Blake's father nodded. "I'm happy for you, Son. I know you'll be a good father."

"Coming from you, Pa, that means a lot to me." Blake cleared his throat, and Jean Luc thought he saw the sparkle of a tear in the man's eye.

Jensen cleared his throat and stood, offering a hand to Blake. "Congratulations."

"I'm happy for you." Jean Luc added his voice to the other men's. "You're a lucky man."

"Not lucky." Blake exchanged a glance with him. "I'm blessed beyond imagining." The joy radiating from Blake was nearly as warm as the fire in the parlor as they joined the ladies.

Anna looked up as Jean Luc approached her, her expression shifting between uncertainty, excitement, and affection.

"Could you show me the way to your father's library? I wanted to look for a particular volume he mentioned during dinner." Jean Luc knew his excuse was weak, but it was the only way he could think of to separate her from her family for a few minutes.

Anna nodded and rose from her chair. As she put her hand on his arm, he could feel the weight of Blake's gaze. He smiled in what he hoped was a conciliatory way. "We'll be right back."

The lamp in the hallway flickered as they passed it. Anna stopped long enough to pick up one of the tallow candles lying next to the lamp and light it before leading him to a door at the end of the hall. "The library's in here."

Instead of entering the room, Jean Luc reached in his pocket and drew out the carved seagull, holding it in his open palm to present it to her. "I'm sorry, but I couldn't find a box to hold this."

Her mouth formed an O of surprise. "For me?"

"Yes." His throat closed up. Jean Luc swallowed hard and wondered what to say next.

Anna took the tiny bird and held it up. "It's beautiful."

"Not as beautiful as you." Remembering what he'd planned to do, Jean Luc dropped to one knee in front of Anna. His heart threatened to explode out of his chest as he took her free hand in his, but he was determined to say the words he'd been practicing since Blake invited him for dinner the day before. "Anna, I have admired you since we first met. You're dedicated, resourceful, hardworking, and a woman of abiding faith. When I look at you, I see the gentle side of Jesus, and I find hope for a happiness I know I don't deserve. I love you, and I hope you'll consider spending the rest of your life at my side."

Silence answered him. Jean Luc's pulse sped up further. Was she going to reject him? He looked up at her and saw tears in her eyes.

"Anna, why are you crying? Don't you understand? I want you to marry me."

"Yes, I understand, John—Jean Luc, and I would like to. . ." Her voice faded into silence, and she shook her head.

He could hear the resignation in her voice and knew she was about to turn down his offer. His heart clenched. "Do you love me?"

Anna nodded.

His pain diminished somewhat. If she loved him, surely they could work out any other problems.

"I'll marry you—"

He stood and tried to take her in his arms, but Anna held him off with an outstretched arm. "Please let me finish."

Jean Luc nodded and stepped back to give her some breathing room.

"I fell in love with you before I really knew who you were, and now that I do, I find myself concerned about the past you hid from me. I cannot marry you until you have dealt with that past." Her gaze begged him to understand her words. "It's not right for your parents to be grieving your death. As soon as the river opens up again, you need to return to them and let them know the truth. Then I'll marry you."

Now it was his turn to be silent. Could he do it? Could he return to Natchez and face them? Could he bear their condemnation? Calm filled him, the whisper of Christ reassuring him. He would not be alone no matter what happened. "I'll do it."

"Good." Her smile of approval warmed him. "There's one other thing."

Jean Luc raised an eyebrow. "I'm beginning to feel like Jason and the Argonauts."

Anna giggled. "I don't need a golden fleece. I want to go to Natchez with you. I want to meet your parents and be there to support you."

This time when he moved to embrace her, Anna did not demur. He wrapped his arms around her and held her close to his heart. When he covered her lips with his own, emotion welled up in him. Love, tenderness, protectiveness, and a myriad of other feelings he couldn't even name. All he knew was that he, like Blake, was blessed beyond all imagining.

Chapter Thirty-five

Camellia was tired of chaperoning "the lovebirds," as Blake called Anna and Jean Luc. She'd been given that responsibility in Cape Girardeau when Jean Luc left his ship and took up residence at a boardinghouse in town. Now that they were back aboard the *Water Lily*, she could relax. There were way too many people aboard for the lovebirds to need an assigned chaperone.

Bidding Aunt Tessie and Reverend Matthews good-bye the day before had pulled at her heartstrings, but as soon as the paddle wheel began churning the muddy water, Camellia began looking forward to returning to Mississippi.

With an hour to fill and warm sunshine outside, she wandered up to the pilothouse to see what her father and Jasmine were doing. As she stepped onto the hurricane deck, she heard her little sister's voice.

"Why did Jesus want to make people suffer?"

Papa was standing behind the wheel, but he took his gaze from the river and frowned at Jasmine. "Who told you Jesus wants anyone to suffer?"

"Blake's papa said it yesterday in church."

He frowned for a moment before understanding dawned on his face. "Oh no, Jasmine, you misunderstood what he was talking about. Jesus was not happy with His disciples because they weren't letting some youngsters through to talk to Him. He told them to let the children come closer. That's what it means when the Bible says, 'Suffer the children to come unto me.' And He reminded His disciples that all of us have to believe in Him with the same open faith that children have."

Camellia didn't know why she hung back a bit. She only knew she didn't want to interrupt their conversation. She stood at the top of the stairwell, feeling the importance of this moment in her heart.

"So He liked children?"

"Yep. In fact, He loved them. And He loves you, too."

Jasmine tossed her hair over one shoulder with a flick of her wrist. "I love Him, too, Papa. I want to be close to Him like those children in the Bible."

Her sister's words took Camellia back to the day she had confessed her faith in Jesus. She had been even younger than Jasmine was now, but she had known exactly what she was doing.

"Tell me what you know about Jesus."

Why was Papa questioning Jasmine? Why didn't he tell her she was saved?

"He is God's Son who was born a long, long time ago in a stable. When He grew up, He did miracles like healing people who were sick or lame or blind. The important people were upset with Him, and they killed Him and buried Him in a cave."

"That's very good, Jasmine. I can tell that you've been listening closely in church. So why do we talk about Him? After all, He's been dead for a long time."

"No, He hasn't." Jasmine looked toward her father. "When His mama went to the cave where He was buried, He wasn't there anymore."

"Where was He?"

Camellia could see Jasmine's shoulders bend forward as she considered how to answer Papa's question.

"He rose from the grave and told His friends not to worry. He said He was going to heaven to make houses for them."

"That's exactly right, honey. I'm so excited for you." Papa hugged Jasmine. "Once you ask Jesus into your heart, the rest of your life will be different. Are you ready to take that step?"

Camellia's little sister nodded. "Yes, Papa, I want Jesus to fill me up with His love."

Unable to contain her joy, Camellia clapped her hands. Both Papa and Jasmine turned to where she stood. She ran forward and embraced both of them. "I'm so happy for you, Jasmine."

"Let's pray together." Papa glanced back at the river to check their progress. Then he put an arm around each of them and closed his eyes. "Father God, we come into Your presence with hearts of thankfulness, praise, and joy. We give thanks for these my daughters who are Your children. Thank You for revealing Yourself to them, and thank You for letting me witness their abiding faith firsthand. Please accept Jasmine into Your fold and watch over her as You do for all your children. Keep us ever mindful of You and Your wondrous plans for our lives. . . . Amen."

"Amen." Camellia and Jasmine chorused the word at the same time.

Looking out on the winding river ahead of their boat, Camellia thanked God again for this day, her sister's faith, and the wonderful Christian examples in their family. On a beautiful morning like this one, everything seemed perfect. Even the war seemed a continent away.

&

"Grant is obsessed with winning Vicksburg."

Jonah stared at his brother across the counter at the shipping office. Eli had aged a decade since the war began. His hairline had faded back, making him look more like Father, and the furrows on his forehead had deepened since the last time they'd been together. "Yes, but for good reason. If we can only gain control of Vicksburg, we'll choke off the supply lines and communications of the Confederacy."

"I know." Eli put a hand over his mouth and coughed long and hard. When the paroxysm was over, he drew a handkerchief from his pocket and wiped his forehead.

Jonah wondered if the physical changes in his brother were more from illness than advancing age. "You sound terrible."

"I'm better than I was a week ago." He reached for the goblet sitting on the desk in front of him and took a long swallow of water. "Renée and I have both recovered, but the children are still struggling with fever and chills. We are just thankful it's not yellow fever."

A shudder passed through Jonah at the dread his brother's words caused. With the privations of war and the arrival of summer, an outbreak of yellow fever was likely.

Eli put down his water. "You're not going to get me off the subject of General Grant. Is it true he's trying to dig a tunnel around the city of Vicksburg?"

"Yes, it's true." Jonah sighed. Concentrating on the campaign strategy of his leaders was better than worrying about the future.

"Does he think he's trying to change the course of a meandering stream? That's the Mississippi, the Father of Waters. He must have no concept of its strength. The spring rains have already begun. The floods will wipe out his efforts and probably kill a lot of good men."

"I know. The water is already threatening the dikes at New Orleans."

"You've been to New Orleans?" Eli's expression turned eager. "Is Sarah still holding court? How are Mama and Papa?"

"Well enough, although Father almost shot me when he realized I was wearing a Union uniform."

Eli chuckled. His cough returned with a vengeance.

Jonah wished he could do something to ease his sibling's symptoms. The thought took him back to the days when Camellia tended him so gently. Nostalgia and yearning swept through him, but he'd become adept at pushing those feelings to the back of his mind. "I think you should go upstairs and rest." He pushed himself up from the leather chair on the opposite side of his brother's desk.

"Visiting with you is as good as any tonic my wife has given me." Eli stood, too, stepping around his desk to give Jonah a hug.

"What does your doctor say?"

Eli threw him a rueful glance. "Doctor? We've not seen one of those for the past month."

"There's help at the fort."

"But they're needed to tend the soldiers."

"That's a ridiculous notion. I can find someone to at least prescribe a remedy for your cough."

"Don't worry about us. God will provide."

Jonah put a hand on Eli's shoulder. "Perhaps He is providing. . . through a brother with the right connections."

"Just pray for us."

"Always." The love he felt for his sibling swelled up. Before Jonah could form the words to express his affections, someone knocked on the library door.

Eli's frown returned as one of his servants poked her head into the library. "I'm sorry to disturb you, sir, but you have visitors."

"I thought I left instructions that we are not receiving."

The young woman bobbed her head. "They are from out of town."

No matter who the visitors were, they would not want to remain in a sick household. Jonah looked at his brother. "Why don't you let me go and explain the situation?"

"I wouldn't mind your support." Eli swallowed hard to suppress yet another cough, and the two of them walked to the parlor.

When they entered the room, the first person Jonah saw was Blake Matthews. His heartbeat increased a notch. Then he realized that two ladies were with the man—and one of them was the only woman who'd ever turned his world upside down. His mouth turned as dry as a desert. "Camellia."

While Eli greeted Blake and Lily, Jonah could hardly keep his eyes from devouring Camellia. She was wearing a yellow dress almost the same color as her hair. In combination, they formed a halo around her that made him think of angels.

His brother indicated the sofa and chairs. While he explained the situation in his home, Jonah took a seat next to her. A thousand contradictory impulses attacked him.

"What are you doing here?" Her voice was barely more than a whisper.

"This is my brother's home." He saw her cheeks redden and wished he could recall the words. He hadn't meant his answer to sound so insolent.

"Of course. I just thought you would be in Confederate territory somewhere gathering information. But I see you are wearing your true colors now."

The venom in her words opened a gulf as wide as the river between them. A gulf he knew he couldn't bridge. She was as dedicated to preserving the Old South as he was to changing it.

"I thought you would be in Vicksburg with people who think like you do." The sarcasm in his voice was a mask for the pain in his heart. Why did this one woman cause so much emotional turmoil in him? She didn't even have to try to be aggravating. Her presence in his brother's parlor was enough.

"As a matter of fact, I've spent the last several months in Cape Girardeau."

His jaw dropped. "With Yankees? Have you had a change of heart?"

"Not that it's any of your business, but Blake's family lives there. His father was in a bad way, so we went up to see if we could help."

Jonah snapped his mouth shut. She was right. She didn't owe him an explanation. He had absolutely no claim on her. But that didn't stop the curiosity consuming him.

"Camellia." Her older sister's voice interrupted their private conversation. "Did you hear that? Eli, my sister has learned so much about taking care of the sick and infirm that she now carries her own medicine bag. It's chock-full of everything your poor family could need."

Eli's gaze met his own. A thankful prayer filled Jonah's heart at the answer God had sent before they'd even made their requests. Perhaps he would even get a chance to explore the changes in Camellia while she was here.

Chapter Thirty-six

Camellia hummed a song as she climbed the stairs, a tray with bowls of warm broth in her hands. Although she missed her sisters, taking care of the Thornton boys and Renée had filled her time.

Blake had returned to the *Water Lily* with Lily and Jasmine as soon as they realized the danger, but he had come to check on her and the Thornton family daily.

She bumped open the boys' bedroom with a hip. "How are y'all doing this afternoon?"

Brandon and Cameron were out of bed, studying their lessons in one corner of the room. Remington, the youngest, had been the first one to catch the croup, and he was the slowest to recover from its ravages.

Setting the tray between the two older boys, she walked to Remington's narrow bed. He was propped against several pillows, his dark hair falling over his forehead. "I'm ready to get up."

Although she sympathized with him, Camellia shook her head. "One more day to make sure the fever doesn't return."

He groaned and rolled his eyes. "It's not fair. Cameron and Brandon don't have to stay in bed."

"At least you don't have to read this awful poetry." Brandon made a face at the book in his hands.

"Or find the answers to equations," Cameron chimed in. He put down his pencil and reached for one of the bowls of broth. "This smells great."

Remington looked toward the table. "Can I at least get up and eat at the table?"

"Your fever is gone." Camellia reached for his wrist and checked his pulse. It was no longer rapid and thready. "I think it will be all right."

Pleasure entered his face, but the youngster did not throw off his covers. "You'll need to leave, then. I only have on my nightshirt."

Camellia nodded. "Be careful, though, and get right back into bed as soon as you're done." Exiting the room, she checked on Renée before heading back to the first floor. Everyone was on the mend. She should be able to rejoin her family in the next day or two.

She saw Jonah before she was halfway down the staircase, and her cheeks flamed in reaction to his intense gaze. Why did he always affect her this way? Straightening her shoulders and taking a deep breath, Camellia continued her descent after a brief pause. She wanted to check her appearance before facing him, but retreat was not an option. "Hello, Jonah."

He nodded his head in greeting. "I was looking for Eli."

Of course he was not here to see her. Why should he be? Jonah had left her behind after she'd thrown herself at him the last time they were together alone. Her pride rescued her from making a fool of herself again. "He's at the shipping office."

"I'm glad to hear that. How are your other patients?" Jonah's gaze slammed into her.

Trying to keep her heart intact, Camellia told herself his eyes were the color of wet moss in a swamp. "Mostly recovered. They don't really need me anymore."

"I'm sure you'll be glad to be back with your family."

"Yes, Blake and Lily have promised to stop in Vicksburg so I can check on Thad and Jane."

His lips lost their supercilious curve. "You must be kidding. I cannot imagine the Rebels will let you make a landing."

"Don't worry." She wondered if he regretted telling her to fix her interest with Thad. Or did he even remember giving her advice? The incident that seemed so clear in her memory apparently had no place in his. "Blake has spent some time in Vicksburg, and he has friends who will vouch for us."

"I hope you don't intend to stay there. General Grant has made that town his main target. When Vicksburg falls, the town's residents may well pay a high price for their resistance."

She could not believe the man's effrontery. Who did he think he was to attempt to advise her? "It's really none of your business what my plans are."

Green fire seemed to shoot from his eyes. "You really haven't changed at all, have you, Camellia? I should have known it was only a vain hope on my part that you might have set aside your childish tendencies, but you are a socialite at heart, and you will never change."

His words struck her heart with deadly force, their power shattering the protective wall she'd erected between them. Tears burned at the corners of her eyes. "At least when the South wins this war, I'll have Thad to care for me. I'll be surrounded by my loved ones while you either flee northward or land in prison for your betrayal of our way of life."

The color washed out of his face, and Camellia realized she'd gone too far. She opened her mouth to take the words back, but it was too late. Jonah turned on his heel and strode out of the house, slamming the door behind him.

Camellia sank onto the bottom step and rocked back and forth as anguish burned her heart. She ought to be glad they had been so honest with each other. Now she knew without a doubt they could never be happy together. But as she considered her future, she wondered if she could be happy without him.

❧

"Good morning, sunshine." Renée's familiar greeting brought Camellia's head up.

She planted a smile on her face for her friend's benefit. "I'm happy to see you up and about."

"Not as glad as I am to be out of my bedchamber." The short, dark-haired woman was pale, but Camellia could see the determination in her eyes. "I don't know how to thank you for all you've done since you got here."

Even though sadness lingered deep inside her heart, Camellia felt a sense of contentment in the knowledge her skills had helped the Thornton family recover their health. "It's my pleasure."

"Have you seen Brandon and Cameron?"

"They've gone to open the shop with Blake and Eli." Camellia rose from her place at the table and went to the sideboard to help Renée get some breakfast.

Renée pointed to the toast. "I think that's all I want to eat."

Her nursing sense took over. "You need something more substantial than that." Camellia spooned scrambled eggs onto the other woman's plate and added a slice of cured ham.

"That's enough." Renée laughed. "I don't want to be as large as a cow."

Remington dashed into the room then, his normal high spirits in evidence since he'd thrown off the effects of his illness. "I've finished my lessons. May I walk to Pa's shop?"

Renée kissed him on the forehead. "I'm glad you feel so much better, but I think you'd better stay inside today."

"Aww, Mama." He broke away from her, picked up a plate, and filled it with slices of crisp bacon.

Camellia put Renée's plate on the table and returned to her seat. "Blake said Jasmine and Lily are planning to visit again this morning."

"Really?" Remington was already chewing on bacon as he sat next to her. "I like Jasmine. She's funny."

Camellia and Renée exchanged a glance. Camellia doubted her sister would appreciate his description of the impromptu theatrics she'd performed for him during her visit the day before.

She sipped her coffee as she listened to Remington's rapid-fire comments and his mother's calm responses. Renée obviously knew how to respond to boyish enthusiasm.

"How much longer will you stay with us?" Renée's question interrupted her musings.

"Lily is anxious to get to Natchez."

"I can understand that. She'll want her family around her when the baby comes."

Camellia nodded. As long as she had the chance to visit with the Watkinses in Vicksburg. She had no doubt she could wrangle an invitation from Jane to stay with them. And Lily seemed amenable to allowing her to remain behind since she'd conceived the idea that Camellia was in love with Thad. And she was. . .or at least she would be as soon as she was near him again.

A flash of lightning, followed by the crash of thunder, made all three of them jump.

Remington's voice rose an octave. "Is that cannon fire?"

Camellia glanced toward the window and shook her head. "It's just another spring storm."

Renée shook her head as rain peppered the window. "I feel sorry for the soldiers outside in this deluge."

Where was Jonah? The question trembled on Camellia's tongue, but she could not voice it. She had not seen the man since Tuesday. Not that she cared, but she did want to apologize for her angry remarks. He had a right to his opinion the same as she did.

Had he been sent somewhere to spy once more? Or was he on board one of the naval ships? She shuddered to think of his pointing a cannon at the bluffs of Vicksburg.

"It's been a stormy spring." Renée pushed back from the table. "Eli says the river is high now and likely to flood."

"Lily will probably be more anxious than ever to depart." Camellia put down her coffee cup. "I suppose I'd better get my things packed."

Renée sighed. "I wish we had more time to visit now that I'm feeling better. I can never repay you for taking care of me and my household."

"You would do the same for us." Camellia folded her napkin and put it on the table. "In fact, Eli's parents—his entire family—have done the same for us already."

"They are a wonderful, giving, faith-filled family." Renée stood and shook out her skirt. "I am worried about Jonah, however."

Camellia's heart thumped. Had he been hurt again? Was that why he had not returned to his brother's home? Was he wounded? Her hands itched for her bag of medicines. If he was hurt, she wanted to treat him now that she actually knew what to do to speed up his healing. "Where is he?" Raindrops peppered the windows, and Camellia noticed how dark it had grown in the dining room.

Renée moved to light some of the candles in the room. "He's gone south where the fighting is the worst."

Which probably meant he'd once again donned his Confederate uniform and gone in search of information to pass along to the Union. She wondered if he would be caught this time.

"Eli and I pray for him every night, and for all of the soldiers fighting in this terrible war." Renée hesitated a moment before continuing. "I hope you don't mind that Lily told me about your Confederate beau. I know you have a good heart, dear, and you cannot be responsible for the person it chooses."

Camellia's cheeks felt as bright as the candles Renée had lit. She wanted to blurt out the truth. Of course she cared for Thad and worried about him. He was her best friend's brother. And he was handsome. . .and rich. . .and a good man, besides. The type of man she'd always yearned to marry. The type of man she would marry. Her head could and would rule over the desires of her heart.

Chapter Thirty-seven

We have family in Natchez." Lily felt like a parrot. How many times had she explained to the hard-faced Union soldier?

"Yes, ma'am, I appreciate that fact. But I need you to understand what's going on here."

Lily glanced past his right shoulder to the ships forming a floating city next to the bank. Soldiers, covered wagons, and horses made a raucous caravan of supplies from boat deck to the city of tents set some distance from the water's edge. "It looks like a great deal of enterprise to me. Do you plan to have a permanent settlement here?"

"That's not for me to say."

"Of course not." Lily tapped a foot as she waited for Blake and his Union escort to return from their inspection of the *Water Lily*. A movement in her stomach made her put a hand on her midsection.

The officer's gaze followed her movement, and an expression of surprise and awe came over his face. "Why don't you sit down, ma'am?"

"I believe I shall." Lily tried to reassure her sisters and Anna with a look of confidence as she returned to the seat she'd vacated when the Union soldiers first boarded their boat.

Camellia's gaze burned Lily's shoulders as she sat.

Anna reached out a hand to her. "God will protect us."

"Of course." Lily squeezed her hand before releasing it. "We'll be on our way in a few minutes."

"I hope so." Camellia picked at the lace on her sleeve.

Lily frowned at her sister as the soldier stepped out into the passageway. "Be careful what you say. I don't want us delayed any more than necessary."

Shouts from outside drew their attention to the single window. A string of logs had been laid to form a path for people on foot. One of them had apparently sunk under the weight of the foot traffic, leaving three hapless men standing thigh deep in thick, black mud. Their plight was causing great merriment from others as they tried to escape to drier ground.

After watching their lack of progress for a minute or two, Lily turned her attention back to the others. "Those poor men. I don't understand why everyone is laughing instead of offering to help them."

Blake strode into the parlor. "We'll be under way in a minute. Next stop, Vicksburg."

Jasmine clapped her hands, while Anna and Camellia looked relieved.

Lily stood and moved toward him. "Perhaps we should try to bypass the port there to avoid further delays."

"We cannot." Camellia tossed a desperate glance in her direction. "I must check on Jane and her family."

"I know we planned to do that, but I'm not sure the Confederates will even allow us to land there."

"But we have to try. I haven't received a letter from Jane since Christmas, and I'm very worried about her. Please, you must let me go see about her."

Lily glanced at her husband's tight face. She could tell he was leery of making the attempt. "Why don't we wait and see what the situation is in Vicksburg? Then we can decide our best course."

Camellia's eyes filled with tears, but she nodded, her heart obviously broken at the news that she might not get to see her beau.

Lily's own heart ached for her. She left her husband's side and sat down next to her sister. "We'll do everything we can to check on them."

"Thank you." Camellia pulled a handkerchief from the sleeve of her gown and used it to dash away the tears trying to escape her eyes.

Jasmine moved toward them, too, her dark eyes troubled.

Lily put her arms around both of her sisters. The hug they shared warmed her. "I love y'all so much. I'd do anything to make you happy."

As the *Water Lily* chugged away from the Yankee encampment, she thought about the families that had been torn apart by the war and sent a prayer of thanks to God for keeping the three of them together.

❧

Camellia ran the last few steps to the picket fence that surrounded Jane's family home. As she reached for the gate latch, the front door flew open, and a glad cry came from the young woman standing there.

"Jane!" Camellia picked up her skirts and dashed forward.

Jane met her in the middle of the front lawn, and the two friends embraced. "I can't believe it's really you."

"I know. It's been so long." Camellia leaned back and frowned. "Why didn't you answer any of my letters?"

A frown marred Jane's pretty face. "I didn't receive any correspondence from you at all. I thought you had forgotten all about me once you and your family went north."

"I wrote to you every week, telling you all about Blake's family and Cape Girardeau."

"None of them got through." Jane shrugged. "So I had no direction to put on a letter to you. But come inside, and you can tell me all about it."

"I only have half an hour to visit. Then I must return to the docks or Lily and Blake will come looking for me."

"Half an hour? That's not nearly enough time. You cannot leave me again so soon. Why don't you plan on staying for a while? I know my mother and Thad would love to see you."

Camellia gave her a hug. "I was hoping you would invite me. Maybe together we can convince my family I should stay."

"It will be perfect. Thad comes by to check on us every day, so your family can have no qualms about your safety." Jane pulled her up the steps and into her home. "I'll collect Mother and my cloak, and we'll go to the boat together to convince them."

Carried forward on the wave of her friend's enthusiasm, Camellia watched as her plan came to fruition. Jane's mother, an older version of her daughter, accompanied them to the *Water Lily* to convince Blake and Lily to let her remain. She didn't feel any pangs of regret as she stood next to her trunks and waved good-bye to her family.

On the ride back to the Watkinses' home, Camellia asked them what had been happening since she last saw them.

"We lost the steeple of the Baptist church to a Yankee shell." Jane pointed out the window. "And some of our slaves have dug a cave area for the family. We've retreated to it twice this winter."

Mrs. Watkins shuddered. "It's a terrible inconvenience."

"But better than braving death when the shelling begins."

Camellia couldn't imagine the fear these women had faced. "You are both very brave."

"Thad tells us to pretend we are staying in a medieval castle." Jane rolled her eyes. "I cannot quite manage that, but it is an adventure to make the place habitable."

Would she have to go to the cave? A frisson of fear slid through Camellia. Perhaps she should not have been so hasty to insist on remaining. At the end, Lily and Blake had left the decision up to her. Camellia had not hesitated at all, but now she wondered if she'd been foolish. Deciding it was too late to question her choice, she sat back against the cushions and prayed for God's protection.

Feeling better because of the peace that entered her heart, Camellia listened to Jane and her mother discussing the high prices and scarcity of even the most basic foods. Flour and sugar were almost impossible to find and certainly beyond the means of any but the richest of Vicksburg's inhabitants.

"Miss Claiborne told me last week that her father has taken apart their smokehouse," Jane reported.

Camellia asked, "Why ever would he do such a thing?"

Mrs. Watkins sniffed. "They boil the wood for water for broth."

"Are things so desperate?"

The carriage slowed to a halt as Jane nodded. "We may have to consider doing the same thing."

Camellia shook her head. She waited for Mrs. Watkins to disembark before turning to her friend. "I hope we can visit the hospital later."

"Of course." Jane climbed down and straightened her skirts. "I go over there nearly every afternoon. It's my Christian duty to offer succor to our brave soldiers."

The prospect of becoming involved with the hospital made Camellia feel much better. No matter what privations she might face, it would be worth it if she helped their soldiers heal. Aunt Tessie had taught her so much. She welcomed the chance to put her skills to work.

❧

The hospital slouching at one end of Pearl Street had serviced the sick and infirm for about ten years. Sunlight peeked between a pair of dark clouds and highlighted the ill-tended lawn, giving the area a foreboding air. Some of the windows had been covered with boards, probably to replace windowpanes shattered by enemy shells.

As the carriage dropped them off, Camellia wrapped her hand around the handle of her bag of medicines and ointments and lifted her chin. No matter how grim the setting or how difficult her self-appointed tasks, she was determined to make use of the talent God had given her.

A nun greeted Jane at the door, her face enclosed in a white wimple. "Thank you so much for coming again today, Miss Watkins. I know how much your visits mean to our young men."

"It's the least we can do, Sister Alice. We may not be able to fight in the battles, but we can support those who do."

Camellia waited behind them as the sister mentioned some of the men whom Jane must have visited in the past.

"Please excuse me." Jane turned to her and pulled her forward. "This is my dearest friend, Camellia Anderson."

"Welcome, Miss Anderson. It's kind of you to volunteer."

"I am eager to be of service, Sister."

Before the nun could answer, a groan from the room behind her focused all of them on the reason for being at the hospital. Sister Alice nodded and turned to the open door. Jane pulled her skirt close to her legs and followed the nun into the first room.

The smell reminded Camellia of the horrendous days on their trip from Jacksonport. But the number of patients then had been much lower than the number of men whose cots filled every available inch of floor space. Little room remained between the cots to allow them to maneuver. Now Camellia understood why Jane had insisted they leave off their hoops. Their voluminous skirts would have seriously impeded their progress.

The first bed they came to held a young man with dark, feverish eyes.

"Hello, Ray." The nun bent over him, raising her voice to counteract the moans coming from the other cots. "Look who I brought to see you today."

The poor fellow seemed oblivious to them. He moved his head back and forth on his pillow and made unintelligible noises, something between a grunt and a moan. He was obviously in a great deal of pain. His cheeks were splotchy, and his eyes bore a bright, fevered glaze.

"He seems much worse today, poor thing." The nun straightened and looked toward them. "I prayed with him last night, but today he is not even coherent."

Camellia put a hand on his forehead. His fever was dangerously high. If they didn't do something to remedy the situation, he would likely die before the day was out. Reaching for the bag at her feet, she opened it and looked for her bag of mint leaves. "Do you have a bowl of water and some clean rags?"

Sister Alice's face froze for a moment as she considered Camellia's question, but then she nodded and disappeared from the sickroom, returning a moment later with the required items.

Camellia sprinkled some of the crushed leaves into the water and stirred, watching as the water turned green. She soaked the rag in the treatment, pulled it out, wrung the excess water from it, and placed it on the soldier's forehead.

The result was immediate. He stopped tossing his head, and the glaze in his eyes dimmed a little.

She was relieved to see the calming effect of her treatment.

"You're an answer to prayer." The nun's voice was filled with joy and wonder. "We've been running low on supplies, and no one has the time or temerity to venture into the woods to collect fresh herbs."

Her hope gave Camellia a feeling of satisfaction. This was the Lord's doing. He had put her in this place at this time to do His will. It was an exciting, humbling idea. "I don't have enough for everyone, but we can begin by treating the most serious cases."

"This is wonderful." The nun steepled her hands and bowed her head. "Thank You, Lord, for providing in our time of terrible need." She was silent for a moment as she communed with God. Then she raised her head, determination in every line of her face. "Let's get to the kitchen and see what we can do."

Camellia closed her bag and nodded. She glanced toward Jane, who was already moving to another bed where she took the hand of the soldier and began talking to him in a cheerful manner. Each of them had something she could offer the men here. She hoped it would be enough to make a difference.

The hours sped by as she measured out dosages and gave them to the patients according to their needs. She ran out of willow bark first then camphor. By the time they left the hospital, her bag of medicines was much lighter, and every muscle in Camellia's back ached. But satisfaction overrode her pain. "We make a good team."

"I don't know that my part is important." Jane glanced at her. "But I cannot believe how much you learned in Missouri. You are saving lives."

"Don't be so modest. I may have some medicine to help relieve them, but you give them hope by talking to them and reminding them of their homes and families. Without the will to get stronger, no amount of medicine can heal them."

Camellia could see that her words had struck a chord with Jane. Her head lifted, and tears made her eyes gleam in the dusky light of late afternoon.

Jane reached for her hand and gave it a quick squeeze. "I'm so glad you've returned to Vicksburg. And I know someone else who will be equally delighted to see you."

Knowing her friend was referring to Thad, Camellia smiled. "I can't wait to see him, too."

"General Pemberton keeps him fairly busy, but I hope he'll be at home for dinner tonight."

Camellia looked down at the soiled material of her gown. "I hope I brought enough clothes with me."

Laughing, Jane linked arms with her. "If not, we'll have to share like we did at La Belle."

The words brought back happy memories. Her life had taken so many unexpected turns since then. Suddenly the time she'd spent in New Orleans seemed unimportant. But without it, she never would have formed this link with Jane. In these uncertain days, such friendships seemed especially important, so she was determined to treasure this one.

Chapter Thirty-eight

*D*inner had almost ended when Thad Watkins appeared in the entrance to the dining room. "Am I too late to dine with you?"

His mother shook her head, the dark curls on either side of her jaw quivering. "Of course not."

"Look who has come to join us." Jane pointed toward her.

"Camellia?" He turned his handsome face in her direction. "Is it really you?"

She pushed back her chair and stood. "It's so nice to see you, Captain Watkins."

Thad took two long strides to reach her and wrapped her in his arms.

Jane giggled, but when Camellia emerged from his embrace, she caught the look of disapproval from his mother. Her face heated, and she stepped back to put a proper distance between them. Her heart was pounding so fast in her chest, she felt like she'd run across the city. Putting a hand on her chest, she glanced back up at him.

"You're as beautiful as ever." His eyes made her think of warm chocolate.

She couldn't help the thrill that shot through her in response to his compliment and admiring gaze. "We're embarrassing your mother."

He cleared his throat and looked past her to his parent. "Please excuse my enthusiasm, Mother. I forgot myself for a moment in the excitement of seeing her here."

"Even though we are caught in the midst of war, we must not forget propriety. If we do, then it will not matter whether or not we win."

He left Camellia to move to his mother's chair and drop a kiss on her raised cheek. "You're right as always. Please forgive me. I promise to be more circumspect."

Camellia slid back into her chair and put her napkin back in her lap while one of the servants laid a fresh setting for Thad. Her heartbeat returned to normal as she watched him interact with his family.

The shadow of a beard darkened his chin, giving him a slightly dangerous look. But his smile was as bright as ever. "How have you been since leaving Vicksburg last fall?"

Jane passed him a basket of yeast rolls. "Camellia has learned how to be a doctor."

"Is that right?" His smile dimmed a bit.

"Not really." She shot a look of warning to Jane. Thad might not approve of women doing such masculine work. "You remember my brother-in-law, Blake Matthews?"

He nodded.

"We went to visit his family in Cape Girardeau, Missouri, because his father had been in an accident. Blake's aunt was caring for him, and she showed me some of the basic treatments she used."

"Don't be so modest, Camellia." Jane turned to her brother. "Even Sister Alice was impressed with her today. She has asked us to come back to the hospital again in the morning."

"I don't know if that's such a good idea." Thad's face wore a frown as his gaze moved between the two of them. "Now that it's growing warmer, yellow fever may settle on the hospital. I wouldn't want to see either of you getting sick."

"I agree." Mrs. Watkins pushed back her chair. "I think we should plan an outing instead."

"That's an excellent idea, Mother. I can ask for a few hours off tomorrow and take you ladies on a picnic."

Jane clapped her hands, but Camellia felt little enthusiasm for the idea. "But we promised Sister Al—"

"Don't worry about that." Thad put down his fork. "I'll send a note explaining that you've been detained. She ought not be so dependent on you anyway. I'm certain the doctors at the hospital have more than enough experience to take care of our soldiers."

Unable to protest further in the face of their enthusiasm, Camellia desisted. She didn't like the idea of disappointing the nun, but she was not free to follow her own inclinations. Perhaps she could at least use the outing to gather fresh herbs and roots to replace what she had used today. As her host and hostesses began to make plans, she made a mental list of what she would need. She was determined to use her time wisely and continue the work God had set for her to do.

❧

A distant thunderstorm woke Camellia from her troubled dreams. She stretched her hands over her head and wondered if it would rain all day. She was so tired of spring showers that turned the streets into muddy bayous and raised the level of the waterways surrounding the city. The storm would also put an end to the picnic and to her plan to gather medicaments.

Another clap of thunder sounded, this time much closer. She looked toward her window. The thick curtains stopped her from seeing much, but flashes of lightning shone around their edge.

As they faded, someone began banging on her bedroom door.

Camellia sat up and pulled the sheet up to her chin. "Who's there?"

"Camellia, wake up." She recognized Thad's deep voice. What was he doing outside her bedchamber? "Get dressed quickly and come downstairs."

She heard his footsteps as he walked away. What was going on? She pushed back the covers and put her bare feet on the floor.

Another knock on the door heralded one of the maids, who entered with a lit candle. "I'ma help you dress, ma'am." The girl sounded terrified. "We's all going to the caves."

More claps of thunder sounded, and Camellia realized what she was hearing was not the sound of nature. The city was under attack. The house shook as a mortar struck somewhere nearby. Would the next one land on top of the Watkinses' home?

The maid used her candle to light a three-pronged candlestick on the mantel. The additional light chased away some of the shadows in the room, making it easier for the two women to work.

The maid picked up the navy blue skirt she'd worn at dinner the evening before and shook it out. Camellia started to untie the collar of her dressing gown but realized it could serve as a chemise. The skirt went on over it, and she thrust her arms into the matching blouse, buttoning the cuffs with trembling fingers as the maid addressed the back closures Camellia could not reach. In record time, she was presentable, even though her hair was in a single braid and her nightcap was still attached to her head. The screams of the mortar fire made her head pound as she grabbed her bag of medicines and ran down the stairs.

Thad was pacing in the foyer.

"What's happening?" She had to raise her voice to be heard over the noise.

Thad looked grim. "It looks like the whole Yankee fleet has decided to converge here. But don't worry. We're too high above the river for them to be able to send soldiers into the city. The poor fellows would be mowed down by our boys before they got halfway up the bluff."

His reassurance brought her some relief. "Then what are they doing?"

"Probably just trying to rob us of a good night's sleep."

Jane tromped down the stairs, her hair still in a braid like Camellia's. "Then they are succeeding."

Mrs. Watkins was right behind her. She carried a candle in one hand and an ornate box that probably held her jewelry in the other. "Are we ready to go?"

Thad nodded and opened the front door.

Billowing smoke made all of them cough. Camellia couldn't see much through it except for the red and yellow flames from a nearby house that had caught fire. She climbed into the carriage after Mrs. Watkins and Jane, moving far enough over for Thad to sit next to her on the rear-facing bench.

"I can't come with you." He stood for a moment in the opening to the carriage, his face drawn.

Mrs. Watkins put down her jewelry box and reached for her son's hand. "You can't send us to the caves alone."

"It will be all right, Mother. You know Thad has a duty to fulfill." Jane pulled her mother back. "We'll be safe in the cave."

Thad threw a relieved glance at his sister before turning to Camellia. "I'm afraid we'll have to postpone our picnic."

Another mortar screamed overhead as if making fun of his statement. She waited until it sailed past before answering him. "Don't worry about that or about us. Jane and I will take care of your mother. You need to focus on keeping yourself and your men safe."

He took her hand and raised it to his lips. "Thank you for being so brave."

Although she didn't feel particularly brave at the moment, Camellia summoned a smile. "We'll be praying for you."

As soon as he let go of her hand, Thad stepped back and slammed the door shut. They heard his command to the driver, and the carriage moved forward.

She closed her eyes and began to pray that God would protect them and allow them to survive the night.

The ride through town was slow but steady. The shelling seemed a little less constant as they escaped the center of Vicksburg.

Swaying with the movement of the carriage, Camellia finished her prayer and opened her eyes.

Mrs. Watkins slumped in a corner, her handkerchief hiding her face.

Jane peered out of the carriage window, looking for all the world like she was no more frightened than if they were making a morning call. "We're almost there." The carriage stopped, and she pushed open the door without waiting for the coachman to dismount. "Come along, Mother. The sooner we're inside, the better you'll feel."

The cave was not as bad as Camellia had imagined. She had to bend over to navigate the entrance, but once inside, she found the roof sufficiently high so that she could straighten. Some of the household slaves must have already come over and lit the candles that glowed from alcoves in the wall. The dirt floor was covered with a rug, and several wooden chairs had been brought from the house.

"The bedrooms are separate from this room." Jane pointed to a corridor to her right. "We only dug two of them—one for females and one for any men."

"What about your slaves?"

Mrs. Watkins looked at her as though she'd grown an extra head. "What about them?"

Camellia glanced around for a secondary corridor. "Where do they sleep?"

"Outside. They're much hardier than you think."

She cringed at the cold note in the older lady's voice. Did she think the slaves didn't need protection, too? They were the ones who had dug the cave system for the family. It was inconceivable to her that Mrs. Watkins hadn't thought to provide a safe place for them to shelter. Yet she wondered if Aunt Dahlia and Uncle Phillip wouldn't agree with Mrs. Watkins's assessment. Camellia glanced at Jane and saw the same incomprehension in her friend's gaze. Was she the only one who thought the slaves deserved space in the cave?

Another anchor to her long-held affection for the Southern way of life fell away. Camellia could not imagine thinking so little of other human beings.

Mrs. Watkins yawned. "I think I'll lie down a little while. Do you have anything for a headache in that bag of yours?"

Camellia considered the question before nodding. "I have some chamomile for a soothing tea. Is there somewhere I can brew it?"

"We have a fire pit right next to the entrance." Jane took her mother's arm and headed for the back. "I'll come out to assist you as soon as I help Mother get comfortable."

Camellia picked up her bag and retraced her steps, taking a deep breath as she emerged into the cool predawn air. Several of the slaves were sitting around the fire Jane had mentioned, but they scrambled to their feet as she approached. "I'm sorry to disturb you, but I need to prepare some tea for your mistress." Spotting a pot to one side of the fire, she moved toward it. "Is there any water already drawn?"

The little maid who had helped her dress stepped forward. "Yes, Miss Anderson. I can fill that from one of the buckets."

"If you'll show me where they are, I'll be glad to do it for myself." Even as she spoke, Camellia realized how much she had changed in the months since she'd left New Orleans. The haughty student at La Belle Demoiselle was gone. Hopefully, she would never return.

Chapter Thirty-nine

Jean Luc wanted to turn and run from his parents' house. His throat was tight with fear. Why had he come? Why hadn't he said no to Anna?

Because she was right. The answer in his head didn't quiet his fear, but it did give him the strength to raise his hand and knock. They had talked about this moment several times during the voyage from Cape Girardeau, and he'd thought he was ready. But now he wasn't so sure.

"I'm right here with you, and so is God."

Anna's whispered reminder buoyed him. He reached for her hand, squeezing it to show his appreciation.

The door opened a few inches, and the familiar face of their butler appeared. "We have a side entrance for tradesmen."

"I'm not a tradesman." Jean Luc turned his head so the man could see the unscarred side of his face.

The butler gasped. "Master Champney? Is it really you?"

Jean Luc nodded. The butler pulled the door open the rest of the way and bowed. "Your ma and pa are in the library, sir. And they're gonna be so happy."

The welcoming look in the older man's eyes warmed him further. "Thank you, Carson. I hope you're right."

"Oh yes, sir. You're gonna be the prodigal son for sure."

Offering his arm to Anna, Jean Luc stepped over the threshold. "I'll announce myself."

Carson bowed once more and reached out a hand for Jean Luc's hat.

The house seemed unchanged, as though frozen in time. Ornate furniture from Europe clogged the hall, and his long-dead ancestors stared down at him as he escorted his fiancée toward the room the butler had indicated. He stopped for a moment and faced Anna. "Let's say a prayer."

"Of course." Her smile was as slow as ever, dawning with the stately radiance of the sunrise.

He took her hands in his own and bowed his head. He didn't know exactly what he wanted to say to God, but after a moment the words seemed to flow out of him. "Lord, thank You for this woman who is lending her strength to me. Please help my parents forgive me for deceiving them, and help them understand why I did what I did. I know how wrong it was, and I'm sorry for hurting them. Please help me to be the son they deserve, one who honors them in the way You always intended. Thank You, Lord, for hearing me. . . . Amen."

"Amen," Anna echoed. She stood on tiptoe and planted a feather-soft kiss on his cheek. "I'm so proud of you."

Jean Luc took a deep breath and pushed the library door open. His father was seated at his mahogany desk, a pile of papers in front of him. He looked up as the door opened. "What is it?"

His mother, seated in her favorite chair next to a southern-facing window, gasped and dropped the needlework in her hand.

"Papa? Mama? It's me, Jean Luc."

His father rocked back in his chair as though blown back by a high wind. "Jean Luc?"

Mama sprang from her chair and took a step forward before crumpling to the floor.

All three of them rushed to her side. Jean Luc picked up her head and shoulders and placed them on his lap. Anna bent over him and waved a handkerchief in front of his mother's face.

Papa fell to his knees on the other side of Mama. He picked up one of her hands and chafed it, but his dark eyes devoured Jean Luc's face. "Is it really you, my son?"

He nodded, overwhelmed by so many emotions he could not speak.

His mother's eyelids fluttered open, and a beautiful smile swept across her face. "You have come back to us."

Both of the men helped her regain her feet and led her back to her chair.

"Your mother never truly believed you were dead."

"I am so sorry. I didn't want to bring more shame to you," Jean Luc blurted out, forgetting the speech he'd practiced. "I almost died in the explosion of the *Hattie Belle*. When I came to, I was so ashamed of what I'd done. Of the pain I had caused my friends and family. . . . I didn't know what else to do except disappear."

His mother put a hand on his arm. "You should have known that we would rather have you with us no matter what happened. We love you, Jean Luc. Nothing you do or fail to do can ever change that."

"She's right." His father held out his arms to him. "I am the one who should be asking for forgiveness. I realize now how hard I was on you."

Jean Luc stepped into the embrace, hugging the dear man with all his might. "No, Papa. You were right to expect me to be a man. I'm the one who let both of you down."

"No, it was my fault."

"Why don't you all agree that none of us are perfect except Jesus?" Anna's calm voice broke through their conversation. "That is why He died for us, after all. We have many things to forgive of one another."

His parents looked toward Anna as though they'd only just realized she was in the room. Breaking free of his father's hold, Jean Luc swept a hand in her direction. "Please allow me to introduce Miss Anna Matthews, the reason I finally found the courage to return to you and the woman who has agreed to become my wife."

A brief pause filled the room. His parents looked at each other and smiled.

Mama pushed herself up from her chair and put an arm around each of them. "Welcome to our family, Miss Anna Matthews. We've been waiting for you for a very long time."

And Jean Luc knew everything was going to be all right.

ع

"Port Gibson has fallen, and still Pemberton won't send us out to face the Yanks." Thad paced across his mother's parlor, pounding one of his fists into a cupped palm. "He's going to cost us the whole war."

"Perhaps he thinks you need to stay here and protect the citizens of Vicksburg." Mrs. Watkins poured warm tea into a cup and offered it to her daughter.

Jane took the proffered cup. "I heard he's nothing more than a transported Yankee himself."

Camellia knew she should probably keep her opinions to herself, but she didn't think the man's reputation should be shredded by gossip. "I thought he was a hero in the Mexican War."

"That's true." Thad stopped his pacing. "But it's also true that two of his brothers are fighting for the Union."

Not wanting to start an argument, she desisted. Sometimes she caught Thad looking at her with a question in his gaze as if he still wondered exactly when she'd discovered that Jonah was a Union sympathizer. He wouldn't be happy if he knew the truth. But she had no intention of telling him. Nor did she have any intention of telling him about the time she'd spent with Jonah and his brother's family in Memphis right before coming here.

"Don't you agree, Camellia?"

She came out of the fog of her thoughts when she heard her name. All three were looking at her. "I'm sorry. I missed what you said."

"We were discussing whether or not we should leave Vicksburg." Jane put down her tea. "I think we should remain here and do whatever we can at the hospital."

Camellia nodded. She and Jane had spent a great deal of time working with the soldiers. "Besides, you've always said we are safe here. With its high bluffs and command of the river, Vicksburg will stand strong until the war is over."

Thad looked troubled as he considered them. "I don't know if that will hold true now that Grant and his army have gained a foothold in Mississippi. Especially since our general seems content to remain hiding in his garrison."

"I don't want to be so far from you, either." Mrs. Watkins nibbled at a cookie, one of the last they were likely to have given the rising cost of sugar. "We have our cave to run to in case of need."

"If you're certain, I must admit that I like knowing you are close by." Thad sat down on the sofa near Camellia's chair. "But I want you to promise that you'll consider limiting your time with the soldiers at the hospital."

Camellia's heart fell to her toes. She didn't like to cause further worry when Thad had so much on his mind. "The doctors have begun to rely on Jane and me to take care of the cases that are not so desperate.

Every day more soldiers are being brought in." She put a hand on his arm. "If you could see them in such pain and fear."

He covered her hand with his own. "Your tender heart is leading you astray, Camellia. I know you want to help, and I know you think that you are filling a need, but I want you to consider your health and your reputation, as well as Jane's." His gaze was sincere.

Camellia wanted to yield to him, but she couldn't form the words to tell him so. "I cannot stop going."

"Why? Why is this so important that you will risk my displeasure and my sister's well-being?"

Camellia pulled her hand from underneath his. "If you would come by and see what we do, perhaps you could understand."

"I don't have time for sightseeing. I am doing all I can to keep the Confederacy together." His voice hardened. "I don't want to forbid you, Camellia. I'd much rather you stopped voluntarily."

"Thad! You cannot mean what you're saying. Camellia and I are not in any danger, nor are we risking our reputations."

Jane's interjection stopped Camellia from answering him directly. But he had chosen the wrong way to win her compliance. No matter what happened, she was determined to continue her work at the hospital. He had no power to force her compliance, and if he tried to stop her, she would simply remove her belongings to one of the hotels in town and continue her work. Her shoulders straightened.

Thad held up both hands. "I'm sorry. I shouldn't have said that. I suppose it's just an effect of the strain I'm under."

Camellia kept her hands relaxed in her lap. She would not let him see how angry he had made her. Over the past weeks, she had thought she might actually be falling in love with Thad Watkins. But she had been mistaken. She could never marry a man who did not think her work as important as his own. Nor could she be married to someone with such a strict notion of what was acceptable behavior for a lady.

It wasn't as if she wanted to go dancing down the street in her nightclothes. She was trying to provide succor and support for wounded Southern soldiers. One day he might be wounded himself. While she did not wish such an eventuality on him, she thought if it happened, he might finally understand why she would not stop her work.

❧

Jonah chewed on a piece of hardtack and wondered when the army would move again. They had forced the Confederates to retreat all along their route inland across central Mississippi. Some said they would be going south next, to Port Hudson, where they would join up with General Banks and overrun the stronghold before moving to Vicksburg with a force greater than that of the Confederates.

After spending more than a week bivouacked in the small village of Port Gibson, Jonah found himself agreeing with the ones who thought Grant would continue forward to Jackson, the capital city of Mississippi, and cut off the railroad supply lines running between there and Vicksburg. If he managed that, the city on the river would be cut off from all hope of success.

Cage, the man who had first befriended him when they fought side by side in Missouri, limped over to where he sat and lowered himself to the ground. "We'll be on the march again before the end of day."

"Where to?"

"Edwards Station." Cage nodded to the north.

Satisfaction filled him. Grant was not going to wait for Banks. He was going with his bold plan to put a stranglehold on Vicksburg and force its capitulation. "I told you so."

Cage bumped him with his elbow. "No one likes a smart aleck."

"I can't help it if I'm smarter than you." Jonah laughed at his friend.

"And I can't help it if someone knocks the stuffing out of you."

Jonah sobered. "You've been a good friend, Cage. Your friendship is one of the few things I will treasure from this war."

"You can try to flatter me all you want, but I've seen who you truly are. You're nothing but a know-all and a pain, besides." Cage's grin took the bite out of his complaint. "But I guess I've invested this much time in saving your sorry hide, so I may as well continue watching your back for a little while longer."

Shouts ended their conversation as the men around them began gathering their meager belongings and wrapping them into their bedrolls. It was time to march.

Tossing his hardtack into a knapsack, Jonah stood and looked out across the unplanted fields surrounding the army. He wondered what the people in Port Gibson would do for food next winter. How long could they continue fighting against a superior force? When would they realize that they could not, would not win? He hoped it would be soon.

"Have you gotten any letters from your lady love?" Cage fell in beside him.

Jonah rolled his eyes. "Just because I kissed a girl doesn't mean I'm in love with her."

"Oh, ho!" Cage's eyes grew wide. "You kissed her? And she's an innocent?"

"Of course she is. She's a family friend. Her sister and my sister might be kin they are so close."

"Then you must be serious about her."

"I am not. She's all wrong for me." Jonah ran a finger under the collar of his uniform, wishing the wool didn't sting. Or was that his conscience? Why had he kissed Camellia? And not just once, but two times. As Cage had pointed out, she was an innocent.

He could close his eyes and still feel the wonder of that first kiss—the way her lips had parted in surprise and the way she had felt in his arms. And when he'd left her in Jacksonport, he'd done it again. And again she had responded to his caress as though there was some connection between them.

Perhaps he should have kissed her again in Memphis. Maybe that would have halted the harsh words between them. But if he had, he might have lost all control over his senses. He might have asked her to marry him. And he didn't want to find himself chained to some spoiled beauty for the rest of his life.

Cage was watching him, his gaze understanding. "Sometimes the heart knows what the head will not admit."

"Her faith is nothing more than a sham. She has no ideas in her head except clothes and money and finding a husband. Camellia Anderson is definitely not the type of woman I should marry."

"What you should do is not always the best thing."

Jonah looked at him. "Would you stop spouting such nonsense? You are not even married yourself. What do you know about it?"

Cage looked out over the fields, his gaze vacant. Then he shook himself and looked toward Jonah. "I once fell in love with a girl, but I let her get away from me. I thought she was not good enough for me, not serious enough, too focused on worldly matters."

It sounded to Jonah that the man must have met Camellia or

someone very like her. "What happened?"

He shrugged. "She married another man and is a wonderful wife to him. I saw that what I had mistaken for materialism was nothing more than immaturity."

Later that night when they bedded down, Jonah thought about Cage's story. Was he making a mistake to resist Camellia? Or was he being careful not to become unequally yoked?

Jonah wasn't sure, so he began to pray for an answer from the One who knew exactly what was in Camellia's heart. He prayed for discernment and wisdom, and he prayed for the patience to wait for God's answer.

Chapter Forty

The sound of marching feet brought Jane and Camellia out onto the front porch. Line after line of gray-coated soldiers passed the house, bayonets resting on their shoulders.

Jane pulled a handkerchief from the sleeve of her blouse and waved it at them. Grins and salutes answered her gesture. "Aren't they handsome?"

Camellia felt sick to her stomach. Yes, these men were clean and well outfitted. They seemed spirited and eager to get to the battlefield. But she couldn't help thinking about their destination. Fighting, killing, or perhaps meeting death itself. How many of the men now writhing in pain at the hospital across town had marched off in the same manner? "I wish I could tell them to turn back."

Jane stopped waving at them and turned to look at Camellia. "What?"

"Don't you see? Your own brother is amongst these soldiers. Aren't you worried about him? How many of these handsome men will return to Vicksburg? How many of them will soon be nothing more than corpses lying on a blood-soaked field?"

"That's not something you should be thinking about right now. Think about the victory they will win for us."

Camellia shook her head. "Whether the army wins a victory or not, many of these men—perhaps even Thad—will come back to us with grievous wounds. . .if they return at all."

"I knew it!" Jane grinned at her. "You're in love with Thad."

She couldn't believe her friend had drawn that conclusion from her words. "I am not in love with your brother. I'm only worried about him like I am about all of these men."

"I don't care what you say. I know the truth." Jane stuffed her handkerchief back into her sleeve. "You're only angry with him because he doesn't want us to continue going to the hospital. But don't worry. You'll soon change his mind."

"I don't want to change his mind because I'm not in love with him." Camellia's temper rose in reaction to Jane's teasing and her concern about all of the soldiers. She clenched her jaw and pointed a finger at Jane. "And if you make comments like that to him, you'll be leading him to believe something that is completely, absolutely, totally false."

Jane lost her smile. "Are you trying to throw me off by denying your feelings?"

"No. I am telling you the truth." Her irritation faded as she saw the hurt look in her friend's eyes. "Look at me, Jane. You know me better than most. Do I look like I am lying to you?"

They locked gazes, and Camellia tried to communicate all of the frustration and sadness she felt. A part of her would like to fall in love with Thad, but that was the old Camellia, the girl who wanted nothing more than a pampered lifestyle as the privileged wife of a planter. Now she knew she wanted more from life. She wanted to make a difference. And being married to someone like Thad would prevent her from even trying to reach her goals.

Jane sniffed. "I suppose not."

"Good. Then please respect my feelings." Camellia put an arm around Jane's waist. "I care for Thad like a brother, not as the man I want to marry."

"Are you in love with someone else?"

The question caught her completely by surprise. All of a sudden she could see Jonah Thornton's green eyes, auburn hair, and crooked grin. She could almost hear his distinct New Orleans drawl and feel his hand touching her cheek right before he kissed her. She tried to banish the memory and concentrate on answering Jane, but it was no use. Her cheeks flamed.

Jane's gaze sharpened. She stepped back and frowned. "You are! Who is it? You cannot hide it from me. Is it one of the doctors at the hospital? Is that why you are so anxious to keep going there?" Her mouth dropped open. "Or is it one of our patients? It's that tall, dark-haired, extremely handsome captain. What is his name. . . ? Oh, Luke Talbot."

Relieved that her friend had not discerned the truth, Camellia shook her head. "Of course not. He's married. Didn't you see the pretty girl who came to the hospital to visit him? I hope he doesn't have to lose his leg."

One of the passing soldiers called out to them, and Jane let the subject drop. As she waved to him, Camellia's mind whirled. She suspected the interrogation was only postponed, and she would have to do a better job of guarding her heart if she was going to keep her feelings a secret. At least until she sorted them out for herself. She didn't love Jonah Thornton, did she?

She couldn't. It had to be a mistake. Maybe it was because he'd kissed her. That had to be the explanation. She felt connected to him because he'd taken advantage of her. . .twice. No longer seeing the waves of young men marching past them, Camellia rubbed the back of her hand across her mouth. She would eradicate whatever connection might have been forged between them. It couldn't be love. Could not. The last time she'd seen Jonah, they had argued like a couple of children. She had barely thought of him since then.

As the parade of soldiers dwindled, she began to feel a little better. Jane turned back to the front door, and Camellia followed her inside. If her silly heart insisted on maintaining a connection to the wrong man, she would take one of the herbs in her bag for purging impurities. She had no other choice. Because no matter what her feelings might be toward Jonah Thornton, she was certain he felt nothing but disdain for her.

><

"Why don't they surrender?" Lily tossed the newspaper on the table and pushed her chair back. She was so worried about Camellia. Why had she let her sister and Mrs. Watkins convince her that the area would be safe? If she ever got Camellia under her wing again, she would not let her out of her sight until the war was over. . .if ever.

Blake shook his head. "The Confederates know that losing Vicksburg will split their forces in two. They will be a house divided."

"But they cannot win against Grant's forces. They may have the upper ground, but he can starve them. And I don't doubt that he will if he is forced to."

Aunt Dahlia, sitting on the opposite side of the table, moaned. "You should have brought the girl back here to me. I always knew your traipsing all over the country with your sisters would come to no good end. And now poor Camellia is paying the price for your stubbornness."

The words should not have come as a surprise to her. Aunt Dahlia would never approve of her unconventionality. Uncle Phillip was nodding his agreement with his wife's condemnation. She supposed they had forgotten how her decision to operate a successful steamship had helped support their lifestyle here at Les Fleurs.

"You cannot blame Camellia's situation on Lily." Grandmother sent a disapproving glance at her daughter and son-in-law. "The girl was determined to stay with the friend she made at that fancy finishing school that you encouraged her to attend."

"She's in love with Thad Watkins." Lily tried to push herself up from the dining chair, but her protruding abdomen made the maneuver impossible.

Blake and Papa both saw her difficulty and moved to assist her.

"Thank you." She managed a shaky smile for their efforts. Taking a deep breath, she turned her attention back to her aunt. "While Captain Watkins is not the man I would have chosen for my sister, I know he and his family will do everything in their power to keep Camellia safe."

Aunt Dahlia's face was pinched with worry. Lily knew she should be more sympathetic. Camellia had always been her favorite of the sisters. Lily was too plain, and Jasmine's black hair and violet eyes were too exotic for acceptance into the highest levels of local Natchez society. Camellia's blond curls, creamy complexion, and cornflower-blue eyes made her the perfect candidate. If the war had not come along, she had no doubt Camellia would have been the most popular girl in the city.

"I think you should go after her." Aunt Dahlia's suggestion was like an arrow through her heart. "Put that boat of yours to good use for once."

Blake put an arm around his wife's shoulders while speaking to Aunt Dahlia. "I think you have lost your mind."

Both Aunt Dahlia and Uncle Phillip looked shocked, but Lily could feel a bubble of laughter trying to escape her throat. Trust Blake to support her even though he'd argued against leaving Camellia in

Vicksburg. She leaned against his shoulder and sent him a thankful look.

"The Confederate batteries will shoot at anything that is moving up or down the river right now. When we passed through that area in March, things were already perilous. The only thing we could accomplish by taking the *Water Lily* to Vicksburg is to get her rammed or shot to pieces."

Grandmother cleared her throat to gain their attention. "Maybe her brave Confederate officer would escort her to Natchez if you sent a request."

Now Aunt Dahlia looked scandalized. "I hope you're not suggesting that she travel alone with a man. Her reputation could never survive such scandalous behavior."

"I'm not as worried about her reputation as I am her life." Lily rubbed her belly with a gentle hand as the baby inside shifted. "I would feel much better if she were here with us, but I don't see how we can accomplish that right now."

Papa returned to his place at the table. "We'll have to leave it in God's hands."

Lily nodded. "You're right as always, Papa. God will protect her as He does all of His children."

She had spent a great deal of time talking to God about her concerns as the situation worsened over the past two months. He had not answered her prayer with words, but His peace brought her some comfort.

Still, it was hard not to worry as they followed the progress of the battles taking place to their north. According to the reports of the local newspaper, General Grant had burned a swath through the countryside, isolating Vicksburg from all hope of support. After two unsuccessful assaults, he had decided to lay siege to the city. Lily could not begin to imagine the conditions her sister was experiencing.

"I think you need to lie down for an hour." Blake's voice tickled her ear.

Wondering how she would ever relax enough to sleep, Lily allowed him to lead her from the dining room. "Do you think we could get word to Captain Watkins?"

"I doubt it." His gaze was kind. "But I have thought of someone who might be able to help."

Lily stopped walking. "Who?"

"The Thorntons' youngest son, Jonah."

"Jonah? I doubt he would be any use to us at all."

The look in Blake's eyes told her he knew something she didn't.

Lily stomped her right foot. "Tell me."

He shrugged. "Eli told me he joined the Union army. He's currently with Grant's army and may be in a position to reach Camellia."

Excitement and hope coursed through her blood. Lily threw her arms around her husband, hugging him as close as she could with the baby between them.

A pang caught her by surprise, and Lily tensed.

"What is it?"

Blake's voice seemed to come from a distance as yet another pain struck, stealing her breath with its strength. Lily doubled over and grabbed her abdomen, trying to keep her composure as the truth became apparent to her. "You'd better send for the doctor. I think the baby's coming."

Chapter Forty-one

$\mathscr{J}$onah Thornton! I have a message for Jonah Thornton."

The voice called him from a dream, a dream of secret waterfalls and stolen kisses. With a groan, he rolled over and peeked out from the opening of his tent. "I'm Jonah Thornton."

The messenger's head turned as Jonah pushed himself up. He was young but carried his satchel with obvious pride. Reaching inside it, he produced a white envelope with Jonah's name printed in bold black letters.

"Thank you."

The boy's salute was crisp. Then he looked inside his bag and read the next name. "Tom Waterford! I have a message. . ."

Jonah put his finger under the seal to break it.

"A love letter?" Cage's drawl held a teasing note. "It's about time for the ladies to catch up with you."

His gaze dropped to the bottom of the letter and read the signature. His lips curled. "Yes, and her name is Blake Matthews."

Both of them laughed at the suspicious looks from some of the nearby soldiers.

Jonah raised his voice to explain. "*His* wife and my sister are close friends." He glanced at the stationery in his right hand:

Dear Jonah,
*   Lily and I are sending this note to you in the hope that you*

can help her sister Camellia. You may remember she is the sister whom we came to remove from New Orleans as the city was being occupied by Union forces.

Jonah rolled his eyes. If only Blake knew how closely acquainted he was with the middle Anderson sister, he would probably demand satisfaction instead of sending him a polite letter.

A few months ago, during a trip from Memphis to Natchez, we allowed her to visit friends in Vicksburg. After we reached Natchez, the situation on the river deteriorated further, and we have been unable to secure passage for her or permission to return to Vicksburg.

She is trapped within the confines of the city, and we are unable to reach her. If you could ascertain her whereabouts and conditions and report them to us, we would be very grateful.

Also, if you speak to her directly, you might wish to convey the happy news that she is an aunt to the most handsome little boy named Noah.

We appreciate your help in this matter and remain prayerfully hopeful that we may all survive this war.

With sincerest thanks,
Blake Matthews

Jonah's heart was beating so hard it felt as if it might jump from his chest.

"What's the matter?" Cage touched his arm. "Your face is as white as a field of cotton."

Unable to express the fear that had taken hold of him, Jonah shook his head. He had wondered from time to time where Camellia was. She had even told him she was planning to visit her friend and that pompous captain. But he'd never really thought her family would have allowed her to stay. Perhaps stop by for an afternoon visit, but then she should have gotten right back onto her sister's boat and sailed away to safety. "I have to talk to Grant."

Cage pulled his hand back as though he'd been burned. "General Grant?"

Jonah nodded. He had to sneak into the city and see Camellia to safety. In the past month, the situation inside the city had gotten bad. While the soldiers sniped at each other from their positions in the ravines and on the hillsides, no food had passed into the city for several weeks. The rumor was that the civilians and soldiers had been reduced to eating mule in place of beef and pork and that all the cats and dogs in the city had disappeared.

The townspeople had moved into caves to escape the shells falling into the city. He had to get to her, no matter the cost.

&

Camellia couldn't remember ever being so tired in her life. Her hand went to the small of her back, and she massaged the area.

"How long has it been since you rested?" Sister Alice touched her shoulder.

Looking out the window, she was surprised to see the sun dipping low on the horizon. "I'm not sure."

The nun frowned her displeasure. "You look ready to drop."

"Where's Jane?"

The nun pointed past the rows of cots. "The last time I saw her, she was sitting by some of the new arrivals."

A sigh filled Camellia's chest. Would the steady stream of sick and wounded soldiers never end?

"I'll go find her." Camellia checked the forehead of a soldier who had lost his left arm to a minie ball. It was cooler than yesterday. She pulled a notebook out of her bag and made a notation.

Sister Alice's habit bounced as she tapped her foot. "You need to leave right now, or you'll have to walk back in the dark."

"Yes, ma'am." Camellia smiled at the older lady. Sister Alice could be a tough drill sergeant, but her motives were always good. "I just have to tell Dr. Dickson I'm leaving."

"I'll tell him. You go on."

She knew when she was outmaneuvered. Walking to the outer room, Camellia collected Jane. "Let's go home."

Jane made a face. "You mean to the cave."

"It's safer than staying in town." As if to emphasize her statement, the whistle of a missile made both of them freeze.

The sound had become so common in the past weeks they could tell when it passed their location. The floor shook ahead of the *boom* as it hit another part of the city. Camellia hoped Willow Grove was unharmed.

"Let's go." Jane's dark tresses were limp, and her eyes no longer held a sparkle. It had been ground out of her by the death and sickness they encountered on a daily basis, compounded by the heat of summer, the uncomfortable sleeping cots in the cave, and the lack of proper nutrition.

Obed, the large, quiet slave who had been assigned to accompany them back and forth from the hospital, met them as they stepped outside. Camellia wondered what he did all day while they were inside. She was glad to have his escort, as the soldiers who seemed to inhabit every street of the city might have been a problem otherwise.

Jane kicked a pebble ahead of them. "I wonder how long it will take before the Yankees give up and go home."

"Is that what you really think will happen?"

"Either that or General Johnston's reinforcements will arrive. Thad says if they come, we will squash them between the two legs of our army." She slapped her hands together to illustrate the maneuver. "Vicksburg will never fall."

Another shell whistled overhead. Camellia looked up and saw its arc. No danger. She continued walking. "I don't know. They seem very determined."

They finished their walk in silence. Camellia wanted to reach out to her friend, but she didn't know how. It seemed they had grown in different directions. Jane still wanted the South to win. She didn't see anything wrong with their old lifestyle and couldn't wait to resume it.

Although Camellia deplored the war, she welcomed the change she believed it would bring. She wanted freedom for all slaves. She didn't want to return to the past, not since her eyes had been opened. Balls and fancy gowns had lost their attraction, as had every other aspect of a life of privilege. She wanted to spend her life in more serious pursuits.

Mrs. Watkins greeted them at the entrance to the cave. "I have a wonderful surprise for you girls."

Camellia and Jane exchanged a glance. All either of them wanted to do was eat a little and fall into bed. They'd both had a long day. And tomorrow wouldn't be any shorter or easier.

"What's the surprise?"

Mrs. Watkins giggled like a young girl. "Your brother has brought us a roast."

Tiredness receded as Camellia's mouth watered. For the past week, they'd subsisted on turnips and canned beans. "Where did he find a roast?"

"Who cares?" Mrs. Watkins led the way into the main room. "I thought you girls were never going to get here, and Thad insisted we had to wait for you."

The room that served as a dining room and a parlor had undergone a dramatic change since they'd left this morning. The large dining table from the house took up most of the space. It had been covered with a white cloth that reached to the floor. A pair of silver candelabra sat on either side of a tall vase of fresh flowers that dominated the center of the table. Four place settings, two on each of the long sides of the table, invited them to take seats and dine, really dine, for the first time since they'd retreated to the cave.

Thad stepped out of the shadows, a look of expectation on his handsome face.

Camellia wished for a moment she could be in love with him. But then sanity returned. Thad would make an excellent husband for someone. . .but not her.

"Welcome." He bowed and indicated the table. "If you ladies will take your seats, I'll check on our dinner."

Jane sat on the far side of the table. Before Camellia could slip into the seat next to her, Mrs. Watkins blocked her path. "Why don't you sit on this side? I know Thad would rather sit next to a pretty girl than his mother."

"I thought he was unhappy with me because of our time at the hospital."

Mrs. Watkins sat down next to her daughter and put her napkin in her lap. "He's past all that. His friends are impressed with the work you and Jane are doing. He told me so while we were waiting for y'all."

Camellia folded her lips into a straight line. Was she supposed to be mollified because Thad's friends had judged her actions acceptable? She managed to swallow her irritation as Thad returned, followed by three slaves.

He was so proud of his efforts. And she had to admit the food was outstanding. Thad was charming, telling them amusing stories about men answering roll call wearing only one boot or with a shirt on wrong side out.

Camellia laughed in the appropriate places, but her eyelids were threatening to close in spite of her best efforts. She held her napkin in front of her mouth to hide a yawn. "I'm afraid I must excuse myself." Camellia pushed back her chair.

Thad jumped to his feet and helped her, ever the gentleman. "I have something I need to discuss with you if you have a moment."

Tiredness washed through her. All Camellia wanted to do was climb into her cot, but a glance at Thad's tense features made her ignore her desire. "Is something wrong?"

"No, but I need to seek your advice on a private matter." His smile appeared as he offered his elbow. "Let's step outside."

When they reached the entrance to the cave, a cool breeze lifted the hair from the back of her neck. A group of slaves huddled near the cooking fire, their voices too low for them to hear.

Thad walked her away from them, to the edge of the light from their cave. She sat on a convenient boulder and watched as he paced back and forth in front of her. Another yawn threatened to crack her jaw. If Thad didn't hurry, she would fall asleep before he got started.

When he knelt before her, however, Camellia's sleepiness fled. Thad took possession of her left hand. "I don't know how much longer our troops can hold out. It's only a matter of time until we have to surrender to the Yankees. I'll be taken prisoner, but I'm very worried about what may happen to you."

"Please, Thad." Camellia tried to pull her hand from his grasp, but Thad would not release it.

"Let me finish before you say anything."

She sighed. "Go on, then."

"Mother and Jane have the protection of our family name. It will stop the Yankees from harming them. But you do not have a male protector nearby, and I think we should remedy that. You are a beautiful woman, accomplished and strong. It would give me great pleasure if you would agree to become my wife."

Camellia squeezed his hand. "While I am flattered by your offer, I must refuse. I am fond of you, Thad, and I admire your steadfastness, but I do not love you in that way."

"I will teach you to love me."

Her empathy disappeared, as did the desire to let him down easily. "That's not possible. My heart belongs to another man."

He let go of her then, his face slack with surprise. "Who is he? Is he one of the doctors at the hospital?"

Camellia thought of kindly old Dr. Dickson, who must be at least midway through his forties. "No. And I warn you to stop guessing before you further insult me. I appreciate your offer, but it cannot be."

Thad stood and brushed dirt off his trousers. "Why not?"

"You are going to make some lucky girl very happy." She put a hand on his arm. "And I really wish I was that girl, but we want different things for our lives. Since I've been working at the hospital, I've realized how much I can contribute beyond my looks."

"I rather like your looks."

She grinned at him, relieved when he grinned back. "Thank you for the compliment, Captain. You are quite attractive yourself."

He tilted his head to one side. "In that case. . ."

Camellia pushed herself up from the boulder. "Don't you see? We have a great friendship, but there's no spark between us. When I marry, I want it to be because I cannot stand the idea of living without him."

"You've given me a lot to think about, Camellia." He walked her back to the cave opening. "I'm sorry things didn't work out between us."

"Me, too."

As he strode back toward his station, she thought his step was not that of a man who was crushed by disappointment. That was a relief. She didn't want to hurt Thad, and she hoped he would find a wonderful girl he couldn't live without.

Searching out her own cot, Camellia completed her toilette with a minimum of fuss and climbed into bed, her eyelids closing the moment her head rested on the pillow.

Chapter Forty-two

A loud explosion woke Camellia, the concussion throwing her to the floor. For a moment she couldn't get her bearings. The darkness of the cave was absolute. She felt around her until her hand closed over the foot of her cot. "Jane?"

She heard the snick of a tinderbox, and a candle's flame dispelled the darkness. "Are you okay?"

Camellia nodded. She threw a wrapper over her gown and slid her feet into slippers. "That was close." The idea of being buried alive inside the cave made her heart pound.

Someone came rushing in, and her breath caught. Had the Yankees finally overrun them? But the face that appeared in their doorway belonged to one of the maids. "Please come quick, Miss Camellia. Someone's been hurt."

Grabbing her bag, Camellia followed without question. Was it Mrs. Watkins? Or one of the families who lived in a nearby cave? She prayed as she ran, leaning on God for the courage and strength to meet whatever awaited her.

The sky outside was much lighter than she'd expected after the gloom of the cave. The first rays of the sun peeked above the horizon. That was the direction they headed, toward the field of wildflowers and the old oak tree that had become a shelter for many of the slaves.

The oak tree looked odd to her, and then Camellia realized what was wrong. It was canted, leaning at an angle. Her breath caught, and she came to an abrupt halt.

"Come with me, Miss Camellia." The maid tugged on her arm. "Obed's bleeding real bad. Can you help him?"

"I'll try." Camellia ran to a small knot of women, pushing her way through them until she could see Obed's familiar face.

The wound was nasty. Flayed skin exposed muscle and bone. She used the belt of her wrapper to stop the bleeding and began cleaning the wound. Obed's face was turning gray, and she worried he was dying. "Hang on, Obed. I'm working as fast as I can."

His eyes opened, and he managed a shaky smile. "I'm not gonna go anywhere unless you say I can, Miss Camellia."

She threaded a needle and stitched up the worst of the wounds. At least the bones had not broken. The worst effect would be the loss of blood. If she could get Obed stitched up well enough, he should be okay.

She was finishing her work as a shadow fell across Obed's body. "What are you doing out here?"

Camellia looked up and saw the appalled faces of Jane and her mother. "Obed was hit by a bomb."

"His people will take care of him." Mrs. Watkins's voice was cold. Wasn't she worried about the man at all? Obed had worked for her family for years.

"His *people* have no medical supplies or experience."

Jane rolled her eyes. "Come back to the cave."

"I will when I'm through."

Several moments passed in silence. Camellia mopped up the blood and leaned back on her heels to see what else she needed to do.

"Come along, Mother. We can't make her come with us."

"I don't know what she expects us to do." Mrs. Watkins's voice floated back to her. "We can hardly keep body and soul together. It's all the fault of the Yankees. If they would just go away, we could resume our lives as before."

"Then I pray the Yankees never go away." Camellia's gaze met Obed's. The kindness and patience apparent on his face made her want to weep.

"Me, too, Miss Camellia. Me, too."

ॐ

The boat, Jonah's exit out of the city, was secure from the view of Confederate pickets. He'd gotten the location of Willow Grove from a bewildered prisoner they'd captured a few days earlier. All he needed to do now was get into the city, collect Camellia, and escape without being caught.

"I can set off a small mine at the end of one of our tunnels." Cage held up a torch to show him an artillery shell with a long lead.

Jonah remembered an earlier attempt to gain entrance through one of the tunnels they'd dug underneath the feet of the Confederates. "What will stop someone from shooting me as I emerge?"

"We've learned from our mistakes. This tunnel goes further than that last one. It burrows underneath their defensive positions and continues another quarter of a mile. You should come out somewhere close to the center of the city."

"No matter where it comes out, someone will hear the explosion and come to investigate." Jonah wanted to get Camellia out, not get them both killed.

Cage shook his head. "We'll time it to go off at the same time as a barrage of cannon fire. No one will notice. I guarantee it. Do you think I want you to get shot?"

"Of course not." Jonah clapped his friend on the shoulder. "When can we do it?"

"Give me five minutes."

Jonah went to his tent and pulled out the Confederate uniform he'd worn during the battle near Memphis. It was more than a little tattered, but that shouldn't raise any suspicions. He doubted any of the soldiers defending Vicksburg looked any better. He dressed quickly and met Cage at the mouth of the tunnel. "Are you ready?"

Cage nodded. "As soon as they start firing, I'll blow the entrance. I'll be praying for you."

"No matter what happens, I appreciate your help."

From a distance they heard the order to fire. The night sky lit up as one cannon after another belched out their deadly missiles.

"Godspeed." Cage pressed the detonator.

Dropping into a hunch, Jonah crabbed his way through the tunnel. He prayed for God's protection, prayed that he might reach Camellia, prayed that they might escape safely. The dim circle of the tunnel mouth came into view, and Jonah's heart climbed into his throat. This was the most dangerous time. He stopped to listen for a moment, trying to ascertain if anyone had noticed the explosion and was waiting for him to emerge.

Another round of shells exploded overhead, and he pushed forward, bursting from the ground with all the speed he could muster. Half expecting to meet the blast of a rifle, he rolled in a ball and tried to protect his head. . .and tumbled down a small rise to lie in the middle of someone's backyard.

No one was awaiting him. Jonah breathed a prayer of thanks and pushed himself to his feet. Now if he was seen, he would be just one of the occupying soldiers. He pulled his cap from the pocket of his trousers and put it on, pulling the bill down to hide his features. The chances of running into someone who knew him were not high, but he didn't want to take any unnecessary risks.

Willow Grove had been described as tall and yellow, with columns and a white picket fence. He looked around but found no house to match that description. Time to explore the neighborhood.

No dogs barked at him as he traveled the streets of the town. No cats slinked in the shadows. The only people he saw were dressed in uniforms like his own. He saluted when appropriate and moved past them with the confidence of a man who had a specific destination. It was a tactic that served him well.

Nearly an hour passed before he came upon a house matching the description he'd been given. It was dark, of course. The front door was locked, but a window next to it opened easily, and Jonah stepped into the parlor.

Moving as silently as he could manage, Jonah checked the rooms downstairs. By the time he climbed the stairs, he was certain the house was empty. If they had moved to a cave, he had no idea how to find Camellia. Desperation filled him as he checked bedroom after bedroom. What was he going to do?

"Stop right there, thief." The sound came from the landing behind him. It was a voice he remembered. "Raise your hands and turn around slowly."

Jonah did as ordered. "Hi, Thad. Is this the way you treat your friends?"

"You!" Thad raised the rifle an inch. "I ought to shoot you right here."

"But you don't want to get blood all over the floor, right?"

Thad's mouth twitched a little, and the deadly bore lowered until it was aimed at Jonah's chest instead of his head.

Jonah didn't know if that was much of an improvement.

"What are you doing here?"

"I came to collect Camellia, and your sister, too, if you trust me to get her out of here."

The rifle lowered a few inches more. "You're not going anywhere except prison."

"I can't." Jonah let his hands down. "I hear you have a flea problem there, and I'm terribly allergic."

"You'll be laughing from the other side of your mouth soon. I'm not going to let you slip away again. You've betrayed your people, and you have to pay the price."

It was time to make a decision. If it came to hand-to-hand combat, he felt like he could get the weapon away from Thad, but he might kill him in the process. Then he would never find Camellia, and if he did, she might never forgive him for killing the lout. *Lord, what should I do?*

"Get your hands back up." Thad gestured with his rifle.

Jonah obeyed him, although he only lifted his hands to the height of his shoulders. He rocked forward onto the balls of his feet in preparation to grab the rifle away from Thad. "Do you plan to parade me through town?"

"Th—" Whatever Thad was about to say was lost forever in the screaming whistle of a shell and a burst of light.

The explosion that followed catapulted Jonah through the air. Then the floor rose up to meet him, and everything went black.

Chapter Forty-three

"Thad hasn't been to see us in several days." Mrs. Watkins looked toward her daughter, ignoring Camellia as she'd done for several days. Ever since Obed had been hurt.

Jane pulled at the collar of her gown. "I know. He may be avoiding us." She gave Camellia a piercing look full of accusation.

The night sky lit up with a barrage of shells. Only a few weeks ago, the three women would have run inside the cave for shelter, but now they waited and watched before moving. The direction was wrong to threaten them, so they kept their seats at the mouth of their cave.

Mrs. Watkins waved her fan in front of her face. "The Yankees don't want us to get any sleep tonight."

Camellia wondered if the woman blamed her for the Yankees' persistence. Probably. She felt very unwelcome in their cave.

She and Jane were still going to the hospital every day. They'd come to an agreement to avoid discussing the slaves' right to equal consideration since it was obvious they would never agree on that subject.

They had patched up their friendship, and Camellia was beginning to feel much better. So much so that she had made the mistake of telling her about Thad's proposal. She didn't think her friend would ever forgive her for "breaking Thad's heart." No matter how much Camellia tried to explain that Thad didn't really love her, Jane was determined to defend her brother.

So here she was, stuck living with two women who obviously wished her gone. Camellia wondered how much longer the siege could go on. The soldiers were so weak from starvation that she wondered how they kept alert. Surely General Pemberton would see the futility of continuing to hold out. Vicksburg might be unassailable, but starvation would kill as surely as bullets and mortars.

One of the women who lived nearby came running toward them, her skirts raising a cloud of dust. "Lawson came by a few minutes ago and gave us some bad news."

Camellia's heart fell. What now?

"It's Willow Grove. It was hit by those infernal Yankees." The woman put a hand to her chest and gasped for air before continuing. "It didn't catch fire, thank the good Lord, but your roof is gone."

Jane jumped from her seat and looked toward her mother. "We need to go see about our things."

Mrs. Watkins's face shone white in the light of the torch. "I can't. . . . I don't. . .feel right."

She slumped forward and toppled from the chair.

Jane ran to her, turning her mother over and chafing her hand.

Camellia knelt beside her, wishing she had her medicines. She checked the older lady's wrist. The pulse was weak but steady. "I'm sure she's overheated. You stay here. I'll get a cool cloth, and we'll have her feeling better right away."

It took a quarter hour, but they managed to get a weepy Mrs. Watkins into her bed.

Camellia and Jane stepped outside the cave to discuss their next move. "You stay here and watch your mother. I'll go check on the house and report back to you."

Jane tossed her a grateful look. "Would you?"

"I'll be back before you know it." Camellia set off for town at a brisk pace, a torch in her hand.

The picket fence looked as fresh as it had when she first arrived in Vicksburg. How long ago that seemed. She tucked away her thoughts for consideration later. Right now she had to focus on her task— checking on the house and reporting back to the others.

A window stood ajar. A result of the explosion? She stepped through it into the parlor, holding the torch in front of her while she looked for a candle. Why had she not brought a candelabrum with her?

A satisfied sound escaped her lips as she found a box of candles near the hearth. Lighting one from the failing light of the torch, she took stock. This room looked untouched. Camellia exited and looked up, surprised in spite of herself to see stars twinkling above her head.

The roof had an enormous hole. They would have to get someone here immediately to patch that before a summer thunderstorm drenched the interior of the house.

Foreboding stole over her. Camellia tried to dismiss the feeling as a result of the destruction, but something raised the hair on her arms. Something was wrong in the house. Clenching her jaw, she considered the stairs. They looked secure. She put her foot on the first step, her heart pounding in her chest.

Was that a rustle from the second-floor landing? Probably a mouse or some other small rodent. At least she hoped it was. Lecturing herself silently, she continued moving upward. She would take a quick look around and leave. She and Jane could come back in the morning for a more thorough investigation.

Having made that promise, Camellia rushed up the last few steps. The wallpaper was blackened and smelled awful. It would probably have to be stripped.

Camellia's foot struck something soft, and she almost fell. Her candle showed her a gray uniform. Had someone been in the house when the shell struck it?

A groan made her catch her breath. "Thad? Is that you?" She leaned over the man, careful to keep wax from dripping on him. His features looked odd in the candlelight. Not odd. Wrong. His hair was auburn, his chin shorter. He looked like. . .like Jonah Thornton.

"Jonah?" She touched his face with a trembling finger. "Jonah? What have you done?" Tears blurred her vision. What was he doing in Willow Grove? In Vicksburg?

She snuffed out the candle and put it down on the floor next to his prone body. "Jonah, wake up. Please, you can't die. I love you." She felt the truth of her words reverberate through her. The pain nearly tore her in two.

Camellia put his head in her lap and rocked back and forth. "God, I don't know why Jonah is here, but I beg You to please let him live. Give me the chance to tell him the truth. I promise, God, that I won't let the opportunity escape this time. Only please give Jonah back—"

A hand fell on her shoulder, ending her prayer with a gasp.

Camellia looked back over her shoulder and saw Thad standing behind her. She bent her body further, trying to protect Jonah from him. "Go away. I'll take care of this man."

"I know who he is, Camellia." Thad's hand squeezed her shoulder before letting go. "He was here before the blast. He came to rescue you."

More tears threatened. Jonah was hurt because of her? After what she'd said to him? The clinical part of her mind protected her from the deepening pain. "Would you get some candles? I need to see how badly he's hurt."

Thad nodded and clomped down the stairs.

As soon as Thad reached the first floor, the man in her lap stirred. "Jonah? Do you hurt anywhere?"

He grinned up at her. "I've felt better, but being this close to you almost makes the pain worth it."

Anger replaced her fear. Camellia pushed him out of her lap. "You're not hurt at all. Have you been conscious the whole time?"

"Ow!" He rubbed the back of his head.

"How much did you hear?" She stood and brushed the dirt off her dress.

Jonah scrambled to his feet. He put a hand under her chin. "Enough to know that you're leaving Vicksburg with me tonight."

A part of Camellia wanted to push his hand away, but she was caught by the look in his eyes. "I am?"

"Yes, you are." Thad had come back upstairs more quietly than he'd departed. "Both of us heard you, Camellia. I know now why you turned down my offer."

She finally found the strength to push Jonah's hand away. "I'm sorry, Thad."

"Don't be." He sighed. "I think I realized the truth when I first saw Jonah here. I was so angry. I wanted him to pay for taking you away from me. But then when I came to and heard your voice. . . I'll always carry the shame of what I tried to do to him."

Camellia started to move to him, but Jonah put a hand on her arm. When she looked at him, he shook his head.

"Don't be so hard on yourself." Jonah's voice was gravelly. "I might have done the same thing in your place."

A slight smile appeared on Thad's face. "Thank you for that. Do you need help getting out of here?"

Jonah seemed completely recovered as he looked up to judge the amount of light in the sky. "I think we can still make it if we hurry."

The two men needed to stop talking about her as if she wasn't even here. "What about my medicine? My clothes?"

Thad and Jonah shared a look. A look that mixed empathy and disdain. Thad turned away, but not before she saw the grin on his face.

"You'll have to leave all that here." Jonah put an arm around her waist. "I'll buy you all the clothes your heart desires, and New Orleans has several apothecary shops, so don't worry about your medicines. We have to leave right now."

"I have one more thing to do." She pulled away from him and walked to where Thad stood.

He turned to face her. "You really do need to leave, you know."

"Thank you." She put a hand on his cheek. "I'll never forget this."

Thad pressed a quick kiss into her palm. "And I'll never forget you." He looked to Jonah. "Take care of her."

Jonah nodded and held out his hand. "Are you ready?"

Camellia put her hand in his. "Yes."

They walked hand in hand through the town and passed two sentries, neither of whom questioned their apparent early morning tryst. One of the men even had the temerity to wink at them. Camellia wondered if her cheeks were rosier than the predawn sky.

Jonah leaned over and put his lips on her ear. "Getting out of town is a lot easier than getting in."

When she was sure they were far enough from the sentries to speak openly, she turned to him. "How did you manage to get in at all?"

"I crawled through a tunnel." He described his efforts briefly before taking her in his arms.

"I'm so sorry for the things I said to you in Memphis. I understand now why you cannot support the South and what it stands for." She stared at the gray collar of his Confederate uniform, thankful it was only a costume. "I've seen the futility of the fighting—the death and pain men are causing each other. When I thought you were a casualty—" The horror of those moments threatened to overwhelm her again. "You shouldn't have put yourself at risk for my sake."

"I would have crawled a dozen miles farther and faced even death itself to rescue you." He put a finger under her chin and lifted it until their gazes met. "I love you, Camellia Anderson. I love the strong, committed woman of faith and integrity you've become."

"I love you, too, Jonah Thornton. I think I always have."

When his lips closed over hers, Camellia wondered how and why she'd ever resisted Jonah. He was the perfect hero for her—a gentle man with a heart of gold, a will of iron, and a love for the Lord that would always guide him. She thanked God for keeping him safe and for opening her eyes to the truth so that they could be together—together serving Him in all of their endeavors, no matter what the future held.

Epilogue

*W*hy is the boat rocking so much?" Camellia asked the question over her shoulder, her blue gaze meeting Lily's in the reflection of the mirror. "We haven't broken away from the dock, have we?"

Lily stood in the doorway and watched as Tamar arranged Camellia's blond curls around her face. She had always been the beauty of the family, but her face glowed with excitement on this, the day of her wedding. "Don't worry. I'm sure it's only the guests arriving and moving around in the main parlor." Perhaps a change of subject would calm the bride's nerves. "Wasn't it nice of Jean Luc's parents to offer their luxury steamship for your wedding? It's a shame Jean Luc and Anna could not come, but they've been busy in Missouri since the baby was born."

Camellia's expression bunched. Apparently she would not fall for Lily's ploy. "What about Mr. and Mrs. Thornton? And Jonah? Is he ready?"

Lily sympathized with the concern she detected in her sister's voice. She could remember her own wedding day. The fear of the unknown. . .the concern over the future. . .wondering if she was making a huge mistake. Of course all of that had disappeared when she saw the look of adoration in Blake's face as he stood tall and straight in front of the altar. And the same would be true for Camellia.

"Of course he's ready." Tamar answered the question for Lily. "Jonah loves you. He loves you the way Blake loves Lily."

"And the way Jensen loves you, Tamar." Lily smiled and moved toward the fancy dress suspended from a wooden rod in one corner of the stateroom. The skirt consisted of three deep flounces, each edged with wide lace. A bodice of matching white silk was decorated with floral fasteners and had short, puffed sleeves. Across the bed pillows lay the lace veil that would drift behind Camellia as she floated down the aisle in front of her friends and family. "You'll be a beautiful bride, dearest."

Camellia's expression mellowed, and a dreamy look replaced the concern in her eyes. "I've wanted to be married since I was a little girl."

"I have to admit I once worried you might select a husband for the wrong reasons, but you resisted the temptation to choose status over substance." Lily turned to the dressing table and reached to give her sister a hug. "Jonah Thornton is a fine Christian man. I know the two of you will keep God at the center of your lives, and He will bless your union."

"Amen." Tamar tweaked an errant curl into place.

Tears sparkled at the corners of Camellia's eyes.

"Don't you go crying and mess up that beautiful face." Tamar shook a finger at Camellia's reflection. "Tears aren't what you want to remember about your wedding day."

Camellia sniffed. "You're right."

"What's going on in here?" Jasmine bounded into the room with the enthusiasm and energy of youth. "Are you crying, Camellia?"

Camellia shook her head and dabbed at her eyes with the lace handkerchief Tamar handed to her.

Lily smiled at both of them, but her words were directed toward her youngest sister. "You'll understand better when it's your turn to get married."

"I'm not going to get married." Jasmine turned up her nose. "I'm going to be an actress with my own show and loads of admirers."

Tamar gasped, but Lily was not surprised. Her youngest sister had a talent for dramatic pronouncements. "That's good. You're too young to be thinking of marriage anyway."

Jasmine flipped her hair over one shoulder, her exotic violet-hued eyes scornful. "I don't care how old I am, I'll never get married. I want to be free to follow my dreams."

Lily exchanged a knowing glance with Camellia. Jasmine's words mirrored the sentiments each of them had once expressed. Camellia had used the same reasoning when she wished to go to the finishing school in New Orleans, and Lily had used it when explaining to her relatives why she had bought her first riverboat. But both she and Camellia had been much older than Jasmine was now. "Let's not worry about that. Today is Camellia's special day. The whole town is coming to share in her joy."

Chastened by the reminder, Jasmine nodded and lowered her nose. "You're right."

Lily's stomach churned, and she spread a hand over it below the blue ribbon around her waist. A thrill shot through her. She was expecting again, she was sure of it. But as she'd told Jasmine, today was not the day to focus on anything except Camellia and Jonah's happiness. Her announcement could wait. Even Blake didn't know yet.

A knock on the door was followed by Blake's voice. "Are you ladies ready? Everyone is here, and there's a nervous young fellow pacing the deck above you."

"We'll be up in a few minutes." Lily carefully took the wedding dress from its hanger, and she and Tamar lifted it over Camellia's curls. "Tell Jonah not to worry."

They heard his footsteps move away and breathed a collective sigh before turning to the next task—fastening the tiny pearl buttons on the back of the dress as well as the florets on the bodice.

Jasmine brought over a pair of white kid gloves and handed them to Camellia as Tamar and Lily secured the long veil in Camellia's hair.

When they finished, Lily stepped back to admire the picture her sister made. "You are so beautiful, inside and out."

Camellia took a deep breath, smiled, and nodded. "Thank you for letting me find my own way to happiness, Lily."

Lily nodded, and she sent a prayer of thanksgiving to God for their blessings. She opened her arms and gathered both of her sisters close for a hug.

"Now, don't you mess up Camellia's dress." Tamar's admonition ended the hug. "Lily, you and Jasmine go on to the parlor. I'll follow to make sure Camellia's train is straight when she makes her grand entrance."

Lily hesitated a moment, but then she felt Jasmine's arm around her waist. It was time to let Camellia go start her own family. She pulled Jasmine closer as they made their way to the crowded main room.

More than one hundred chairs were arranged in neat rows, and nearly every seat was occupied. It seemed the whole town had decided to attend Camellia and Jonah's wedding.

She and Jasmine took two chairs on the front row next to David and Blake, who was holding Noah. Grandmother was seated past them, with Aunt Dahlia and Uncle Phillip filling out the row.

Papa stood next to the podium, his smile as wide as the Mississippi. Jonah, standing next to him, still looked a little pale.

No wonder, given the fact that he'd only returned to Natchez from the war a month earlier. When Lily and the rest of the family tried to convince him to wait until he fully regained his health before marrying Camellia, he had replied that he had waited far too long already. He would marry his bride as soon as his parents arrived from New Orleans.

Lily leaned forward and looked to her left, sending a smile toward Mr. and Mrs. Thornton. Who would have thought that the friendship they had offered so many years ago would end in the union of their families? God, of course. It amazed Lily that she could be so blind to His purpose until she looked back in time. But seeing His guiding hand was a comfort she relied upon. No matter what circumstances or challenges they faced, He was always there.

Her thoughts were cut off as the buzz of conversation died down. She looked back to the entrance of the room and saw Camellia standing in the doorway, her skirts flowing around her like fluffy white clouds. Lily and the others stood and watched as she advanced, seeming to float forward like a cloud. When she reached the front of the room, Jonah stepped toward her, his adoration for Camellia plain to see.

He took her hands in his own, staring into her eyes as though she was the only person in the room. He repeated his vows as instructed, never looking away from her. When Papa pronounced them man and wife, Jonah swept back Camellia's veil with one hand and captured her face with the other. His whole attitude was one of love and devotion. What a wonderful man Camellia had fallen in love with.

"I love you." Blake whispered the words in her ear as he put an arm around Lily's shoulders.

Looking up at her husband, Lily thanked God again for her

blessings—for giving her a dream and helping her to follow it. "I love you, too."

Lily's heart seemed likely to burst from happiness as she returned her attention to Camellia and Jonah. They ended their first kiss as a married couple. Jonah tucked his bride's hand under his arm, grinning at the audience as Papa introduced them.

Mr. and Mrs. Jonah Thornton began their new life. . .together.

Diane T. Ashley, a "town girl" born and raised in Mississippi, has worked more than twenty years for the House of Representatives. She rediscovered a thirst for writing, was led to a class taught by Aaron McCarver, and became a founding member of the Bards of Faith.

Aaron McCarver is a transplanted Mississippian who was raised in the mountains near Dunlap, Tennessee. He loves his jobs of teaching at Belhaven University and editing for Barbour Publishing. A member of ACFW, he is coauthor with Gilbert Morris of the bestselling series "The Spirit of Appalachia." He now coauthors with Diane T. Ashley on several historical series.

Discussion Questions

1. This story is in large part Camellia's spiritual journey. At first, she selfishly follows her own ambitions. But circumstances begin to point her toward her talents of nursing the sick and wounded. What abilities and attributes does she possess that lead her to discovering this gift? Do you think God puts certain things into us from our "creation" that help reveal his will for our lives? Camellia also changes in her outlook on her lifestyle. How do her newfound abilities play a part in her "awakening"?

2. Jonah's convictions drive his actions throughout the story, leading him to go against most of his family and spy for the North. Was he right with the choices he made that turned him away from his parents? Are there times God would allow us to forsake our parents' teachings? How should we handle these situations to be pleasing to God? Jonah struggles with moral issues that come up as a result of his spying. Is lying ever the right thing to do in situations like this? Check out stories of spies in the Bible, such as the story of Rahab hiding the spies (Joshua 2) and the incident of the woman hiding two friends of David who were going to warn him of Absalom's plots (2 Samuel 17).

3. Blake's spiritual journey is continued in this book, as he must deal with his father and the animosity he has felt for him. Was it right for Blake to wait as long as he did to approach his father? Often as adults, people come to realize that some actions of their parents they thought were bad were actually for their good. How did this apply to Blake's situation? Do you feel that Blake's father was solely responsible for their situation or did Blake have a part to play in it, too?

4. John Champion's story was particularly fun for us to write in this book. We so enjoyed showing the complete redemption of this man. In this redemption, should he have been more straightforward in letting Blake know of his father's accident and illness, or was he right in the way he did it? In helping Blake, should he have realized he needed to go to his parents as well? Do you think God sets up certain times for us to have necessary conversations with others, such as what John and Blake needed to do, or do you think we should take those opportunities as soon as they come, as God simply directs us to live at peace with others?

If you enjoyed *Camellia*,
be sure to read *Lily*. . .

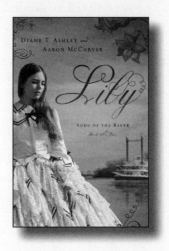

Determined to avoid a marriage of convenience,
a Mississippi belle tries her hand at a riverboat venture.
Will she find love while navigating danger?